AWAKEN

DAUGHTERS OF THE SEA SERIES

KRISTEN DAY

Edited by: Stacy Sanford
Formatting and Cover Art by: Daydream Designs

This is a work of fiction.

All of the characters, organizations and events portrayed in this novel are a product of the author's imagination. Any resemblance to persons, living or dead, actual events or organizations is entirely coincidental.

To Mom and Stacy - thank you for believing in my dreams and catching me when I fall.

Praise for Awaken Daughters of the Sea #2

"I definitely was not prepared for what happened in this book. I loved Forsaken, and now I love Awaken. If you're a fan of the young adult genre and love paranormal and mythology, you will definitely love this trilogy from Kristen Day. - *Book Lovin Mamas*

"I would without a doubt recommend people read this, it's worth purchasing and reading a few times. I know before the next one comes out I'll probably reread these. Kristen Day is a great writer who really knows how to yank you into the worlds she's created". - *Reading in the Window Seat*

"After obsessively completing Forsaken, the first in this series, I was anxiously awaiting Awaken's release...and Kristen Day did not disappoint. Another beautifully written, intriguing, and well-developed novel that goes much deeper than the first. Awaken is an amazing story with honest characterization, and beautiful imagery. Most definitely add this one to your library!" - *Between the Bind*

"Tear jerking, heart wrenching goodness. This book screams READ ME NOW!" - *Behind The Pages*

"Book one was just a teaser to prepare us for the awesomeness of this book!! There is more action, more suspense, more evil and more twists and turns. And when you get to the end of that final page... Well, prepare to be left reeling!!" - *YA Book Addict*

"Awaken is packed with suspense, romance and a few twists I definitely didn't see coming. I cannot find the words to tell you exactly how much I loved this book. It exceeded my every expectation. Day has created a fantastically quirky cast of characters for us to fall in love with and in doing so she has made it impossible for me to stop reading these books". - *Girls *Heart* Books*

"I am at a loss for words. Once again, Kristen Day molds a fantastic storyline that keeps you on the edge of your seat. A great series for fantasy and mermaid lovers alike.".- *The Librarian's Bookshelf*

"I have no idea how I am going to describe my feelings while reading this. I could write a million words and still not succeed. Or I could just leave this blank because I am so awestruck by the story. It was unputdownable! Exciting. Thrilling. Adrenaline-raising. And that is the greatest praise a book can ever get!" - *Book Addict*

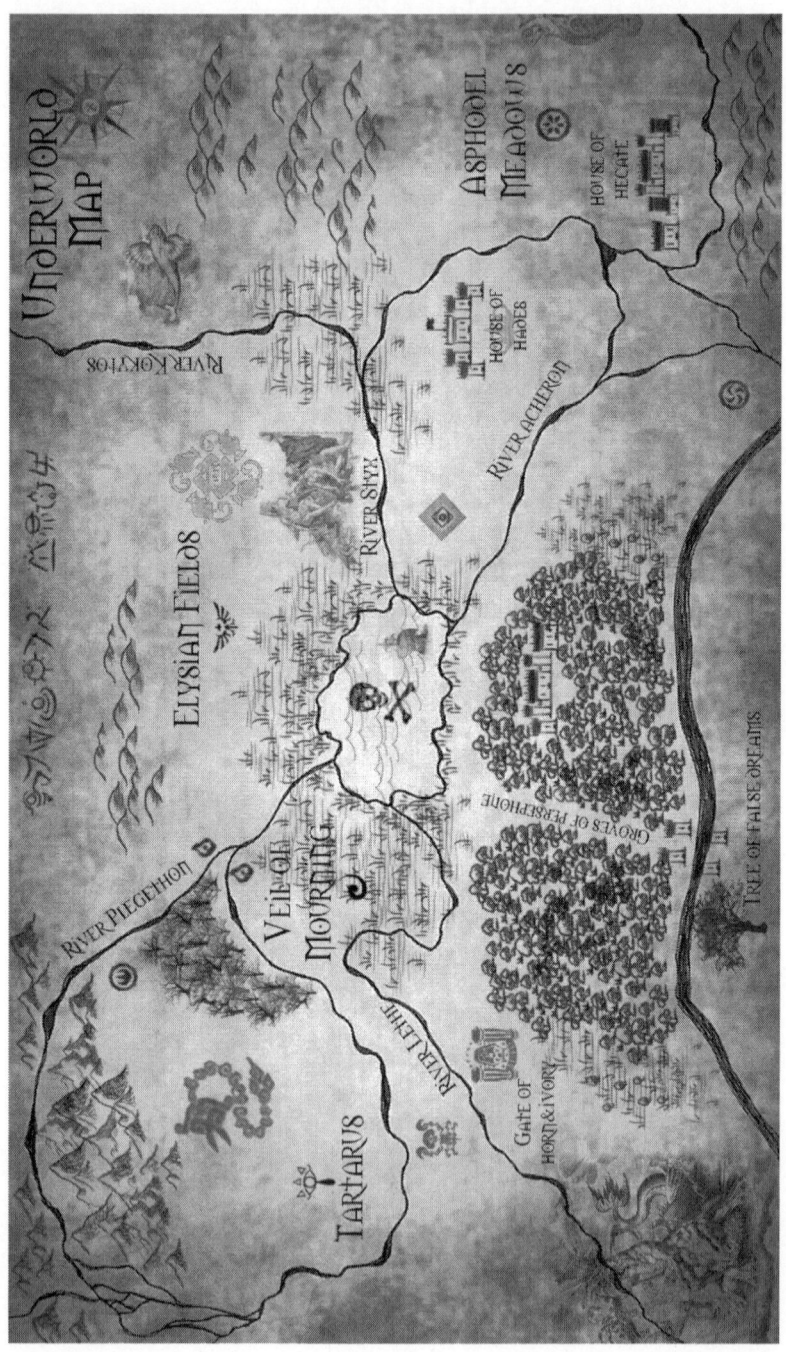

Prologue

The familiar call of seagulls diving for fish amongst the crashing waves pulled him from his restless slumber. His tired, bloodshot eyes opened and gazed upon the same weathered stone ceiling looming above. As they roamed down the sloped wall where he kept count, he pushed back the agonizing hopelessness encasing his heart. Another long night behind him simply meant another long day before him. He swung his legs over the side of his cot and gently placed his worn feet on the stone floor. It was always bitterly cold in the morning. He shivered as he glanced down at his too-skinny legs and the dirt that clung to his calloused feet. His ragged cotton shorts now hung low around his emaciated waist, and his faded blue shirt had been discarded long ago; traded for a sunken-in bare chest. He smoothed down his gray hair and thick beard and wondered if today would be the day.

Sighing, he stood and collected the conch shell he kept hidden within a crack in his counting wall. He found the last mark and bent down to add yet another. He never counted days; only nights. The darkness always brought out his worst nightmares and he was continually amazed he had made it through so many. Thousands of marks littered the wall before him; a diary of solitude and sheer will captured forever in stone.

As he did every morning, he padded over to the window and looked out over the rolling sea. The lone window of his small room faced east, allowing him one pleasure amidst the hell that had become his life. Sunrise. At first, each sunrise brought only tears to his eyes while the slow ache in his chest grew, threatening to wrack his body with a sadness no man should bear. What those brilliant colors dancing across the sky stood for only served as a reminder to his unending loss. Another night bereft of her loving arms. Another day without her magical presence. Over the years the pain had receded, but her memory never faded. Neither did the seed of hope she had planted so long ago. It grew every day; branching out and becoming the only thing that kept him alive. Many nights he peered out of his window at the white sand far below. He thought of how easy it would be to end this torture and return to her. But he knew he had a bigger purpose, and he would not let her down. He would endure and wait until his heart beat no more.

Once a week he was allowed to stroll along the beach and speak to the others, but it was only a brief illusion of freedom. They could feel the eyes that watched their every move. The others had become his only companions. For years there had only been seven, but a couple of months ago a newcomer arrived. He heard her anguished cries at night, and her deep despair was evident in the scratches along her arms; the victims of her own fingernails. She, too, finally succumbed to the seclusion and hopelessness; becoming void of emotion and as hollow as the rest of them. His thoughts moved back to the present and to the brilliant ball of light inching its way above the horizon. This was when he felt closest to her. He closed his eyes and called upon the memory of her ever gentle, loving eyes.

"My love, I have lived to see yet another dawn cast its light upon this wretched spit of land. Thankfully this dawn brings new hope for my weary soul. You appeared to me in my dreams once again last night, but for the first time I heard the sweet melody of your voice. You spoke to me and breathed life back into my withered heart. You told me to be patient; to remain steadfast. You assured me the hour is growing near, and I know the words you speak are true. Indeed, it is almost time."

I felt her suffocating presence before she ever appeared. A silent, bitter darkness slithered its way into my heart; eclipsing the light in my soul and chilling me to the bone. The hair on the back of my neck rose as the air surrounding me turned frigid. I wrapped my arms around myself and glanced at my classmates to see if anyone else noticed the sudden climate change. That was the moment she walked through the door.

The incessant clicking of her black stiletto heels against linoleum announced her entrance, and I could have sworn I heard a collective gasp of shock and awe. The black leather mini skirt hugging her hips was strategically ripped on the sides, showing an inordinate amount of skin, and her white tank top stopped just short of a diamond studded belly ring. Flowing golden hair the color and consistency of honey cascaded down her bare shoulders as she strode the rest of the way into the room with a slight swagger. The impatient manicured hand she placed on her hip oozed of arrogance, and even the large stone pendant dangling from her necklace couldn't compete with her overwhelming beauty. A tiny diamond stud adorned the side of her nose and when my eyes travelled up to hers, the icy darkness began to envelope me once again. My entire body shivered as her rich, caramel-colored eyes caught mine for a brief instant before looking expectantly at the teacher. Mrs. Leone cleared her throat and shook her head, suggesting that she was just as taken by the newcomer as her students were.

"Class, this is Lorelei's newest transfer, Nadia Trice. She has travelled all the way from California to be here. Please make her feel welcome." Apparently satisfied with Mrs. Leone's introduction, Nadia raised her perfectly shaped eyebrows at her audience; wordlessly daring anyone to question her arrival. She dramatically brushed the hair off her shoulder, sauntered down the middle aisle before making herself at home in an empty desk diagonal to mine. While the rest of the class remained captivated by her dark, sexy style, I noted the sarcastic smirk playing across her glossy lips and the calculating gleam in her eye. I squinted as I caught a glimpse of something I'd never seen before. Not only could I still feel the darkness emanating from her, I could actually make out light gray tendrils swirling in the air around her. They had a smoke-like quality as they curled around her and floated out from her body. When her heavily lashed eyes met mine, the smoky tendrils suddenly disappeared and she turned back around abruptly. Her long, slender fingers began carving something into the top of her desk. With her fingernail. As I followed her finger, I noticed she wasn't carving the wood as much as she was burning it. As she dragged her nail across the desk, the wood beneath immediately smoldered and darkened; leaving a slight smell of burning embers.

"As usual, for the last fifteen minutes of class you will meet with your research groups." After we divided up into our groups, her eyes flitted toward Nadia and then slid in my direction momentarily. "Nadia will be joining...." She inspected some papers on her desk while I sent up a silent plea she wouldn't pick our group.

"Lexi, Stasia, Maya, and Lyric," she announced. Damn.

Nadia inclined her head ever so slightly as Mrs. Leone steered her towards our group. As she breezily pranced across the room with a grin laced with amusement,

Maya groaned inwardly and I concentrated on not staring at the gray tendrils that had reappeared around her body.

"Lexi, Stasia, Maya, and Lyric," Nadia mimicked Mrs. Leone's shrill voice and contemplated our outfits before taking a seat; clearly unimpressed. As we all stared back at her, shocked into silence by her obvious disrespect, I felt the already suffocating tension in the air thicken. Oblivious to Nadia's adverse effect on everyone, Lexi beamed at her with pure adoration wrapped securely in unmistakable envy.

"Hey Nadia! I'm Lexi! I am so excited you get to be in our group!" she gushed; not taking a breath before launching into a hundred questions. "So, where did you come from in California? Was it near the beach, too? What were the guys like? I love your shoes! Where'd you get them?"

Nadia appeared to take it in stride, as if she was used to throngs of loyal fans showering her with compliments and occasionally offering up their first born if she'd pose for a picture.

"San Diego," she responded flippantly. "But the guys were worthless. Only good for one thing." She winked and I thought Lexi was going to offer her a BFF heart necklace right then and there.

"Oh my God. I know exactly what you mean!" she huffed, and crossed her arms in contempt. Maya's clear blue eyes darkened considerably as she glared at them both.

"So Stasia, what are you doing for fall break?" Lyric asked loudly, attempting to drown out Nadia and Lexi's self-involved chatter. Tomorrow marked the beginning of fall break, but I remembered fall breaks extending much longer at my old high school in Atlanta. Classes were cancelled Friday and Monday, but would resume on Tuesday. They really should consider calling it fall 'long-weekend' instead. Fall 'break' was definitely false advertising.

"Just staying here. By the time I get home, I'd have to turn right back around and come back." I shrugged my shoulders and hoped she wouldn't ask me anything about 'home'. My adoptive parents, Doris and Charles Whitman, requested that I come home for Fall break, but after explaining how short a time I would be able to spend back in Atlanta, they agreed it would be better to wait until Thanksgiving.

"Everyone I've talked to is staying here, too. Plus, the weather's supposed to be good. I definitely see some sun, sand and a good book in my future." Maya grinned dreamily.

"Speaking of reading, we need to talk about our paper." Lyric frowned at Lexi and Nadia. "I think having another member of the group will give us an added advantage." As we brought Nadia up to speed on our research, I realized I hadn't seen a trace anywhere on her body. And with so much of it showing, I found that to be a little odd. But then again, it could be anywhere. I also couldn't help but wonder which order she belonged to. Although she was beautiful, she didn't quite fit into the Siren category. Being that she was a girl, it only left the Tydes. I shuddered at the possibility. Since that fateful weekend of the Cimmerian Shade Ball last month, I knew my life would never be the same. But what I hadn't expected was the intense pride and sense of protectiveness I would feel for the Order of Tydes. I had a greater understanding of what being a descendant of the Nereids truly meant. Not only did I find my original home on the Fortunate Isle, I found my true destiny as well. As the only child of Thetis I was the Chosen future leader of the Tydes...which included the Sirens, and they weren't too happy about that.

My whole world had immediately shifted; aligning my heart and soul to the new path I must walk. As terrified as I was at the prospect, it didn't hold a candle to how I felt about returning to school that following Monday. The rumor mill had been working overtime as it twisted and mangled the truth about what happened that night on the Isle. Thankfully, I had three incredible roommates who helped me wade through the litany of accusations and whispers. Depending upon the Order of the person, I could receive anything from an icy glare to a joyful hug. Most Sirens shunned my very presence, while the Tydes and Sons sent loving praise my way. It was an awful divide that seemed to foreshadow something larger to come.

Isadora's death was covered up by a fabricated 'car accident' on the mainland that same weekend. It didn't fool anyone, but it kept them from asking too many questions. The former teacher at Lorelei had been replaced the very next day. Kira was completely healed by the water of the Lagoon, and Priscilla stayed away from me for the most part. As the Maven, or high mistress of Lorelei, she could easily keep an eye on me without my knowledge. She was fully aware of my upcoming journey, and I expected some sort of retribution at any time. I tried to lose myself in my school work as well as retrieve any sense of normalcy to my life, no matter how remote. I knew what I had to do. I knew what my future held. And I would face it head on. But until then, I just wanted to be plain Stasia for a little while longer.

"Stasia."

"Huh?" I snapped out of my thoughts.

"We need something to, um, 'show and tell' as it relates to Thetis, so we were kind of, well…we were hoping…" Maya asked shyly.

"Oh! Sure, yeah, not a problem," I assured her with a smile as soon as I realized what she was asking. As if on cue, the temperature in the air around me plummeted and I felt a precise pain between my eyes. I automatically met Nadia's piercing stare. Images began to flood my mind with the ferocity of a freight train. Vivid flashes of faces, landscapes and colors whirled before me, throwing off my

14

equilibrium. The last image I saw was a massive tree teeming with activity. It appeared to be lit by an inner glow, which gave it an otherworldly quality. I became entranced in its beauty until the image was ripped away. In true plain Stasia fashion, I had fallen out of my chair.

"Stasia! Are you okay?" Maya and Lyric were instantly at my side, helping me up. I tried to regain my balance and stop the world from spinning, but it was the venom in Nadia's voice that forced me to find my center once again.

"Violate my mind again and I will end you." Her eyes sparked with fury, reminding me of a bolt of lightning. "I'm the last person you want to mess with." Amidst a cloud of swirling smoke only I could see, she vanished out the door and out of sight.

"What did you do to her?" Lexi shot me an accusing glare. I was too stunned to react to her hostile tone.

"I didn't do anything to her," I claimed, although I was fast becoming the one that needed convincing.

"Whatever," she dismissed me, as I tried to wrap my mind around what had just happened. It was exactly like seeing the sea turtle's memories that first weekend at Lorelei. But, this had to be different...right? I had an affinity for sea animals, not people. But I couldn't deny what I saw. Did I unknowingly reach into Nadia's mind and see her memories? Did I hurt her? How did I do it? My frantic thoughts were halted once I noticed Nadia's work of art still burned into the top of her desk. It was only one word.

Penance

Claiming sickness, I was granted permission to skip the rest of my classes that afternoon. I texted the most amazing guy on earth (who also happened to be my boyfriend, Finn) to let him know I wouldn't be in last period, and walked towards Maren Hall in a hurry. I had to do some serious thinking and clear my head. Literally.

"'Trophy Wife', 'Come to Bed Red', or 'No Prenup'?" Phoebe asked as she placed three small bottles on the coffee table in front of her.

"I still think you should go with 'Fishnet Stockings'," Carmen suggested; glancing up from her homework.

"What happened to normal colors like 'Baby Pink' or 'Red No. 5'?" Willow wrinkled her button nose at the bottles and settled onto the couch beside Carmen.

"Who wants to paint 'Baby Pink' on their nails when you can paint 'Take Him to the Cleaners' on them instead?" Carmen disputed; reading the bottom of a bottle with a grin.

"Nothing says I'm girlfriend material like the color 'Call Me Irresponsible'," I added after inspecting several of the already rejected colors of polish. Phoebe had a habit of repainting her nails to match her outfit, shoes, or favorite candy of the week. She had more nail polish in her collection than you could find at any one store. It was pretty impressive. Her most recent revision was in preparation for her date with Ian. After attending the Ball last month, they had become inseparable.

"Speaking of irresponsible, have you guys heard about the new girl?" Carmen asked with revulsion. My heart hardened as the memory of this morning's incident with Nadia replayed in my mind.

Phoebe's head peeked out of her bedroom, mid-outfit change. "I heard she transferred from the House of Metis in California because she got heavy into drugs."

16

"She's in my history class, and I can tell you she definitely won't be crowned Ms. Congeniality anytime soon," I informed them with a frown.

"I heard she was in the Order of Nymphs," Carmen added, and put down her spiral notebook.

"Like a marsh Nymph? Or a river Nymph?" Phoebe guessed from her room.

"I guess it's possible she could be either of those." Willow bit her lip in deep thought.

"Okay wait, I'm confused. There are more than four Orders?" I asked Willow; seriously considering creating that dictionary again so I could keep all of them straight.

"There are many Orders, but the Nymphs are the descendants of the Oceanids. While we're all connected to the sea, they're connected to specific bodies of water. So a river Nymph would be connected to one particular river," she explained.

"So that would mean there are pond Nymphs and lake Nymphs?" I deduced.

"That's right, and the body of water they are connected to would be determined by which Oceanid they're descended from; kind of like how our abilities work," Willow attested.

"Maybe she's a mud puddle nymph." Carmen snickered.

"Or a sewer nymph." Phoebe giggled from the bathroom where she was brushing her brown, blonde and red multi-colored hair again. Willow just rolled her eyes at them, but I could see the wheels turning in that brain of hers.

"There are so many kinds of Nymphs it would be hard to know for sure, but I have a feeling we can rule out sewage and puddle nymph." Still giggling, we all looked up at the same time when we heard a knock at the door. Phoebe gasped and started rushing around her room in an effort to finish getting ready. I stood, grabbed the doorknob and swung the door open.

Expecting Ian, my heart faltered when a pair of deep blue eyes collided with mine. The hint of a smirk played on Finn's lips as he leaned confidently against the door frame.

"Hi there." An amused smile crept across his face.

"Hi yourself." I beamed up at him, while my legs promptly turned to rubber. No matter how many times I laid my eyes on him, he always managed to take my breath away. Maybe it was the way his dark hair fell into his eyes or the sexy darkness he emanated. Maybe it was the way his jeans hung perfectly on his waist or the way his shirt clung to the muscles of his arms and chest. Maybe it was the person beneath it all who I knew would gladly risk his life for mine. I was pretty sure there was no way to pin it down. He just had that something. Plain and simple.

"Who is it?" Phoebe came sliding to a stop beside me dressed in an eclectic, bright purple, asymmetrical dress. I watched as her face turned from expectant to surprised, and finally landed on disappointment.

"Expecting someone else?" Finn teased her. She instantly turned a nice shade of bright pink, which only caused his smile to widen. "Don't worry. He'll be here soon. When I left he was fixing his hair for the hundredth time."

"What can I say?" a rich, deep voice sounded behind Finn as Ian stepped into the doorway. Dark denim jeans and a pale yellow polo shirt accentuated his dark skin and hair. "Phoebe deserves no less than absolute perfection." He looked Finn up and down and scrunched his nose in my direction apologetically. "Unfortunately, Finn falls into the 'less than' category."

He easily dodged Finn's playful punch, but being the quicker of the two, Finn still managed to mess up his short dark hair. In an attempt to save Ian's dignity and our suite (I'd seen those two fight each other before and it wasn't pretty), I grabbed Finn's hand and dragged him the rest of the way into the kitchen. Ian just winked at him and clutched Phoebe's hand, already leading her out the door.

"Don't wait up!" she called out to us as she closed the door behind them, already giggling. Armed with a witty remark I turned to face Finn, but he gripped my waist and jerked me close; instantly erasing any words I was about to say. I breathed him in and tried my best not to melt into a Stasia-sized puddle at his feet. His blue eyes darkened and he smiled knowingly as he bent down and gingerly kissed my eager lips. A flood of tingles assaulted my spine and the only thing that saved me from losing myself in him completely was Carmen's exaggerated sigh coming from the living room.

"What I'm about to say truly comes from a place of love." She paused for dramatic effect. "Spare us the lovey-dovey crap and go make out somewhere else."

"You know, you really should tell us what's on your mind more often." I chuckled at her. In response, Finn cloaked us both; sending a sparkling net around our bodies and shielding us from sight.

"Ew. Just 'cause I can't see you, doesn't mean I don't know what you're doing," she shot back to the place she assumed we were still standing.

After Finn uncloaked us, I planted a kiss on Carmen's cheek and watched her wipe it off in mock revulsion. We ducked into my bedroom for privacy, but after catching a glimpse of my disaster of a room, I instantly wished I had cleaned up that morning. My bedspread and sheets had somehow twisted into a pile of fabric at the foot of the bed, clothes were draped over every surface, and books were scattered across the blue shag rug. Thankfully Finn didn't seem to notice. He shut the door, swept the hair back from my face and inspected me with genuine concern.

"For a girl who's supposedly sick, you sure are beautiful." He raised a skeptical eyebrow at me and drew me close. The proximity of his warm body scrambled my thoughts, but somehow I managed a halfway coherent response.

"You should see me when I'm well." I leered up at him. The corners of his mouth lifted up into a crooked grin and his blue eyes danced with amusement. His retort was a soft, slow kiss that left me reeling.

"Nothing could diminish your radiance. Not a fever," he smiled slyly, "and especially not a fake fever."

"I don't know what you're talking about. I'm burning up." I put a hand to my forehead.

"You're definitely hot…" He reached for my hand and kissed it, then sat down on the bed. His blue eyes changed from amused to serious in a nanosecond, and I sat down gingerly beside him.

"There's something we need to talk about," he started, eyes down.

"Okay…" My heart plummeted to the floor; fearing what he wanted to talk about. No conversation that started with we need to talk ever ended well. It was usually followed by an it's not you, it's me.

"It's about your journey to the Underworld." He sighed in frustration, but the amount of relief I felt had me suppressing the urge to do cartwheels around the room. A discussion around my journey, I could handle. A discussion around him breaking my heart, I couldn't bear. I forced myself to focus.

In order to fulfill my true destiny and become the leader of the Tydes like my mother, I would have to face the current, self-appointed leader Keto, who just happened to be a Siren. But before I could do that, I had to complete my essence in order to become a true Goddess once I turned eighteen. Unfortunately, there were far more things I didn't know about my journey than I did know. I knew I would have to die for my soul to be released and enter the Underworld. Once there, I'd have to swim in the River Styx, which would complete my essence. I knew my whole journey would be in vain if my soul couldn't find a way to leave and return to my body. If I failed to return, my soul would spend the rest of eternity in the Underworld while my shell of a body remained trapped in this realm forever. Most importantly I would let down my family, my friends, and all Tydes. I couldn't let that happen.

"We have a problem. I talked to my mom today and she reminded me of something."

"Okay..." I said hesitantly. This didn't sound good.

"There are only four days during the year when a mortal's soul can voluntarily cross into the Underworld." He glanced at me with worry evident in his eyes.

"That doesn't sound too difficult. What are they?"

"That's where it's going to get tricky. You have to take the journey before you turn eighteen, right? So we need to know which of those days falls before your birthday. Those are the ones we'll have to choose from."

"Well my birthday's in April, so..." My words faded quickly as understanding hit me like a sledgehammer. I gaped up at him with dread and whispered slowly, "I don't know my true birthday." I put all of my attention into inspecting a rogue string on my comforter as the gravity of the situation sunk in. When I was found on the police station doorstep as a baby, there were no records of my birth and no documentation to confirm my birth date or true age, so the doctors could only guess at my age, and therefore my birthday. April seventeenth had been decided upon as a stand-in date, but my true birthday would forever remain a mystery. Or so I thought.

"The next two days you could go are in November and February," he continued.

"But it's the second week of October - November's too soon!" I pleaded; searching his eyes with paralyzing panic. The fear that immediately clutched my chest at the thought of taking the journey so soon had me hoping my true birthday was indeed after February. "What's so special about those four days?"

"They're the only days of the year when the veil between the two realms is thin enough." He watched me carefully to make sure I was following along before he continued, "So, in order to know when you'll go to the Underworld, we have to find out when your real birthday is. If it's before February, and you're forced to go next month, we'll have to start preparing you now."

An idea occurred to me and my eyes lit up. "The Isle! If I was born there, there's got to be a birth certificate somewhere, right?" My excitement was replaced with disappointment when he averted his eyes and pressed his lips into a straight line.

"Unfortunately being born on the Isle means you definitely do not have a birth certificate."

"So you don't have one either?"

"Birth certificates are only useful for government records, and no one knows the Fortunate Isle exists except for our kind. And even that number is low because of its secrecy. Same thing goes for social security numbers. I don't have one of those either."

"So there really are no records to show I was ever born," I concluded, disheartened.

"Records are only kept for those who can't or won't remember." He supported my hand in his. "I think I know how we can find out when your true birthday is, but we can't do it here. I have a feeling the Sirens are all watching you pretty closely." He raised an eyebrow and beamed with excitement. "So we'll need to go somewhere remote to practice."

"Practice what?" His only answer was a slow smile.

"You'll see. But first you need to tell your roommates to get packed. We're all going on a little trip for fall break."

"So let me get this straight. Fall break on the Outer Banks in a massive beach house?" Carmen's eyebrows shot up. "Why are we still sitting here?!"

She sprinted out of the kitchen mid-bite to pack her clothes. Phoebe had just returned from her date with Ian and we were all perched on bar stools sampling Willow's newest recipe for white chocolate brownies topped with macadamia nuts; or, according to Carmen: the best thing since Channing Tatum. I peered at my other roommates and hoped they'd agree to go just as easily.

"You had me at 'Ian'." Phoebe sighed and pretended to fan herself, but the big, goofy grin on her face was anything but forced.

"What other guys are going besides Ian and Finn?" Willow asked apprehensively. "This isn't a couples-thing, is it?"

"I think he's bringing his other roommates Ricker and Cage, along with another guy, but I don't know his name. He said it's a big house-"

"More like a mansion...the Sons' beach house is crazy big!" Carmen shouted from her room.

"So there'll be plenty of room and it's definitely not a couples' thing, I promise," I finished.

"Did you say Ricker?" Carmen reappeared.

"Do you know him?"

"Unfortunately," she muttered and disappeared again. I looked at Phoebe with a question mark in my eyes.

"There's major history there," she whispered. "But don't ask her about it. She'll bite your head off."

"What kind of history?" I asked, intrigued.

"It's kind of a love-hate relationship, but somehow they always find their way back to each other," Phoebe explained in a low voice.

"It's a hate-hate relationship...end of story," Carmen bellowed from her room.

"See? She's a little touchy about it," Phoebe warned me with a giggle.

"This could be entertaining. I'm in," Willow finally conceded. Phoebe squealed, wrapped her in a hug, and then ran off to her room to pack. Following their lead, we finished off our brownies and retired to our rooms. The plan was to meet Finn and the rest of the guys at the marina in the morning. The Sons' beach house was located near Cape Lookout, which was at the southern corner of the Outer Banks, north of Lorelei and Bald Head Island; only a six hour boat ride on the Sons' yacht.

Long after I went to bed, I still lay awake staring intently at the ceiling above. I was secretly hoping the answers I needed would magically present themselves across its smooth surface, but after examining it for more than an hour, I raised the proverbial white flag in defeat. The only thing I had succeeded in identifying was the white paint peering back at me with the same blank stare I felt on my own face. The incident with Nadia was pushed to the bottom of my priority list in lieu of the new development in my journey. Unfortunately, the number of questions far exceeded my number of answers. Trepidation had begun to outweigh most of the excitement I felt about the long weekend ahead. What did Finn mean by 'practice'? And how did he plan on figuring out my birthday on a remote island in the Outer banks? Unless the answer was hidden away in a buried chest, I wasn't too sure how this was going to work. What happened if we discovered my birthday was before the November date? Or even already past? Would I just be out of time and out of luck?

No wonder I couldn't sleep. The weight of the world was growing pretty heavy on my slim shoulders. Giving up on any chance of rest, I rolled out of bed and ambled across my room. I softly touched the twelve dried black roses still hanging beside my mirror and couldn't stop the unexpected smile that fought its way onto my face. A glowing heat spread through my chest, and the simple fact that I wasn't going to have to do this alone immediately lightened the intense pressure on my shoulders. Finn would be with me the whole time. I didn't know if I could do this, but maybe we could. We would figure this out together. Of that, I was 100% sure. Whatever life threw at me, I would deal with it and overcome it the same way I had my entire life; with strength and courage. I fingered the triskellion charm hanging around my neck that matched my trace and felt it warm beneath my touch; reminding me who I really was. I'd faced adversity before. Not only as Hannah, but also as Anastasia. This test would be no different. As I laid back down, Finn's words to Keto floated through my mind...She will prevail...she will prevail...

Blue. Stretching out for miles. But not just any blue. A deep indigo hue of epic proportions that captivated my soul and enriched my heart. I knew I was having a reverie, but besides that I was completely at a loss. I stood on stark white sand as fine as powder with towering limestone cliffs in the shape of a crescent at my back. The beach was in the shape of a crescent as well; the cliffs blocking any view except for the expansive sea before me. I was mesmerized by the contrast of the dazzling white cliffs against the mystical blue water. Where was I? Taking in my surroundings, I had an odd sense that I was very far away from my body. I could only describe it as a feeling of extreme freedom; to the point it was frightening. I shoved the highly unsettling feeling back in my mind and tried to concentrate on why my soul would have come here. I pivoted slowly, trying to find anything that would give me a clue. Upon closer inspection, I noticed a section of cliff behind me had actually been altered. It had been chipped away to the extent that a large block-like structure emerged from the stone. With several hollow squares resembling windows, it could have been a five story building carved into the limestone. Suspended high above the sand, it was the perfection of camouflage. Clink...clink...clink. My head swiveled side to side, finding movement on the sand several yards away. A man. Where had he come from? ...Clink. He was collecting something. I held my breath, even though he shouldn't be able to see or hear me, and moved closer. The warm air blew his gray hair and beard to the side; revealing weathered skin and sunken cheeks. Only wearing thin shorts, his body appeared starved for nourishment as well as for cleanliness. He methodically scanned the beach, bending carefully when he found a particular shell. He dropped it in a small basket with the others, which caused the clinking sound I heard. I moved closer still, accidentally stepping on a small piece of driftwood. It broke beneath my weight and the old man immediately glanced up, startled. Serene, blue-gray eyes met mine and I froze. I was overcome with a feeling of déjà vu and the world faded to darkness around me.

       I opened my eyes and saw that I was back in my darkened room. Confusion heavy on my heart, I pushed back the covers and headed for the bathroom to splash refreshing, cold water on my flushed face. Where had I just been? And who was that man? I pulled my hair up into a bun, checked out my reflection in the mirror and gasped. I quickly let my hair back down and leaned in closer. Well that wasn't something you saw every day. Thin streaks of aqua now highlighted my messy blonde hair. The streaks shimmered slightly in the bathroom light. It was kind of pretty; ethereal almost. Unless it spread and I ended up with a head full of blue hair. I giggled at myself and jumped back in bed. If I woke up looking like Smurfette in the morning, so be it. I was too exhausted to worry about it.

"Seriously? Permanent highlights?" Carmen crossed her arms over her chest with disdain. "Do you know how many people would kill to have those?"

"Something tells me aqua wouldn't be their first choice of color." I laughed and adjusted my bags as we walked out of Maren Hall on our way to the marina.

"Maybe you'll start a new trend!" Phoebe shrieked. "I can already picture the cover of Glamour magazine: Blue highlights: Not just for sea Goddesses anymore…"

"Somehow I don't think it's going to catch on, Phoebs." I couldn't help snickering at her, but I was also secretly hoping Finn wouldn't think they were weird. My heart skipped several beats at the thought of him. I couldn't wait to spend an entire weekend with him, even though I had no idea what we would be doing. Of course, we could be cleaning the beach house from top to bottom and I wouldn't care as long as we were together.

Once arriving at the marina, three very tan, very good-looking dark haired guys met us on the boardwalk and took our bags. Ian, with his black onyx necklace and diamond stud earrings catching the light of the sun, and two guys I assumed were Cage and Ricker. Although Finn talked about them, I had never actually met them. Ian wrapped his arm around a glowing Phoebe and kissed her gently on the lips, while the other two glanced back at the yacht. If I thought it was impressive the night of the Ball, it blew my mind in the daylight. Several times larger than Olivia's, the Sons' yacht dwarfed all other boats docked in the marina. From what I could tell there were four levels, as well as a large deck on the bow and stern. On the top level a smaller, more secluded deck overlooked the rest of the boat.

"Aren't you going to introduce Stasia to your friends?" Carmen looked expectantly at Ian.

"Cage, Ricker...Stasia." He gestured at each of us in the world's shortest introduction ever.

"Nice to meet you." Cage smiled genuinely at me and then made a face at Ian, who was too busy kissing Phoebe to notice. Cage's full head of curly dark hair and warm brown eyes matched his laid back style, and his plaid swim trunks told me he was ready to get this vacation underway. I instantly liked him. Ricker was a little more reserved, with short hair and light blue eyes. He was tall with a lean build, and simply nodded his head at me. I saw Carmen narrow her eyes at him as he twisted on his heel.

"Finn and Liam are already on board," Ian informed us as the six of us ascended the ramp attached to the back deck.

We entered through the same door we had the night of the Ball, but instead of continuing into the sitting area, we climbed a small staircase. The second level could best be described as the ultimate man cave. On the far side of the room a pool table, foosball table, air hockey game, and a couple old-school arcade games littered the deep red carpet. Directly in front of us were several large black leather couches and fluffy armchairs facing a large flat screen TV on the wall. In the corner a small kitchenette housed a refrigerator, microwave and sink. Maybe this was where the Sons were while everyone else was hanging out at school. You'd have to drag me off of this boat if I had unrestricted access to it.

Someone was splayed across one of the leather couches watching ESPN, but he jumped up at our entrance.

His pale skin and unruly blond hair that he kept tucking behind his ears made him stick out like a sore thumb amongst Ian, Ricker and Cage. He had warm green eyes that darted shyly toward Willow. He effortlessly hopped over the back of the couch and introduced himself with a cute boyish smile.

"I'm Liam," he announced, before Ian could introduce me. His khaki shorts hung low on his hips; his blue plaid boxer shorts peeking out below a white t-shirt. His height and the impressive muscles of his upper body had me placing him in the Triton category. He had to be at least six feet-four inches tall! My assumption was confirmed when I caught sight of a trace in the shape of a trident along his calf as he inched his way closer to Willow.

"I'm Stasia," I told him.

"Charmed." He bowed to me and glanced back at Willow; clearly trying to impress her with his theatrics.

"Nice to meet you." I held back a chuckle.

"Finn's upstairs. He told me to send you that way when you got on board." Liam gestured up another small flight of stairs. It was no wonder most wealthy people were always in shape. When your boat has five flights of stairs and your house is a million square feet, you either needed roller skates or plenty of stamina. I left the others and headed upstairs in search of Finn.

The next level of the yacht held a small sitting area with a glass door leading to the control deck, but it appeared to be empty. I continued climbing the stairs to the top level, hoping to find him there. At the top of the stairs, I stepped into a modest bedroom. Old world nautical artifacts decorated the room. An antique telescope sat on a tripod in one corner, a seventeenth-century compass and octant sat on the nightstand, and a weathered wooden ship's wheel hung on the wall above the bed. A low bookshelf full of books and more artifacts ran the length of one wall. A photograph in a simple black frame caught my eye and I strode over to the shelves to get a closer look. It was a younger Finn in the arms of Natasha; him laughing while she looked down at him with unending love. It made me smile, but also sent a wave of sadness through my heart; reminding me of what I never had. As I scanned the rest of the shelf, something else jumped out at me.

A double-bladed axe lay on its side; the serrated blade glinting in the sunlight. The handle was encrusted with diamonds and black onyx, which gave it a menacing, but captivating appearance. I slowly ran my finger over the jewels and noticed something engraved on the blade. Finn's full name was written in an elaborate script. It was beautiful and deadly, just like its owner. Engrossed in its splendor, I almost missed the savage presence looming above on the next shelf. As my eyes flitted upward, they were trapped in the chilling, gaping eye sockets of an actual skull and crossbones. But this wasn't bought in a costume store, this was the real deal. Its crooked teeth were slightly yellowed with age, and the bones themselves were more of a brownish color. The two long bones were held together with what looked to be an old piece of rope, and the skull sat atop them. My blood turned to ice and I fell backward; tripping over the black braided rug covering the wooden floor. Unable to tear my eyes away from its haunting stare, I jumped out of my skin at the sound of Finn's low, ghostly voice.

"I see you've met my father."

I spun around clumsily and encountered Finn's stormy blue eyes watching me curiously. Wearing a gray shirt and black swim trunks, he looked sexier than ever. The corner of his perfectly shaped mouth lifted ever so slightly into a crooked grin, while I did everything I could to calm my racing heart and stop my feet from running back down the stairs.

"You...your father is...dead?" I knew the look on my face screamed of shock and horror, but I had no control over it at this point.

"Technically, yes," he breezily clarified for me. He stepped over to the skull and crossbones and rested his hand on top of the skull, while I tried not to shiver visibly. Apparently keeping your father's bones in your bedroom wasn't disturbing to him at all. I was hoping any other skeletons in his closet weren't actual skeletons.

"Technically?" I shivered again.

"His body is dead, but his soul is very much alive." He smiled lovingly at the skull and took a step toward me.

"So he's a...ghost?" I guessed, knowing full well I didn't believe in ghosts. His slight leer turned into a full blown smile as he started laughing.

"Don't let him hear you say that." He chuckled again and I did a quick survey of the room for fear his dad was hanging around listening to us. Finn looked at me apologetically and took my hands in his. "Ghosts are fickle souls who will forever be lost and broken. They were awarded no true resting place in the Underworld, so they walk the realm of the living. My father is anything but lost or broken."

Glancing back at the double axe, the skull and crossbones, and then around his penthouse bedroom on a million dollar yacht, I searched his eyes. Still stormy, they swirled with hues of deep blue and gray, but the tenderness in them was unmistakable. He rubbed my cheek and pulled my rigid body close. All I could do was stare up at him, still in shock.

"Who are you?" I whispered in awe.

"Here ya'll are!" We both jumped at Cage's voice bursting with excitement. He stood at the top of the stairs, a little out of breath, and his brown eyes danced with mischief.

"Don't you think it's about time we headed out into the deep blue yonder?" he asked as he shielded his eyes with his hand; peering out the window and into the distance. We snickered at him and descended down to the third level. As Finn and Cage maneuvered the yacht out of the marina with expert precision, I went back down to the second level to find my roommates. As I might have guessed, Phoebe and Carmen were locked in a battle at the air hockey table while Willow played referee. At the moment, she was trying to convince Carmen that Phoebe's last move was indeed legal.

"Hey Stasia!" Phoebe's eyes darted up for only a second, but long enough for Carmen to strategically send the puck flying into her goal.

"Hey! No fair!" Phoebe pouted.

"Okay, I disqualify you both for being so annoying," Willow said as she threw up her hands in defeat and walked over to me.

"Liam told me it should only take about six hours to make it to Cape Lookout from here." I noticed her face redden as she said his name.

"I think somebody has a crush on Liam," I teased her.

"Maybe," she said sheepishly, and then leaned closer. "I think he's kinda cute…"

"I think he thinks you're kinda cute too," I whispered back, and her bright green eyes got wider.

"You really think so?"

"What are ya'll talking about?" Phoebe called out from across the room. She and Carmen continued their game, minus the referee.

"How Willow likes Liam," Carmen answered for us a little too loudly.

"Carmen!" both Willow and I scolded her.

"Who likes Liam?" Ricker asked as he bounded down the steps with none other than Liam. Willow gasped and her face turned bright red. She immediately shot a warning look at Carmen, who just grinned and shrugged her shoulders. I caught Liam glance hesitantly in Willow's direction with hope evident in his eyes.

"We were talking about Liam Hemsworth," Phoebe tried, but Ricker just sneered at her and then Willow, knowing she was making it up.

"Uh-huh." Ricker smirked.

Willow grabbed my hand and yanked me onto the couch away from Liam and Carmen's big mouth, which was still in full swing.

"Why don't you go find someone else to annoy, Ricker?" she snarled at him.

"Why don't you do us all a favor and stop talking, Carmen," he snapped back.

For the next five hours we tried to keep the two of them from ripping each other's eyes out as we exhausted the pool table, Pac-man, foosball table, and two mobster movies, along with a case of Orange Crush and a couple bags of soft pretzels. Thankfully we had good weather and calm seas, so we were making excellent time. When everyone moved outside for some fresh air, Finn held me back.

"I want to show you something," he uttered in a low voice with a dark smile.

"As long as it doesn't involve more bones." I shook my head vehemently.

"You have my word. It's back upstairs in my room." My stomach clenched at the thought of his empty bed, as well as his father's skull and crossbones. I wasn't sure which one I was more afraid of.

"So why do you have your own bedroom on a yacht that's used by all of the Sons?" I questioned him as we climbed the stairs. He ran his hand through his hair before answering.

"Well, I guess you could say I use it more often," he responded vaguely.

"Why's that?" I prodded further. He glanced at me out of the corner of his eye before speaking again.

"Because it's my yacht."

I almost tripped up the stairs. "You're telling me you have your own yacht?" I blurted out; not believing him for a second.

"That's right."

"Are you also going to tell me the beach house is yours, too?" I challenged.

"Of course not!" He laughed at me, as if owning a beach house at the age of seventeen was ludicrous but owning a yacht wasn't. "My family's been around for a very, very long time. Over the years, money just tends to…collect. Your family's no different, Pasha."

He grinned, clearly amused. I hadn't thought about that. Technically I had a huge mansion on the Fortunate Isle. What else did I have that I didn't know about?

"Touche." I snickered. Doing my best to ignore his father's skull staring us, I followed Finn out onto the deck adjacent to his room. The view was magnificent. Sparkling blue water stretched out in every direction, soothing every cell in my body. The deck beneath our feet also held several comfortable-looking lounge chairs and one massive Jacuzzi. I couldn't imagine how incredible it must be up here at night under the stars.

"I haven't had a chance to tell you how beautiful your hair is." Finn gently played with an aqua highlight and I was hopelessly caught in his intense gaze. "It brings out your eyes. It's incredible."

"I don't know how it happened. I went to sleep last night and they just appeared."

"It's all a part of the transition. Your body's slowly transforming as you get closer and closer to your eighteenth birthday. You'll become stronger as well." I remembered how easy it had been to push Noah down on the sand a couple months ago.

"But why now? Why last night?" I wondered; absently fiddling with the hem of my navy shorts.

"Being a direct descendant, you must have been exposed to something from your past or direct bloodline. That's why most Chosen descendants don't have to take a journey to the River - their essence is filled through the presence of their family or something that represents their family." He smiled shyly at me. "That's another reason why I gave you the aquamarine necklace."

"Because aquamarine represents my mother?" I connected the dots.

"Right," he confirmed.

"I had a reverie last night, but I have no idea where I was. There was an old man there."

"Maybe that's why your soul was drawn to him," he suggested as his eyes lit up with excitement. "Because he was in your past or a part of your direct bloodline."

"What about you?" I questioned. "Are you a direct descendant?" Unfortunately instead of an answer, Finn walked back into his room and returned with an object clutched firmly in his hand.

"This is for you," he said as he dropped it into my open palm. It was heavy and solid as I rolled it back and forth with my fingers. I wasn't really certain what I was looking at. It was a large black stone, smooth in texture and oval shaped. A smaller red stone was encased by the black stone; peeking out at various points along the exterior.

"It's a black onyx surrounding a fire agate stone," he expounded; seeing the question already in my eyes.

"It's beautiful…" I whispered. It shimmered in the sunlight as it rolled back and forth in my hand. The black and crimson hues playing off of each other created an effect similar to a campfire; the dark coals supporting and feeding the brighter red flames. It was warm in my hand and sent energy up my arm the longer I held it. "What's it for?"

"It has many uses, but for our purposes this weekend it will act as a kind of homing beacon. Once we begin, you'll understand. Until then, keep it close." He watched me with reverence and moved closer to wrap his arms around my waist.

"I will," I breathed, and slipped my arms around his neck. I rested my head on his solid chest and closed my eyes. I felt so safe with him; so protected. My heart warmed as he sighed happily and squeezed me to him even tighter. The hand that lightly rubbed my back tensed and his fingers trailed down the small of my back; cinching my lavender tank top as if they couldn't keep themselves from travelling farther south. I looked up into his deep blue eyes and was surprised by the passion burning within them. He gripped the fabric tighter, leaned his forehead against mine and closed his eyes; his breath suddenly measured. Witnessing his restraint, my heart melted and then rapidly lit fire; erupting in a tidal wave of longing that crashed over me and washed away any trace of resistance. I tilted my head upward and brought my lips dangerously close to his, which caused the need swirling within me to become almost unbearable. As his breath caught ever so slightly, he opened his eyes and gave in to the heat pulsing between us.

His velvety lips met mine and I felt the passion increase as each kiss became more intense; hotter. As my knees went weak, I reached out for the railing behind me to steady myself. He pressed my body against it and I held on for dear life. He wrapped an arm around the small of my back, his hand squeezing my waist, while the other wrapped around my shoulders and pulled me impossibly close. My body went limp as he slowly caressed the tender skin below my ear; his embrace the only thing holding me upright. My legs had become numb with pleasure and my arms were now holding onto him, struggling to keep up with his fervor.

My heart was on the verge of exploding when he stood quickly, lifted me up and carried me inside. Which was good, because there was no way my legs would have gotten me there. He gently laid me down on the bed, his lips never leaving mine. Unable to get enough of him, I pulled him down on top of me, eager to feel the length of his body pressed against mine. I ran my fingernails down the taut muscles of his arms and heard him groan as he kissed my neck. The tickle of his breath suddenly in my ear had my body responding in a way that threatened to cause the thin string of control I still had to unravel completely. Then someone knocked on the door.

"Hey Finn?"

At Ricker's voice, Finn jumped off of me in a flash, almost tumbling off of the bed in his haste. I stifled a laugh with my hand, but failed miserably when it came out as a snort.

"Yeah?" Finn's voice came out rushed and hoarse.

"The lighthouse is coming up on our bow. I think we've passed the house," Ricker informed him.

"I'll be right there!" he called out, and gingerly sat on the edge of the bed. I crawled over to where he sat and wrapped my arms around him, kissing him square on the cheek. The rush of adrenaline still running through my system made me a little hysterical and I couldn't stop giggling. Unfortunately for me and my need for oxygen, Finn grabbed me and began to tickle me relentlessly. Laughing so hard that my stomach began to hurt, he finally relinquished his attack and left me gasping for air.

"As soon as...I find your...weakness, you're in...trouble," I threatened him through shallow breaths, falling short of convincing.

"I'll be sure to sleep with one eye open." He laughed at me and kissed me one last time, leaving me gasping for air all over again.

While Finn hastened down to the control room to right our course, I strolled back out onto the deck. From this viewpoint I could see only water, but as the yacht made a wide left turn, a thin strip of land appeared. A towering lighthouse rose majestically from the sand, silently watching over the Cape and surrounding ocean. The black and white diamond design told me that this was the Cape Lookout Lighthouse. Past the regal lighthouse, long expansive beaches were backed by massive rolling sand dunes and a forest of trees that resembled the live oaks on Bald Head. The lighthouse was the only sign of civilization I had seen thus far. There were no vacation homes, shops, or sunbathing tourists dotting the beaches. I leaned over the rail and tried to pinpoint our exact destination, only to find more vacant beach and cresting waves.

With a thrilling rush of excitement, I dashed downstairs to join everyone else. I found them on the bow of the boat admiring the untouched landscape.

"This part of the Cape is actually called the Shackleford Banks," Liam pointed out to us. "It's still mainly uninhabited and looks exactly like it did in the time of Blackbeard."

"Who's Blackbeard?" Phoebe inquired; still gazing at the beach.

"He was a pirate who frequented the waters around North and South Carolina. Eventually his ship, the Queen Anne's Revenge, ran aground sailing into Beaufort Inlet, which is just north of here. He was killed in a bloody battle at Ocracoke Island," he explained further, and his eyes turned wistful.

"Wow," Phoebe marveled, eyes wide. Willow eyed Liam with glowing admiration and I could tell she was impressed by not only his good looks, but his mind as well. I smiled to myself and searched again for our elusive destination.

The yacht slowed and came to a complete stop in a seemingly random spot. The sound of the anchor dropping had us all looking at the other Sons standing on the deck with one question on our faces.

"How are we going to get to the beach?" Carmen was the first to ask; skeptically measuring the distance between the yacht and the beach.

"We'll just have to make a swim for it," Ricker said as he shrugged his shoulders with a twinkle in his eye.

"Swim?" Phoebe peered over the side of the yacht apprehensively. "But won't our stuff get wet?"

"Then I'll be staying on this perfectly dry yacht," Carmen clipped; regarding Ricker with a chilly expression. The massive yacht still wasn't large enough for both of them. They were too much alike.

"Be my guest." Ricker stepped towards Carmen with hostility apparent in his tone.

"You'd like that, wouldn't you?" Not to be outdone, Carmen stepped towards him as well.

"As a matter of fact I would," he challenged her.

"Good. 'Cause I'm not staying anywhere near you!"

"Oh, my feelings are so hurt!" He pretended to clutch his stomach, then narrowed his eyes at her. "You think I want to stay anywhere near you?"

"Well, good! I don't want to hear your annoying voice and smell that god-awful cologne that's been making me gag for the last six hours!"

"You think that's bad?! How about hearing you complain and whine for the last three ye-"

"Nobody's making a swim for it," Finn interrupted him; appearing behind us suddenly. "So stop fighting about it." He shot a look at Ricker, who immediately looked down at the deck and stepped away from Carmen. It still surprised me how much the other Sons revered Finn. Liam threw his strong arm around Finn's shoulders and smiled wickedly at everyone.

"Who's ready for a little James Bond action?" He wiggled his blond eyebrows at us. The guys took off towards a miniature elevator, while the girls trailed behind uncertainly. After three trips (it was a really small elevator) we all stood in a snug, darkened room. Someone hit the lights and a nice-sized dinghy materialized before us. It was completely black and matched the stealth appearance of the yacht it was housed in.

We piled in along with our luggage and Finn hit a few buttons on his phone. Suddenly we were drenched in sunlight as a ramp slowly lowered from the back of the yacht, providing immediate access to the ocean. Sharing a tentative look with Phoebe, I held on tightly as a conveyer belt below the dinghy moved us to the top of the ramp. I heard myself shriek as the boat flew downward and landed hard in the water. With another command via Finn's smart phone, the ramp lifted; disappearing into the bottom of the yacht. He started the dinghy's small motor and we were on our way. As we neared the breakers, Finn leaned over and dragged the tips of his fingers through the water. The waves ahead of us immediately stilled, providing a smooth channel of passage leading to the beach.

Finn's gaze flickered up and met mine. His deep blue eyes danced across the small raft and directly into the depths of my heart. Our friends, the raft and the ocean disappeared when he smiled, and an explosion of emotions shot through my body.

"Is that the house?" Phoebe exclaimed. Her voice broke through my thoughts and I followed her awestruck eyes. Past the wide beach and expansive sand dunes, a sprawling estate blended in perfectly with the landscape.

"That's it!" Ian smiled with pride. We all lurched forward as the raft ran up onto the beach. We gathered our things and trudged up the sand toward the house's boardwalk; walking above the dunes and small brush that skimmed the bottom of the wooden slats. The full estate came into view and my first thought was that it belonged in the Hamptons, not on the Outer Banks of North Carolina. The white cedar shake exterior complemented the mass of trees that skirted the grounds, and we followed the winding stone path around a sparkling pool and up to an inviting patio. Ian stepped forward, produced a set of keys, and we entered an elaborate sunroom furnished with lush plants and wicker patio furniture. A glass door led us to the main living area.

"Wow," Willow gasped, and I agreed with her astonishment whole-heartedly. Crisp shades of white, cream, and brown greeted us as we took in the overflowing couches, chairs and pillows. I was immediately drawn to the substantial wooden coffee table sitting amidst the furniture. I ran my fingers along its length, mesmerized by its beauty. Surprisingly, it sent that familiar tingle up through my arm that typically only sea animals could evoke. The wood itself was dark, very weathered and smooth to the touch, and I could tell the wood of the table was extremely old; this was only one of the many identities it had taken during its long life. I looked around the rest of the room and noticed several other pieces made from the same wood.

"This place looks like a Pottery Barn showroom!" Phoebe chirped; coming to stand beside me. "Did you see the kitchen?"

We explored the rest of the residence and were blown away again and again by each new room we entered. We eventually found the bedrooms, which were quickly claimed. Willow and I would be sharing a room, while

Carmen and Phoebe commandeered the one across the hall. Finn and Liam grabbed the next one, while Ricker, Ian and Cage immediately headed for a loft overlooking the main room that contained several beds and a massive flat screen TV on the wall.

"Oh my God, you guys! Come look at this deck."

I followed Carmen's voice out to what I thought was just a patio, but after stepping outside, I saw it was anything but. An outdoor gathering area constructed of stone was spread out before us. The biggest grill I ever laid eyes on was encased in gray stone and faced an elaborate fireplace that reached at least ten feet tall. A litany of beautiful couches and chairs were set up for conversation and relaxing. Past the deck was an extensive backyard full of colorful gardens, divided by winding walking trails. They overflowed with everything from hydrangeas to impatiens, and the array of colors was magnificent. A small, gray stone bridge crossed a sparkling creek that ran along the outside of the property and disappeared into the cluster of yaupon trees beyond.

As my gaze drifted to an elaborate fountain that adorned the center of the gardens, my heart stopped and my blood ran cold with fear. She wore a blue dress that skimmed the top of her bare feet. Long blonde hair fell below her shoulders, untouched by the summer breeze, and her thin arms hung limply at her sides. The pale skin of her face offset the bright green eyes that stared straight at me. Not completely opaque, I could actually see through her body and onto the stone path behind her. Expressionless and unblinking, she stood completely still while a cold sweat broke out on my forehead.

"Are you okay?" I vaguely registered Carmen's voice next to me.

Her bare feet became transparent as she turned languidly and drifted away. I contemplated going after her, but the grotesque sight of her back stopped me dead in my tracks. Her skull appeared to have been caved in, and her blonde hair was matted with dark blood. The back of her blue dress was shredded, revealing long, jagged gashes in her skin. A bloodcurdling scream began to fester in the pit of my stomach, but I clamped a hand over my mouth before it escaped.

"Stasia?"

As she disappeared amongst the trees, I deliberately turned my head towards Phoebe; not trusting my legs to remain where they were. They wanted nothing more than to run as fast as possible back to the yacht and back to Lorelei. I lowered my hand and took several deep breaths.

"Please tell me you guys saw that," I managed; my tone deadpan.

"Saw what?" Phoebe glimpsed back and forth between the backyard and my still panicked expression.

"The girl." I stared at them wide-eyed and realized I was alone in my terror.

"What girl?" Carmen wrapped her arms around my shoulders and led me back into the house. "Come on, let's go inside." Once inside, my phone began to ring in my pocket, so I found a quiet hallway and answered it. Shock still fresh in my system, I reminded myself I had to talk.

"Hello?"

"Hey girl, how are you?"

"Hey Kira!" I attempted to sound chipper.

"Are you okay?" Apparently I wasn't a good actor.

"Um…yeah, yeah I'm alright," I stumbled. "I just have a lot on my mind."

"You didn't go home for Fall break?"

"No, we actually decided to come to Cape Lookout with Finn and his friends to stay at their beach house for the weekend," I explained.

"Really? I've heard it's beautiful out there," she gushed.

44

"I love it so far, but we kind of have an ulterior motive for coming somewhere so remote." I went on to tell her our plan for the weekend and my attempt to contact my mother.

"Do you think it will work?" she asked; her tone full of doubt.

"I don't know. But Finn seems to think it will, so I'm going to give it a try."

"Just be careful, okay?"

"I will, I promise," I assured her. "I'll come see you as soon as we get back to Lorelei."

"I want to hear all about it and if you need me, don't hesitate to call."

"Thanks Kira."

"Are you sure we can't just Google it?" Phoebe threw out to the group. After stuffing ourselves with the delicious lasagna Willow made for dinner, we were all hanging out in the living room discussing the unfortunate nuances of my ever-complicated life. Finn and I explained my most recent dilemma: not knowing my true birthday and its effect on when I had to make the journey to the Underworld. Phoebe was completely convinced we could figure it out using the internet, but I think she was just trying to make me feel better.

"Why can't you just ask her?" Cage, who had been quiet for the entire conversation, asked Finn.

"You know that's not how it works," Finn retorted, his voice clipped. My memory sparked to life and I recalled a conversation that Finn and I had about my mom. He told me that she had been ecstatic that I chose the name Anastasia when I came to Lorelei. So…he obviously had a way of communicating with the dead.

"That's right! You said you'd talked to her before. Why wouldn't you be able to talk to her about this too?" I asked him, hopeful.

"I didn't say I talked to her, I just said she was happy about you choosing Anastasia. Someone else relayed that particular message to me." As Willow, Carmen, Phoebe and I stared at him in confusion, he sighed in defeat and continued.

"I can't talk about anything I see or hear in the Underworld. It's not that I don't want to…I physically can't." He ran his hands through his hair, clearly uncomfortable.

"Oh my God!" Phoebe gasped. "You've actually been to the Underworld!?"

"Of course he has, he's the-" Ian started to explain, before Finn shot him a steely look that instantly quieted him.

"I'm not getting into that tonight. Right now we need to concentrate on Stasia and figure out when she was born. Unfortunately, this is the only way." Finn took my hand and squeezed it, but it did little to ease my anxiety surrounding his solution. The fact that I had been able to see my mother before that first fateful vision, had given Finn an idea. He believed I could contact her somehow during a reverie and communicate with her. Obviously I wasn't too optimistic about my chances of success, considering I didn't even know how to control my reveries. I had no idea how to contact my mom and communicate with her. The only thing that gave me an ounce of confidence was Finn's unfailing conviction. If he believed it would work, I would give it everything I had. Where that would get us, we'd just have to wait and see.

"The first thing we have to do is practice, so that's what we're going to do tonight. I'll take her down near the lighthouse so there aren't any distractions," Finn maintained.

"No way. We're going too. What if something happens?" Willow disputed.

"The less people around her, the better; and besides, tonight will only be practice. I promise she'll be fine. You have my word," Finn declared. Willow sat back but crossed her arms; not completely convinced.

"You guys, I'll be fine, really. Chances are I won't be able to do it anyway, so you'd just end up getting really bored watching me sleep," I quipped; hoping to elicit some smiles, but my roommates weren't finding the humor in the situation.

"Tomorrow night when we try it for real, you all can be there. But tonight she needs to concentrate," Finn attested. He stood abruptly and walked towards the kitchen, which effectively signaled there would be no further discussion.

"So what are the rest of us going to do tonight?" Phoebe's green eyes lit up as she surveyed everyone else. I took the opportunity to go after Finn. The whole contacting-my-mom-thing didn't damper the fact that I was going to spend time with him on the beach all night. I discovered him in the hall collecting blankets from the walk-in linen closet.

"You ready?" He smiled at me with obvious enthusiasm. I could tell he had no doubt I would be successful. I wished I felt the same way.

"Ready as I'll ever be."

"Control is all about awareness. You have to be cognizant of everything around you at all times; that means your body and especially your soul." Finn and I arrived at the Cape just after sunset. Traces of orange and pink still enveloped the sky, but the world around us had grown increasingly lurid. I made sure to inspect the beach for any signs of unwanted, bleeding ghosts. So far, so good. I really wanted to mention it to Finn, but I knew I should be concentrating on the task at hand. Besides, I was probably just hallucinating. Maybe I'd had a mild sun stroke? It could happen. I wiped her ghoulish face out of my mind and tried to focus.

The night air was heavy with moisture, with only a slight breeze blowing in from the ocean. Brilliant stars sparkled down on us from above, silently observing my first of many lessons. We sat Indian-style; facing each other on a soft fleece blanket just below the sand dunes of the beach. The imposing Cape Lookout lighthouse stood to my left; hypnotizing me with the slow rhythm of its revolving light as it methodically scanned the ocean. To understand exactly what I was about to attempt, Finn was in the process of telling me exactly how reveries worked. He held my hands in his while the skull and crossbones trace on his forearm shimmered in the light of the stars.

"Close your eyes."

"Close my eyes?" Was I going to sleep already? He nodded, so I shut them and tried to sit up straighter in the

48

hopes I would be prepared for whatever he was about to throw my way.

"Now tell me what you see," he instructed.

"Um...nothing." I heard him snicker. I frowned but kept my eyes closed.

"Just because you have your eyes closed, doesn't necessarily mean your eyes have stopped seeing. So, try again. Tell me what you see." After a long moment of awkward silence, a flash of light swept across my eyelids and they flew open.

"The lighthouse! I saw its light!"

"Good - now close your eyes again, but this time tell me what you hear," he told me calmly. I listened closely, but the sound of the ocean drowned out the possibility of hearing anything else.

"I just hear the waves crashing."

"Good, now tell me what you feel," he prompted without missing a beat. I concentrated on my bare skin that was in direct contact with my surroundings.

"The softness of the sand...and the wind," I claimed, and opened my eyes again. I took notice of how oddly exposed I felt with my eyes closed.

"Good. Just like humans, your five senses are attached to your physical body. So when you want your soul to be back in your body, you concentrate on those five physical senses. Whether it's sight, touch, or hearing, latch on to whichever one is strongest at the time." He paused to make sure I understood, and then continued. "But with the addition of essence to our souls, we have another sense that humans don't have."

"We do?" Things like spidey vision and sonic hearing ran through my thoughts.

"You've been using it all along, you just didn't know it," he revealed. He threaded his warm fingers through mine; sending tingles across my skin. His features softened and he suddenly appeared more vulnerable.

"What do you...sense about me?" he requested shyly. I automatically diverted my eyes to the patch of blanket between us. I had a feeling that incredibly sexy, alluring and good-looking weren't the answers he was looking for, but they were exactly what came to mind. My heart began to beat wildly as I searched for a way to describe what I 'sensed' about him without sounding like an obsessed groupie. I closed my eyes like I had with the other senses and opened my mind.

"The main thing I sense is...darkness." As soon as the words were out I realized how awful they sounded, so I rushed to clarify. "But it's not a bad darkness. It's more like a warm-summer-night kind of darkness, not the monster-under-the-bed kind of darkness." Wow. Great explanation...for a six year old. I should have stuck with sexy, alluring and good-looking.

"Monster under the bed?" he remarked, seeming to enjoy my obvious discomfort. I began to describe how I used to take a running start and jump on my bed in order to avoid the monster that was surely lurking underneath, waiting for the opportune time to grab my ankles and eat me alive. Thankfully, before I could embarrass myself further, he continued.

"So how exactly do you sense that darkness?" He arched a dark eyebrow at me.

"I....feel it. Not in the same way that I feel the sand or the wind. I just...know it's there."

"Jackpot. That's your other sense kicking in." He smiled at me with pride. I pondered whether or not my 'other sense' included seeing darkness as well. Nadia's darkness was definitely the monster-under-the-bed kind. Before I could ask, he rose to his knees; eyes gleaming with excitement.

"Time to practice, Pasha."

Ignoring the turmoil growing in my stomach, I positioned myself on my back and gazed up at the stars with consternation. Finn crawled around to the crown of my head; simultaneously erupting into a fit of laughter.

"You might want to try and relax. It works better that way," he sneered down at me.

I glared up at him. "Go ahead and laugh, but you aren't the one sprawled out on a blanket like a science experiment." Still smiling, he leaned down and lightly kissed me on the forehead.

"You've done this a dozen times, there's nothing to worry about. I promise." He ran his fingers gently through my hair. "I'll be right here the whole time."

"Promise?" I peeked up at him, requiring a little more reassurance.

"I promise," he assured me. Satisfied, I closed my eyes and commenced to taking long, deep breaths. "First thing I want you to practice is separating your soul from your body, but not letting it go anywhere. Since you know it's going to happen, try to relax your mind and allow yourself to let go. If you don't wake up in five minutes, I'll wake you up."

"Okay, but usually I just wake up somewhere else during the reverie. I don't ever remember separating from my body."

"This time you're doing it voluntarily, so you should be able to remember the experience. Now, try and relax." I focused my ears on the roar of the ocean and allowed the soft wind to caress my skin. Feeling Finn's eyes on me, I cracked open one eye and observed him.

"I can see your nose hairs."

"I bet closing your eyes would help."

"I can see your Adams apple, too," I said, suppressing a giggle.

"You're about to see me tickle you if you don't close your eyes and concentrate," he threatened me with an incorrigible smile. When I failed to do so, he lunged forward; convincing me he was going to launch a full blown tickle attack.

"Okay! Okay! I'll close my eyes, I'll do it! I'll do it!" I squealed and attempted to squirm away from his torturous hands that hovered precariously above my stomach. After my giggles died down, Finn continued to run his fingertips through my hair and I finally felt my body relax. I listened to my own breathing and felt my conscious mind center as it began to grow numb with sleep. I forced myself to direct my focus inward, and automatically endured a slight dizzying sensation. My immediate response was to steady myself in order to curb the uncomfortable feeling, but I made myself endure and give into the weirdness. As I continued to spin, I let go absolutely; quickly sinking. I descended farther and farther until I was simply suspended in a world of weightlessness. I hesitantly opened my eyes.

Stars. I failed. I was still lying on my back, staring at the sky trying to go to sleep. But if that was the case, why did I feel so light all of a sudden? I tentatively sat up and scanned my surroundings. I wasn't on the beach anymore. Odd. I was...above it. I steeled myself and peered down. What I saw would remain with me for the rest of my life. It was as unsettling as it was miraculous. My body lay peaceful and unmoving below; eyes closed. Finn was observing my face intently, still clutching my hand. It melted my heart and made me smile down at him lovingly. Suddenly I began to move. Finn and my body continued to grow smaller and smaller as the ocean spread out before me. Where was I going? I wasn't supposed to go anywhere! I needed to go back! As panic raced through my veins, I tried to remember what Finn told me. Senses. Something about senses. I closed my eyes and listened. All I could hear was the sound of wind as I flew out over the water. I listened harder, but couldn't hear anything else. I opened my eyes and looked for the lighthouse's revolving light. Where was it? Was I too far away already? Feel. What did I feel? Finn had been holding my hand. I looked down at my hand and tried to feel his palm in mine. I closed my eyes and concentrated harder. Warmth. A soothing touch. I could feel it. I squeezed it to make sure I wasn't imagining things.

"I did it!" I shot up; filled with overwhelming elation. "I did it!" I turned to face him and launched myself into his open arms. Laughing, he tumbled backwards and hugged me back while I continued. "I saw my body! And I saw you! I did like you said and concentrated on my senses to get back to my body. I felt your hand and all of a sudden I was back!"

"Never a doubt in my mind." He kissed me, and then carefully brought me back down to reality with his soothing words. "Now, let's see if you can take it one step further."

I collected myself as much as I could, then sat back down and faced him with eagerness. "Okay, what's next, Professor?"

"Next is purposefully going somewhere. We'll need to pick a place relatively close so you can practice directing your soul, and also coming back to your body at will."

"Would Bald Head be considered relatively close?" I proposed, but he shook his head in disagreement.

"Let's start with the yacht. If that goes well, you can try Bald Head."

"I can live with that," I conceded. This time as I lay back down and gazed up into Finn's eyes, relaxing my body came much easier to me. After several minutes, I began to feel the numbness, the dizziness and sinking, and then finally the weightlessness.

Stars. Again. But this time I knew right away. I remembered that the lightness meant I'd succeeded in separating from my body. I immediately sat up, glanced down and saw my body lying below me with Finn once again holding my hand. Infused with excitement, I scanned the water in search of the yacht. I could just make out the white hull in the distance. Keeping my eyes locked on the yacht and concentrating on moving towards it, I felt a pull in that general direction. I glanced down to witness the ocean blurring beneath me as I picked up speed. As the yacht began to get closer and closer, I started to panic. How did I slow down? What if I hit the boat? Then what happened? Unfortunately, I didn't have a chance to find out as I reached the boat and proceeded to fly right past it. The pull I felt became stronger; holding me hostage and increasing my speed. The dark water below me and the star-filled sky above melted together into one continuous blur. I had no idea where I was headed, but I knew one thing for certain: I was no longer in control. My head exploded with pain and the world went completely black.

I gasped as I took in the spectacle before me. I was precariously perched on the top row of some kind of stone coliseum. At least a thousand people crowded the levels of seats that rose impossibly high into the night air. Seemingly carved out of a mountain, the coliseum encircled the main attraction far below. The modern lights towering above me shone down on the large circle that everyone was watching. Cheers and stomping feet filled my ears as I tried to understand what they were so enthralled with. I saw the figures of two men in the circle. They looked like they were fighting, but to be sure I needed to get closer. I carefully made my way down the stone steps nearby and arrived at a lower level that allowed a better view. Before I could focus in on the fighters, my eyes caught on a woman sitting directly across the circle from me. She was crying. Natasha! Beside her sat the same older looking man I had seen that night at the Ball. The one Finn claimed was just a friend. A cheer rising from the crowd averted my attention back to the fight. The two men were already beaten and bloodied as they continually lunged for each other. Their dark hair shining in the artificial light, they wore only black shorts. Their muscular bodies were tense with the anticipation of their opponent's next move. One in particular moved with quiet stealth. He was always one step faster than the other; his movements more fluid. His bloody hands were wrapped in a type of brown leather that extended from his fingers to his wrists, sort of like a glove…leather…glove…Finn. Finn! I squinted in an effort to see past the bruises and swollen eyes. It was definitely Finn. That's also when I noticed the array of weapons littering the circle; a double bladed axe attached to a handle encrusted in onyx and diamonds being one of them. What was happening? And why was I here? Another cheer came from the crowd as Finn was able to throw the other man down and reach for his axe. But before he could wrap his hands around the handle, his opponent jumped to his feet and tackled him to the ground. He raised a silver, menacing sword above Finn's chest and a collective gasp came from the crowd.

"Stasia! Wake up!"

My eyes flew open and I scrambled to my feet. My heart was beating wildly and I was drenched in sweat. Finn was still sitting on the blanket, watching me with concern.

"I'm not going to watch you die!" I screamed at him. Confusion washed over his face as he stood and walked towards me slowly; somehow knowing the turmoil that was racing through me. He held his hands up.

"I'm not dying, Stasia. I'm fine. See?" He continued taking steps toward me.

"Stop!" I warned him as I tried to catch my breath and still my frantic pulse. He stopped advancing immediately and held his tongue. What had just happened? That wasn't a reverie. Well it was, before… it was a vision. I let out a ragged breath and dropped to the sand below me in defeat; closing my eyes.

"No more secrets, Finn. If I'm going to start having visions like that, I need to know what's going on with you." I felt his presence in front of me as he sat down on the sand beside me. I met his worried gaze.

"What did you see?" he prodded carefully; a shadow falling over his features.

"My reverie changed into a vision," I breathed. "You were fighting. You were in a huge stone coliseum and there were tons of people watching, like it was some kind of sick sport - they were cheering for you to kill each other!" I yelled, exasperated, but his handsome face turned blurry as the tears collected in my eyes. "Even Natasha was there, as well as the older man from the Ball."

His eyes fell to the sand before meeting mine once again; pleading, almost fearful. He reached out slowly, took my hand, and gently ran his finger over my trace. His touch calmed my nerves immediately and I felt the tears finally spill over and roll down my cheeks.

"I can't tell you everything, Stasia. I wish I could, but I just can't," he whispered, and swiped a tear from my cheek. My eyes dropped to my triskellion trace in disappointment, and I ran a finger across the swirls that extended all the way to my ring finger.

"I just need to understand. You always tell me I can trust you, but you need to know you can trust me too. It goes both ways. Nothing you tell me will change the way I feel about you. I love you, Finn. Please just tell me something. Anything."

"I love you too, Stasia. You're everything to me and I never want to lose you. Unfortunately that means having to keep certain things from you. For your safety."

"I can take care of myself!" I threw at him in desperation.

"I know, I know." He moved closer, grasping my hand; desperately wanting me to understand. "You're so strong, Stasia. But there are forces in this world - evil forces - that are almost impossible to overcome. I would never forgive myself if I let anything happen to you." The sorrow in his eyes unraveled my resolve.

"I just need to understand. I want to be there for you like you have been for me. We're in this together." He searched my eyes and I saw the war playing out in his mind; trying to decide what to divulge.

"Charon," he whispered.

"What?"

"Do you know who Charon is?" he asked quietly. I nodded.

"He's the God of the Underworld."

"Right. All the Sons of Daimon are descended from him," he added.

"Why aren't you called the Sons of Charon?" I asked curiously.

"He's been known by many different names, Charon being the most recent, but Daimon was the name he was given at birth." He took a deep breath and continued, "Every five hundred years the Prime, or leader of the Sons, steps down. But his successor has to be a direct descendant of Charon; a true Son. That successor becomes the new leader at the age of eighteen; as well as becoming immortal. Until then he's referred to as…the Scion." He paused as my eyes got wide. "Charon is my father, Stasia. I was Chosen to be the next Prime."

A wide smile spread across my face and my heart filled with unabated pride. I leaned forward and smothered him in a hug.

"Oh, Finn! That's incredible!" I exclaimed, but my excitement wasn't reciprocated. I sat back and examined his face with confusion.

"It's an amazing honor, but there are sacrifices a Prime has to endure. Many sacrifices. You witnessed the first in your vision." His features darkened and his eyes filled with sadness. "The Scion isn't just appointed as Prime, he has to earn his place as leader. So, in order to become the Prime, on my eighteenth birthday I must kill the current Prime." Understanding crept into my heart, tearing it in two.

"That means…." I couldn't say the words I was thinking.

"I have to kill my own brother," he finished for me; his voice oppressed with obligation and defeat.

"But….why?" I furrowed my brow. Would I be strong enough to kill my own sibling in order to fulfill my rightful destiny?

"All true Sons return to the Underworld to serve under Charon once they complete their time as Prime. But it's also the first test of sacrifice for the new Prime. It's been that way for thousands of years."

"That's what you've been practicing for…" The image of Finn on the ground in my vision flashed before my eyes. "But what if he kills you first?"

"He'll remain the Prime and my soul will be sent to serve under Charon in his place." My heart froze in fear. That couldn't happen. I couldn't lose him.

"Your soul…" I exalted quietly.

"Since I'm a direct descendant of Charon, my soul already belongs to the Underworld. That's the 'darkness' you feel." He held up air quotes and grinned at me with amusement. I couldn't help but wonder once again what that meant about Nadia, considering I could actually see her darkness, but I tried to push that thought out of my head.

"What other sacrifices will you have to make?" I asked; a sense of dread filling every fiber of my being. I couldn't imagine how lonely it must be for him.

"My own sacrifices, I can handle. I've come to terms with my destiny," he claimed with creed. "It's the price the people I love will have to pay that I can't bear." The muscle in his jaw flexed with anger.

"What price do they have to pay?" I asked hesitantly.

"Stasia-"

"Here they are! I found them!" Phoebe was jogging up the beach towards us, followed by several other shadowy shapes resembling Ian, Willow and Liam.

"Hey you guys!" She waved at us. Automatically thinking something was wrong, I jumped up and met her near the water's edge.

"Is everything okay, Phoebs?" I asked her.

"Of course! We were getting worried about you guys. You've been gone for a long time." She gave me a hug and smiled at Finn. "Plus we got tired of listening to Ricker and Carmen fight, so we left Cage to deal with them and went for a little midnight walk!"

Deciding I'd been through enough for one night, we decided to give it another try tomorrow afternoon. If that went well, we'd try to contact Thetis later that night. I had to admit I was relieved, but I was quickly losing any faith that I would be able to pull this off.

Click….creeek….click….creeek… The cloak of night was still heavy on the world when I woke up with a start. Click….creeek….click… Trying not to wake Willow, I slid out of the covers and tiptoed over to the large bay window in our room. The sound was coming from the backyard; the gardens. From my vantage point they were shaded under a light veil of dew, glistening in the moonlight. Creeek…click…creeek…click… The sunshine-filled rooms of yesterday had morphed into something darker and more menacing as I made my way out into the hall, down the stairs, and towards the back deck. The hair on my arms lifted and I felt my heart thumping faster against my chest. The image of the ghost's blood-matted blonde hair and shredded skin flashed in my mind, and I almost ran back upstairs..

I peered out of the window into the gardens beyond, when the sound of a door shutting upstairs had me clamping a hand over the scream trying to escape my mouth. I closed my eyes and took deep breaths. Some Goddess I was - scared of a door shutting. I rolled my eyes and stood up straight. I had nothing to be afraid of. As I reached for the door handle, I realized it was already ajar. I steeled myself and stepped out into the crisp night air. Click....creeek....click...

A rolling mist had set in and it swirled around the garden in a magical cadence. The savory fragrances of the flowers invaded my senses and the sound of the ocean rushed in my ears; submerging me in its fury and strengthening me. Although there were seven other people inside, I felt completely isolated. The world around me had come alive with energy. It pulsed in every flower, every leaf, and every blade of grass as I walked along the stone path. I sensed their acknowledgement of my presence as clearly as if they had spoken it aloud. The cool mist swirled and settled on my bare skin; initiating me into the ethereal world I had just entered. Click....creeek...click...

Now I could tell the sound was coming from along the edge of the gardens, near the side of the house. I circled back and inched my way to the corner of the house. Click...creeek....click... Holding my breath, I leaned forward to get a better view. Click...creeek....click... I leaned a little farther, a little farther...and lost my balance.

Sprawled out on the grass, spitting dirt out of my mouth, I looked up into the surprised eyes of Carmen and Ricker. They were sitting (extremely close, by the way) in an old wooden swing, rocking back and forth. As it swung backwards again I heard the creeek of the chains and the click of the hook catching a bent chain link at the top. I scrambled back to my feet and a new wave of embarrassment hit me as I realized my thin shorts had moved much higher during my fall from grace; revealing one very bare cheek.

"Stasia? What are you doing?" Carmen asked; guilt and shame written all over her face.

"I, um, heard a noise and was trying to figure out what it was. But I found it. Along with...ya'll," I spit out clumsily. "So I'll just...um...yeah. Good night!" I took off back down the stone path, eager to put as much distance between myself and that awkward encounter as possible. I finally made it back to the fountain and perched on the side of it in an effort to collect myself. I could even feel the frenzy I caused the plants in the garden with my little stunt. Slowly, the world went back to the calm of several minutes ago and so did my heartbeat. I hopped off the fountain and started down the path towards the house when I saw something out of the corner of my eye. Probably more terrifying shutting doors and swinging swings, I chuckled at myself as I turned around to see what it was - and froze mid-step.

She stood near a rose bush several meters away. Tears were streaming down her cheeks and she gently reached out to touch one of the blooms. As her transparent hand went right through it, she closed her eyes and wept softly. Not daring to chance a breath, I stepped closer. Her eyes fluttered upward and met mine. A coldness washed over me as she turned and walked towards me. I couldn't move. Couldn't scream. I just watched in horror as she eyed me curiously and came ever closer. She had deep green eyes that blended in with the lush garden of plants surrounding us. They held a certain warmth; an innocence. She couldn't have been more than fifteen or sixteen years old. Those green eyes searched my own; pleading with me.

"Hi," I whispered, so softly I barely heard it. She shifted and faded slightly; her body blurring in response. She stilled and glanced to the right as if she heard something, which gave me an even closer view of her exposed skull, covered with blood and matted blonde hair. Her eyes flickered back to mine and I immediately noticed the glassy fear that suddenly consumed her.

"Hurry," she said in a low, urgent voice right before disappearing. The effect her actual voice had on my already frazzled nerves was immediate and crushing. Somehow my legs carried the rest of my body back inside and up the stairs without incident. Sliding back in between the sheets, I noticed how violently I was shaking. I closed my eyes and rolled into a ball, completely underneath the comforter. My makeshift cocoon began to work as the shaking subsided. Unfortunately the hollow fear had already clawed its way into my soul, and I didn't know if it would ever let go. I'd just had a conversation…with a dead girl.

"I knew it!!" Carmen exclaimed and sat up in a flash, narrowly missing her Orange Crush can. It rested precariously in the sand, along with several magazines and a bag of chips. We were lying out in the soothing heat of the sun while the guys struggled to surf the less than ideal waves crawling toward the shore.

"You did not! None of us did." Phoebe rolled her eyes and continued to construct a sandcastle with one powerful finger. She was resting on the edge of her towel, wearing an adorable white and black polka dotted bikini with a white scarf wrapped around her unruly hair. She reminded me of a modern day Jackie O. With multi-colored hair.

"I did! I swear!" I'd filled my roommates in on my reverie-turned-vision, as well as what Finn and I had discussed about his destiny, although I made sure to clear it with him this morning before I said anything. I didn't want to betray his trust, but I also needed to talk to my friends about what happened. Apparently, a good number of people at Lorelei already knew of Finn's destiny; most of them being close with the Sons, like Liam or long-time girlfriends.

"What about the reverie training? How'd it go?" Willow peered at me from behind her gold aviator sunglasses. They matched her yellow and gold Quicksilver bikini perfectly.

"Not so good. I have a long way to go if I'm going to contact Thetis," I sighed. "I'm not sure I'll be able to do it at all." I wiped some renegade sand off of my leg and readjusted the top of my pink and blue striped bikini.

"Are you still going to try it tonight?" Carmen asked.

"I have to at least try, even if I fail miserably. There's too much riding on this not to."

Phoebe abandoned her sandcastle and flipped over onto her stomach. "Did you guys hear anything weird last night?" Carmen's eyes immediately darted toward me. "I thought I heard talking... I could have been dreaming, though..."

"I didn't hear anything. Slept like a baby," Carmen declared a little too quickly, and silently pleaded with me through her dark eyes.

"Nope, didn't hear a thing," I supplemented; reaching for the chips nonchalantly.

"Huh. I guess I was just hearing things." Phoebe chuckled and shrugged her shoulders.

"Was it the voices again? You know they aren't real, right?" Carmen joked with her.

"They aren't?" Phoebe played along; eyes growing wide with feigned disbelief. "I guess I won't have to shave your head and smother you with a pillow like they told me to, then."

As they continued to bicker over the different ways to kill each other, I thought about my eerie encounter last night with the ghost of childhood past.

"Do you guys believe in ghosts?" I asked them as off-handedly as I could.

"Ohhh, I love ghost stories!" Phoebe cooed.

"I think she meant actual ghosts, Phoebs," Carmen corrected her, and then regarded me. "Of course ghosts exist, silly."

"How can you be so sure?" I contended.

"It's a proven fact. They're the souls that have no place in the Underworld. They're cursed to roam Earth forever," Willow explained ominously. I know I stared at her a little too long, as a similar comment from Finn bounced around in my head.

"Finn should know all about ghosts if he's destined to be the Prime," Carmen replied. "You should just ask him what he thinks." Phoebe must have recalled my strange comments from yesterday because she perked up with excitement.

"Did you see her again?" she looked at me. "You know - the girl you said you saw yesterday?"

I brushed my finger over my trace and squinted up at her with loathing. "Yeah. Last night."

"Awesome!" Phoebe rejoiced.

"It was about as awesome as a razor burn," I protested with disgust. "She looked normal enough from the front, but when she turned around I could see her bloody skull and slashes in her skin."

"Who is she?" Willow asked quietly.

"I have no idea. But she actually said something to me last night." Their jaws dropped as they fervently waited for me to continue. "She seemed scared of something, but then just said 'Hurry'." I shrugged my shoulders. Did all ghosts talk in one word fragments? It would be next year before I got a complete sentence out of her at that rate.

"Hurry?" Carmen slathered more tanning lotion on her legs as she spoke. "Hurry and do what?"

"I wish I knew."

"Maybe she knows you're going to try to contact Thetis, but she wants you to hurry for some reason?" Phoebe suggested.

"We should see if we can find some history about the island. If she was young, there's got to be a story about how she died," Willow analyzed. I wasn't so sure that I wanted to attach a name or specific story to the ghost. That would make her more real. I was more comfortable with the possibility of her being a rare side effect of heat stroke.

I averted my gaze to the ocean. The guys were sitting on their surfboards talking, occasionally scanning the water for a surfable wave. Finn, shirtless and God-like, ran a hand through his wet hair and my pulse immediately quickened. How was it possible to look that good? The muscles of his chest and shoulders glistened in the sun as it shone down on his wet skin. My body ached to touch him. I wanted to wrap my arms around him and get lost in those soft lips. Suddenly, I got an idea. I smiled slyly and rested my hand on top of the sand next to my towel. I didn't know if it would work, but I had to give it a try.

I gathered up all my energy, centered it and focused it down my arm and into the sand. I pulled from my love for Finn, my leftover fear from last night, and my anxiety about contacting my mother; channeling all of it into the feathery sand beneath my fingertips. As I watched on apprehensively, the waves became more frequent and slightly larger. I concentrated harder and blocked out everything else except the waves and the energy flowing out of my fingers. Higher and higher the waves rose, becoming more and more powerful. Finn met my gaze as the other guys cheered at the suddenly larger waves.

A sense of pride filled me when a glowing smile broke out across Finn's face before he began to paddle out with the other guys. The longer I did it, the easier it was to muster up the energy and channel it. Adrenaline pumped through me each time one of them caught a massive wave and called out to one another in excitement.

"Stasia!"

The sound of my name startled me and I instinctively lifted my hand from the sand. The rush of energy that slammed into me knocked my breath away and I collapsed into a heap on my towel; reeling with dizziness and panting. I'd forgotten about that unfortunate aftereffect. Several woozy seconds later, I propped myself up on my elbows and tried to focus on something stable. At the moment the world was spinning at a dangerous pace.

"If you tell me you were making those waves from the beach, I'm going to piss myself," Carmen growled at me; crossing her arms.

"Okay, I wasn't making those waves." I rubbed my temples and smirked at her.

"I can't even do it in the water, but you can do it from the freaking beach? Unbelievable," she muttered, clearly displeased with herself.

"That's what you call talent." Phoebe applauded my experiment; making me smile.

"I didn't know if it'd work…" I admitted shyly.

"Hey, who hit the off switch on the wave machine?" Cage sprinted up to our towels and tumbled down with the grace of a two ton elephant. I noticed a small black ring on his pinky finger that had to be black onyx as he shook out his curly hair; spraying cold water all over Phoebe and Carmen.

"What are you? A cocker spaniel?" Carmen scowled in his direction. As you might expect, that only prompted him to do it again while she scrambled to her feet to avoid the water. A cooling shadow fell over me and I squinted up to see Finn gazing down at me. The sun was at his back, making him look like a dark angel - just like the first time I'd seen him; providing evidence that he wasn't only in my dreams. My heart quivered at the thought. He held out his strong hand to me and yanked me up from my towel so quickly my feet left the ground; catching me securely around the waist. The sudden feel of his skin against mine was magnified by the warmth of my skin contrasting with the cool feel of the water dripping off of him. His eyes swirled with shades of dark and light blue, culminating into one breathtaking color that had me hypnotized. I swept the dark, wet hair back from his brow and pressed my lips to his. He tasted like the salt water rolling down his skin, and my insides turned to mush as he kissed me back with urgency. With our audience groaning and yelling at us to get a room, he released his grip and set me down gently; arms still draped around my waist.

"You become more amazing every day." His eyes smiled at me, but his features softened with sadness. I furrowed my brow in concern, but the look was gone before I could say anything. That was also the exact moment Phoebe fell in love.

"Oh my God. You guys..." She stood calmly; eyes transfixed on something down the beach. We followed her star struck gaze and my mouth dropped open. Four golden brown horses with blond manes were trotting down by the water's edge in our direction. A smaller colt trailed behind precariously on his lanky legs. They were slightly smaller than the horses I'd seen and there were no saddles, no tags, and no sign of ownership.

"I can feel them..." Phoebe marveled with fascination, "but I don't get it. They aren't connected to sand."

"These horses would be." Ian beamed down at her.

"They're Shackleford ponies. Wild horses," Liam informed everyone.

"Wild?" I gawked at Liam in disbelief.

"They're the descendants of horses that survived shipwrecks or were left for dead. They were originally brought over on Spanish ships in the sixteen-hundreds," he educated us further.

"Descendants..." Phoebe whispered, completely enthralled in the horses. "Just like us..." She began to walk, as if in a trance, towards the horses. Feeling her presence, they all glanced up at the same time and stopped dead in their tracks. The colt bumped into the larger horse in front and teeter-tottered on two scraggly legs before regaining his balance. Carmen giggled behind me. After a moment of simply observing Phoebe, the horses changed course and headed directly for her.

"Phoebe-" Ian warned, before she held up a hand to let him know it was okay. He remained where he was, but I knew he was ready to protect her at a moment's notice. Feet glued in place, we watched in awe as the horses reached her. A tense silence ensued as Phoebe and the horses stared at one another for several minutes before we saw any sign of movement. With unabated love she began to stroke the lead horse's mane as he nuzzled up against her shoulder. As if on cue, each subsequent horse allowed the same as they each nuzzled her in an endearing display of respect. It reminded me of how the sea turtles reacted to my presence so many weeks ago. It was as if each one wanted to acknowledge her presence individually. As the last horse trotted back down the beach, Phoebe turned and raced back up to where we still stood frozen in suspense.

"That was the most amazing thing that's ever happened to me!" She bounced up and down with exuberance. "Did you guys see that?! They were so...innocent. They were pretty confused about me at first because I wasn't a horse, but they could still sense me. After they got over that, they opened up a little more." She placed a hand over her heart. "They're so happy here."

"They aren't the only ones," Finn whispered to me; hugging me tight. My heart soared as I wrapped my arms around him; never wanting to leave his side.

The sun was just beginning to sink below the horizon as Finn and I made our way down to the beach for my second lesson. A bubble of anxiety lodged itself in my throat and I wasn't sure if I could go through with it. What if I had another vision? What if the ghost girl somehow showed up? And what was she scared of? I mean, she was a ghost. Besides glimpsing her reflection in a mirror, I couldn't think of anything she could possibly be scared of.

"Do you really believe in ghosts?" I questioned Finn on our way down the boardwalk. He shot me a curious sideways glance before answering.

"Of course. Ghosts are as real as you or me. Like I was telling you back on the boat, they're just souls that have no resting place in the Underworld."

"So what's wrong with them? Why don't they have a place in the Underworld?" I began to wonder why the ghost girl wouldn't have been allowed entrance.

"When a person dies, their soul is given admittance to the Underworld by Persephone. If she deems them broken or not at peace, she sends them away. The only place they have to go is back to this realm."

"I saw one yesterday," I blurted out carelessly.

"A ghost?"

"She was a young girl with blonde hair." I scrunched my nose. "But her head and back were all gory. It wasn't a pretty sight." He chuckled at my repulsion.

"You'll find that certain lost souls seek you out. Especially the ones that have some past connection with the sea. They'll feel that shared connection with you."

"I'm not sure I want to have any kind of connection with a ghost," I proclaimed; shaking my head. "Can they ever go back to the Underworld after they've been refused the first time? What if they become…unbroken somehow?" Was it possible the ghost girl needed my help?

"They can keep trying to get into the Underworld, but ultimately it's up to Persephone whether or not they're allowed to enter."

"So, who's Persephone?"

"She's the Queen of the Underworld."

"The Underworld has a Queen? Who's the King?" I didn't realize the Underworld had its own version of the Royal family.

"Hades is the King, but Persephone didn't exactly choose or want to become the Queen. When she was a Goddess in this realm, Hades abducted her and took her back with him to the Underworld."

"He…kidnapped her?" I made a mental note to stay as far away from Hades as possible during my journey. He nodded, and I saw the abhorrence in his blue eyes. He scuffed the sand up as he took each step; sending a shower of sparkles through the air. Also shimmering in the low light was the trace on his forearm. Oddly enough it didn't remind me of his father's bones; Finn's trace was completely his own.

"To make matters worse, before she escaped he deceived her. If you consume anything grown in the Underworld, your soul is tied to that realm forever; you're trapped. Do you remember the pomegranate trees at the Ball?" he asked and I nodded.

"You said they were the fruit of the dead."

"Right. Pomegranates grow everywhere in the Underworld and they have many meanings, but it's also how Hades trapped Persephone. He tricked her into eating pomegranate seeds, therefore tying her soul to that realm forever."

"Oh my God."

"Over the centuries her bitterness and resentment grew, changing her into a very vicious and relentless Queen. She's not to be messed with," he affirmed with creed.

"Hell hath no fury like a woman scorned..." I muttered; fascinated by Persephone's tragic story. Then it hit me. I looked up at him. "I'll have to get past her in order to enter the Underworld, won't I?"

"Yes."

Excellent.

The stone in my hand was hard and cold, but my small hand conformed easily to its jagged shape. According to Finn it would act as a beacon; something to absorb my energy and make me more visible to my mother. Not that I was shooting for that just yet, but he wanted me to practice with it. I lay once again on a soft fleece blanket, eyes closed, with Finn rubbing my hair to help me relax. Unlike the first time, I had a better idea of what was in store. As the numbness surrounded my mind and I began to feel slightly dizzy, I thought about the day I would have been born. I wondered if my mom would have been in a great deal of pain. I wondered how my father felt, and if I was born at night or in the morning. I wasn't sure why that mattered, but I guess I was just curious. The last thing I remembered was anticipating that floating feeling of my soul lifting above my body and wondering why it wasn't happening.

Waves of pain wracked my body and I squeezed my eyes shut. I heard voices but they were muffled. Then I realized why. My own screams were drowning them out. Suddenly the pain receded and my body collapsed. Sweat rolled down my brow and I felt myself smile, although I couldn't imagine what I had to be happy about amidst all the pain. My breathing was ragged and I could feel the exhaustion hovering over my body.

"It is time to rest," a voice informed me. Someone was still rubbing my hair, but that definitely wasn't Finn's voice. It was a woman. I turned my head to the side and opened my eyes with effort. Long, wavy dark brown hair swept past large green eyes and a heart-shaped face punctuated by a wide smile. I closed my eyes again and took a deep breath, allowing the oxygen to strengthen my weary muscles.

"How is she?" Another woman's voice. I kept my eyes closed.

"She's doing great. Her body will heal quickly," came the answer.

Footsteps sounded and I felt a strong presence. It was as if it was calling to me; signaling its arrival. Warmth spread from the aquamarine necklace around my neck to my heart and I felt myself smile again.

"She has arrived, my love," said a man's voice. When I opened my eyes, a handsome man stood beside the bed I was lying on. His dark hair appeared disheveled as if he'd been running his hands through it, and his blue-gray eyes were wet with tears. He exuded happiness, and the joy within shone through his bright smile. Not until I looked down into his arms did I understand what he was talking about. Carefully, he shifted the bundle and transferred it to my outstretched arms. The strong presence I had felt was wrapped in this soft, silky blanket. Tears rolled down my cheeks as I gazed down into her bright blue eyes; the color of the sea.

Squirming and watching me with wonder, she reached towards my face and my heart broke with the weight of my love for this small being. But why was I holding a baby? And who were all of these people surrounding me? None of it made sense.

"What time is it?" I asked, not sure why it mattered.

"Twelve-fifteen. She was born several minutes after midnight," he answered.

"My vision was right." I breathed a sigh of relief. "January first. She is the new beginning." I looked back down into her eyes and watched in amazement as she observed her new surroundings; grasping the blanket and kicking her tiny legs.

"What will you name her, Thetis?" a white haired man with a white coat asked. I smiled at the handsome man beside me and then admired the baby in my arms.

"Anastasia Nemertes Theophanides."

I snapped back to the present with immeasurable speed; sitting up even faster. I heard Finn's gasp of surprise at my sudden movement and I twisted around to face him. I tried to speak, but unfortunately nothing came out. My expression was frozen in shock and complete and utter disbelief at what I just experienced.

"What happened?" Finn observed me with a mixture of concern and amusement. The amusement probably stemmed from the way my mouth gaped open and my eyes bugged from their sockets. With the speed of a snail, I covered my mouth with the hand that wasn't holding the stone. I hoped that would lessen the permanent deer-in-headlights look.

"What is it? Is everything okay?" Finn had taken the stone from my other hand and threaded his fingers through mine in an effort to calm me. It didn't work.

"I…" I croaked. "I…was her…"

"You were who?" He furrowed his brow in bewilderment. Tears, churning with every emotion known to man, pooled in my eyes and splashed down my cheeks. I had no idea where to start explaining what I'd just seen; it was so overwhelming. I simply continued to stare at him like I had lost my mind. His widening grin didn't do much to help that association. Before completely bursting out into laughter, he grabbed me and held me close; rocking me back and forth slowly. I closed my eyes and tried to calm the shaking that had taken hold of my body. Finally I felt like I could open my mouth without a string of inaudible noises spewing out.

"It was amazing," I managed. Finn patiently waited for me to continue; allowing me time to put words to my thoughts. "I was her. I was watching through her eyes. I witnessed my own birth." My sentences came out choppy and slightly deadpan, but the important thing was that they came out. Now it was Finn's turn to be shocked. I felt his breath catch against my back as he released me and I turned to face him. A giggle snuck out when I saw the same deer-in-headlights look on his face.

"You...saw the past?" he searched my eyes; stunned. I nodded. "And you saw it through your mom's eyes?" I nodded again and waited for him to tell me I had gone stark raving mad. "Do you know what that means, Stasia?"

"That I need anti-psychotic drugs?" I guessed with heavy sarcasm.

"It means you have Antiquity." He stared at me with wonderment.

"Is that some sort of disease?" I cringed, but when he laughed the knot in my stomach loosened.

"It's an ability. An amazing and rare ability, I might add." He winked at me.

Another rare ability? I was going to end up on the endangered species list at this rate. My face must have mirrored my thoughts because he laughed again.

"The memories of our ancestors are passed down from person to person. But you wouldn't know it because most people can't access them. You, however, do have that ability." He brushed back a piece of blonde hair that had blown across my cheek. "You were seeing your mother's memories."

"Her...memories? And you're saying she passed them down to me?"

"That's exactly what I'm saying," he confirmed. The blood drained from my face as I remembered the most important thing I'd learned.

"Finn...I know my true birthday," I said slowly, and his eyes widened ever so slightly. "It's January first." As I said it, an unsettling realization dawned on me. I would be taking my essence journey very, very soon.

"No - the marshmallow goes on first," Phoebe declared, as she closely inspected the melting blob of marshmallow on her stick that was hanging precariously above our makeshift beach fire pit. After my successful afternoon searching for my true birthday, we decided to celebrate at precisely S'mores-thirty with a beach bonfire and blankets. The night was cool and refreshing, with a light breeze blowing off the ocean. The smell of sea grass and salt swirled amidst the embers, tickling our noses with a warm brew of seductive fragrances. The thickening clouds above warned of thunderstorms, but we volunteered Phoebe to do an anti-storm dance if warranted. We were gathered around the fire, roasting the first marshmallows of the evening while we watched the flames dance and light up the night. The reflections of our shadows flickering across the sand sent my imagination running wild. I could almost picture the first explorers arriving here several centuries ago, cooking their food in this very same fashion. Unfortunately for them, S'mores hadn't been invented yet.

"No, the chocolate goes on first, and then you squish the marshmallow off the stick with the crackers…like this." Carmen tilted forward and stole the marshmallow blob from the end of Phoebe's stick between her graham crackers.

"Hey! That's mine!"

"Noth amymore." Carmen grinned as she stuffed the entire sandwich in her mouth.

"I hope that goes straight to your butt," Phoebe muttered in a huff.

"Nothing wrong with a little extra cushion…" Carmen shrugged and began preparing the ingredients for her next S'more. I caught a fleeting glance between her and Ricker that involved grinning and a wink, but it could have been a trick of the flames. I still hadn't gotten a chance to talk to her alone about seeing them cuddled up on the swing last night. I glanced beside me at Finn, who had been unusually silent and thoughtful all evening. Phoebe and Ian were next to him, then Carmen, Ricker and Cage, with Liam and Willow on my other side to complete the circle.

"Well you're both wrong," Cage piped up; his dark curly hair bouncing as he talked. "First, you pop a graham cracker in your mouth, then the chocolate goes in." He carefully blew on his roasted marshmallow and proceeded to pull it off the stick with his teeth. "And them you adth amother gwaham cwacker…dewicious." We all doubled over with laughter as he smiled; sending crackers crumbling and marshmallow dripping out of his mouth and down his chin. I could tell Finn's laugh was forced, so I squeezed his hand and leaned my head on his shoulder, hoping to comfort him. He peered down at me and grinned, but his blue eyes were despondent and sorrowful. Before I could ask him what was wrong, he scrambled to his feet.

"The game should be on by now….ya'll coming?" he addressed the other guys, who eagerly jumped up too. He bent down and kissed me softly on the lips before glaring out at the obscure ocean and turning on his heel to follow the rest of the guys to the house. There was a highly anticipated football game on tonight that they wanted to watch, which left us girls to our own devices. I watched him saunter down the boardwalk dejected; head down and shoulders slouched forward.

"What's wrong with Finn?" Willow asked, following my eyes.

"I'm not sure. I thought he'd be happy we figured out my birthday, but he's been quiet and distant all night." I ran a finger over my trace absently and watched it shimmer in the firelight.

"Maybe he's just worried about you," Phoebe offered with consoling eyes.

"Yeah, maybe so," I agreed, not really convinced.

"Well I've got an idea that'll take your mind off of him." Carmen leaned in with a diabolical smile. "I think we should do a séance and see if we can figure out who your ghost girl is!"

"I don't know if that's such a good-" I started.

"A séance! Oh my God, that's the best idea I've heard all weekend!" Phoebe squealed.

"Do you think it would really work?" Willow wondered aloud; biting her lip.

"Beats me, but what can it hurt?" Carmen answered flippantly. I could think of a few things it could hurt - my already unstable sanity being one.

"What do we need?" Phoebe hopped to her feet, anxious to gather supplies.

"Really guys, I don't know if we should do a séance." I shook my head in doubt.

"Come on, Stasia! It'll be fun! Plus, maybe we'll figure out who she is and what she wants," Phoebe advocated. As always, her enthusiasm was infectious.

"If it gets too weird or freaks us out, we'll just stop," Carmen urged. I looked to Willow for backup, but she just shrugged her shoulders and left the final decision up to me.

"Okay, but I don't feel good about this," I warned, but they ignored my dismal tone.

"Okay Phoebs, we'll need some candles, a lighter, some sea salt and a flower from the garden, since that's where Stasia last saw her." She inclined her head at Phoebe, who ran off in a flurry of anticipation, and then began to tidy up the bonfire site.

"So, Carmen...." Willow raised a conspiring eyebrow at me before continuing. "What's up with you and Ricker these days?"

"Me and Ricker?" Carmen's eyes shot to me in a flash.

"I didn't say anything, I swear!" I pleaded.

"It's pretty obvious, Carmen. You could cut the sexual tension with a butter knife," Willow snickered.

"There's nothing going on anymore. He's the last person I'd want to hook up with. He is so annoying and he talks too much. Plus, he's too sarcastic and tries to push my buttons all the time. It's so annoying. He is so annoying."

"You said that already." Willow chuckled again.

"Well, that's because it's true. He's....annoying," she made a face of disgust.

"I've seen the way he looks at you when you aren't looking," Willow provoked her. And it worked like a charm.

"Really?" Carmen twisted around, eyes wide, before catching herself. "Not that it matters or anything. I could care less how he looks at me."

"You are the worst liar ever," I accused her, and couldn't help laughing at her futile efforts to hate him.

"I don't know what you're talking about. He walks around like he's God's gift to women... showing off his nice body and flashing that sexy grin every chance he gets..." she trailed off as we started laughing. A guilty smile crept across her face and she looked down. "Whatever."

"I'm back!" Phoebe scampered down the beach with as much finesse as Bigfoot. "I found everything we need!"

Deciding to let Carmen off the hook for the time being, we abandoned our fire pit and helped her set up a circle several yards away using only the candles for light. Five minutes and one sea salt fight later, we were sitting in true séance fashion. Carmen lit the four white pillar candles and placed them in an oversized hurricane glass that Phoebe had stolen off the mantel in the living room. A ring of sea salt encircled them, while another ring of salt surrounded us; creating the official 'circle'. The blood red rose Phoebe plucked from the garden lay in the sand in front of Carmen. Its soft petals had collapsed in on themselves; heavy with the finality of nightfall. The thorns protecting its long, slender stem were a vivid warning to anyone who dared to touch it. As I stared at its unending beauty, I sensed its will to live falter after being severed from its life source. Carmen's voice broke into my thoughts and I tried to pay attention.

"Okay, so here's the plan. We want to contact a specific ghost, so first we'll do a chant to calm our thoughts and energy, and then we'll reach out to her. While we are calling out to her I'll be burning the rose to release its energy into the air. It will help draw her spirit in." She sat up straighter. "Now, we'll need to close the circle during the calming chant. To do that, we just hold hands. Try to center your energy and breathe slowly."

"What if we contact a bunch of ghosts and they all attack us?" Phoebe's eyes grew wide with alarm.

"That's not going to happen, trust me," Carmen answered nonchalantly.

"What if we contact something other than ghosts?" Willow asked with apprehension.

"That's not going to happen either," Carmen declared. With a descending cloud of fear looming over our circle, we timidly held hands and, following Carmen's lead, closed our eyes.

"I am peaceful, I am strong. Though darkness sometimes seems so long. For day must follow every night, everything will be alright. I am peaceful, I am strong. Though darkness sometimes seems so long. For day must follow every night, everything will be alright. I am peaceful, I am strong...." We began chanting softly with her, centering our energy and opening our minds. The warm breeze swirling around us dwindled and I felt my entire body relaxing; filling me with a serene sense of self.

"Now that we've closed the circle and calmed our souls, we must remain within this space to call upon her spirit," Carmen instructed us in a low, eerie voice. We opened our eyes and glanced around with trepidation. The candles still danced, the sea salt still lay on the sand and the flower remained in front of Carmen. But I could tell something was different. I just couldn't put my finger on it. Carmen began the second chant as we watched on in fascination.

"Guardians of the Spirit realm hear and guide my plea. This sacred place in time and space was created just for thee. So bring her forth, the hour is near; our hearts and minds revere. On this night, I ask you thrice: Appear. Appear. Appear." She began to repeat it again, but this time she vigilantly lifted the rose and dangled it above the jumping flames of the candles. I held my breath as she lowered it inch by inch; an agonizing display of torture playing out for the sacrificial flower. I made myself look away as the fire withered and blackened its petals; a steady stream of smoke ascending silently into the heavens. Willow and Phoebe were hopelessly entranced in the burning rose at the center of the circle, gazing at it with wonder. That's when I felt the darkness.

It crept along my spine and penetrated my soul with a quickness I couldn't defend. As the air in my lungs stifled and chilled, I looked around to see where the feeling was originating from. The other three girls were still staring at the rose, unaware of the evil that had arrived.

"Carmen, I think we should-" I whispered.

"Oh my God." Phoebe's strained voice and stricken eyes had us following her shocked gaze to the sand dunes at my right. Not a word was said. Not a sound was made. No one so much as took a breath as our eyes met hers.

Dressed in the same faded blue dress, she was poised several feet away watching us curiously. Her flowing blonde hair still hung down below her shoulders, and her thin arms remained limp at her side. Her bright green eyes locked on me and I watched as a shadow of fear crossed her features. In that instant I could tell the darkness I felt wasn't emanating from her. With a start, I felt something else. Phoebe's hand. And it was currently crushing every bone in mine. I squeezed it to let her know everything was going to be okay, but I wasn't even sure I believed that, so it probably wasn't very reassuring. As the ghost girl continued to stare at us, I tapped into my 'other' sense, as Finn had called it, in an attempt to figure out where the evil chill was originating from. It simply seemed to be all around me; not approaching from one specific direction.

"What's your name?" Somehow Carmen had found the courage to speak.

"Bianca."

The blood vessels in my left hand were threatening to burst under the pressure of Phoebe's vice grip, but this time I gripped back just as hard. When Bianca spoke, it resembled a soft echo riding on a light breeze. It lightly tickled your ear drums, but also resonated deep within your soul.

"Why are you here?" I mustered up the nerve to speak; hoping she could enlighten me on why she kept appearing to me.

"You called me," she responded plainly. She furrowed her brow, somewhat confused at my question.

"Why have you been appearing to me?" I tried again with more tenacity.

"She makes me," she answered matter-of-factly; her voice bereft of lightness. My heart leapt to my throat, and I tried to exude calmness despite the explosion of terror and hysteria that engulfed me at her foreboding words.

"Who's....she?" I asked carefully; hearing the unsteady waver in my voice. She glanced around and began to close in on our circle.

"The Reaper," she whispered.

I heard Willow's surprised gasp as well as Phoebe's high pitched squeak of fear, but my own terror was so all-consuming, I was having trouble breathing. Glancing sideways, I noticed that Phoebe's face had completely drained of color as she continued gawking at Bianca.

"She is close," Bianca warned as her green eyes flitted toward the ocean and then back to us. She stopped at the edge of the sea salt ring and peered down at the scorched rose lying at Carmen's feet; its petals now decrepit and charred. Her placid face fell as her eyes glistened with translucent tears of mourning.

"The living always fail to understand the plight of the dead," she breathed; face pained. Suddenly she looked directly at me in a panic. "The beacon - it calls to her, too. Use it wisely. She-"

Her words cut off abruptly and I felt it again in earnest. As I looked on with dread, her slight body trembled and blurred before us. My own body became wracked with waves of icy daggers; relentlessly slicing into my heart and causing a piercing pain that echoed out from my chest. I bent over in agony; attempting to catch my breath and to understand what was happening. The trace on my wrist and hand had taken on a brackish color; absorbing the darkness pulsing through me. Bianca's image stabilized before she spoke.

"Careful, girls," her crisp voice became layered and forced. "If you call...you might just get an answer." She chuckled, but the sound came out as more of a growl.

Bianca's once serene features contorted into a smirk and her bright green eyes darkened considerably; becoming the greenish-brown color of a murky sea. The pain in my chest suddenly dissipated.

"Bianca?" Carmen asked cautiously; observing her with suspicion.

"I don't think that's Bianca anymore..." Phoebe murmured to Carmen. Willow swiftly clamped a hand over Phoebe's mouth.

"Ah, Bianca...nice girl. A little too talkative though." A sly smile slithered across her face and she scrupulously began to circle us. I regarded her aversion to the outermost salt ring.

"Then...who are you?" Carmen spat at her. Her hostile and annoyed tone towards the ghost paralyzed us with fear as we awaited her answer. Thankfully Bianca only laughed again, but her murky eyes collided with mine and her steps stalled behind Phoebe. As she raised an eyebrow, I realized with dismay that I knew exactly who she was. Suddenly the piercing pain in my chest exploded and I slipped into unconsciousness.

When I snapped open my eyes again, I saw that the world had been transformed. The lightness I felt told me my soul had been involuntarily snatched from my body, but the fact I could see myself slumped over below was the more glaring clue. Phoebe, Willow and Carmen were scrambling around me, calling my name and rolling me over to my back. My mind reeled as I tried to figure out what had just happened. As one startling possibility slammed into me with force, I locked onto the eyes of my true attacker.

"What did you do?!" I screamed at her. She just rolled her eyes at me and shook her head, moving closer.

"Relax. You're not dead. I just wanted some...privacy." A wicked sneer spread across her glossy lips and her golden eyes twinkled. The fact that I hadn't just experienced my own demise calmed me instantly. Now I was just pissed off.

"Why are you here, Nadia?" I shot back with annoyance, narrowing my eyes at her. She stood before me, appearing darkly ethereal in a long, black strapless maxi dress with an imposing pendant necklace taunting me from her neck. The deep red stone shimmered with the orange and yellow of a dancing flame as she stepped towards me with fluent grace.

"Fire agate. Isn't it simply amazing?" she purred and touched the stone. "It represents perfection…naturally." She curtsied; alluding to her obvious arrogance. My thoughts catapulted to the beacon Finn had given me; the fire agate emerging from the onyx.

"So why are you here?" It was amazing how her presence could ruin a perfectly good night. "I just wanted to size up my competition…or lack thereof…" She scrunched her nose at me.

"This isn't a game, Nadia." Finn's voice swept over me like a warm blanket on a cool autumn night as he stepped out of the darkness of the dunes. The fervor in his tone was unmistakable.

"Oh, isn't that sweet? Our dark Prince Charming has come to the rescue." She snickered and continued to glare at us. Finn was instantly in her face; menacing and terrifying.

"Release her soul," he commanded with chilling calmness.

"But I was having so much fun!" she pouted, reaching up to touch Finn's cheek. He swatted her hand away and her eyes turned steely, her tone sarcastic. "Uh, fine. But only because you asked so nicely."

I was instantly overcome with the sensation of my soul slamming back into my body with immense speed. I opened my eyes to the disturbing sight of my roommates in an all-out panic. Willow's blue eyes were filled with tears;

desperately attempting to heal me and wake me up. They smothered me with relieved hugs when I managed to sit up.

"Oh my God, are you okay!?"

"What happened?!"

"I didn't know what to do!"

I hugged them back and scanned the beach frantically in search of Finn. "Where's Finn?" I asked no one in particular.

"Finn?" Carmen scratched her head and examined me with confusion. I sensed movement to my left and Finn's dark figure stepped out from behind a shadowed sand dune.

"Are you okay?" He approached me, his blue eyes heavy with torment.

"I am now." I latched onto him and he gently kissed my forehead.

"What happened?" Finn addressed the other three girls. Phoebe stepped forward, her eyes darting between the dunes and the water, probably for fear of another ghost appearing and waging an attack.

"Well, we were having a séance and there was a ghost - and then she changed into somebody else - and then Stasia passed out - we didn't know what to do or what happened to her!" Her words spewed from her mouth with desperation.

I looked down at the hourglass trace adorning her ankle and the white sand beneath her feet which had begun to tremble and shift from her frenzied emotions.

"Phoebe, calm down. You're going to cause an earthquake." Carmen wrapped her arm around her. Phoebe grinned sheepishly.

"No more séances - I think we've had enough excitement for one night." Finn's eyes flitted down to mine with adulation, but the storm brewing behind them told me he was trying to make light of the situation for the other girls' sake. A river of dread trickled down my body;

saturating every pore with fear. While my roommates headed for the boardwalk, I held Finn back.

"So how do you know Nadia if she just transferred from the House of Metis?" I asked him, trying not to sound too accusatory.

"I've known Nadia for a long time." He turned to face me. "She is from the House of Metis, but she also graduated last year. It would seem she's pretending to be someone she's not. I haven't figured out why, but I think I have a good idea." Another chill ran down my spine as I remembered seeing the gray smoke swirling around her, not to mention the sickening feeling I got whenever she was around.

"So if she's not a transfer student, then who is she?"

"Do you remember me telling you about Persephone?" he asked hesitantly.

"Queen of the Underworld...Jaded...Don't mess with her," I counted off on my fingers.

"Right." He nodded, amused at my offhanded attitude. "Nadia is Persephone's daughter." Well that explained a lot.

"She's...princess of the Underworld?" I asked incredulously, and Finn chuckled darkly.

"I guess you could call her that, but she's mainly just a direct descendant like you and I." So I had something in common with the princess of darkness. Super.

"But wouldn't that make her a Goddess? If her father's the King of the Underworld and...well...a God?" I asked, perplexed.

"Persephone isn't the most faithful of spouses. Nadia's father is an Oceanid, which puts Nadia in the Order of Nymphs and technically, just a descendant," he explained. "But a very powerful and immortal descendant, whose soul belongs to the Underworld." More excellent news. Then a puzzle piece clicked into place within my thoughts.

"The smoke is her darkness," I murmured to myself in disbelief.

"What'd you say?" Finn looked up in surprise.

"I've seen this gray smoke coming off of her and I couldn't figure out what it was. But if her soul belongs to the Underworld, it would be the darkness I'm seeing, right?"

"So you can see it?" he said with the same amount of surprise.

"Yeah," I confirmed carefully. I didn't know if that was good or bad.

"Stasia, that's awesome! Do you know what that means?" I looked at him blankly, hoping he would enlighten me. "That will help you immensely in the Underworld." He rubbed his chin, thoughtful.

"But won't everyone in the Underworld emit the...smoke? And why don't you have any?"

"Unfortunately, the 'smoke' you see isn't darkness," he said slowly, taking my hand in his. "It's evil." Every hair on my body stood on end and my eyes widened. I was seeing...evil?

"You can sense it too, can't you?" he asked. I nodded my head; still in shock.

"It's definitely the monster-under-the-bed kind of darkness - I mean evil," I corrected myself. I still couldn't believe what I was saying. "So what about you? Can you sense it, too? Can you see it?"

He nodded. "That's how I knew something was wrong. I sensed her arrival," he explained, his voice drained.

"But I'm not connected to the Underworld like you. Why can I see it and sense it? And how do I shut it off?"

"It goes along with that 'other sense' that all descendants have. However, yours is apparently extremely advanced...like mine." His blue eyes smiled down at me with pride. "One of the perks of being a direct descendant." If by "perks" he meant harrowing abominations. I couldn't believe I had argued with someone who literally dripped with evil. I was suddenly thankful that I didn't know that critical piece of information at the time. I would have needed a change of shorts.

"So what exactly does she do in her spare time, besides pretend to be in high school and crash séances on remote islands?"

"She serves under Persephone right now, but I've heard she'll be the next leader of the Nymphs. I don't know how much of that is true, though." He shrugged and wrapped his arms around me. That was when I remembered what Bianca had called her. I looked up at Finn with alarm.

"Bianca, the ghost, called her 'The Reaper'. What exactly does that mean?" I steeled myself for the answer, because I had a feeling that the job description of The Reaper didn't include picking flowers or feeding unicorns.

He chuckled, sensing my fear. "It's not as scary as it sounds - well, unless you're a ghost." I thought about the terror that filled Bianca's eyes each time Nadia was near and shivered. "She escorts the souls Persephone rejects back to this realm. She can control ghosts and even merge her soul with ghosts who aren't strong enough to ward off her advances."

"That's how she did it…" I marveled to myself.

"Did what?" Finn asked curiously.

"Before she forced my soul out of my body, she merged with Bianca and talked to us. It was creepy." I shivered again and Finn hugged me tighter.

"Now that you know who she is and what she's capable of, you'll be a little more prepared next time." Next time?

"It wouldn't hurt my feelings if I never saw her again," I declared resolutely.

"Unfortunately, I don't think that's an option," he warned in a low voice; heavy with bitterness and distaste.

Twelve

"Pasha."

The sheets beneath me were cool and soothing as I listened to the wind stirring against the window pane above my head. The night was undisturbed, but I had the odd sense that something was coming; something of great consequence and reprisal.

"Pasha." I cracked open a sleepy eye. Finn knelt beside the bed, his handsome face only inches away. "Come to the beach with me," he whispered with a ghost of a smile and mischief swirling in his blue eyes. It had to be past two in the morning, but warmth for his adventurous spirit filled my heart and I grinned at the almost boyish hope that garnished his face.

After assembling several blankets and one curious canvas bag, contents unknown, we were on our way down the boardwalk towards the deserted beach. The intoxicating smell of wet sand and sea grass filled my nose, and the roar of the ocean greeted me as I took in the captivating scene we found ourselves immersed in. The quarter moon hanging above cast a silver lining on every dune, every sleeping flower, and the shoulders of the dark angel walking beside me. It created a magical backdrop to an otherwise ordinary scene.

The tantalizing allure of the rolling ocean curled around my soul and teased me with its promise of freedom. I closed my eyes and smiled happily, seduced by its magnificent power. Finn chose a soft spot of sand to spread out the thickest of the blankets. He knelt down and absentmindedly searched through the large canvas bag.

Maybe it was the magical moonbeams shining down on us, maybe it was the events of the weekend filling me with renewed courage, or maybe it was the way the light danced on his dark hair and strong shoulders, but either way I peered over the proverbial edge, smiled at the mysteries lurking below, and jumped. I crawled over to him and took his hand slowly; calling his attention. I threaded my small fingers through his and he turned to face me with a crooked grin, both of us on our knees.

"Come swimming with me," I said, more timidly then I had intended. My heart leapt into the air and my pulse quickened at my own courage. He glanced down at our clothes and then back at me with questioning eyes. As his answer, I kept his gaze and carefully pulled the strap of my blue tank top down my shoulder, revealing a pink bra strap. I reached up to pull the other strap down when he suddenly clutched my wrist.

Never breaking his suddenly intense gaze, he moved closer and caressed my cheek. Assuming he was stopping me from making a fool out of myself, I felt an embarrassed grin cross my face. I held my breath as he lightly ran his fingers down my neck and onto my shoulder. With obvious wonderment, he removed the other strap of my tank top, revealing another pink bra strap. His now hooded eyes met mine once more and I became lost in the powerful emotions I saw shining from them. He dragged a finger over the bottom of my tank top; sending shivers along the bare skin beneath.

He gingerly pulled my tank top over my head and tossed it down on the blanket. My thin undergarments did little to protect me from the cool ocean breeze, but I was too nervous to notice. With trembling fingers I gripped the bottom of his cotton t-shirt and tugged it over his head, revealing his sturdy, muscular torso. The moon shone down onto his bronze skin and his blue eyes softened even further. He climbed to his feet, took my hands and pulled me up with him. Taking another deep breath, I hastily shrugged off my shorts. Unfortunately as I stepped out of them, my big toe caught the inside seam. If you've ever tripped up a flight of stairs, dropped something valuable down a drain, or slipped on a patch of ice, you can empathize with the sudden mini heart attack that clutched my heart. I saw myself crashing face-down in the sand, shorts tangled around my ankles and my butt in the air. Thankfully, back in reality, Finn caught my arms and righted my body before the inevitable epic fail came to fruition.

As his amused, deep blue eyes took me in - bare, vulnerable and now completely mortified - a sudden tsunami of insecurity rushed over me. Despite my shorts mishap, I told myself this was no different than wearing a bikini. Unfortunately the evasive wind flowing through the thin fabric disagreed.

An entirely new feeling swept over me as he let his own shorts fall to the sand, leaving only thin plaid boxer shorts. My heart hammered against my chest and my hands began to sweat as he stepped forward and touched my cheek lovingly.

"You are so beautiful," he professed; amazement glittering in his eyes. His shaded features darkened even further and he became serious. "I've always just gone through the motions of life; always preparing for what was ahead of me and never letting myself feel too much. I never let myself hope for more." His eyes searched mine and I felt my knees go weak. "But you. You've changed everything. You make me want to be something better. You've transformed my world in a way I didn't think was possible, and suddenly life has a million possibilities. Even normal things are suddenly extraordinary, because I get to share them with you. You've taught me who I really am and most importantly, who I want to be."

As I tried to figure out how someone like Finn could possibly feel that way about me, I realized he had no idea the impact he'd made on my life. The walls I held onto so tightly before had all been washed away by his love; leaving the door open for a new, happier me to emerge and flourish. This new life was exhilarating, if not scary, and I couldn't believe I had someone as amazing as Finn to share it with. Unfortunately I had no idea how to put that into words. A tear escaped as I smiled up at him and gave it a shot.

"Everything I've been through, everything I've endured has led me back to you. I'm beginning to realize just how much I've lost, but I can also see how much I've gained. You're my life now, Finn. You're my home. The one place I truly belong is right here…with you." Another runaway tear slid down my cheek as he kissed me lightly on the lips and gave me a lopsided grin.

"You're breathtaking when you're vulnerable," he whispered, and I started to squirm beneath his intense gaze. "And just as cute when you're nervous," he chuckled.

"I am not nervous." I put my hands on my hips but felt the heat rise to my face. I should just wear an electronic ticker across my forehead that broadcasted all of my emotions to the world.

"And you're not bright red either," he teased; reaching for me. I stepped back and smirked at him. I drew a line in the sand with my toe and glared back up at him.

"I stay over here, you stay over there," I declared, but he reached across anyway. "That includes your arms," I scolded him.

"I hate to tell you, but these arms are about to throw you in the water."

"Only if they can catch me!" I challenged him and took off into the waves. The ocean spray chilled my bare skin and the rough, foamy waves crashed against my body, but with the splashes of my pursuer right on my heels, adrenaline filled me and I dove in head first. The water was clear and calm beneath the waves and I instantly felt at home. I took a breath of water and reveled in the comfort of my lungs expanding and filling my body with energy. I swam as fast as I could until I was sure Finn had stopped chasing me. I confidently turned to look back when a dark-haired torpedo flew towards me; clasping his arms around my body and taking me on a spiraling, dizzying journey that left me disoriented and woozy, but not enough for me to give up on the fight. My spinning eyes found him and I lunged forward; grabbing his ankle. The tips of my fingers grazed the four onyx beads dangling from the strap of leather and pulsing warmth spread through my fingers and up my arm. He kicked free and I watched him swim around me; resembling a shark circling a potential meal. And if he wanted me, who was I to tell him otherwise?

Suddenly, slimy fingers wrapped around my legs and tightened with a jolt. I looked down to see a forest of kelp below me, several of which were securely twisted around my calves. This could not be happening again! I looked up at Finn in a panic as I began descending at a rapid pace; pulled down by the massive seaweed I was supposed to have an affinity for. I was beginning to seriously doubt that claim. This was the first time I'd been attacked by kelp, the largest of seaweeds, but that didn't do much to calm my nerves. Even though there was no possibility of drowning, I still felt a twist of fear take hold of my stomach.

"Finn!" I yelled up at him. But he just shrugged, grinned widely, and waved back at me. Some dark Prince Charming he was. The thought of Nadia's words sent my imagination running wild as a sharp image of Keto flashed in my mind; her kelp dress draped over her body. An entirely new sense of terror filled me and I began to struggle against my bonds. Trying to calm myself, I took a deep breath of cool salt water and closed my eyes. I concentrated on what I 'felt' from the kelp. Surprisingly, I only got a sense of playfulness and anticipation, so I focused on relaxing my body as it pulled me farther and farther down into the depths of the ocean.

Finally my legs were freed; allowing me the chance to evaluate my surroundings. I'd never been claustrophobic, but that was quickly changing amidst the giant swaying stalks of kelp. They towered around me in every direction and blocked any view of the world above. It reached towards the surface as a whole, searching for any inkling of sunlight that may filter down to those depths. I suddenly felt very small and insignificant. All at once an overwhelming sense of infinite patience and wisdom drenched my soul and instantly calmed my nerves. I got an odd feeling that the forest was welcoming me.

As I parted the thick curtains of kelly green, tiny electric sparks shot through my arms; making me smile. That was when I realized I was far from lost. If anything, I'd been found. As the soft blades brushed against me, I began to catch glimpses of a clearing up ahead. I swam through the edge of the dense forest and a hauntingly tragic scene stretched out before me; taking my breath away.

Naked planks of iron splintered up from the ocean floor, which created an eerie skeleton that would forever point accusingly up at the surface it would never again see. Several algae-covered cannons lay near the main wreck, along with other bronze and iron structures I didn't recognize. The entire wreck site oozed with history and reverence, shadowed by a tragic end. Amidst the field of debris, one object in particular had my full attention. She was poised at what used to be the bow and she was looking directly at me.

She was a dark garnet hue; rusted and aged to perfection by the waters of the Atlantic. Her eyes were kind; gazing at me with a look of serenity and truth. She had long, flowing hair that elegantly disappeared behind her shoulders with a crown of flowers adorning the top of her head. Her body was at least ten feet tall and the scales running down the length of her were intricately crafted, leading down to a sweeping fish tail. She was magnificent. I swam closer, completely mesmerized by her enchanting presence. She was made that much more magical by the effects of the ocean slowly devouring her surface. Algae and moss clung to her features, while tiny sea creatures made their homes within her nooks and crannies. I slowly reached out and ran my hand along her side.

A litany of images assaulted my mind in the span of two seconds. Raging seas. Colossal waves. Dark skies. I pulled my hand away in surprise and stared up at her serene face with wonder.

"She was attached to the front of the ship. They believed she would give them protection and safe seas." I turned to find Finn several yards away, partially obscured by the shadows of the kelp forest. I was reminded of the first time I'd seen him at The Hole. I was right. He didn't belong amongst the flowers, birds or sunshine. He belonged beneath the waves where the sun scattered instead of shined, where time became muted, and where darkness protected. He was a part of the ocean as much as the ocean was a part of him. Just like me. Just like the forgotten Sea Goddess before me who was lost to the sea so many years ago.

"She's amazing…" I grinned at him, contemplating the irony of her final resting place. "…apparently not very effective, but still amazing."

"You wouldn't believe how many shipwrecks are off the Outerbanks of North Carolina. It's referred to as the Graveyard of the Atlantic." His eyes suddenly seemed far away. "So much history…so many souls lost…"

"When I touched her I saw a bunch of images…just like I experienced with the sea turtles."

"You have an affinity for all things connected to the ocean, not just the animals," he explained. I immediately reverted back to the memory of Nadia accusing me of violating her mind. Then I remembered something else much less threatening.

"What about the coffee table in the living room? I felt something from it, too. Where did it come from?"

"This shipwreck." He grinned and swept his arms out, encompassing the whole wreck site.

"This shipwreck? It's the wood from this ship?" I stared back at him.

"Pretty cool, huh?" He grinned.

"Very cool..." I said; inspecting a circular object below.

"After it sank, the Sons salvaged the wood from it. It had been sitting piled up in storage, so we decided to make something out of it. We're good with our hands." He winked at me and I rolled my eyes, even though I was secretly impressed. I swam closer to the main skeleton and marveled at how large it had been. The spine of the ship remained hidden beneath the sand, but its ribs were massive. I swam inside what would have been the belly of the ship and imagined what it must have looked like. Out of the corner of my eye, something glinted in the sand. I kicked down further and zeroed in on the unknown object. I could tell that only part of it was sticking out, so I plunged my hand in the soft, forgiving sand and plucked it out.

"Wow," I breathed in pure amazement. The stone fit into my hand perfectly and warmed when I gripped it. Its iridescent white color was enhanced by the tiny striations throughout. It was smooth and shimmered even more than my trace as I turned it back and forth in my hands. It was simply beautiful.

"Find some buried treasure?" Finn asked with an amused smile. His dark hair danced in the current and his deep blue eyes had swirls of light blue, courtesy of the ocean waters.

"Wouldn't you like to know." I arched an eyebrow at him and closed my hand around my find; putting it behind my back.

"I've already found my treasure," he inferred with a wicked grin.

"You are so cheesy." I shook my head at him and smiled.

"You like it," he accused me.

"That's completely beside the point," I said at the same time a yawn took my mouth hostage. I didn't even know it was possible to yawn underwater. Finn came up behind me and hugged me; leaning down and kissing my cheek.

"I think it's time to go back up to the beach," he said with a suspicious smile.

If I thought the breeze was chilly on my bare skin before swimming in the ocean, I obviously wasn't thinking about what it would feel like after the fact. Still only wearing my bra and underwear, Finn wrapped me up in a huge, fluffy beach towel decorated with snowmen, which I found wildly ironic, and the icicles on the end of my nose slowly begun to melt away. Huddled on the blanket with only my nose and eyes peeking out, I observed Finn emptying the mystery canvas bag of its contents. First to come out was a round Tupperware container. Next was a small black box, a corked bottle of liquid, and a small shot glass. If he thought I was about to do shots with him, he was sadly mistaken. I'd be asleep long before I could set down the glass.

"It's not what you think,' he said without looking at me, but I knew he was referring to the highly skeptical look plastered all over my face. "It's coconut milk…from the Fortunate Isle." This time he glanced up at me and smiled knowingly. Relief washed over me, quickly replaced with curiosity and excitement. I had no idea what this was all about, but I couldn't wait to find out.

He sat up straighter and something resembling devastation rushed into his eyes. "I have some bad news."

"Okay…" I unwrapped the part of the towel cocoon covering my head and gave him my full attention. Coming in second to 'we need to talk' were conversations starting with 'I have bad news'. The devastation I saw in his eyes travelled across his features, which caused my heart to break.

"The day you'll have to take your journey to the Underworld will be November second."

"November second…got it." Sounded like a harmless date to me. "Why is that bad?"

"It's the Day of the Dead," he clarified, paused, and then took a deep breath. "It's also my eighteenth birthday."

"Your birthday's on the Day of the Dead?" Realizing quickly that wasn't the little nugget I was supposed to get out of his explanation, I hastily continued. "What does that mean for my journey?"

"What that means is that I won't be able to go with you." Yep. Definitely bad news. My heart sank to my feet and I felt the blood drain from my face.

"But…why not?" I asked slowly, even though I was pretty sure I already knew the answer.

"I'll have to fast in solitude for two days leading up to the night of my birthday, which is when I'll be required to kill my brother; making me the new Prime. So I'll be taken somewhere to begin fasting on October thirty-first, All Hallow's Eve - or as everyone else calls it - Halloween."

"I can't do this without you," I declared, and an overwhelming sense of dread began to fester in my gut.

"You'll have to, Pasha. I'm so sorry."

"But I don't know anything about the Underworld! I don't even know what to do if, by some miracle, I do find the river, and I definitely don't know how to get past Persephone!"

"We have two weeks to prepare. I'll make sure that you're ready, and my mother will be there that day to help you. She'll be able to get you into the Underworld, but you'll have to do the rest on your own." As my own destiny began to fall through the cracks, I thought about the risks Finn would be taking.

"And what if your brother kills you first?" The festering dread now morphed into hysteria and fear. "I can't lose you, Finn." I tried to push down the massive panic attack I could feel coming on.

"I can assure you that won't happen. I've been working out." He tried to make me laugh, but fell abysmally short. "And that's why I brought this with me." He picked up the small black box, opened it carefully and produced a bracelet of small black beads from the velvety lining inside.

"Give me your foot," he instructed, and I stuck one leg out. Apparently what I thought was a bracelet was actually an anklet. He secured it around my left ankle as the beads glistened in the moonlight. The same pulsing warmth I felt earlier from Finn's beads began to flow up my leg; encasing my entire body and lifting my frenzy of emotions. Black onyx. "Since I can't be with you, I wanted to give you something to remind you how important you are to me. I have no doubt you'll be successful."

"It's beautiful, Finn." Not to mention its protective energy was bringing my heartbeat back down to a normal speed.

"Just one more thing. We're going to head back to Lorelei tomorrow, since now we know how soon the date of your journey will be. However, we will begin preparing...tonight." He reached for the bottle of liquid and I realized how old it looked. It was in the shape of a wine bottle, but had no markings or labels on the outside; just a single cork in the top. It had turned hazy with age and I noticed that Finn handled it with care. He shook it gently before uncorking it; filling the shot glass with coconut milk and handing it to me. As I expected, it had a milky quality to it and smelled just like, well...coconut.

"The closer you get to your eighteenth birthday, the stronger you will become. The rest of your abilities will begin to show themselves and sharpen. However, we need to speed up that process. Anything connected to your ancestry will help pull out your abilities and strengths. So coconut milk from the Fortunate Isle will be a part of your diet for the next month. One shot glass worth, each day," he instructed.

I'd never had pure coconut milk before, but I liked coconut, so it couldn't be too different, right? I turned up the shot glass. It tingled my throat on the way down and steadied my nerves even more. It didn't have much taste, except for a hint of coconut.

"Not too bad." I smiled.

He took my glass and placed the bottle, shot glass and black box back inside the canvas bag. He held the Tupperware container with his palm like a waiter, swept it in front of me dramatically and pulled the lid off; bowing his head formally. Hoping for dessert, I was disappointed at what I was presented with.

He just smirked, and in his worst British accent announced, "Next on the menu for my lady: an exquisite course of fresh Atlantic seaweed from the Fortunate Isle."

"I'm allergic," I tried.

"And I'm British." He snickered sarcastically; making me laugh.

"You couldn't have brought some oranges or mangos? Maybe a kiwi or two?" I asked cynically.

"You have the strongest connection to seaweed...as did Thetis. So just like the coconut milk, you'll need to eat some each day." I inspected the slimy mass of green in the container.

"Why do I feel like I'm on 'Fear Factor'?"

"The tarantulas and cow intestines are next," he warned; his tone overly foreboding. I would have to keep my gag reflex in check around him. I wouldn't last a minute on that show. I shoved his shoulder lightly and tentatively selected a short string of seaweed to eat. It was slimy to the touch and I had no idea what it would taste like. I tried to convince myself it was no different than lettuce. It didn't work.

"Okay, here goes…" I closed my eyes and dangled it above my mouth dramatically; head back, eyes closed…and dropped it. The taste exploded in my mouth, but to my surprise I didn't immediately spit it all over Finn. It was similar to collard greens, just a lot more salty. And uncooked. And cold. But besides that, it wasn't terrible. I opened my eyes to catch Finn in the middle of a gigantic yawn.

"Leave some oxygen for the rest of us," I teased him. He just laughed and spread out another blanket. Was he making a makeshift bed for us? When he pulled two pillows I recognized from the couch out of the canvas bag, I glanced up at him in surprise.

"We're going to sleep out here?" I asked; trying not to appear too eager. Sleeping on the beach in the arms of the hottest guy on earth was exactly what I wanted to do.

"Of course."

I quickly abandoned my towel cocoon and traded it for a pillow and blanket next to him. My emotions immediately went into overdrive as I remembered what we were wearing…or more accurately…not wearing. He pulled me to him and I tucked my head in the crook of his neck; breathing him in. My body recognized the safety of his arms and it instantly relaxed into them. I felt a new kind of vulnerability wash over me, but it wasn't frightening and I didn't try to fight it. It felt more like a freedom; a letting go. Our exhaustion stifled the fire that always erupted when our bodies were this close; leaving us with a more raw form of intimacy, made up of pure acceptance and unabated love. It was amazing. And just as powerful.

"Sweet dreams," he murmured as we both drifted off to sleep.

Fourteen

I stood before a rustic, weathered wooden door and rose up onto my toes to peer through the small square window secured with five thin, but strong metal bars. I grasped the wrought iron knob and turned. It gave way under my grip and the door swung open with a low groan. My bare feet shuffled along the cold, cement floor as I cautiously stepped through the doorway. Something felt very off. I felt...separated from myself, and the perceived distance was substantial and unsettling. The lightness I sensed told me I was having a reverie, but I didn't remember leaving my body. Where was I? The indistinctive room where I currently stood refused to unlock any clues surrounding my whereabouts. A small cot with a single threadbare sheet occupied the far corner, and one lonely square window gave passage to the afternoon sun streaking across the floor. A modest chest of drawers leaned against one wall; a collection of seashells camouflaging the top. I started to advance towards the window to see if the view would stir any memories, but my feet were suddenly frozen to the floor as my eyes traveled upward. The entire unassuming wall to my left was scarred with a countless number of lines. Each of them measured at least four inches long, all running vertically. They appeared to have been scratched into the stone wall, leaving them jagged and archaic. As I scanned row after row of lines, I realized there must be thousands of them. My feet thawed enough for me to step tentatively and I approached the wall with bewilderment. I knelt down and ran a finger over what I assumed to be the freshest line. Below it on the floor lay stone shavings; etched out to make way for the line. It was as if someone was keeping count. A subtle inner pull abruptly diverted my attention to the window. I straightened, shuffled to the window and steeled myself as I peered out. When my eyes found only an expansive blanket of deep blue, an unexpected bout of vertigo took my equilibrium captive and I leaned up against the window pane to keep my balance. The cool glass on my forehead eased the queasiness, and I tried looking down instead of out. The soaring elevation of the room was dizzying. The white beach far below was in the shape of a crescent moon, caressed by the rolling waves, while the cobalt blue hue of the water tickled my subconscious.

Small, dark forms milled about on the sand or in the surf, as if they had been let out for recess and were enjoying their limited time outside. When I spotted one figure several meters from the others, my memory flashed and I knew this was a place I'd been before. I stood on the sands of that same beach - the beach where I saw the old man for the first time. And he had seen me. I peered closely below at the figure with the gray hair blowing in the wind. Without warning, his head snapped up and his gray eyes met mine. Even from this far away I could see the shock on his face. Whatever he had been holding was dropped and forgotten on the soft sand at his feet. When I blinked, I was knocked off balance by an intense moving sensation. The world around me swirled with colors and sounds before abruptly stopping. And then all was still and dark.

When my eyes adjusted to the sudden blackness, I noticed I was sitting against something rough with my knees pulled to my chest, like I was hiding from something. When I took a breath, the frigid air sliced into my lungs and pierced my throat as it rushed back out through my nose. I shifted my rigid body to the right and heard the crunching sound of dead leaves. The dank, mildewy stench condensed in the air around me and something scampered across my big toe. I let out a surprised yelp; pulling my feet even closer to my body. I heard a noise from what must have been outside of whatever I was being housed in and froze in terror. A bright light penetrated the darkness and shone directly into my eyes. I squeezed them shut and lifted a defensive hand.

"You done?" a raspy female voice demanded from behind the one-hundred watt light blinding me. In my effort to understand what was happening, the allotted time for my answer apparently ran out. "I said...you done?" she repeated with teeming annoyance.

"With what?" I asked from behind my hand; squinting around the brightness. Suddenly a strong hand encircled my arm, yanked me onto my knees and dragged me out a door. After the metal edge of the storage building slashed my left thigh, sending a sharp pain down my leg, I landed face-down in a patch of mud and weeds. I made an effort to lift myself up and wipe the hardened mud from my skin, but the same hand slammed into my shoulder; spinning my small frame around and landing me right back in the mud, this time on my back. I glared up into the bitter face belonging to a woman in her mid- forties. Her brown hair rested limply against her round face and neck. Her bloodshot brown eyes matched the mud I was currently splayed in, and were emphasized by the dark circles hanging beneath. The wooden spoon clutched in her hand and the radiating pain from both hands reminded me what had prompted this unfounded punishment. Accidentally grabbing a pot with bare hands, I scorched the skin across my palms and spilled the pot's contents onto the kitchen floor. Although the floor was already stained from years of disregard, she supervised as I cleaned up the mess with Clorox and water; sending seething pain into my fresh burns. When the tears started flowing, I was thrown into the shed. Crying was not allowed in our house. It would upset him. And neither I, nor the angry woman glaring down at me wanted to upset him. The severe repercussions would make the singed skin of my hands feel like a loving hug.

"Get up!" his booming voice exploded from the right of us. He stumbled down the brick steps and seized the fabric of my sweatshirt; lifting me to my feet in a split second. "You think that burn feels bad?! You'll wish you just had a burn when I get done with you!" He swayed closer and I flinched; twisting my head to the side and anticipating the pain. Instead of hitting me, he secured my arm in his much larger hand and contorted it at an odd angle. One more twist of his wrist and I heard a loud pop followed by an immense pressure. The pain that shot up my arm made my knees buckle and I collapsed back in the mud. I felt the cool wetness against my cheek right before I blacked out.

I heard a scream and shot straight up; eyes wide open with alarm. Suddenly aware that the earsplitting scream was coming from my own mouth, I put my head in my hands. In an instant, sturdy, protective arms enveloped my body.

"Stasia! What's wrong? What happened?" Finn. I shut my eyes and allowed my body with its severely frayed nerves to fall into his stable one. He brushed several unruly strands of aquamarine and blonde hair back from my tear-stained face.

"I just...I had a reverie-" I breathed; forcing down the sobs I could feel pulsing in my throat and demanding to be released. He held me close until my breathing had calmed and the last of my tears had dried up. He pulled away to look at me. And gasped.

"Pasha your eye!"

"If you tell me they've changed colors again, I'm going to scream," I threatened; my tone deadpan. Finn just chuckled lightly, sat up, and inclined my head to the right as he examined me closer. He smiled but remained quiet.

"Lemme guess. Pink? Orange?" I joked with him as he continued to inspect my face.

"It's not your eyes, it's your eye." His blue eyes watched me adoringly and I wondered how I was going to explain one aqua eye and one...purple or yellow. "You've acquired another trace."

"Another...trace?" I stared at him; utterly confused. "On my eye?"

"It's under your eye, Pasha," he laughed at me and touched a finger to the skin at the outer corner of my eye. "It's right here." Relief that my eye color hadn't changed was trumped by the mystery of an unknown addition to my features. Nothing says 'freak' like a glaring trace on one's face.

"Are you sure it's a trace? Aren't I only supposed to have one?" I asked him; hopeful. His sly smile told me he was more than sure.

"It's rare but not unusual," he explained with pride. "The most powerful descendants - direct, Chosen, or both - can have multiple traces."

"So what does it look like?" The suspense was now literally killing me. I was close to running back up to the house in search of a mirror, when he started to dig in the canvas bag.

"Hold on..." He pulled out his IPhone and handed it to me. I held it up like I would a mirror and thankfully the moonlight was bright enough to create a slight reflection on its dark surface.

Below the outside corner of my left eye was a small shape that was hard to make out in the phone's semi-reflective surface. I inclined my head towards the moon so the light would shine more on my face.

"Oh, wow," I murmured as my new trace became visible. Just like my hair, this was going to take some getting used to. It was the same blue as my triskellion trace

111

and greatly resembled the infinity symbol; the number eight turned on its side.

"It's absolutely beautiful," Finn exalted. He furrowed his brow. "Didn't you say your hair changed color after another reverie you had?"

I thought for a minute. "You know, you're right. It did..." I paused and realized both reveries occurred in the same place; the crescent-shaped beach. With the same older gentleman picking up shells. I launched into an explanation of the two reveries and the older man I saw carefully sidestepping the nightmare of my past that had followed.

"You must have a connection with the old man," he speculated. "I would guess he's an ancestor."

My heart skipped a beat. "Like....like a grandfather?"

"It's possible," he told me. I looked out over the waves to the dark horizon. An ancestor. I hadn't thought about it before, but it would only make sense. My father wasn't immortal, so he would have had a family. A family that didn't know about me. My growing hope withered at that gloomy possibility. Either way, I knew that if my soul found its way back to that place, I would be compelled to find out.

"So if the reverie wasn't upsetting, what was?" Finn eyed me curiously and rubbed my back. I had completely forgotten about the dream my reverie morphed into.

"Just a bad dream," I muttered.

"What was it about?" he asked gently.

"Just stuff from the past..." I trailed off. A sigh laced with a whimper made its escape. "Why can't I just get a good night's rest like normal people do?"

"Because you are far from normal." Finn smiled down at me; the depths of his blue eyes alleviating my suffering.

"Lucky me."

He chuckled and readjusted the blankets to shield us from the cool wind that flowed off the waves. The sky was only beginning to lighten, so I curled up in his reassuring embrace.

"I'm the lucky one, Pasha."

"Are you sure you didn't murder somebody?"

"I'm definitely about to murder somebody," I threatened; leering at Carmen. My newest trace had become the talk of the trip back to Bald Head as we hung out on the second level of the boat, watching more movies. As was to be expected, everyone was throwing out guesses as to what my trace could mean; murder being the most recent hypothesis. My trace wasn't a teardrop, which apparently signified how many people a gang member had killed, but that didn't stop them from running with it.

"Maybe you did it in your sleep? That's why you don't remember!" Phoebe figured.

"That must have been why I saw a bloody knife laying on the floor last night." Cage snickered and watched me suspiciously. "It's all making sense now…"

"Yeah, this whole 'future leader of the Tydes-thing' is just a ruse. She wants us to think she's all honorable and trustworthy, but just when you least expect it - WHAM! Knife to the chest. Lights out." Ricker pretended to stab himself dramatically. Ian shook his head at me from the other couch as if deeply disappointed at my unthinkable deception.

The rest of the trip was, for the most part, drama-free except for the once again glaring eyes of Carmen and Ricker. How two people could go from hating each other back to loving each other, and then right back to hating each other in one weekend was beyond my comprehension. It also sounded awfully exhausting. Willow and Liam tiptoed around each other, both waiting for the other to make the first move. Finn was all business, as he was intent on starting the preparations for my journey right away. Since we only had three weeks, my regimen would start immediately. Strength training in the ocean, memorizing a map of the Underworld, and a regular diet of slimy seaweed and coconut milk awaited me once we returned to Lorelei. The fact that Finn wouldn't be accompanying me did, in fact, force me to raise the bar for myself. If I had to do this without him, I would soak up every piece of knowledge I could until the time came.

Upon returning to Lorelei and Maren Hall we ran into Olivia, who was coming out of the elevator as we were getting on.

"Hey Olivia!" I grinned at her. As someone who had earned the nickname 'Bee-yotch' from my roommates, we were extremely surprised when she'd offered up her yacht and accompanied us to the Fortunate Isle. After finding out her mother was the therapist who coordinated my move to Lorelei, I began to see her in a new light. Underneath the attitude was a good person. Her dark hair had been straightened and her dark eyes were accented by smoky eye makeup. Her long black dress skimmed her black stilettos. She looked like she was going on a date. Either that or a funeral.

"Stasia," She smiled at me in greeting, and then acknowledged my roommates with a sly nod of the head. "Stasia's groupies."

"You better be glad my hands are full," Carmen threatened her with a smirk. We stepped onto the elevator and Olivia stuck a hand out to stop the doors from closing.

"Just to warn you – there's some people snooping around your suite." She raised an eyebrow. "They said they were looking for a girl named Hannah." I let go of the bag I was holding and my stomach dropped to the floor. The Whitmans were here? At Lorelei? In my suite?

"Didn't you lock the door when we left?" Carmen asked Phoebe.

"I thought so..." Phoebe frowned in thought. My roommates didn't know my previous name, Hannah, because I changed it to Anastasia upon my arrival to The House of Lorelei.

"I think I know who they are," I admitted to Olivia, still in shock.

"Oh, good." She let go of the elevator door. "See ya!" She disappeared around the corner in a cloud of strong-smelling perfume. Phoebe and Carmen looked at me expectantly.

"It's my adoptive family," I said with a disconcerted sigh.

"So who's Hannah?" Phoebe questioned.

"Me," I answered. "That was my name before I changed it to Anastasia."

"And they don't know about any of this?" Carmen swept her arms out; alluding to our ancestry and Lorelei's true purpose.

"Nope," I sighed again, but Carmen just smiled.

"This is going to be fun," she said with a sneer and a twinkle in her eye. I could only pray Laura Beth hadn't come with them. Carmen would eat her alive. After Phoebe had to physically push me off of the elevator, I braced myself and we entered our suite.

"Hannah, darling!" Dee Whitman embraced me in an awkward hug. She wasn't usually the hugging type. She was usually worried it would wrinkle her clothes. Currently her dark green tweed skirt and dress jacket matched the black and green plaid shoes accentuating her feet.

"Hi Dee." I looked past her to see who else had come. "So...what are you guys doing here?"

"Now that's no way to greet your family after such a long time! We wanted to surprise you!" She threw her arms up in somewhat-forced excitement. "Charles and Laura Beth are out on the balc- Hannah Whitman! What is that thing on your face?" She grabbed my chin and yanked my head to the side in horror.

"I got a new tattoo." I held my breath and hoped she would keep her composure in front of my roommates.

"We'll talk about that later, young lady," she threatened in a low voice and scowled at me. She masked her distaste with her High Society face, typically reserved for people she believed to be beneath her. She turned to Phoebe, Willow and Carmen.

"And these must be your little roommates!" She introduced herself to Carmen, Phoebe and Willow while I took my bags into my bedroom. Unfortunately, all I could think about was how to make them leave. I wasn't prepared to reconcile my old life with my new – colorful life, and I wasn't even sure it was possible without a nuclear explosion occurring.

"Well hello, Hannah," Charles Whitman greeted me as I walked back out into the living room. I gave him a warm hug and he froze for a split second as he zeroed in on my newest trace. I glimpsed the person standing behind him with her hands on her hips. "Hey, Laura Beth."

"Hey," she snipped. "So, all four of ya'll live here?" Her skeptical green eyes scanned our suite like it was a smelly locker room.

"On Wednesdays we sleep in our closets and eat off the floor," Carmen answered breezily. "Luckily the rats and cockroaches only come out at night."

All color drained from Laura Beth's face as she did a quick scan of the carpet for rodents. Phoebe stifled a giggle disguised as a cough and I could feel Dee's weighty stare on me.

"She's kidding," I assured Dee and quickly made all of the necessary introductions; hoping that would suffice in changing the subject. I should have known better.

"So why are y'all here?" Laura Beth's eyes washed over my roommates with disdain. "Did you get kicked out of your normal schools or something?" To my adoptive family this was a school for kids with behavioral or psychological problems. I felt an uneasy feeling creep up my spine as Carmen cleared her throat accepted the challenge.

"I tried to kill my ex-boyfriend." Carmen replied with a shrug, and then gestured toward Phoebe nonchalantly. "Phoebe was caught making out with a german sheph-"

"This school isn't any different than any other school," I interrupted and shot Carmen a threatening look. She just smiled back at me.

"Dr. Campbell assured us Lorelei was an upstanding school with high credentials," Dee announced to the room and then zeroed in on me. "If it is anything less, I expect you to tell me so I can take appropriate action."

"No, no - I love it here!" I heard the underlying panic in my voice. The last thing I wanted was for Dee to take me back to Georgia. I lowered my voice back to normal. "I've made some amazing friends-"

"And she's got a hot boyfriend-" Carmen winked at Laura Beth, who's jaw promptly dropped.

"A boyfriend?" Charles raised a shocked eyebrow.

"It's nothing, really," I hurriedly denounced her claim. "Just a guy I've been seeing for a while."

"He's not 'just a guy'," Phoebe rolled her eyes at me. "He's the future leader of the-the..,the water polo team." She clamped her mouth shut as she realized what she almost let slip.

I moved to sit down on the couch before I strangled Phoebe. I almost threw up but thankfully, words came out of my mouth instead. "So what brings you guys down this way?"

"We're actually on our way to Virginia for the week. Do you remember Uncle Stephen and Aunt Josie?" She didn't wait for my answer. "We've been invited to stay with them this week and I couldn't imagine not swinging by and seeing our other daughter!" Laura Beth's expression as she stared at me was comparable to a laser beam.

Willow jumped into hostess mode immediately as she made sure the Whitmans had something to drink and pretzels to snack on. The longer they were there, the higher my blood pressure rose. My calculations gave me another hour before a heart attack would bring a fitting end to the day. The next hour involved Dee catching me up on all the latest gossip and extravagant parties as if I was remotely interested. As long as the conversation was off me, Finn, or the House of Lorelei, I would listen and nod until my head fell off. Finally Laura Beth stood and crossed her arms impatiently.

"I'm hungry," she announced. "and it's going to take forever to get off this island."

"You have a point, dear," Dee smiled at her, grabbed her purse and stood. "If we want to get to Virginia before it gets too late, we'll need to get going."

"I couldn't be happier that you are enjoying Lorelei, Hannah," Charles hugged me goodbye. I squeezed him and felt a twinge of regret. He would be the only family member I'd want to share some of my new life with. But I know that was not possible. He took my hands in his and looked at me lovingly. "Please take care of yourself and let us know if you need anything."

"I will," I assured him as Dee put a hand on my shoulder.

"Behave yourself," she instructed me and then lowered her voice. "If I see one more tattoo, I'll yank you out of this school in a heartbeat." Her eyes flitted toward my roommates as her tone became even more hushed, "And I'm not sure I trust that Carmen."

She said her name like she was a dog who might have rabies, but for some reason her threats made me smile. Although Dee was strict and closed-minded, she had opened her home to me, fed me, clothed me, and attempted to raise me as she would her own daughter. I wave of nostalgia washed over me and I placed a hand on hers.

"Thank you," I said with genuine gratitude. "...for everything."

For a moment, she stared at me in shock, but quickly gathered herself and smiled uncomfortably. "You're welcome, dear."

After saying their goodbyes to Phoebe, Carmen and Willow, they filed out of the door stiffly and I closed it solidly behind them. I leaned against the door, let out a breath, and instantly felt lighter.

"They weren't too bad," Willow tried with a smile. I chuckled at her.

"Yes, they were just maaaarvelous," Carmen squealed in her southern accent and clapped her hands together. If a person needed distraction from her foster family and an impending, possibly perilous, journey to the Underworld, my suite would be the place they'd find it.

"I love you guys," I snickered.

"In the late eighteen-hundreds, the house and surrounding land were owned by a wealthy doctor; living there with his wife, three daughters and two sons."

The next night, we were huddled on the balcony of our suite enjoying the pink and orange colors dancing across the ocean as the sun majestically announced its departure. We had lain around the living room most of the day watching movies and taking naps. It was exactly what I needed. We ordered a pizza for dinner and decided to eat outside since the weather was so nice. As talk turned to Halloween, Phoebe insisted on telling me the story of the old Drake House near campus that was rumored to be haunted.

"They were very active in the community and well known up and down the coast. One summer, one of the daughters dropped dead for no apparent reason. Another daughter was soon to follow, and then his wife began to show the same signs of sickness. Apparently in an effort to save his family, the doctor began to dabble in alchemy. Soon he was consumed with an obsession to not only save his wife, but to bring his daughters back. One weekend, the family didn't show up for church on Sunday. No one thought much of it until the doctor failed to make his house calls the next day. A friend of the family decided to drive out to the house to see if everything was alright." She leaned towards me and raised her eyebrows for effect. "What she found would shock the whole island. Their blood was smeared across the walls, leading up the stairs to the family's bedrooms. All of the children were still in their beds, face-down and now soaked in their own blood. They had all been beaten to death and were missing one vital thing..." She paused; her eyes sparkling with excitement. I held my breath; anticipating the punch line that didn't disappoint. "...their hearts."

Chills ran down my spine and I wrapped my arms around myself. Contemplating the tragedy of young, promising lives ripped away from innocent children prematurely sent my thoughts to Bianca. Not only had she been killed, but she was now destined to aimlessly wander the earth realm as a ghost. Phoebe, reveling in the chilling response she was eliciting, continued her story.

"His wife was found in her bed, also dead. Her heart had been removed as well. Not until they searched the underground cellar did they find the doctor. His body was found on the floor, a surgical knife in one hand. He had sliced through his own chest and his heart had been ripped from his body."

I peeked at Willow, whose face had taken on a sickly green tint, and at Carmen, who was nervously biting her fingernails.

"According to the story, the doc did find a way to raise the dead, but something went very wrong and he raised a demon instead. They say the demon possessed him and made him take his family's hearts out and then his own."

"Did they find the hearts?" Willow's soft voice wavered. Phoebe shook her head solemnly.

"They were never found. Only one piece of evidence was ever found. Written on the cellar door in blood was one word: Penance."

I clasped a shaking hand over my mouth and my veins rapidly hardened to ice. The world began to spin and I grasped my chair to steady myself. Penance. That was the same word Nadia had burned into her desk. But this was just a story - it wasn't real! Right? Bianca had called her 'The

Reaper'. Was there something Finn wasn't telling me about Nadia? He said she escorted the rejected souls back to the Earth realm, but was it possible that she took souls as well? As a sick type of punishment to the living? As it would happen, the word 'reaper' meant to harvest, and the word 'penance' meant atonement; the righting of wrongs. As this new, startling possibility hit me, I leaned back in my chair, utterly petrified.

"You okay Stasia? You don't look so good." Willow placed her hand on my arm and a healing tingle spread through my body; settling my stomach. I couldn't tell them what I'd seen. They didn't know Nadia was the one who had paid us a visit during our séance, and I didn't want to make a big deal out of nothing. It was probably just a coincidence. But what if it wasn't? Would Bianca know? Is that why she's so scared of Nadia? I wished I could talk to her again. I squeezed the bridge of my nose. A couple days ago I hadn't even believed in ghosts, and now I was wishing I could speak to one? I really had to get myself together. This was ridiculous. It was just a haunted house story. Every town in America had one. It wasn't real. I looked up at my roommates, who were watching me with concern. You'd think they'd tire of my unstable mental health and sudden emotional breakdowns, but they never complained.

"Yeah...I'm okay. I just got dizzy all of a sudden." I summoned a convincing smile onto my face and Phoebe continued.

"Anyway, over the years several families moved into the house, but they would always leave within a few months. They say the family still haunts the house...searching for their stolen hearts."

"Dinner just isn't the same with a family of ghosts digging in the food searching for their hearts," Carmen snickered.

"We should go!" Phoebe squealed with delight and clasped her hands together, nearly knocking over Carmen's Gatorade bottle.

"To the Drake house?" Willow gulped and turned a light shade of green again.

"We don't even know how to get there," Carmen contemplated Phoebe's idea with skepticism.

"I know exactly where it is! It's easy to get to - promise!" She batted her big green eyes at Carmen.

"What about the Halloween party?" Carmen argued stubbornly.

"Halloween party?" I finally discovered the ability to speak again.

"Every year there's a Halloween party in The Hole. They move all of the tables and make it real spooky. It's actually really fun!" Phoebe's features lit up with enthusiasm. "We could do both! Go to the party and then find the Drake house! Come on, it'll be fun! Plus, I've been wanting to go since I got here and this is our last year," she begged.

"Do you think dead doctors like sexy nurses?" Carmen narrowed her eyes and wiggled her dark brown eyebrows.

"Please tell me you aren't going to dress up as a sexy nurse again," Phoebe snarled at Carmen with frustration. "That's what you wore last year!"

"If it ain't broke, don't fix it." Carmen shrugged her shoulders and twirled a dark brown lock of hair around her finger.

"It's kinda overdone," Phoebe contended; scrunching her nose.

"And your sexy cop outfit isn't?" Carmen challenged her. "Six other girls wore the same costume last year."

"Yeah, but I was the only one with a pink uniform and fishnets." Phoebe rested her hands on her hips with indignation. "And I'm going to be something different this year anyway."

"Fishnets? Seriously?" I gawked at Phoebe. I would never be able to pull fishnets off, but somehow I knew they looked absolutely amazing on her.

"When did Halloween turn into an excuse for girls to dress up like cheap sluts?" Willow chastised no one in particular; shaking her head.

"Don't knock it 'til you try it." Carmen grinned shrewdly.

"So what do you guys think?" Phoebe prodded us again. I had to admit, I was a little curious about the Drake house and what, if any, connection it may have to Nadia.

"Are you sure you know where it is?" Willow asked. Phoebe shook her head vehemently, and then looked to me for my consent next.

"It would be kinda fun..." I started, and Phoebe jumped up and down in her seat. Two yes's and one to go. We all turned our attention to Carmen.

"Alright, but if a demon takes over my body and forces me to cut your heart out, don't blame me," Carmen cautioned her.

"I'll just come back and haunt you every chance I get," Phoebe challenged her with a steely expression.

"In your pink cop uniform? Ohhh, I'm shaking with fear already," Carmen countered sarcastically.

"You guys really shouldn't joke about that," Willow chided. "If the legends about the Drake house are true, you'll be eating your words."

"I personally think the doc just went crazy and decided to slaughter his whole family. Probably cooked up the hearts and ate them himself," Carmen theorized.

"Eww! Don't say that!" Phoebe shrunk back in revulsion while Carmen smiled in triumph.

"Make no mistake," warned a deep, foreboding voice behind us. "Demons are very real."

"Ever heard of a doorbell?" Carmen scowled. "You can't just go jumping out of the shadows anytime you feel like it."

"But it's so much more fun," Finn smirked at her and then easily met my gaze. He leaned against the doorframe with inherent confidence. He was dressed in jeans and a gray t-shirt, while his handsome face was eerily shaded with the living room light at his back. "Plus, I brought something I think you guys will be very interested in…" he teased cryptically. My tortured heart proceeded to hurdle up in my throat.

"The map?" I choked; my voice coming out an octave higher than I intended.

"The map," he confirmed smugly. Willow gasped and a silence fell over our small balcony. All at once everyone bounded into the living room with renewed exhilaration.

"I'll get markers!"

"I'll get a notebook!"

"I'll get the pixie sticks!" The stampede halted long enough for us to give Willow a curious glance.

"I always eat candy when I study," she explained and shrugged her shoulders.

We posted up at the coffee table like a pack of kids waiting for ice cream, eager to catch a glimpse of an actual map of the Underworld. Finn produced a large, unassuming piece of paper rolled up and secured with a rubber band. Either The Sons had incredible preservation techniques, or this was a printed version.

"Shouldn't it be…older?" I scratched my head.

"I was only able to bring a copy of it…," he justified with a slight grin. "The actual map is thousands of years old, not to mention it's housed in a remote, undisclosed location; unknown to most descendants." The gleam in his eye told me he wasn't including himself in the 'most' category. I could only imagine the kind of information he was privy to. I wondered what it must be like to be Finn Morrison, future Prime and hottest guy on earth. Being that sexy must come with immense responsibility and pressure. Oh, and the whole future-Prime-thing must be hard, too. I giggled at my own thoughts; consequently attracting odd looks from my roommates.

Finn, apparently used to my random outbursts, carefully unrolled the map; spreading it out on the table and securing its unruly corners with Phoebe's teal and white tile coasters. A blanket of stillness cloaked the room as we gazed upon the most impressive map we had ever seen.

Although it was simply a photocopy, it was clear just how ancient the original map had been. The hand drawn creatures and places were created with the artistry and perfection of DaVinci. The normal lines that sectioned off specific parts of the Underworld were layered with exquisite sketches of each important landmark. Scribbled notes and headings covered the extent of the paper, but they were written in a language I didn't recognize.

Carmen looked up at Finn with uncertainty. "Please tell me you know whatever language that is?"

"Of course," he confirmed; flashing an exceptionally charming smile in my direction that stopped my world for a millisecond. Didn't he know how dangerous that smile was? There were only so many things that could stop time, and his smile ranked up there with the time warp continuum.

"Uh, he's been to the Underworld, remember?" Phoebe retorted, stunned by Carmen's failure to see the obvious.

"Well that doesn't mean he knows what all these crazy symbols are supposed to be!" Carmen incited defensively.

"He doesn't need symbols when he's been there and seen the real thing."

"Well he's not going, so what's in his head isn't going to help her!" Carmen threw back at her.

"I believe that's what your notebook is for," Finn inserted; chuckling at their heated debate over his legitimacy. Carmen crossed her arms at him and a smug grin spread across Phoebe's face as Finn continued. "What Stasia needs to concentrate on are the major landmarks, the path leading to the river, and most importantly, the passageway leading back to this realm."

I inspected the map once more and began to feel a numbness crawl up my fingers and into my arm. I couldn't do this. The farthest place I'd ever been to was the High Society of Atlanta with its embellished etiquette and society rules. I'd never even been to a foreign country, and now I would be travelling to a different realm? By myself, no less. At that little jewel of self reassurance, my entire body succumbed to the numbness and a determined panic scratched its way into my heart. It wrapped its prickly fingers around me and stifled my ability to breathe. I stood deliberately and walked back out onto the balcony in a debilitated stupor. The light wind coming off of the ocean swirled around my face and I tried to take several deep breaths. The roar of the dark waves gradually filled me with a peace like nothing else could…well, almost nothing else.

"You can do this, Pasha." Finn's sure voice caressed my ears as he stepped behind me and wrapped his warm, steady arms around my shaking body. He leaned down and planted a kiss on my cheek, and then stared out at the ocean with unwavering certainty.

"What if I can't?" His unshakeable confidence in me continued to leave me flabbergasted.

"What if you can?" he disputed my doubt with amusement.

"What if I let everyone down?"

"What if the ocean dries up and sharks become the new higher intelligence?" he speculated; his tone serious and reflective. The panic in my throat turned to slight hysteria and a bubble of laughter fought its way out. Finding a chink in my armor, he kept going.

"What if my hair falls out and I grow a head of spaghetti instead?" he questioned me; still deeply thoughtful.

"I'd grab some Ragu, parmesan cheese, and a fork," I giggled. He laughed and turned me around to face him. His features softened and his earnest gaze captured my undivided attention.

"What if you are the strongest person I know, and I'm certain you don't have it in you to fail?" He grinned at me. His comforting words soothed me and I felt the panic dissipate into only a slight ripple of anxiety.

"I wish I could be as confident in me as you are."

"Which is exactly why you will succeed. Modesty is an important virtue that always leads to courage. This won't be the first time you'll rise above adversity and come out stronger. You have no idea how amazing you are, Anastasia." He gave me another hug as I breathed him in. "Let's go inside and give you the weapon you'll be concealing on your journey."

"Weapon?" I questioned; perplexed. A kickass cat woman suit with hidden ninja stars and exploding diamond earrings popped into my mind. He smiled wickedly at my question.

"Knowledge."

SEVENTEEN

"It's like the map in the Legend of Zelda game!" Phoebe squealed. She was met by our vacant stares as she glanced around. "You know - the Wii game? Twilight Princess? Except Stasia isn't Link, so I guess she'd be considered the princess, who's actually Zelda..." she trailed off in deep thought.

"Your talking privileges have been revoked for the rest of the night," Carmen declared solemnly, right before Phoebe threw a pixie stick at her. "Mmm...red. My favorite."

"There's only one way in and one way out," Finn divulged to me in all seriousness. "Both of which will test your character and fortitude. Once you reach the entrance, Persephone will be your first challenge."

"This could so be in the Legend of Zelda game," Phoebe muttered. Carmen shot her a look while I prayed Finn wouldn't mention the whole part about dying in order to reach the Underworld. I didn't want my roommates to completely freak out and insist I back out. This was too important to just give up on. I was hoping we could discuss the details of my imminent demise at a later time. I shuddered as I contemplated my own death and urged myself to pay attention as Finn kept talking, pointing down at the map with insistence.

"Persephone will have to approve your entrance and allow you to pass through the groves and continue on towards the river." His piercing gaze was somewhat daunting. Or maybe it was the fact that I wasn't looking forward to coming face-to-face with the infamous Queen of the Underworld. Something told me we would never be 'besties'.

"Will Persephone know she's there, or does she need a big parade to announce her entrance?" Carmen asked as she vigorously jotted down notes. Willow had a pink highlighter poised above the map, ready to highlight at a moment's notice. I couldn't help but smile at their devotion.

"Persephone will know. She always knows when a soul enters her groves," Finn affirmed despairingly.

"So, what exactly are the Groves of Persephone?" Phoebe asked, scanning the map intently. This would be the perfect time to develop a photographic memory. Unlikely at best.

"It's where the pomegranate trees grow, right?" Willow presumed. Finn nodded.

"The only trees in the Underworld are located in Persephone's grove. Before she was trapped in the Underworld she was the Goddess of spring growth, so it's only natural that she has her own grove. The variety of trees is immense, however Willow's right; it's mostly dominated by pomegranate trees." Finn ran his hands through his hair. "Unfortunately, her decision to allow a soul passage is truly her own. She'll decide based on what she sees within that particular soul."

"So that's it? She either lets you in or she doesn't?" Carmen complained; clearly appalled at Persephone's undisputed power. "I think that's a load of crap," she contested and crossed her arms in defiance.

"And it is, but the chances of her denying Stasia entrance are pretty slim. Only the most broken of souls are turned away. Stasia is anything but broken." He smiled at me, alluding to my declaration several months ago on the beach. No matter the level of his certainty, I still viewed myself as broken. I'd chipped away at my self-doubt, but I couldn't be sure if I'd ever live up to the elevated image Finn had of me. I frowned at his handsome face.

"But I'll still have to talk to her regardless, right?" I maintained.

"Yes," he answered simply, with a gloomy undertone I didn't miss.

"Excellent." The prominent sarcasm dripping from my voice had Finn chuckling.

"She's not that bad," he claimed, but I'd believe that when I saw it. He scooted to the edge of his seat and indicated an invisible path on the map that Willow promptly highlighted. "Once you head north and through the grove, you'll run right into Charon's Marsh. It's where he collects the souls and takes them to the parts of the Underworld where Persephone has decided they belong." A crushing, foreboding cloud settled over me.

"Wait - is she going to decide where I 'belong'?" I asked; holding up air quotations at the word belong. The last person I wanted deciding where I belonged would unanimously be the jaded Queen.

"Your soul will still be technically attached to a body in this realm. You wouldn't be permitted to enter the parts of the Underworld where body-less souls reside, so you won't need to worry about that." I let out a breath I didn't realize I'd been holding.

"So tell me again what four sections of the Underworld the body-less souls are sent to?" Phoebe pulled her hair back in determination and tapped the highlighter against her chin.

"The Asphodel Meadows is where normal, everyday human souls reside. It's the largest section of the Underworld," he explained.

"So…basically heaven?" Phoebe guessed; setting a bowl of roasted almonds down on the table.

"I guess you could call it that." Finn grinned at her connection. "It's an expansive space full of springs and life, so definitely the kind of place humans would consider to be heavenly."

"Then there's The Vale of Mourning. It's a section reserved for those who take their own life - commit suicide. Unfortunately the number of souls resting there is much higher than you would imagine." His face fell in despair for those tragic souls, and I hopelessly fell in love with him all over again. I shook myself and tried to focus. This was not the time to be drooling over him. I needed to remember this.

"The Elysian Fields is what I'm the most familiar with. It's where the souls of Gods and Goddesses reside. Namely, your mother." He watched me knowingly. "There are no words to describe the grandeur and majesty of the Fields." His features turned wistful and he seemed to smile to himself, as if remembering a fond memory. I wished again that I had the ability to see into his mind.

"Finally, there is the section called Tarturus." His eyes flitted toward Phoebe. "Or as humans would call it, Hell." Phoebe gasped and Carmen choked on her Gatorade mid-sip as he continued. "I've only seen it from afar, but it's not a place you'd ever want to find yourself. Raging fires and continuous pain follow every soul; torturing it for eternity. But it's only reserved for the most demented of souls. I don't believe any of us fall into that category." He glanced around at his immediate company, then continued, "No need to worry, the rivers of the Underworld divide the different sections, making it impossible to get anywhere without Charon's assistance. You couldn't get into Hell if you tried. Metaphorically or literally."

"Comforting." I shook my head in astonishment, but Finn just laughed and popped some almonds in his mouth.

"So all these rivers feed into Charon's Marsh, right in the middle of it all." Willow gestured at the squiggly lines on the map that signified the different rivers. "Which one will Stasia have to find?"

"There are five rivers in the Underworld," Finn contended. "They all feed into Charon's marsh in the middle, which is how he carries the souls to the different sections. The rivers are not to be taken lightly, however. They each shelter secrets of their own between their unassuming banks."

"What do you mean?" Phoebe asked, completely entranced.

"Three main rivers circle the different sections of the Underworld. The River of Fire surrounds Tarturus and-"

"The River of Fire!?" Phoebe's eyes widened in fascination.

Carmen looked at him skeptically. "Is it actually a river of fire?"

"I guess it would be better described as a river of lava." Finn shrugged his shoulders, as if a river of lava were no big deal. "Let's just say you don't want to fall in it." He chuckled at himself, but Phoebe's face paled at his words.

"The River of Forgetfulness surrounds The Vale of Mourning." He paused; anticipating more questions. Phoebe didn't disappoint.

"Forgetfulness? So does that mean it makes you forget things? Is that why it's around the Vale of Mourning? So those souls will forget whatever made them kill themselves?"

"Only if a soul drinks from its water, will they forget. The amount they drink will determine how many memories will be erased. It can be very tempting for those souls who have many memories they'd like to forget."

"But if you erase the bad, how will you be able to appreciate the good?" Willow pondered.

"I have a million memories I'd like to forget, but they also made me who I am. I wouldn't want to forget them," I divulged quietly.

134

"I agree, but unfortunately the souls of the Vale of Mourning have succumbed to their pain. They are weak and the river is all too tantalizing," Finn stated.

"How sad..." Phoebe gushed, as he described the third important river.

"The River of Unbreakable Oaths surrounds the divine Elysian Fields. It's also called the River Styx." He nodded his head at Willow, who quickly turned it a bright neon pink and tapped her chin in deep thought again.

"So how exactly does Stasia get there?" she asked studiously.

"She'll need to reach the end of the groves, where she'll run right into the marsh. Following along the marsh to the east, the River Styx will be the first river she'll come to." He pointed to the place where the River Styx met Charon's Marsh on the map. "The mouth of the river meets the marsh in spectacular fashion, creating a large waterfall. So, she'll need to follow the banks of the river until she can no longer hear the waterfall."

"Large waterfall..." Willow mumbled, as she set to changing more of the map to pink.

"So how does it work? Does she run and cannonball into the river or simply stick a toe in?" Carmen asked; scribbling again in the notebook.

"She'll have to completely submerge herself in the waters of the river. But the current is extremely strong, hence the swimming lessons." He raised an eyebrow at me. Carmen had been tasked with giving me swimming lessons, and I was dead set on putting them off for as long possible. Finn turned his attention to me. "You'll need to avoid any rocks or boulders as you flow down river. Then you'll go over the waterfall; landing in the marsh and ensuring your immortality."

"Did you just say I'd have to go over the waterfall?" I asked; dumbstruck and praying I heard him wrong.

"That's exactly what I said." He looked up at me, his face solemn. I could tell he didn't like this any more than I did, but his resolve had grown into an understanding and acceptance of what must happen. Alternately, my resolve was still crawling around in diapers.

"Right. Go over massive waterfall. Got it." I swallowed and tried not to start shaking again.

"You'll make your way out of the marsh and walk west along the River of Forgetfulness. But no matter how thirsty you are, do not drink from it." He looked at me with intensity. "When you see the groves of Persephone appear to your left, you'll know you're almost to the Gates of Horn and Ivory."

"The Gates of Horn and Ivory are real?" Willow's big blue eyes grew impossibly larger. Finn shook his head in confirmation.

"I can assure you, they're all too real. And Stasia will need to pass through them in order to get back to this realm...and her body." My stomach lurched and I held down the queasiness that ensued. I had no idea what the Gates of Horn and Ivory were, but I could only hope they weren't lined with flesh-eating spiders the size of buses busily spinning webs; perfect for capturing detached souls.

"Let me guess, there's a big fire breathing monster she'll have to slay with her sword in order to get the golden key and save the princess?" Carmen's eyes darted toward Phoebe, who crossed her arms and glared back at her. Finn just rolled his eyes.

"The only big monster Stasia will have to face is herself."

Eighteen

"Did you just call me a big monster?" I joked with him, trying to hide the paralyzing fear that had taken hold of every fiber in my body. The three almonds that broke free from the shaking of my hand as I reached into the bowl betrayed me.

"The most incredibly, beautiful monster in the world...," Finn retorted with a smirk.

"There's that charming side I just can't resist," I teased, and swatted at him playfully. He caught my still-shaking hand and pulled me close, instantly making me feel better. He turned to address my roommates.

"The Gates are actually 'The Gate'. Depending on the soul's integrity, it will either be made of ivory or horns. The catch is that the soul won't be able to tell which it is when they walk through it."

"So what's the difference? Why does it matter?" Phoebe asked curiously.

"If the gate is made of horns, they'll pass through without a problem. But if it's made of ivory, they'll be refused exit and trapped in the Underworld to serve under Persephone. Forever," he declared with finality.

As I attempted to swallow the latest piece of bad news, a knock sounded at the door. We all jumped out of our skin and Phoebe let out a surprised yelp. Finn just grinned wickedly and his blue eyes sparkled as they shot towards Willow.

"Oh yeah, I forgot to tell you. I invited Liam over." He shrugged innocently.

"What?" Willow's face flushed the same bright pink color of her highlighter, and then she immediately jumped up and frantically began to tidy the room.

"You did?" I couldn't help wondering what Liam would add to the conversation.

"You don't knock. You invite people over. You do realize you don't live here, right?" Carmen put her hands on her hips and glared at Finn, but he was too busy eyeing Willow with obvious amusement to care.

"You might want to answer the door." He unsuccessfully covered up a chuckle when Liam knocked again. Willow shot Finn a warning look and smoothed down her unruly blonde hair. As she opened the door, Liam sauntered into the suite looking quite proper in khaki shorts and a green polo shirt that offset his blond hair nicely. He also appeared to be extremely nervous. He grinned shyly at Willow, who just stared back at him speechless. An intervention might be in order for those two. At this pace, they might go on a date by next spring.

"Hey Liam! Come on in and make yourself at home," I greeted him from my spot on the couch; elbowing Finn as he snickered at the nervous silence hanging between the two of them.

"What's up everybody?" He came into the living room and gave Finn a slight head nod; the universal guy greeting. Willow sat down on the loveseat; making room for him. He smiled at her politely and sat down. I caught Carmen roll her eyes at his careful manners.

"Alright, where were we...?" Finn glanced down at the map and ran his hand through his dark hair once more.

"The possibility of Stasia getting trapped in the Underworld and serving under Persephone forever?" Carmen speculated; innocently shrugging her shoulders. I put my head in my hands.

"Which is not going to happen." Finn's eyes darkened and he squeezed my arm in sympathy. "As I was saying, once she gets through the gate, her soul will reunite with her body and she'll wake up."

"Will she be immortal?" Phoebe asked quietly.

"Not yet...she will only have planted the seed. She won't become fully immortal until her eighteenth birthday," he explained.

"Wow," Phoebe marveled.

"So how will she actually get into the Underworld?" Willow asked, and I planted a vice grip on Finn's hand; hoping he wouldn't give her a detailed account of my approaching departure.

"That's why I invited Liam over. I'd trust him with my life, and along with my mom, they'll be helping Stasia make the switch to the realm of the Underworld." The switch. I guess that was one way to describe the ending of my life.

"I have some experience in that particular field," Liam inserted.

"Dying?" I asked, exasperated. Then I realized what I said. I felt the stares of my roommates as their mouths gaped open in horror.

"I guess you could call it that." He glanced at Finn; wearing his discomfort on his face at the same moment that Carmen stood up. I instantly made the assumption that Finn warned him not to use any words centered around death.

"Okay, whoa. Back the stinking fruit truck up." She stared at me. "Did you just say dying?"

"No," I lied outright. Carmen shot an accusing glare at Finn and then back at me.

"You have to DIE to get to the Underworld!?"

"Well-" I started.

"Oh my God," Willow said quietly.

"You what!?" Phoebe put her hand over her mouth.

"You guys-" I tried again, but just as I suspected, they were completely freaking out. When they all started talking at once, Liam stood and held up his hands to get their attention.

"I can explain everything if you guys will calm down." Three pairs of irate eyes zeroed in on Liam and I watched as he physically shrank back. "My grandfather created a serum that allows descendants who don't belong to the Underworld to enter that realm. It has been in my family for several generations and we continually perfect it. It will be what keeps the link between Stasia's soul and body strong while she's in the Underworld."

"Serum, schmerum. All I heard was blah, blah, blah...Stasia has to die."

"Technically, yes. But it has never failed. Natasha has used it many times and never had any issues," Liam pleaded.

"And just how do you plan on killing our best friend and future leader?" If Carmen's eyes could kill, Liam would be the one dying, not me.

"That's part of the serum as well. We'll hook up an IV for Stasia and slowly let the serum enter her bloodstream. Once her soul separates, we'll monitor the amount of serum within her body until she returns."

Although Finn hadn't completely explained everything that would happen when I 'died', Liam's detailed explanation actually made me feel much better about the whole situation. Especially if Natasha had used it before. She wouldn't put me in harm's way.

"Would we be able to be there? I'd feel a lot better about this if I could be close to her," Willow told Liam calmly, but I could tell she was holding back her emotion.

"I think that could be arranged." He smiled at her.

"It better be arranged," Carmen threatened.

"I definitely want to be there." Phoebe's bottom lip began to quiver.

"If Finn trusts Liam, then so do I - and I especially trust Natasha. They won't let anything happen to me," I tried to console them. Finn smiled at me encouragingly. "I need you guys to trust them too."

My roommates reluctantly nodded their heads in agreement, but it was obvious they were extremely uncomfortable with this twist in the journey. After Finn and Liam left, we stayed up for a while longer talking; however my bed was calling, so I retired to my bedroom before everyone else.

Lightness. A reverie? But where was I? Everything was pitch black. I couldn't see my hand in front of my face. Suddenly I felt myself flying though space, tumbling towards an unknown destination. The temperature dropped and I stopped abruptly, landing on my hands and knees. Even though I had no idea where I was, I could see a little better. It was still dark, but my eyes had adjusted enough to see several yards around me. The ground beneath me was hard and dusty; stirring up into my eyes and causing me to cough. The air smelled of smoke and I got the odd sensation that I had been taken to a recently burned forest, void of any life. I wiped the parched earth from my knees and stood carefully, right before something suddenly struck me from behind, sending me skidding across the sooty ground. I wiped my eyes and frantically glanced around, preparing for another attack.

"Who's there?" I scanned the blackness around me but found no one. I heard shuffling feet all around me, but I still couldn't make out any shapes. My breathing came in shallow spurts as fear crept around my heart and entered my frenzied thoughts. I tried to stand but was pushed from behind a second time, finding myself back on the ground. That was when she materialized in front of me.

"You did this," her ghastly sounding voice came out ragged and forced. Her gray cloudy eyes glared down at me. My stomach lurched at the sight of her sunken skull and hallowed face, beaten and bloodied, but there was no denying who stood in front of me. My dead foster mother, who was killed by my foster father when he hit her with a baseball bat…seconds before I shot him.

She inched closer and I slid backwards on my backside, trying to put distance between us. Just like Bianca, she was transparent; allowing me to see the blackened ground behind her. She reeked of mildew and rotten flesh. Paralyzed by fear, my legs stopped responding to my commands. I sat there stunned and helpless as she moved even closer; peering down at me with pure hatred.

"You did this," she repeated with quiet rage.

"No. He did. He killed you," I managed shakily.

"Liar!" she roared; blood spewing from her mouth."If it weren't for you, we would have been happy. If it weren't for you I'd still be alive!" Her form blurred as the anger rippled through her body. Finally my legs began working and I scrambled to my feet; backing away from her.

"You did this!" she repeated again, and something about her forced voice caught my attention. Her gray eyes changed to an even darker gray and laughter erupted from her bloody mouth. Then she disappeared. I collapsed into a heap on the ground, trying to catch my breath and remove her disturbing image from my mind. As the instinctual terror receded, it changed into a more powerful instinct: survival. I began to run. With no way of seeing what was in front of me, I held my arms out in order to avoid running into something. Or someone.

"Anastasia." I whirled around at her voice, and the breath caught in my throat as recognition hit. Her bright red hair was blowing in a nonexistent wind and her eyes shone with madness.

"Nicolet? What's happening? Why are we here?" I asked, hoping for an ally in this desiccated hell.

"You did this." She glared at me, completely ignoring my questions.

"No-" I began, but she was quick to step forward and interrupt me.

"This is your fault! If it weren't for you I'd still be alive!" Crushing guilt slammed into me as I lost my balance and fell to the ground again.

"Nicolet, I'm so sorry!" I pleaded.

"Liar!" she shouted, suddenly standing over me. Her green eyes turned dark and she berated me with accusations."This is all your fault! You killed me! You did this...!"

On and on she continued screaming at me. I curled into a ball on the blistered ground and clamped my hands over my ears. I squeezed my eyes tightly shut, hoping she would go away. I tried to remember what Finn taught me about controlling my reveries, but I couldn't think straight. I felt helpless to protect myself.

Blaring silence filled my ears. Was she gone? Or was she just waiting for the opportune moment to murder me? A crawling panic spread across my chest as I tentatively opened my eyes and looked around. There was only darkness. I jumped when something tapped my shoulder and spun me around.

"Boo!" Nadia was inches from my face, her dark eyes smiling. "I thought you'd like to see some of your old victims – I mean friends..." Then I was falling. Endlessly falling into a bottomless pit of despair and guilt that I hoped I would never wake up from.

I sat straight up; gasping for air and drenched in sweat. I looked around frantically, but only saw my own darkened bedroom. I pulled my shaking knees against my chest and closed my tear-filled eyes. I accepted what I already knew. Nadia had found a way to not only enter my reveries, but to control them as well.

Nineteen

"My bronzer is leaking off my face," Phoebe screeched in her best Jersey Shore accent, and then collapsed into a fit of uncontrollable giggles.

"I'm going to have to veto that costume. I'm not going to a Halloween party with...that." Carmen turned her nose up at the Snooki costume Phoebe was parading around in. A tacky wig full of dark, coarse hair that sat at least two feet off of her head completed the outfit.

"If people start dressing up as me for Halloween, please do me a favor and shoot me." Willow shook her head and perused the rack of pirate costumes.

A week after Nadia invaded my reverie, we went to the mainland to one of the hundreds of Halloween stores that seemingly popped up out of nowhere during the month of October. I hadn't told anyone what I suspected about Nadia's ability to now terrorize not only my waking hours, but my reveries as well. I hoped I was just imagining things. I didn't particularly want to consider that it had actually happened. The idea that someone else had control of my soul was too terrifying to consider. Maybe if I stashed it away with my other repressed memories, it would magically vanish.

"What do you guys think about this?" I held up a white chiffon Greek Goddess costume.

"You can't go as yourself, silly," Phoebe informed me casually and put the Snooki wig back onto the mannequin's bald head.

"But I'm not a….oh." I smiled sheepishly and hung it back on the rack. Carmen pressed a red bathing suit against Willow, tossed a red rescue tube over her head and nodded in approval.

"You're welcome," she told Willow with a smirk, who looked down at herself and grimaced.

"There is no way I'm going out in public dressed up like a Baywatch lifeguard."

"You could so pull that off, but you'd have to run around The Hole in slow-mo." Phoebe laughed and showed us her best impression of the slow motion Baywatch run.

"Stasia! You should go as the Corpse Bride! Look at this one!" Carmen came running around the rack, waving a white dress. She placed the veil over my head and held the dress up to me. It was actually kind of pretty.

"Not bad. I'll go try it on," I made my way to the dressing room with Phoebe on my heels with some sort of red and white striped ensemble she wanted to try on. I smiled to myself as I slipped the form-fitting white dress over my head and zipped it up. The bottom of the dress was cut in a ragged fashion to appear torn, and several slashes ran along its length as if I'd just been stabbed. It was slit up the side all the way to the top of my thigh; showing a lot of leg. The strapless bodice was trimmed in black, and the accompanying veil flowed down to my shoulder blades. I pulled on some lacy thigh highs and turned around in front of the mirror. Some white makeup, a little fake blood and a ratty hairdo would do nicely. My new aqua highlights actually helped the otherworldly look.

I shimmied the dress off; deciding to leave the big reveal for Halloween. I left the dressing room in search of my roommates and found them gathered around Phoebe with questioning looks. When Phoebe turned to face me, I understood why she was being met with such skeptical looks. She wore a skin-tight red and white striped dress with red and white stockings that came up past her knees. A red hat with a white ball sat precariously on her head.

"What am I?" she quizzed me; standing very stiffly.

"A candy cane?" I surmised, and Carmen laughed so hard she snorted. Phoebe's face fell slightly while she waited for Carmen to collect herself.

"No! I'm 'Where's Walda'!" She twirled around, still thrilled with her find.

"That's it. I'm picking out your costumes from now on," Carmen informed her sternly; giving her a light push towards the fitting rooms. Phoebe slinked away to change back into her clothes.

"What'd you think?" Willow asked me, gesturing to the dress in my hand.

"It's coming home with us for sure." I smiled.

"Good, now you can help me figure out what I'm going to wear. I'm at a loss."

"Maybe you and Liam should come up with a couple's costume." I wiggled my eyebrows at her.

"We'd have to be a couple first." She shook her head in confusion, and then let out an exasperated sigh. "I can tell he likes me, but he just won't do anything about it! He hasn't asked me out or even tried to kiss me, and I'm definitely not making the first move," she declared stubbornly.

"You just make him nervous. Give the poor kid a break! Want me to get Finn to talk to him?" I winked at her.

"No!" she said a little too frantically. "I mean, I want him to ask me out when he's ready. I just wish he'd hurry up." She grinned.

"Jackpot!" Carmen came around the corner holding a sexy nun outfit. "I was born to be a sexy nun," she announced dramatically with a devilish grin.

"Oh my God, Carmen! It's so P.E.M.!" Phoebe ran up behind her from the fitting rooms. I looked at Willow, but she just shrugged her shoulders; as clueless as I was.

"P.E.M.?" I prodded.

"Pure Effin Magic," Phoebe clarified with a telling smirk.

"Oh my God, this is it!" Willow jumped up and down as she pulled something from the rack. "This is exactly what I've been looking for!" I couldn't help but smile at the costume that could have been made just for her. It was a flowing, ethereal lavender dress straight out of a fairy tale.

"Cinderella?" Phoebe rubbed her chin.

"Cinderella wore a blue dress, Phoebs," Carmen corrected her, but didn't offer a guess of her own. Fortunately this dress belonged to the only Disney princess I ever liked. Probably because I had a lot in common with her.

"Rapunzel," I confirmed simply with an adoring smile. As Phoebe and Carmen caught on, their faces lit up.

"Hair extensions! You need hair extensions! I'll put them in for you!" Carmen was already sizing up the length of Willow's hair, while Phoebe took a close look at Willow's eyes; pinching her cheeks.

"And you need glitter on your eyelids. It'll make your eyes sparkle..." she explained. Willow sent me a subtle look that screamed 'get them off me before I murder somebody'.

"Oh my God - is that Kim Kardashian?" I squealed and pointed out the window.

"Where!?" Phoebe and Carmen spun around, just in time for me to grab Willow and pull her away.

We headed back to Lorelei with three winning costumes and four others for the undecided Phoebe. She justified her unnecessary purchases by telling us she'd return the ones she didn't wear. But I had a feeling they had all just found a permanent home in her closet. Back on the ferry, we followed the sun as it set below the horizon and cast warm colors across the sky.

"Did you guys hear that girl Nadia went back to California?" Carmen asked us.

"She did?" My breath caught in my throat at her name. She hadn't been in class for a week, but I definitely wasn't losing any sleep over it.

"I guess she didn't like it here." Phoebe shrugged her shoulders, but I knew there had to be much more to her disappearance than that. As much as I didn't like seeing her evil smokiness and being in her chilling presence, not knowing where she was or what she was doing was even worse. They always say to keep your enemies close, right?

"I'm glad she's gone. She just gave off bad vibes," Willow scowled; visibly shivering. Maybe she felt a hint of Nadia's evil nature without realizing it.

"Same here. Something about her just didn't add up," I agreed as my phone vibrated in my pocket. Finn.

Ur goin to be the most beautiful dead bride ever

How in the world did he know what costume I bought? I looked around the ferry to see if he was spying on me. Then I remembered.

Either ur stalking me or u had a vision bout me

Yes

Yes ur stalking me or yes u had a vision bout me?

Stalked u in a vision

Ur impossible

Thank you

That wasn't a compliment

Then why r u smiling?

Good night, Finn

So I was right

Good night, Finn

Night Pasha - luv u

Luv u 2

Later, as I crawled under the cool covers of my bed and closed my eyes, I made an effort to stop the rush of thoughts that were splashing around in my head. November second was now only a week away, and I still didn't feel ready. I doubted I ever would. How did you prepare yourself to die and travel to another realm?

"I like your room."

I sat up so fast I got whiplash. As soon as the world stopped spinning, I noticed her standing in the corner of my room in that same blue dress. Her blonde hair flowed down her shoulders and a shy smile danced on her colorless lips.

"Bianca?" I squinted at her, trying to make sure it was actually Bianca and not Nadia dressed up in ghost clothing. She walked out of the shadows and towards my bed; stalling once she got to the soft rug.

"You remember me!" The surprise in her wispy voice was unmistakable.

"Who could forget their first ghost sighting?" I joked; attempting to make light of the situation. Unfortunately it had the opposite effect on Bianca.

"I haven't always been a ghost." She drifted closer and actually sat down on my bed. The bedspread didn't give under her weight. But then again, she must weigh next to nothing. I wasn't sure if the jitters in my throat were from the whiplash or from the actual ghost sitting next to me, so I just chalked it up to a combination of the two. "I had a good life...or so I thought." She smoothed her bloody dress and hung her head as sadness pulled down her beautiful features.

"I thought my mother loved me," she looked up at me with desperation, "but I guess in the end, she...didn't."

"What...happened to you?" I wasn't sure if I wanted to know the answer to that, but I couldn't help but ask. It just seemed so tragic. Her life had been cut short before it could even truly begin. And now she was left to wander the earth until the end of time? That couldn't be the way her story ended.

"I'm...I'm not real sure. I mean, I remember mother getting real mad at me and me crying, pleading with her that I hadn't done it." She looked down at her transparent hands wistfully. "But she didn't believe me. She wouldn't listen. And then everything went black and all of the sudden I was floating above my body. I was only fifteen."

Fear splintered in her eyes. "That's when I met her."

"Who?"

"The Reaper," she whispered, and a shower of shivers cascaded over my skin.

"Nadia?"

"Yes. She took me to Persephone, and then she brought me back here after I was...rejected. Now I really am cursed. I'll always have to answer to her."

"But why? Why did Persephone reject you from entering the Underworld? I mean, you don't seem, well, broken." I wasn't sure how to say it, so I stole Finn's description of the rejected souls.

"If The Reaper finds a soul she wants to have, she will stop at nothing to obtain it - even if that means influencing the living. Persephone grants her daughter any wish she may have."

"You mean..." I was having trouble speaking, as Bianca was unknowingly confirming my fears about Nadia's true intentions.

"I believe The Reaper coerced my mother into killing me." Her bright green eyes flitted up to mine, hesitant. "She wanted my soul."

I was completely speechless for several minutes as I accepted what I didn't necessarily want to believe. Nadia had taken Bianca's soul. Another piece of the puzzle clicked into place. At the séance, she ripped my soul from my body...so she obviously had the ability to play with people's souls like her own personal play toys. She knew exactly what she was doing. And she appeared to be incapable of feeling any remorse.

"Does that happen...often?" I asked gingerly. What I really wanted to know was if some version of Nadia had coerced the infamous Drake doctor, and probably many more unfortunate people across the centuries.

"I don't know." She shrugged. "I don't know why she'd want my soul. I'm nothing special." The wheels in my head started turning.

"What happened to your mother? Where is she?" I asked quietly.

"I'm not sure. She never came back to the island we lived on...the island you and your friends visited."

"So you did live there," I surmised.

"Yes, but that was nearly twenty years ago. After my death, my mother insisted the island was cursed. She told everyone a story about me becoming possessed by evil and attacking her. She told them it was self defense. She said she was scared of what I might do to my sister. I would never hurt anyone! Especially not my sister!" She shook her head. "Mother knew that. She would never accuse me of something that cruel. That's why I believe it was The Reaper all along." A stray tear ran down her cheek as sadness took hold of her again. "My sister would talk to me at night. I think it made her feel better. I tried to talk to her, but she didn't hear me. And then they left."

"You had a sister?"

"A twin sister. I called her Cissy. I don't know what's become of her."

"I'm so sorry, Bianca. And even though you may not believe me, I understand what you're going through a lot better than most. I know how it feels to be alone."

"But I don't feel so alone now. I...I followed you here. I didn't want to be by myself anymore."

"As far as I'm concerned, you are always welcome here."

"Thank you." She grinned and then became solemn. "But it's not safe for me to be around you. Nadia will find me, and then she will find you."

"Nadia already knows where I am. And besides, I'm not scared of her," I lied.

"But that's the thing - you should be. You have no idea what she's capable of. As you witnessed with me, she can possess ghosts. She can control us; use us."

"She can't control me. She can't use me. And I'll do everything I can to protect you from her."

"But you can't fight her! She's immortal! She's strong! That's why you have to hurry and make the journey before she finds a way to ruin it for you!"

"You know about me?" I asked with surprise.

"Yes. You're the next leader of the Tydes. I've heard Nadia talk about you." She glanced down at her hands and back at me through her lashes, as if she was afraid she'd anger me. "She's not very fond of you, and she doesn't want you to fulfill your destiny."

"I've definitely gathered that, but I just can't figure out why." I rubbed a hand over my face in frustration.

"I was a Siren," she whispered.

"What?" I looked up at her with astonishment.

"I was a Siren," she repeated tentatively. "I never knew anyone in the other Orders. Your friends – are they Tydes too?"

"Yes," I confirmed, and she smiled shyly again.

"Can I be your friend?"

"Of course you can, Bianca. You'll always be my friend."

Twenty

My alarm clock was in the process of burning a blue two-thirteen a.m. into my retinas as I wondered for the hundredth time how I was going to coax myself into falling asleep. After Bianca left, I crawled under my covers and tried to pretend that all was right with the world and I had nothing to worry about. Unfortunately I wasn't good at lying to others, and was especially not good at lying to myself. To ward off the blue glare of the clock, I reached over and turned on the small lamp sitting on my nightstand. Not sleeping for the next week was not an option, so I needed to think this through. Although my journey was in one week, I liked to think that the first part of the journey was all falling into place. I felt pretty good about it, all in all. It was the part where I had to aimlessly wander around the Underworld by myself that was chewing at my conscious, and several things were reinforcing that fear. The fact that neither Priscilla (nor any other Siren for that matter) had made a threatening appearance or tried to slash my throat in the middle of the night was at the forefront of my mind. Something about their absence was extremely unsettling. I knew Priscilla hadn't forgotten about me or my journey, and regardless of Keto's warning, Priscilla wasn't the type to just sit back and watch. I was afraid she still had her hand in this somehow.

The other issue weighing on my mind was Nadia. She showed up out of the blue, crashed the séance, haunted my nightmares and stole the souls of innocents on the side. What did she have against me? What difference did it make to her if I fulfilled my destiny or not? Finn's speculative comments sounded in my mind. She was possibly the next leader of the Nymphs. Was she power hungry? Did she not want an equal to compete with? I was definitely still missing something. I just wished I wasn't stuck in my bedroom, allowing my thoughts to make laps inside my head. And then it dawned on me.

Reveries. I wasn't stuck! I knew how to control them! Instead of being the sitting duck, waiting helplessly for Nadia to turn up again, I could go find her. I could seek her out. Adrenaline began to shoot through my already alert system as I considered what I was about to attempt. Could I do it? What if something happened? Finn wouldn't be there to save me or wake me up. But then again, I couldn't always depend on him to fix my messes. I needed to practice on my own, too. And what better way to practice than to go searching for my arch nemesis? I mean, what could go wrong? Well…besides everything?

Before I had the chance to talk myself out of it, I turned over on my back and closed my eyes. Without Finn to run his fingers through my hair, I decided to listen to my breathing instead. I took deep and slow breaths, listening to the sound of the air rushing in and out of my lungs; all the while willing my soul to separate from my body. It took longer than it did on the island, but eventually the numbness shadowed my mind. I turned my focus inward and immediately felt the dizziness. I fought the urge to steady myself and open my eyes. Instead, I concentrated on the spinning and the freedom I felt. I began sinking, sinking, sinking…and then I stopped.

I peeked out, careful not to move. Inches away from my ceiling, I immediately yelped with surprise and giggled at myself. I did it! I glanced down at the unsettling picture of my own body lying motionless in my bed and felt a rush of excitement at what I had done. Suddenly I was on the other side of the room. And then right back to the other side.

I was a ping pong ball, bouncing around my room without a single ounce of control. I had to get this figured out before I broke something. Ignoring each wall I bounced off of, I suppressed the excitement and tried to focus on the task at hand. Nadia.

I pictured her face. Her clothes. The smoky tendrils lifting and swirling off her skin. And I began to move. Through the wall (yes through the wall - talk about strange) and out of Maren Hall completely. The night air caught me and I felt myself riding on the breeze. I continued to picture Nadia, as well as attempting to zero in on her evil energy. Somehow it seemed that the wind itself was carrying me where I needed to go. An image of a leaf floating down from a tree popped into my mind, and I relaxed and let it take me.

When I opened my eyes, I immediately fell to the floor in a heap. Apparently the landings were going to need a bit more work. Movement on the other side of the room caught me by surprise and I leapt up; flattening myself against the wall. Realizing that a lamp was shining directly on me, I groaned inwardly and moved several feet to the right and out of the bulb's illumination. I had a bad feeling that The Reaper of souls would be able to see my soul as clear as day. A woman with long blonde hair shut the window on the opposite wall, and wrapped her arms around her body as if warding off the cold. She sauntered over to a large stone fireplace in a ruffled blouse snugly tucked into a black pencil skirt, and leaned down stiffly to turn up the gas a notch; sending the bright flames dancing higher.

As the dim light caught her face I gasped. It wasn't Nadia. I had somehow brought myself to none other than Priscilla's house! Too bad GPS didn't work in reveries. My sense of direction was greatly amiss. I was about to begin concentrating on Nadia again when a knock came at the door. Priscilla briskly made her way to the other side of the room and swung open the door. I slapped my hand over my mouth to squelch any sound that might try to seep out.

"Nadia! So nice to see you again!" Priscilla cooed, instantly reminding me of Lexi. Nadia slid into the light of the fire dressed in a deep purple silk blouse and black skinny jeans, topped off with zebra print peep toe shoes. Her golden hair was braided down her back, and the disparaging look on her face did nothing to help slow my pulse.

"Priscilla," she greeted her; annoyance heavy in her tone.

"Sit down, sit down…" Priscilla suggested cordially, but Nadia ignored the offer.

"I'm only going to ask this once. Does she know?" Nadia stated; boiling madness stalking just below the surface of her calm façade. I immediately assumed they were talking about me and held my breath.

"I'm working on it, but I haven't been able to-"

"Answer the question," Nadia gritted through her teeth, but then laughed. "For a second there I forgot who I was talking to. Let me try again." Her features darkened and twisted into something terrifying. I pressed against the wall at my back as she pointed at Priscilla. "Give me a straight answer or I will end your pathetic, useless life."

"She doesn't know," Priscilla whimpered.

"Perfect." Nadia's features returned to mysteriously beautiful as she stealthily glided across the room and stood before Priscilla, who cowered in her presence. Something about the scene playing out before me was off. Priscilla was much older than Nadia, but in the scheme of things Priscilla was nothing more than a pesky eyelash to the Princess of the Underworld. Power always trumped age. As she continued, the telltale evil smoke began to waft up from her skin and slowly tether around the room, unbeknownst to Priscilla.

"It doesn't surprise me, really. He's always been such a gentleman." She rolled her eyes."I, on the other hand, look forward to crushing her simple, wretched dreams. It will weaken her further."

Was she talking about Finn and me? Anger heated in my veins and my fingernails pressed into skin as I balled my fists up at my sides.

"We must make sure she doesn't find out about the Sacrifice," Priscilla inserted carefully.

"And what of Natasha?" Nadia implored as she absentmindedly picked up a mermaid figurine and inspected it. Natasha? She had to be talking about us. But why? And what 'sacrifice'?

"She's been too busy with the details of his upcoming fast and fight."

"Let's make sure it stays that way." She raised a perfectly waxed eyebrow at Priscilla, inferring that she was delegating that responsibility to her. Suddenly she furrowed her brow and glanced around the room curiously. I froze in fear and tried to remember how to leave. A connection. What could I connect to?

"Priscilla. I do believe we may have a visitor..." Nadia's eyes scanned the room meticulously, looking for the presence she sensed. My presence. Sheets. My body was in bed. I closed my eyes and thought about the cool, soft feel of them on my skin. The room started to spin wildly and I landed hard.

My eyes flickered open in panic, but miraculously I found myself back in my body sitting up in bed breathing hard and shaking. That was way too close. And extremely disturbing. What was Finn not telling me? Nadia said it would crush me!? Wouldn't it dawn on Finn that maybe he should warn me? Or Natasha? If it was that dire, why hadn't she told me? What did Nadia know that I didn't? If it had something to do with my journey, which was, in fact, seven days away, I deserved to know! And what sacrifice did they not want me to know about? A sacrifice I would have to make? Feelings of betrayal and mistrust crept up into my heart, but I couldn't let myself overreact. Natasha cared about me. She wouldn't betray me. Would she? Would Finn?

Four a.m. came and went. Five a.m. Six a.m. The more time that went by, the more desperate and anxious I became. Unable to lie still any longer, I decided to get up. I opened my closet and pulled down the valise my mother left me. 'Valise' was just a fancy word for chest, but this chest was anything but ordinary. I ran a finger over the intricate designs and unhooked the latch. I pulled out the onyx stone and anklet Finn gave me on the yacht. I secured the anklet around my leg, noticing how the stone warmed in my hand, even causing my trace to shimmer and brighten. They both immediately soothed my soul. In search of more comfort, I latched my mother's aquamarine necklace and my own triskellion necklace around my neck, and then slid her ring on my finger. All three warmed at my touch and sent waves of courage through me; pushing away my fear.

I slumped onto my bed, allowing my legs to hang off the edge, and closed my eyes. I clutched the stone against my chest and concentrated on centering myself. I was strong. I was smart. I would make it through this just like I had everything else in my life. I just needed to take action based on fact, not assumptions. Assumptions were the seeds of poison that destroyed lives. My foster dad, Charles Whitman, always said that assuming makes an ass out of u and me. At the time I laughed and brushed it off, but now I saw it was all too true. I had to stay true to what I knew, and I needed to listen to the other sense that was strong within me. It wouldn't steer me wrong. I needed to talk to Finn. Tonight. I'd ask him to come over tonight. If I could make it through my Monday classes. And that was one massive if.

I thought about my mom and whether or not she'd been through something like this. Who did she trust? Who did she not trust? Did she go through a lot of pain in her life, or was it smooth sailing? For some reason I wanted to know. I felt closer to her now, but the consequence of that was knowing just how much I truly needed her. All I had were things. Just things.

"No."

"You must allow a great amount of deliberation for this decision. It is not to be taken lightly."

"You think the gravity of my situation has been lost to me?" a voice threw at her; exasperated, but also shaken. It was coming out of my mouth, but it wasn't mine. The turmoil inside me was threatening to rip me apart, piece by broken piece. The pressure it caused on my heart was unbearable. Beneath that flood of turmoil flowed a hazy river of confusion that struggled to understand what was happening. Who was this woman beside me? My body felt different; heavier. When I glanced down at my hands, I realized why. I was...pregnant? How did that happen? I mean, I knew how that happened, but I also knew I hadn't yet partaken in the all important, well, prerequisites to pregnancy. Theoretically that left only a couple other options. Either I was dreaming, I was experiencing someone else's memories, or I had woken up in some alternate universe. All of which were entirely possible. I was banking on it being the second, however. Not in control of my motions or words, I knew I was only watching what was happening. I had no involvement whatsoever. I was merely a spectator.

She covered my shaking hand with hers and sighed. "Thetis." She looked into my eyes with patience, confirming my assumptions. "I do not presume to know how hard this must be for you. I would never claim to be strong enough to make a decision of this magnitude. I trust you will choose wisely. I just want to ensure that you have considered each and every consequence." I recognized her voice from the last memory I shared with my mother, however this was the first time I had actually seen her. She was amazing. Flowing blonde hair, highlighted by pale streaks of white, reached her lower back and cascaded over her shoulders. Her bright blue eyes contained a strong presence of wisdom; the depths of which held courage and strength that seemingly surpassed her youthful features. She appeared to be in her late twenties; carrying a grace and dignity that refused to be overlooked. She greatly resembled the portrait I saw of Thetis on the Fortunate Isle.

"The only consequence I must consider is that of her safety," Thetis declared with conviction.

"And what of the Tydes? Who will become their leader?" she asked gently.

"I have seen it, Amphitrite. She will return…in time." Thetis sighed and I felt my head shake."But if I do not provide her with the refuge she needs now, she will not live long enough to grow in years and take her rightful place as leader." I wracked my brain for the name Amphitrite. I'd heard it before, but couldn't quite place it.

"Visions can change, dependent on the course a person may choose to take. There is a chance she will not make it back to us," Amphitrite reminded her.

"That is a chance I must take. For her. For all of us."

"But you are our leader-" she pleaded.

"She is my daughter!" Thetis roared. "The people we love must always come before position and obligation. Without them, the foundation we stand upon would falter and collapse! Everything we fight for; everything we believe in would perish along with it!" My body stood as Thetis did and began to pace; unable to contain the war of emotions playing out within her heart. "As a leader, I can control neither the fate of the Tyde Order nor the Nereids from which they are descended. But as a mother, I can ensure a future for my child. And that, Amphitrite, comes before all else."

"As your sister, I will wholly support your decision. But I must warn you, others will not feel the same."

"They do not yet know of my unborn child, and therefore they will not be privy to word of the childbirth. You must promise to keep this in strictest confidence. It is vital."

"I will not let you down sister, I promise." She smiled.

"Thank you." My hand squeezed hers. "Never question the strength of our bond. It will endure, as will the bond between a mother and her daughter. Even in death." I patted my stomach as a crushing sadness settled on my already breaking heart.

Dawn. The sun was creeping its way across the floor of my bedroom when I finally came to, and I laid there motionless for a good twenty minutes before attempting any activity. Between the reverie, the shared memory and a serious lack of sleep, I was suffering from informational and emotional overload. I was afraid that any sudden movements would result in a catastrophic breakdown; one that I may or may not recover from in the next century. I contemplated whether or not 'irrevocable neurosis' would be an approved excuse to miss classes.

"Stasia?"

Crap. "Yeah?" I answered casually, as if I had no idea why Willow was at my door ten minutes before first period was supposed to start.

"You coming to class?" She poked her head in the door and raised an eyebrow at my position on the bed. I mean, who didn't sleep sideways with no pillow and their legs hanging off the side? It was actually pretty comfortable once I started to think about it. Maybe a soft blanket would be-

"Stasia," she prompted again. I slowly sat up, feeling numb and detached. I nodded my head for no particular reason.

"Be there in a sec," I promised, without making any movement toward my closet.

"Um..okay." She hesitated and disappeared back into the living room. I peered down at my wrinkled t-shirt and cotton shorts. These would not do. I spotted a less wrinkled pair of jean shorts and a mostly folded yellow tee sitting on top of my dresser. Without fixing my hair or so much as peeking in the mirror, I threw on some flip flops and headed for the door.

"Books?" Willow stared at me bleakly. I turned around with the liveliness of a zombie and stalked back to my room in order to collect my books. The rest of the day went much the same way. My feet took my body where it was supposed to go, as my mind dragged behind; kicking and screaming the entire time. However the closer I got to last period, and to seeing Finn, my expertly suppressed emotions started to fight their way outward. My walls were not as thick around him, and although I could pretend to be strong sometimes, I didn't know if I was capable of hiding what lurked behind my walls today. This was foreign territory to me. I wasn't used to having someone who could break down my walls. Or having someone who wanted to break down my walls. In all actuality I wanted to run to him; allow him to hold me, support me and give me a shoulder to cry on. Unfortunately, suffering a mental breakdown in front of the entire class was not an option. So the massive amount of conflicting emotions that were swirling around in my mind and wreaking havoc on my thoughts would have to wait. One hour. I told myself I could do it. I had to.

As I walked into the classroom and met his warm gaze, I swear I heard my carefully constructed walls cracking from the pressure. I wanted to tell him about my disturbing reverie. I wanted to tell him about my amazing antiquity experience. I wanted to tell him that I knew Nadia could enter my reveries. I wanted to tell him I'd made friends with a dead girl. I wanted to tell him I was terrified of my upcoming journey. I wanted to tell him I was terrified of his upcoming fight. And I needed to find out what, if anything, he was hiding from me. My next step coincided with the disheartening realization that my walls weren't going to hold. As the first piece crumbled, followed by another and another, Finn's eyes darkened with concern and his entire body tensed. I stopped mid-step, turned on my heel, and ran.

Thankfully, my seaweed and coconut milk diet had indeed helped my body become stronger and more agile. I made it to the beach in no time, and I wasn't even winded. I didn't stop until my feet hit sand, and once they did, I noticed it. Almost…an acknowledgement. Very similar to what I felt in the garden on Shackleford Banks. I felt everything around perk up at my appearance. The sand beneath my feet danced slightly with each step I took, as if celebrating my arrival. The sea grass growing out of the sand dunes bent ever so slightly in my direction, and the waves reached farther up the beach in my immediate vicinity. I felt…welcomed. Intrigued, I slowly sat down and watched the sand dance beneath my touch. The emotions still coursing through me seemed to drain out, as if the sand was feeding off of it. I closed my eyes and ran my fingertips over the top of the sand, trying not to smile as it tickled my legs; dancing and shifting slightly. I could feel a different kind of energy flowing up my arms and throughout my body. It filled me with the reassurance and acceptance I desperately needed.

I lazily opened my eyes and gazed longingly at the rolling waves. I stood as my feet automatically began to move in their direction. Although I knew it was only salty ocean water, it felt like slipping into a relaxing Jacuzzi filled with silky body wash and soothing bubbles. As each wave crashed into me, I drug my fingers over the top of the water and heard it.

The ocean's song; greeting me, calling me. The beautiful melody filled my ears and soothed my heart. Once again, I felt the raw pile of emotions loosening and slipping away from me; replaced by a calm so peaceful, it didn't seem real. I gently slipped beneath the water and began to swim. The song faded, but the feeling remained, and the more I swam the lighter I felt. The more water my lungs inhaled, the more detached I felt from the world above. It was so freeing, I didn't want to stop. I could have swum to Bermuda if I'd been so inclined, but the search party would have a hard time finding me. Instead I swam along the shore; eventually circling the entire island. Fish of all sizes, shapes and colors would swim alongside me for several meters, before darting away and disappearing into the blue.

The fact that I was not fatigued whatsoever was astonishing to me. I'd just swam around an island. I also began to notice that underneath the water I had an incredible sense of direction, without even thinking about it. I could feel north, and therefore, every other direction fell into place. I could feel the presence of the shore to my left as well as the vast expanse of the deep ocean to my right. My trace was shimmering a beautiful light blue, and for the first time that day I felt like everything was going to be okay. I felt the pulsing warmth of the multiple pieces of aquamarine and onyx jewelry I was wearing; observing with reverence as they seemed to come alive beneath the water.

I had no idea how long I had hidden in the ocean, but for the first time I felt strong enough to go back and face all that awaited me. I silently thanked the ocean for opening its arms to me, and then headed back. When I reached the breakers, I paused. This feeling was definitely new. I could sense a very strong presence. Darkness. His darkness.

He was sitting on the beach; distracted by something he was currently drawing in the sand. His gray shorts and simple white shirt contrasted with his dark features, which had my pulse quickening and spiking erratically. Although his eyes were downcast, I found myself anticipating the effect that their depth and intensity had on me. As I walked out from the waves and up the beach, his hand paused for a split second before erasing his artwork. The darkness I sensed before suddenly reached out and wrapped me in a cocoon of soft caresses. Finn met my surprised gaze with a devilish grin as he leaned back on his arms; taking a long moment to look me over. Standing before him dripping wet, I suddenly became highly aware of the soaked fabric clinging to my skin, as well as the inordinate amount of jewelry I was wearing, but there was a slight chance my just-swam-in-the-ocean hair was an upgrade from my earlier just-rolled-out-of-bed hair. So I had that going for me.

"Better?" he asked knowingly.

That one word held such a variety of meanings, I wasn't sure how to answer. Did I feel better after swimming in the ocean? Yes. Did I feel better after finding him patiently waiting for me on the beach? Definitely. Did I feel better about almost having a nervous breakdown in class? Not in the slightest. Two out of three wasn't too bad.

"Much," I responded simply; putting my hands on my hips and lifting a suspicious eyebrow. "How'd you know I was out there?"

"Lucky guess." He shrugged his shoulders, but the twinkle in his eye told me different.

"You were stalking me, weren't you?" I teased him.

"Only on Tuesdays." His grin widened. "Actually, I just followed the path of destruction you left in your wake. Brought me right to you." I could tell he was suppressing laughter.

"You better be joking."

"I wish I was. See for yourself." I held my breath and glanced up the beach where I ran through earlier. It was as if someone had walked onto the beach and down the sand holding a leaf blower. The sand was blasted outwards in a two foot path all the way to the spot I had sat down on; which was just a larger extension of my path. Then it extended all the way down to the ocean. My eyes widened as I caught sight of the sand dunes, which had literally shifted away from my footsteps.

"Like a bull in a china shop." Finn commenced to laughing so hard, he had to bend over to catch his breath. I had no idea my emotions had that much of an effect on the things around me. An image of Phoebe's feet creating ripples in the sand when she was upset after the séance flashed before my eyes.

I crossed my arms and glared at him. "Go ahead. Laugh it up. But I'm not the one with sand all over me."

He looked up, confused, as I made a circle around him in the sand with my eyes. I pushed my emotions down my legs and into the sand; lifting it above him and letting it shower down on his head. Unfortunately, he immediately disappeared and the sand simply poured off of the cloak he had hidden himself under. He appeared again, completely sand free. Damn. He slowly got to his feet; his features turning sinister. His eyes became stormy while he slowly stepped closer to me; watching me with a steady, dark gaze. If I hadn't known he was joking, I would have been terrified. He was absolutely the most intimidating, menacing thing I'd ever seen. And the sexiest.

"Are you sure you really want to mess with the Son of Darkness?" he said in a low, threatening voice, moving closer to me. My body warmed, my legs turned wobbly and my thoughts began to scramble beneath his stare. I squared my shoulders and steeled my own gaze.

"Are you sure you really want to mess with a future sea Goddess?" I threw back at him with as much antagonism as I could muster.

A nefarious smile cracked his armor and he cocked his head to the side. "More than anything." I fought back a smile of my own, but my lips betrayed me and my heart fluttered against my will.

"Then let's see what you got, Son of Darkness," I taunted him; already coming up with my next plan of attack. Before I had time to think about it, he was inches away from my body. I stared up at him just as he bent his head down. His lips halted so close to mine, I could feel the heat coming off of them. His eyes bored into mine with a repose that erased everything around me except for him. Caught in his gaze and presence, I had no defenses against this assault. And he knew it.

His warm hand settled on my hip and deliberately slid around to my lower back. A light smirk played at his lips as he pulled me against him in one swift movement. I strove to remain indifferent, but I wasn't kidding anybody. Every cell in my body sizzled with the onslaught of his touch. I bit my lip to try and get my focus back, but it only brought my attention to his lips so close to mine. He bent down and barely brushed his lips across my collarbone. His breath tickled my skin and sent shivers down my spine. I closed my eyes and resisted the overpowering urge to react when his almost-kiss crawled up my neck and hovered over my ear. His breath was now coming slightly faster and he held me to him tightly. Again, I willed myself not to show him the affect he was having on me. He straightened; instantly releasing my ear and neck from his torturous closeness. The absence of his warm breath left a longing even stronger than its presence.

I opened my eyes and was instantly caught in his powerful stare. I saw the yearning behind his hooded eyes and stilled all the muscles in my face to make sure he couldn't read it. His eyes flitted down to my lips and back up to my eyes. I raised my eyebrows ever so slightly.

"Not bad." I attempted sarcasm, but it came out as more of a breathless whisper. "What's your next move, dark Son?" Desperation washed over his features and his dark blue eyes reflected his desire.

"Surrender," he breathed. His lips were on mine in a split second and all restraint was erased, replaced with the raging fire that always simmered below the surface any time he was near. Wet clothes and hair forgotten, the only thing I could feel was him. The darkness I felt earlier once again surrounded me in its arms; enveloping me in a warm cocoon of pleasure. I broke our kiss in surprise and looked up at him with delight.

"Before, I could only sense your darkness. Now I can feel it too," I smiled.

"I can feel you too." He grinned, brushed his thumb over my cheek and held me against him.

"You can?" Why was I just now finding this out? A million questions zipped through my mind. "What does it feel like? Can you always feel it? If yours is darkness, then what's mine?"

He chuckled at my litany of questions. "I'm not sure what it is, although I imagine it has something to do with the sea, but it's like a wave crashing over me; refreshing and powerful all at the same time."

"Have you always been able to feel it?"

"Yes, but it's gotten stronger. I've been able to feel your presence from farther and farther away. It's the real way I found you today."

"So you were stalking me…" I teased him. His smug grin was my immediate answer; proving he wasn't embarrassed in the least.

"I was worried about you." He grasped both my hands and watched me with concern. "What happened earlier?"

My eyes dropped to my feet; trying to figure out where to start. He mistook my body language as insecurity. "Why don't we go back to my suite to talk and get you dried off? My roommates went to the mainland, so we'll be alone for a while."

"Are you sure?" I had to admit, I was extremely curious to see what his room looked like; the one place he spent most of his time in. I felt myself begin to blush but if he noticed, he didn't mention it.

"Of course," he confirmed lightly.

We made our way to Rostrum, directly beside Maren. I wasn't sure what to expect out of a guy's dorm - maybe a little plainer? Dirtier? I mean, they were guys, after all. But I was pleasantly surprised. It was identical to Maren, with the exception of the décor. Dark brown tones mixed with white and tan created a soothing ambiance in the lobby, and decorated the framed abstract art on the walls. We rode the elevator to the eighth floor, stepped out into a hallway that resembled the ones at Maren, and stopped at an unassuming dark brown door. Finn searched his pockets for the key, unlocked the door and swiftly swung it open for me.

As I suspected, the layout of the guys' suites were exactly the same as Maren's, but that was where the similarities ended. Finn and his roommates made several additions. Huge, overflowing dark brown leather couches filled the living room to capacity. A foosball table took the place of a dining room table, and a massive flat screen television almost covered the entire left wall. It didn't smell of old gym socks or week-old dirty plates as I had expected, either. It had sort of a clean linen smell; the Glade Plug-ins in the kitchen and living room telling me the reason why. I smiled at the image of a couple of guys trying to figure out how to install the refills.

"Thirsty? Hungry?" Finn asked off-handedly; peeking around the stainless steel refrigerator door.

"Something to drink would be awesome." He produced two bottles of Aquafina and I followed him to what would be Phoebe's room back in my suite. I'd never been in a guy's bedroom either, so I was very curious. Not to mention that something about being in Finn's personal space made me feel giddy.

He pushed open the door for me and quickly disappeared into the bathroom. An obvious extension of himself, his bedroom instantly captivated me. It was dark but cozy, with an air of stature. The window on the far wall was hidden by dark gray curtains; shading the room from the harsh, glaring sun outside. A dark gray bedspread covered the queen-sized bed, while two lamps on either side bathed the room in a warm light. A massive black and white painting above the bed boasted an artistic rendering of a skull and crossbones. Oddly enough, it wasn't creepy or imposing. It was actually kind of...pretty. Two long surfboards stood propped up on the opposite wall next to a flat screen television and a tall, dark wooden dresser. Displayed on the wall above the dresser were four double axes of different sizes.

"Here's a dry towel." Finn handed me a fluffy light gray towel that I immediately wrapped around my body. The normally refreshing air conditioning caused goosebumps to rise on my skin. He grabbed a white t-shirt that read 'Morrison' on the back above a big number three, and a pair of black gym shorts from his dresser. "These should work until your clothes dry."

After he left the room, I peeled off my wet clothes and dried off before pulling on his t-shirt and gym shorts. I rolled down the waistband in an attempt to make them fit better, collected my clothes, and gave them to Finn so he could toss them in the dryer. Several minutes later, we were relaxing on his bed watching reruns of CSI Miami. For some reason I could never get enough of Horatio, who could figure out that the killer was a twenty-five year old Caucasian male with green eyes and an addiction to cocaine from a simple piece of scrap metal. After another one of his cheesy one-liners, it cut to commercial and Finn sat up.

"So, what happened today?" he prompted me gently. I sighed and propped myself up on my elbows; allowing myself to be captured by his endearing concern. The whole confiding-in-others-thing was still relatively new to me. A hazy cloud fell over my heart as I began to re-hash the events of the last twenty-four hours. After divulging the details of encountering Nadia and her ghostly camouflage in my reverie, Bianca's visit, and my second antiquity experience, he shook his head with chagrin and frowned.

"I wish you would have told me all of this sooner. It's exhausting to keep it all inside like that." He reached for my hand. "That's what I'm here for."

"I guess I'm just used to keeping my abnormal problems to myself. I wouldn't want to put that burden on anyone else. Especially not you."

He laughed and rubbed his finger over my trace, sending tingles up my arm. "Neither you nor your abnormal problems could ever be a burden to me. Plus, I happen to have a master's degree in abnormal." He smirked at me.

"There's one more thing," I began, really not looking forward to rehashing my most recent reverie involving Priscilla and Nadia. "I purposefully had a reverie...and I found Nadia."

Expecting a lecture or disappointed look, I was pleasantly surprised when Finn leaned forward and excitement flashed in his eyes.

"Did it work?" he asked eagerly. I felt a smile creep over my face, anticipating his reaction when I told him it had indeed worked.

"It worked a little too well, actually," I hinted at the disturbing details to come.

"Nice! I knew it wouldn't be long before you were gallivanting all over the world in your reveries." He grinned at me with pride. I inspected my hands closely and took a deep breath.

"Finn." I glanced up and watched his smile fade at my serious tone. "What are you not telling me?"

"What do you mean?" he asked; furrowing his brow.

"Not only did I find Nadia, I found Nadia and Priscilla," I explained, and his eyes began to grow stormy as he continued to listen. "Nadia alluded to the fact that there was something I didn't know about - a sacrifice? And that you hadn't told me something. What were they talking about, Finn? What aren't you telling me?"

Twenty-Three

His jaw muscle flexed as he gritted his teeth and collected his thoughts. "Was there any way Nadia knew you were there?" he questioned me. I deliberated for a minute.

"She did say something right before I figured out how to end the reverie."

"She could have been messing with you. I have no idea what kind of sacrifice she could have been talking about." He squeezed my hands reassuringly. I desperately wanted to believe him, but I didn't think Nadia knew I was there until after her and Priscilla's conversation. But Finn wouldn't lie to me.

"She said something about Natasha too; that she hadn't said anything to me either because she's been busy preparing things for your birthday," I told him, and his jaw flexed again.

"I don't know what Nadia's up to," he sighed and I noticed the muscles in his arm tighten as his eyes darkened ever so slightly, "but it looks like she's doing everything she can to curb your focus and make you vulnerable. That's why it will be important for you to keep your head down and concentrate on what's ahead of you." He held my gaze and his tone lightened. "As the future Prime and the future Leader of the Tydes, we have a duty to make sure we are successful in both of our journeys. There are a lot of people depending on us. We have to keep reminding ourselves what's really important."

"What if she's planning something? What if she's in the Underworld during my journey?" I could feel the panic rising in my chest. I wanted nothing more than to be successful, but I felt grossly inadequate to be able to ward off Nadia on her own turf.

"Stasia." He rubbed my cheek, bringing my focus back to him. "You are so much stronger than her in every way that matters. Don't let her get in your head. Don't let her win. Stay focused on what you have to do, and remember who you are."

"I'll try," I muttered, not at all confident.

"This is your destiny, Stasia. This is what you were meant to do. That's more powerful than any spiteful, evil-hearted girl," he proclaimed with such conviction that I began to agree. He was right! This was my destiny, and I wasn't going to let her or anyone else take that away from me.

"You're right," I said, and attempted a smile. "This is what I was born for." I thought about my mom and the tough decision she had to make so many years ago. My parents risked so much just to make sure I would live. "I won't let my parents or the Order of the Tydes down."

"No, you won't." Finn grinned at me. "Like I said before, you just don't have it in you to fail. You simply don't know how."

"You've never seen me try to cook," I quipped.

Finn chuckled. "I bet you can make a mean peanut butter and jelly sandwich, though,"

"Even that's touch and go when it's me holding the knife." I scrunched my nose and Finn laughed again; pulling me close. The axes on the wall caught my eye and piqued my curiosity about his fight.

"So what happens Friday? When you're...taken and then have to fast for two days?"

"Technically I'll be taken Thursday night at midnight," he clarified.

"So do they just pull up in a dark van, throw you in the back, and then peel off down the street?" I asked, only half joking.

"Not quite." He snickered. "I just have to meet the car downstairs at midnight. Then I'll be taken to the place where I'll spend the next forty eight hours. I'm hoping it's got a bed," he wished aloud.

"Is it here or in the Underworld?"

"It's actually not that far from here," he divulged, but didn't explain further. I instantly wished I knew more about the area.

"So you don't get to eat or drink at all?" How did they expect him to fight after they starved him to death?

"I can only have water," he stated simply; resolved to the challenge that awaited him.

"Wow. And then they expect you to fight and kill your own brother." My harsh tone pulled a sneer out of Finn.

"Yes, they do. But it's part of my obligation as the Scion to find the strength within and earn my position as Prime."

"And then kill your brother," I reminded him.

"And then send my brother to the Underworld to serve under our father."

"By killing him," I argued.

"Only his body." This kid desperately needed to learn the definition of 'kill'.

"All I know is if your brother…" I paused, suddenly realizing I had no idea what his name was.

"Maddox," he provided.

"…Maddox sends you to the Underworld instead, he'll have to answer to me."

"I'll let him know." Finn held back a laugh. "Or you can tell him yourself. He'll be the one picking me up Thursday night."

"Well, good," I retorted with contempt.

"I was hoping you'd be there, anyway." He rubbed my hand and his face softened. "I was hoping you'd stay with me that night until I have to leave."

"I wouldn't be anywhere else." My heart warmed at his invitation. "Are you nervous?"

"Not in the least," he announced confidently, and then his shoulders sagged. "What bothers me is that I won't be with you on the most important day of your life."

"But you've done so much to get me ready! And knowing you're thinking about me will be all I need to get me through," I reassured him.

"It's not enough," he seemed to say to himself. "It's not enough." He glowered and his eyes became slightly unfocused. I could practically see the wheels turning in his head. I got to my knees, scooted closer, and stole his gaze in an attempt to break him out of his own thoughts and bring his breathtaking smile back.

"It is enough," I told him emphatically. "And both of us are going to rock this. It's what we do." I shrugged my shoulders, as if taking fateful journeys was an everyday occurrence for us. My random thoughts seemed to distract him from his sullen inner dialogue.

"It is what we do, isn't it?" He chuckled and my heart brightened instantly.

"It sure is," I said matter-of-factly. "In fact, we might just be a power couple like Brad Pitt and Angelina Jolie…minus the twenty kids. They'll call us Finnastasia."

"That sounds like a foot fungus."

"Anafinn?" I tried again.

"Sounds like a blood pressure medicine."

"Well, it's definitely your name throwing it off," I teased him. "'Anastasia' has a slew of possibilities, but 'Finn' is pretty one dimensional." I scrunched my nose at him in dissatisfaction.

"I'll show you one dimensional," he said as he suddenly waged a full blown tickle attack on my unsuspecting tummy, causing me to instantly cave.

"Okay, okay! I take it back!" I continued giggling long after his fingers retreated.

"We'll just have to go with 'Awesome'," I decided with a smirk.

"It does have a certain ring to it. I like it," he concurred, and then leaned back on the pillows with a sexy grin. He ran his fingers through his hair and then rested his hands behind his head with a happy sigh. Although I told them not to, my eyes drank him in as they slowly trailed over every part of his body. His t-shirt did little to hide the muscular build beneath, and the image of him standing on the beach in nothing but boxer shorts slammed into my mind; sending sharp pangs of desire through me. His legs were stretched out on the bed and his relaxed posture told me he was completely at ease in his own space. I wanted nothing more than to run my hands over his stomach and chest; to melt in his arms and feel his soft lips on mine. A flash of heat shot through me and I told myself to get it together. It was a good thing he couldn't read minds. It was only then I realized he was watching me.

"You look good in my clothes," he stated simply with a hint of awe.

"I was thinking about wearing them to class tomorrow," I teased, before realizing what I was saying. "I mean, not that I'm expecting to sleep over, I just…you know what I mean." I grinned sheepishly. So much for getting myself together. Sheesh. He chuckled and I mentally smacked myself across the face. He leaned forward, took my arm, and pulled me down beside him; wrapping an arm around me. I rested my head on his shoulder and made the fatal mistake of draping an arm over his torso. Feeling the incredibly soft cotton fabric of his shirt against the hard body beneath was the tipping point. Suddenly I wanted to touch every part of him, and not just through the fabric of his clothes. Passion spread through me like wildfire and control packed its bags, bought a one way ticket, and flew right out the window.

I lifted myself up until I was looking him right in the eyes. What I saw in them destroyed any restraint I had left. Behind the confidence, beneath the intensity, and hiding amongst the darkness was an innocence so pure it almost blinded me. The wildfire condensed into a river of hot lava that flowed straight to my soul; feeding something even deeper and stronger then love itself. Destiny.

I bent down to kiss him softly, but I should have known that would be a futile effort. He latched onto me with an urgency that was mirrored in my own movements. Instantly on top of him, the feel of his body beneath mine sent a surge of longing that couldn't be silenced, no matter how close I was to him. Somehow I managed to pull his shirt off and couldn't resist kissing every inch of warm skin I could get to. He rolled us over so that I was now beneath his weight; causing every cell in my body to explode with need. He buried his mouth into the crook of my neck and simultaneously thread his fingers through mine; pulling my hands above my head and securing me where I was. It was all I could do not to wrestle out from under his grip and continue touching him.

Knees on either side of me, he sat up and tugged off the t-shirt I had been wearing in a split second; tossing it on the floor as I fumbled with the button of his shorts. Surprising myself with my own boldness, I unzipped them and practically ripped them off of him. He did the same with the already loose gym shorts I was wearing, and I watched as his breath visibly caught in his throat when he looked down at me. Watching me carefully as if I might disappear into thin air, he wrapped an arm around me; picking me up enough to pull back the covers beneath me. I scrambled under them and he slid in beside me; pulling the covers over us and bathing us with soft fabric and security.

My hands, seemingly of their own volition, unclasped my bra and tossed it somewhere, leaving me completely bare and vulnerable. Finn's body instantly stilled as he met my gaze; his eyes shining with astonishment and shock. Lying very still, I watched in anticipation as his now shaking hands cupped me softly and a low moan escaped his throat. The feel of his hands on me sent waves of pleasure down to my feet and enveloped my every thought. Craving those lips, I pulled him back down on top of me. His hands were everywhere at once and I felt helpless to fill the intense crushing need that had taken over my body. At the same time my hands grasped the waistband of his boxers, fully intending to pull them off, he hooked his thumb on the strap of my underwear and we both froze. Breathing hard and filled with something neither of us could seem to control, he gazed into my eyes with restraint and I smiled warmly back at him. When I let go of his boxers and instead rubbed his cheek, he did the same and simply wrapped his arms around me. We lay that way for a long time; allowing the fire we were consumed in to simmer and cool.

Eventually he propped himself up on his elbow and regarded me with a big lopsided grin on his face.

"You're amazing," he murmured with adoration, and then glanced down almost shyly. "You know, I've never had a girl in my bed before."

Honestly surprised at his admission, I couldn't help grinning back. "Well no worries, your track record is still spotless. I'm not a girl, I'm a Goddess." The second I said it, we both collapsed into a fit of laughter. Albeit true, it sounded like a cheesy pick-up line from a movie. After several minutes, Finn was able to quit laughing long enough to flash me a wicked look.

"And that, Pasha, is the understatement of the century."

TWENTY-FOUR

Thursday: October 30th

"Where do they take him?"

"Phoebs, she already told you she doesn't know," Carmen answered for me with annoyance.

"I know, but what if it's somewhere awful? Like a dungeon or a cave? Or what if it's somewhere really amazing like a Spanish castle or The Hilton?"

I snickered at Phoebe's imagination, (along with her belief that a Spanish castle and The Hilton were remotely on the same level) as I placed my valise on the coffee table in our living room; surrounded by my roommates. After the fastest two days known to mankind, I was awaiting Finn's text message to tell me he was home so I could head over to Rostrum and stay with him until midnight.

"I seriously doubt it's a Spanish castle or The Hilton. He said he was just hoping it had a bed, so I don't think he has any idea either," I responded absentmindedly. As I carefully lifted the valise lid, I took a deep breath; inhaling the leftover lavender scent from The House of Thetis, or I guess technically, my house. The fact that I had a house was still beyond my comprehension.

"I just don't know if I could go two days without eating," she professed in horror.

"They give him water, right?" Willow asked; concerned.

"I'm pretty sure he can have all the water he wants, just no solid food," I explained.

"And then he has to fight for his life..." Carmen thought out loud, shaking her head in disgust. I was ready to talk about something else. Thinking about Finn starving and then fighting for his life was quickly bringing on an anxiety attack.

"Okay, you guys." I surveyed my roommates. "Here's everything she left me." I cautiously pulled out each item from the valise and laid it on the table for them to see. We had inspected the items before, but never from the perspective of what, if anything, I should take with me on my journey to the Underworld.

"Hello?" A deep voice from the kitchen called out; making us all jump except for Phoebe.

"Come on in, baby!" she called to him. Ian continued into the suite as Phoebe jumped up and hugged him.

"What is it with Sons and their inability to knock on a door?" Carmen hissed under her breath. He just flashed a smile at her and sat down across the room on the loveseat with Phoebe. He wore snug gray jeans and a bright orange shirt that matched his black and orange wayfarer sunglasses. Somehow the orange of his shirt outshone his diamond studded earrings.

"Did ya'll go on a treasure hunt?" he asked; squinting at the items spread out on the table.

"We're trying to figure out what Stasia should take on her journey with her," Phoebe informed him happily. "This is all of the stuff Thetis left her."

As everyone began to pick up objects and investigate them, I stared at each one, trying to figure out why in the world my mother would have left them for me: three skeleton keys, a dark stone, a piece of rope, a conch shell, and a beautiful aquamarine, diamond and pearl encrusted dagger. I had also been keeping my jewelry and the moonstone I found at the shipwreck in the valise as well. Ian, of course, was instantly drawn to the dagger.

"You should definitely take this," he suggested; looking it over.

"Definitely," I agreed. "I just hope I don't have to use it."

"I don't think I could stab anyone," Willow doubted.

"I bet you could if they were trying to kill you," Carmen speculated.

"Aren't you supposed to be able to hear the ocean in conch shells?" Phoebe held the large shell up to her ear and listened intently. She gave up and handed it to Carmen; already moving on to the piece of rope.

"I think this stone is a hematite," Willow told us from behind her laptop. She held up the stone and examined it further. "Yep, definitely hematite."

Carmen got up and peeked over her shoulder at the screen. "Does it say what it's used for?"

"It says that it absorbs negativity, gives optimism and courage, calms the emotions and treats hysteria," Willow read out loud.

"Hysteria?" Carmen nodded her head in consent. "I could see that being a strong possibility in an Underworld filled with evil queens and rivers of fire." I fought the urge to heave.

"Oh, and it helps maintain the balance between body, mind and spirit!" Willow added. "I definitely think you should make sure you have this with you for the journey."

"Okay...here's the 'taking' pile," I advised. Willow placed the black stone in the space I designated, along with the dagger. I picked up the conch shell and eyed it closely for any sign that it may have a specific use.

"See if you can hear the ocean, Stasia," Phoebe recommended. I held it up to my ear and almost threw it across the room. My shocked look immediately caught everyone's attention.

"I heard...somebody's...in there..." I spit out incredulously. Carmen snatched it from my hand and covered her ear with it.

"I don't hear a thing." She shrugged her shoulders and passed it to Willow, then Ian. No one else heard anything but silence. Ian handed it back to me as I stared at it; waiting for a troll to come crawling out. When it didn't explode or sprout legs, I held my breath and put it to my ear again. Just as before, I heard it immediately. A...mumbling. The sound of someone talking, but it was as if someone had pocket dialed me and I could only hear a muted version of their conversation. I listened harder. There was only one voice; a male.

"I swear I hear somebody talking or mumbling something," I said; hoping I didn't sound too crazy. "And you guys didn't hear anything at all?" They shook their heads and I stared at the shell for another moment before carefully setting it down on the table. If that shell was talking, I wanted it as far away from me as possible. Shells were not supposed to talk.

"What does it sound like?" Willow asked; poking the shell with her finger apprehensively.

"It sounds like a guy mumbling. Kind of reminds me of a pocket dial," I offered my example. Carmen bolted upright, suddenly getting an idea.

"Maybe it's a portal! But only a sound portal! It could even be a different realm or a different time that you're hearing," she surmised thoughtfully.

"I guess it's possible, but I've never heard of anything like that before," Willow countered.

"And why am I the only one who can hear it?" I asked; not enjoying that particular aspect. I didn't need even more reason to think I had a couple of screws loose.

"Maybe it's linked to your family somehow," Willow speculated.

"I don't think I'll be taking that with me," I muttered, and transferred it to my newly formed 'NOT taking' pile on the floor.

I was still perplexed and slightly disturbed by the shell when my phone vibrated in my lap. Finn was back at Rostrum. I didn't want to think about the fact that tonight would be the last time I'd see him until after his fight. Or possibly the last time I'd see him.

"Finn?" Phoebe asked gingerly. I nodded as I wrote him back to say I'd be over in a minute. "Tell him we'll be thinking about him."

"I will." I smiled at her and tried to suppress the agonizing desperation that crept into my bones at each moment's passing.

"How will I know?"

"You won't until afterwards."

"I can't live with that," I pleaded. "Could I come to the fight if I'm back from the Underworld in time?" Finn was emptying the cabinets and refrigerator with more cans, boxes and containers than an entire army could eat.

"They won't allow it, but it might be possible for Mom to talk to you. Text message?" he suggested, after smelling a jar of pickles to see if they were still edible.

"I don't want to find out you've been killed by text message." I frowned at him. "So who does get to go to the fight?"

"One family member can visit me during isolation, but all family and Sons are required to be in attendance for the fight. There will be a ceremony following - regardless of who succeeds." He tapped his chin as he scanned an open cabinet.

"There are no exceptions?" I tried; alluding to myself.

"It's a once-in-a-century event for the Sons. People come from all over the world and security has a huge presence."

"Then they wouldn't notice one more person," I uttered with frustration as he handed me a bag of unopened Doritos.

"Another thing you have to be cognizant of is the time vacuum in the Underworld. An hour there could be three in this realm." That could get tricky.

"Then I'll wear a watch," I declared stubbornly. "Where does the fight take place?" I thought about the stone amphitheatre and where something that old would be located.

"On an island off the coast of Greece."

"Greece!?" I shrieked. "That's so far away! Even if I got back in time, I have no way of getting to Greece!"

"I want you to be there too, but while you're in the Underworld you've got to stay focused on what you are doing. You can't afford even a moment of weakness by worrying about me. I'll be successful. I know I will."

"But my vision-"

"Your vision wasn't finished," he said quietly and took my hands in his. "As far back as records have been kept, only one Scion has ever failed to become Prime. You have nothing to worry about it."

"Only one?"

"Only one."

"Why did he fail?"

"He didn't eat cherry cheesecake beforehand." He licked his lips and gestured at the wide array of various desserts, snacks and drinks he compiled on the bar; all of which were his favorites. My mouth began to water as I took it all in. Several choices were questionable, such as the Vienna sausages (I'm pretty sure no actual meat was used in the manufacturing of those) and pigs feet (anything with the word feet in the name won't get anywhere near my stomach), but I didn't argue. This was his 'last meal' as he called it, which only succeeded in bringing images of death row and electric chairs to the forefront of my mind. Not very comforting. Before I get any more information from Finn about the one Son who had failed to earn his position as Prime, Cage and Ricker came crashing through the door.

"Well hey there, Patience!" Ricker affectionately threw an arm around me and Finn shook his head in annoyance.

"Pasha," I corrected him.

"Okay, Pacemaker, whatever you say." He popped a chocolate chip muffin in his mouth and smiled down at me with it smeared in his teeth.

"You got something in your teeth, Rigor-mortis." I gave him a dose of his own medicine and he grinned up at Finn; food still in his teeth.

"I like her. She's feisty."

"How about you like her from across the room where you can't spit crumbs all over her?" Finn retorted. I laughed when Ricker flipped him off and sat down on the couch across from Cage. ESPN fired up on the giant flat screen television.

"Where's Ian?" Cage asked while flipping through the channels.

"He's at my place," I answered for Finn.

"That dude's whipped," Ricker criticized under his breath.

"Talk about the pot calling the kettle black," Cage shot at him.

"Whatever, man. Carmen can't hold this down," Ricker announced with overly dramatic arrogance; getting a snicker out of Cage and Finn.

"I guess you won't care that she's going to the Halloween party with somebody else, then?" I threw out some bait.

"What?" He vaulted off the couch so quick, I almost missed it. "Are you serious? Who is it? She could have at least told me…" I could see the jealousy fuming in his eyes and stifled a laugh.

"Calm down, Cujo." I suppressed a laugh. "I was just kidding."

His entire body relaxed and he cocked his head to the side; sizing me up. "Well played, Passion. Well played."

"Pasha!" I laughed at him and threw a chocolate covered almond at his head.

"You better get your girl before I have to kick her ass," he told Finn with a leer, but Finn just laughed.

"I'm pretty sure she can take care of herself. You wouldn't last one round," he retorted.

"It wouldn't be the first time you got beat up by a girl," Cage laughed from the couch.

Ricker threw up his arms; exasperated. "Pamela doesn't count as a girl! She's six-feet, two inches tall and weighs two-hundred-thirty pounds! She could bench press my car."

"Still counts," Finn substantiated.

For the next hour I listened to their random conversations and witty insults and just tried not to cry from laughing so hard. After the last doughnut had been eaten and the last beef jerky was torn apart, Finn and I retreated to his bedroom to watch a movie and relax for a while.

A lone backpack was set up in the corner of his room awaiting his departure. Being that he would be kept in isolation for two days and then fighting to the death, I supposed clothes weren't the top priority. I did notice that all four axes had been taken down from the wall, and I immediately shivered at what he intended to do with them.

Halfway through Super Troopers, I nodded off in the warmth and security of Finn's arms. At one point I woke myself up, twitching around. My right leg kicked out and connected with Finn's calf, which only made him snicker. I peeked out of one eye to see him smiling down at me and then snuggled deeper against his shoulder.

"Are you afraid?" I asked quietly; eyes still closed.

"No, not at all," he answered confidently.

"I am," I whispered; mind hazy. "Promise you'll think of me?"

"Every second of every day," I heard him promise, before slipping into the outstretched arms of sleep.

Twenty-Five

The dead leaves woke me up. Scraping across my arms and legs, they trailed their ragged edges across my skin until it split and cracked open; searing my nerves with a relentless burning felt all the way to my soul. The smell of mildew and dead grass filled my senses as I opened my eyes. As soon as I began to move, the razor blade leaves blew away, leaving behind their painful destruction; the blood pooling and dripping to the cold ground beneath me. The air was crisp and the wind was still as I pushed up into a sitting position. A slight fog hovered above the ground, but the full moon above still shone through. Stalking me in every direction were gravestones; tilted and weathered by the rough hands of time. They weren't the marble masterpieces of this century however, they were thin slices of stone sticking up from the earth like rotten teeth; casting eerie shadows across the lifeless landscape. I slowly got to my feet and checked the rest of my skin for any damage. When I looked up, a bloodcurdling scream resonated throughout the dark night. My scream. I clamped a hand over my mouth; instantly swallowing my voice and holding my breath. Eyes wide with terror, I glanced from grave to grave and hoped I wasn't really seeing them. I squeezed my eyes shut in a futile attempt to make them disappear.

Unfortunately no matter how many times I blinked, they were still there. Hovering above each gravesite lay the deceased owner. Completely stiff, hands crossed over their chests and eyes closed, they did not move. Their tattered clothes hung beneath their bodies; each showing varying degrees of transparency, as if some had been dead longer than others. Holding my breath and not daring to move an inch, I scanned the cemetery and searched for an exit. Tall oak trees blocked my view of the perimeter, but I caught the glint of a gate to my right. It was far away, but I thought I could make it.

I carefully inched forward; each footfall painstakingly loud as the leaves crunched and gave way beneath my weight. Another disturbing sound halted my steps altogether. It sounded like two rocks being rubbed together, grinding and moaning at the pressure of the movement. Gradually every grave owner turned its head in my direction; their sunken, dark eye sockets causing my stomach to lurch and heave. As a frightened whimper forced its way out, I carefully bent down; hoping to blend in with my surroundings. I had to think. I had to focus. The lightness I felt told me I was having a reverie. A reverie. I could control those - I knew how. I could get myself out of this! I thought about the sheets of Finn's bed, the warmth of his arms and the feel of his chest rising and falling to his breaths. When several minutes passed and nothing happened, the panic became overwhelming. Why couldn't I get out of this?

I opened my eyes and screamed again. Only this time I couldn't stop. The numerous dead escaped their hovering shackles and were now standing. They blurred and shifted as they began to move in my direction; silent, stiff and expressionless. I half ran, half stumbled down the stone path towards the gate I saw. I felt the grave owners reaching out to me; their bony fingers scraping across my arms and face as I passed. Tears of horror raced down my face as I peeked over my shoulder at the menacing corpses. When I looked back at the path, I ran right into a headstone, knocking it over and tumbling down on top of it. I tried to scramble back to my feet, but the ground beneath me opened up and everything went dark.

The dirt beneath me was damp and soft; soothing my cuts and cooling my face. But as reality came crashing back, my eyes snapped open. Daggers of terror sliced through my heart when I realized what I had fallen into. It was a rectangular hole, walls made of earth and mud; the surface at least ten feet above any chance of escape. I whirled around, making sure I was the only inhabitant of the hole, and then attempted to climb to the surface. The loose dirt gave way and I ended up back on the ground. I wiped my face and attempted the climb again, only ending in the same result. For at least an hour I tried everything I could think of, but to no avail. I was trapped in this God-forsaken grave.

"Hello? Can anybody hear me?" I yelled to the open air high above. "Somebody help me!"

I could feel the tears welling up inside my eyes as a crushing despair eclipsed my soul. Claustrophobia gripped me next; churning the already frenzied panic inside me. I tried to climb again, now knowing I had no other options, but when I looked up my heart stopped. The grave owners were back. Surrounding the grave on all sides, their lifeless faces leered down at me.

"Help me!!" I screamed in desperation. I covered my face and knelt to my knees, overwhelmed by the hopelessness of my situation. I tried once more to escape the reverie. I thought of Finn's soft bed, his loving arms, and the sound of his heartbeat against my ear. If he could just hear me. Maybe if I screamed loud enough my body would also scream.

"Finn!! Finn!!" I shouted his name over and over again. As exhaustion took over, I could only cry quietly and fold into myself. "Finn…please help me…"

Then I felt it. Evil. It pricked at my already bleeding skin; lashing out and encircling my body.

"Doesn't look like our dark Prince Charming is coming to save you today," she purred in mock sympathy and pouted; her eyes flashing. "How sad."

I stood immediately, anger shooting through me. "Let me go, Nadia," I demanded through my teeth.

"Now where's the fun in that?" She laughed and glanced up at the grave owners with adoration. She eyed me, snapped her fingers once, and they all promptly disappeared. I instantly noticed a glaring change in her appearance. Her otherwise golden-brown eyes had taken on a striking metallic sheen, making her appear almost feline-like. They were piercing and haunting; drawing my attention and holding me captive. Her flowing blonde hair now boasted streaks of gilded yellow – a hue normally saved for the most awe-inspiring of sunsets. Flecks of gold sparkled across her skin and I had to admit she was...breathtaking. Her black mini dress showed off her long legs and something else I hadn't seen before: her trace. A jagged lightning bolt ran down the length of her calf; white vines twisting around it. The multiple gold bangles on her wrist clinked against one another as she crossed her arms and stared at me; leaning against the mud wall of the grave.

"Besides, we have much to discuss," she smirked at me.

"The only thing I want to discuss with you is why you won't leave me the hell alone!" I snarled at her.

"Aww, Anastasia." Her eyes flashed again and she smiled sweetly. "Such hostility! And here I am, simply trying to save you from humiliation!"

"Ditch the pretenses, Nadia." I glared at her. "Stop wasting my time."

"I'm only trying to tell you what our dark Prince Charming has failed to explain." She tapped her gold watch and tsked. "He's the one who's been wasting your time."

"My relationship is none of your business," I spit at her.

"Wrong again," she snapped back, and began to step towards me. I stood taller and braced myself for an attack. She pointed a manicured fingernail at me and continued.

"You think he loves you? You think you mean anything to him?"

"I know he loves me!" I lashed out at her, but she just chuckled.

"So innocent." She shook her head at me. "And so stupid. He doesn't love you. He's just using you."

"Screw you." I moved towards her, anger tearing through my veins.

"Tempting...but no thanks. You're not my type." She snickered at her own joke and then turned serious. "On the Day of the Dead, his eighteenth birthday, he will become bound. And no one, not even you, can change that."

"You think I'm going to believe anything you say?" I threw at her with bitterness.

"Won't you?" She smiled wickedly and stepped closer, with evil dripping down her face. I clenched my jaw. "Listen closely, Anastasia. In two days time, your dear Finn will be betrothed..." her smile widened, "...to me."

My jaw dropped to the ground. Finn...betrothed? To her? That wasn't possible. Was it? It fit the conversation I overheard at Priscilla's house, so could this be what she was so eager to tell me? Was this what Natasha had been too busy to tell me? Why wouldn't Finn have said something? He said he wasn't keeping anything from me. He said he didn't know what Nadia and Priscilla's conversation was about in my reverie. Would he...lie to me?

"Betrothed?" I managed, and gawked incredulously into her smug golden eyes. The anger that had consumed me moments before had dried up; uncovering the steady, paralyzing grip of doubt.

"So you see, in his mind there's never been the possibility of a future with you. He knows as well as I do that the true Son of Daimon, The Prime, is required to have a wife whose soul is connected to the Underworld, just like his. He needs a wife who shares the same bond of darkness; who is truly his equal. You could never be that for him. I am his future." Her face darkened and I watched the evil tendrils rolling off her skin, taunting me. "I will be his wife. It has been decided."

"He doesn't want you," I growled at her, my hatred returning at her obvious arrogance.

"That's the best part! It doesn't matter what he wants. My mother has spoken." She shrugged and twirled a lock of honey hair around her finger. "One of the many perks of being the Princess of the Underworld. I get what I want. End of story."

"You're lying," I accused her, my tone lacking harshness. As much as I didn't want to admit it, the fear that she was telling the truth was more than I could bear.

"Tell yourself what you want. It doesn't make it any less true. He knows what's to come. As a matter of fact, go ask him yourself."

The last thing I saw was her blowing a sarcastic kiss at me and disappearing into thin air.

Gasping for air, I sat up abruptly and began to sob uncontrollably. The room around me swam and blurred as I struggled to pull in a steady breath.

"Stasia! What's wrong? What is it?" I felt Finn's hand on my back as I turned to face him.

"Did you lie to me?" I watched him desperately, still holding onto a sliver of hope.

"Did I...?" He furrowed his brow at me. "What are you talking about?"

I scooted to the end of the bed, fearing the worst. "Did you lie to me?! Did you? Tell me the truth!" The walls of my heart slammed shut; locking him out instantly and completely.

"Pasha, slow down! Tell me what happened!" Panic was evident in his eyes.

My legs began to shake as I stood with dizzying speed. He slid off the bed and walked towards me; his eyes frantic. I backed away from him and willed myself to stop crying.

"Betrothed," I stated simply; my voice breaking. Shock crossed his face, followed swiftly by crushing sadness. He slouched on the end of the bed in defeat and looked at the floor. My entire body began to shake as his body language confirmed my fears. Frozen to the spot, I cringed visibly as my heart hardened, turned away and shattered into a million pieces. The weight of it was too much. It cut too deep.

Suddenly I was running. Out of his bedroom and past his roommates. Out of his suite and down the hall towards the elevator. I wanted to be as far away from the catalyst of all these painful emotions coursing through me as possible. This couldn't be happening.

"Pasha, please wait-" he pleaded as he caught up with me. With tears still streaming down my face, I looked into the deep blue eyes of my safe harbor that was no more, and my heart broke all over again.

"How could you not tell me?! Don't you think 'betrothed-to-the-Princess-of-the-Underworld' would be sort of an important topic to discuss with your girlfriend!?" It took my shaking finger three tries to press the button for the elevator.

"It's the last thing I want to happen! I love you-"

"Do you? Do you love me, Finn?"

"You know I do, Stasia!" Tears I had never seen before collected in his eyes.

"When did you plan on telling me this? After your birthday when it was too late!?"

"I didn't want to upset you before your journey-"

"Don't." I put up a hand and walked onto the elevator. He followed and reached for my arm, but I twisted away and stared at him with disbelief.

"How could you do this?" My anger turned into devastation in a split second as I watched the tears roll down his cheeks. I looked away.

"Please don't be mad at me," he pleaded. "I'm going to find a way around it! You have to believe me!"

"I don't have to do anything, Finn. You lied to me."

"I'm so sorry, Pasha. Please-"

"After everything, Finn! After everything we've been through, how could you do this to us?" The elevator doors opened and I stomped out of Rostrum with him on my heels. I stopped and turned, searching his eyes for some kind of answer. I only found love. I pushed his chest in anger and felt my sanity unraveling.

"Don't you know how much I love you? Don't you know I would have spent the rest of my life with you? You ruined it. You ruined everything!" I began to sob and pushed him again. He tried to touch my arm but I backed away out of his reach. Neither of us saw the black limo pull up. Neither of us saw the door open or the two men dressed all in black who stepped out. They grabbed Finn's arms firmly and wrestled him into the car. I watched on in a haze of numbness; detached and fragmented.

"Stasia!" His stricken dark blue eyes disappeared behind the tinted windows. He hadn't even had time to get his backpack. I told myself I didn't care.

Friday: October 31st

Halloween. The day the world celebrated all things dark, macabre and all around ghoulish. It was one of my favorite holidays. Costumes, haunted houses and candy? What's not to like? Even behind the corporate agendas and cheesy commercials, Halloween still represented and revered a world darker than our own. A world I had glimpsed several times in the last several months. Little did the human population know that the existence of evil was certain. The existence of monsters and ghosts was very certain. And there were plenty of things that went bump in the night.

Miraculously, I made it through my classes the next day without one anguish-filled tear. I had a feeling it was because they had already been cried out. After returning to Maren last night, heartbroken and devastated, I laid in bed for hours drowning in my own pain. I was only left with a dull ache, hidden behind walls of reinforced concrete. In a daze I travelled from class to class; my roommates assuming I was simply upset at Finn's departure. Verbalizing it would make it more real, and I wasn't quite ready to do that. So it festered inside of me all day; draining my world of color and happiness. I was actually glad for tonight's distractions. Unfortunately my roommates were beginning to get to know me a little too well.

"I know something happened, and we'll beat it out of you eventually so you might as well make it easy on yourself and spill it!" Carmen raised an eyebrow at me. A stool was set up in the middle of the living room with Willow poised atop. Carmen was prepping her hair for the extensions that would complete her Rapunzel costume. Phoebe was relaxing on the couch, munching on a bag of candy corn.

"She's right." Willow eyed me sympathetically. "We can tell you've been crying...a lot."

I wasn't surprised they could tell I'd been crying. My eyes started to swell if I even considered crying. I was lucky if I could still see after five hours of sobbing. I plopped down beside Phoebe and grabbed some candy corn; tossing it into my mouth distractedly.

"If I tell you, will you promise not to bring it up any more tonight?" I asked them reluctantly.

"Cross my heart and hope to die!" Phoebe giggled beside me. Sugar was the last thing that girl needed. I ran my hands through my hair and leaned forward, suddenly fidgety.

"I had a reverie last night." I peeked up at Phoebe, who had stopped chewing mid-bite. "Besides being absolutely terrifying, Nadia was there."

"Nadia? Why would you see Nadia in a reverie?" Phoebe asked; perplexed.

"Didn't she go back to California?" Willow questioned. I sighed, remembering that I hadn't told them who Nadia really was.

"Nadia isn't who you think she is. I didn't want to scare you guys so I haven't said anything. But you need to know. Especially now." Confusion washed over their faces as I continued. "Nadia graduated from Metis last year, but she's not your normal descendant."

"I knew something was weird about her," Willow concluded.

"What is she?" Phoebe asked.

"Nadia is the princess...of the Underworld." I waited for their reactions. I didn't have to wait long. Carmen dropped the hair she was holding, Willow almost fell off the stool, and Phoebe choked on a candy corn.

"Shut. Up." Phoebe gawked at me.

"The princess of the Underworld? As in Persephone's daughter?" Willow exclaimed in disbelief.

"As in Persephone's daughter," I confirmed.

"Wow. I didn't know she had a daughter." Carmen sat down on the loveseat; eyes so wide I could see white all the way around her dark irises.

"Apparently she was the product of an affair, so maybe that's why?" I guessed. "Anyway, that's not the bad part."

"Having the princess of the Underworld amongst us isn't the bad part?" Phoebe whimpered.

"She can control my reveries somehow, and she pulled me into one last night to tell me something." I paused, not wanting to say it. Tears began to well up in my eyes again and Phoebe scooted closer to me. "Persephone has decreed that on Finn's birthday he will be betrothed...to Nadia." The last part of the sentence came out in a whisper as a sob rose in my throat.

"That bitch!" Carmen shot to her feet, anger flashing in her eyes.

"Wait - what does 'betrothed' mean again?" Phoebe squeaked.

"Basically it means they'll be engaged." Willow turned thoughtful. "But it's more complicated than that. Since they'll both be immortal on his birthday, they'll become bound."

"Bound? I've never heard of that. Is it something only immortals have to do?" Phoebe asked, and this immediately got my attention. I just figured Nadia meant 'bound' metaphorically. I didn't realize they may actually be bound together.

"Their souls are…merged. I don't know exactly what all that entails, but it's irreversible. At some point they would take part in the Myriad Ceremony." We stared at her blankly. "Get married."

"That bitch!" Phoebe growled.

"And Finn never told you anything?" Carmen looked at me with amazement; her anger growing as she paced back and forth.

"No." I squeezed my eyes shut and choked down another sob. "I think that's what hurts the most."

"But Finn can't possibly want to be bound to Nadia!" Phoebe spit out her name.

"Nadia said her mother had 'spoken' and that no one could change it."

"So Finn's just going to go along with it?" Willow asked incredulously. "He's not going to fight it at all?"

I shrugged my shoulders. "I don't think he has a choice. He said he was trying to find a way around it, but he doesn't appear to be trying too hard. I mean, his birthday is in two days! Not to mention the fact that he's in isolation. What does he think he's going to do?"

"I don't get it. Is it because she's from the Underworld?" Phoebe slumped back onto the couch cushion with frustration.

"I believe so. She said something about the Prime being required to be with someone who has a connection to the Underworld."

"I think Nadia just likes ruining people's lives," Willow hissed.

"I think she's just a spoiled brat who has to get mommy to do everything for her. She knows she couldn't get Finn otherwise." Carmen put her hands on her hips.

"Well it doesn't matter now. It's happening and there's nothing I can do about it." I sighed and put my head in my hands. "He's gone. The limo pulled up when we were fighting outside and they just grabbed him and threw him in the backseat! He didn't even get his backpack with all the stuff he was taking."

"His roommates will find a way to get it to him. Or Natasha," Willow attempted to soothe me.

"I just can't believe Ian didn't tell me." Phoebe's anger turned sullen; her eyes growing pained.

"Don't blame Ian, Phoebs. This isn't his fault."

"Why don't we try to find out how it works and see if there's a way we can reverse it? Or maybe you can convince Persephone when you go to the Underworld!" Her face lit up with hope but I shook my head vehemently. "It was his decision not to tell me. If he really wanted to be with me, he would have talked to me before now. We could have figured it out together." I rubbed my trace. "But he didn't. I'm not going to go chasing after somebody who wouldn't do the same for me."

"I'm sorry Stasia." Phoebe embraced me in a hug. I could feel the tears begin to burn in my eyes and the sobs collecting in my throat.

"So now you guys know." I picked up the hair Carmen dropped and handed it back to her. "But the one thing that would make me feel better is to have the best Halloween ever with my best friends."

"Hmm…first we'll have to find you some best friends…" Carmen tapped her chin and smirked at me.

"All I know is that you're going to look amazing as a decaying, rotten corpse bride." Willow grinned.

"Especially after I get done smearing blood all over you…" Phoebe added wickedly. "Bwah ha ha ha…"

"That's the worst evil laugh I've ever heard." Carmen put her hands on her hips and stared at Phoebe.

"I'd like to see you do better!" Phoebe threw back at her. Willow and I grinned at each other as they took turns serenading us with evil laughter. I couldn't help smiling.

"I don't know what I'd do without you guys," I told them adoringly.

"You'd probably be better off." Phoebe shook her head and whispered loudly, "Carmen can drive a person crazy."

"If anyone could pull the crazy out of somebody, it's you, Phoebs," Carmen quipped.

"I'm going to go crazy if you don't hurry up and finish my Rapunzel hair." Willow frowned at Carmen. After Willow's Rapunzel hair had been attached and Phoebe tried to jump rope with it, she set to putting gold glitter all over her face. It brought on a flashback of Nadia's shimmery skin, so I excused myself to put on my costume.

My corpse bride costume was the only thing that brought something resembling a true grin to my face. Something about its ripped fabric and morose style fit what I was feeling inside and soothed me. The sheer lining of the dress felt wonderful against my skin, and wearing a dress made me feel elegant and regal, although technically I was supposed to be dead. I pulled my hair up into a loose bun and picked out some random pieces; giving it an I'm-getting-married look with a hint of just-got-murdered. I pulled on the lacy thigh highs, secured the veil and snickered at my reflection in the mirror. The dark circles under my eyes actually went a long way to make me look dead. Who knew?

I swept across the room to my dresser, secured my triskellion necklace around my neck and slid my aquamarine ring on my finger. They didn't go with my costume, but I felt naked and vulnerable without them. My heart began to crack when my hand paused over the black onyx anklet Finn had given me. I rubbed a finger over its smooth beads and sighed as warmth crept up my arm. I stood in front of my mirror and inspected my outfit. I needed a little something more… I grabbed some white ribbon and wrapped it around my wrist and hand; allowing it to hang haphazardly as if I was once mummified and had broken from my binds. Perfect.

The irony of my costume wasn't lost on me, but I was going to do my best not to think about it. Besides, I was an expert at compartmentalization. I tucked Finn, my journey and Nadia into their own individual chambers far back in the recesses of my mind. I slammed the doors and locked them before tucking the keys away. I knew I could only hide from my problems for a short time, but it was Halloween and I was determined to have a good time tonight. Tomorrow I would open Pandora's box and begin the task of sorting out the cluster that had become my life. My heart clenched as I pictured Finn isolated and alone. No - I was not going to think about him. The only place that would get me was under my covers, crying my eyes out. Although it sounded pretty tempting, I steeled myself and looked in the mirror.

"Be strong. You can do this," I told myself sternly. Unfortunately the person looking back was on the brink of falling apart. I took a deep breath. "Or at least pretend."

Twenty-Seven

"Blood."

"Huh?" I turned to see Phoebe watching me from the doorway, a sly smile on her face.

"You need blood," she repeated and came to stand beside me. "Thankfully, I have some to spare. But don't think you're drinking any. Dead brides don't drink blood."

"And here I'd spent my whole life thinking they did," I said dryly, which made her chuckle. Her sexy vampire costume looked incredible. It was a black leather mini dress with tall black boots and a long, red silk-lined cloak. She had a tiny vial of blood hanging from a necklace, and two fake fangs that popped onto her incisors. She looked deadly and seductive all at once.

"You look great, Phoebs!" I looked her up and down. "Ian might even let you drink his blood." I smiled darkly and raised an eyebrow at her.

"A girl can dream," she snickered. "Now sit down so I can spray you."

"Blood comes in a spray bottle?"

"If you want, I could stab you and let it spray out naturally?" she asked in all seriousness.

"I think I'll go with the spray bottle." I frowned at her.

"I had a feeling you might." She grinned at me and began to spray blood in specific places on my dress. I had to admit, it looked pretty real.

"What's Ian going to be for Halloween?" I asked her as she worked.

"He and Ricker are going as something together, but Ian wouldn't tell me what." She smiled adoringly and a pang of jealousy hit me. I pushed it away resolutely. "Okay, close your eyes so I can do your face."

She pulled out a tube of blood this time and went to work. When she was done, I looked in the mirror and laughed.

"That looks amazing, Phoebs!" I had blood dripping out of my mouth and from the corners of my eyes.

"We aren't done," she instructed. "Come with me." I followed her out into the living room where Carmen waited with something in her hand.

"My God, Phoebe. She looks like she took a blood bath!" Carmen exclaimed, and Phoebe and Willow died laughing.

"You've been waiting to say that all night, haven't you?" I accused her.

"It's possible." She grinned. "Now come here so I can really make you look dead." She proceeded to cover my entire body with thick white powder. Next, she attacked my lips with a light blue lipstick and then two shades of blue eye shadow to enhance the circles under my eyes. Once half the compact was empty, she was happy with her work of art. Fearful I would resemble a dead Smurf, I was pleasantly surprised when I looked in the mirror and simply saw a dead bride; Carmen standing behind me grinning from ear to ear. It was hard for me to look at her without laughing…her sexy nun outfit was the definition of contradiction. She had also lacquered her lips with bright red lipstick. Willow looked like she was born to be Rapunzel. I had a feeling she was secretly wishing she could dress like that every day. She looked like she belonged in a different century.

Thirty minutes later we all stood in the kitchen, marveling over each other's costumes and taking pictures on our phones. A vampire biting a nun. A vampire biting Rapunzel. A dead bride biting a vampire. And last but not least, a nun strangling a vampire with Rapunzel's hair. If that wasn't going on the front of the scrapbook, I didn't know what would.

As we walked across campus, we passed by anything from Lady Gaga in her infamous meat dress (thankfully no hungry animals were trailing behind) to a walking IPhone. Cousin Eddie from Christmas Vacation ran by, along with the Dumb and Dumber guys decked out in orange and blue tuxes. A walking breathalyzer test with the words 'Blow Me' across the front was chasing two Playboy bunnies, and we were almost run over by three sexy crayons (pink, blue and yellow, in case you were wondering). By the time we made it to The Hole we were having trouble breathing from laughing so hard.

We were greeted at the entrance by Kira (A.K.A. Princess Leia) and one of her friends dressed up as Carmen Sandiego. They handed out orange wristbands and ushered us into the The Hole. Or what used to be The Hole. Our normal lunch destination had been cleared of all its tables for standing room only. The stone planters that normally overflowed with colorful flowers were now teeming with skulls, pumpkins and tombstones. Black lanterns had been strung up all over The Hole; dancing and casting an eerie glow over the entire place. Cobwebs and dark purple string lights entrapped the tree branches and enhanced the haunted atmosphere. Several fog machines placed a thick layer of fog at our feet that swirled and danced with the movements of the party goers. The massive amount of people incited an air of excitement and fun I felt down to my bones.

I grinned as the power of the music pumping out of the massive speakers wrapped around me and sent a rush of energy through me. This was exactly what I needed to distract me from everything. We soon merged with the throngs of witches, vampires and sexy nurses and found a spot to dance and hangout.

"You are the hottest vamp I've ever seen."

We all turned to see Ricker and Ian grinning at us. Ian planted a big kiss on Phoebe before she pretended to bite his neck.

"This is a Halloween party, not a funeral." Carmen looked them up and down skeptically. Standing before us in matching black suits adorned with black ties, I had no idea what they were dressed up as until they reached into their coat pockets at the same time and pulled out black sunglasses.

Ricker looked over at Cage.

"I make these look good," he smirked, and they both crossed their arms dramatically.

"IRS guys?" Willow asked; completely clueless as to what they were.

"We are…" Ricker started. Ian finished, "The Men in Black."

"If I get abducted by aliens, you two are the last ones I'd call," Carmen snickered.

"If you get abducted by aliens, we're throwing a party," Ricker countered.

"Whatever. You know you'd miss me," she declared, hands on her hips.

"Doubtful." Ricker grabbed her arm and pulled her close. "But tell yourself whatever you want to get through the day."

"You make me sick." She smiled at him.

"Good," he retorted with a sexy grin. They definitely got the 'Most Dysfunctional Relationship' award.

"This hot vamp wants to dance," Phoebe announced, taking Ian's hand and leading him away.

"So does this hot nun." Carmen looked expectantly at Ricker.

"What are you looking at me for?" he asked, trying to sound surprised.

"Dance," she said simply; venom lining her eyes.

"Nah." He turned his attention to the crowd but couldn't hide the amused grin.

"Do you really want all these people to see you get beat up by a nun?" she threatened.

"Hmm…Maybe you're right," he commented in all seriousness. "I'd hate to get this suit dirty while I'm kicking your ass." He grinned at her almost coyly and she dragged him out to the dance floor with a laugh. I looked at Willow.

"You want to go find something to drink…" I trailed off and followed her eyes to a tall, blond-haired guy in khaki pants, a light blue button up shirt and a brown jacket. A wide brimmed hat adorned his head and a brown leather satchel was strapped around his body. His right hand clutched a leather whip; rolled up and menacing.

He must have noticed us staring, because he turned and grinned crookedly before sauntering across The Hole to where we stood.

"Ladies," Liam greeted us with a tip of his hat.

"Out chasing down crystal skulls on this lovely Halloween night?" I joked with him.

"The much younger version of Indiana Jones at your service," he corrected me. "I haven't yet discovered the Kingdom of the Crystal Skulls. Currently, I'm on a quest to find the Holy Grail." He stood tall and struck an Indiana Jones-esque pose, then removed his hat and bowed formally to Willow.

"You look amazing," he cooed as her cheeks flushed and her blue eyes lit up. Feeling like a third wheel all of a sudden, I stepped back to give them some privacy.

"We're gonna go dance," Willow told me, clearly brimming with joy. "I'll be back."

Watching Willow and Liam walk away, I felt a crushing loneliness darken my heart and rip open my soul; allowing the contents to spill carelessly onto the stones beneath my feet. My thoughts inevitably drifted to Finn, which elicited an immediate onslaught of burning tears.

Instead of pushing them down, I reveled in the pain; reveled in the sadness. To feel nothing at all would be my heart's true demise. He brightened my world in such a way so that his absence created a massive black hole; sucking out any and all light into its infinite depths. What was he doing right now? What was he thinking about? Could he feel my entire being reaching out and craving his presence? Had he found a way around Persephone's decision? No. I couldn't allow my thoughts to travel down that hope laden road. The stakes were too high.

"Don't cry, Stasia."

I let out a yelp when Bianca materialized right in front of me.

"Don't do that! You're gonna give me a heart attack!" I grinned at her through the tears. Her presence swept away a portion of my loneliness. Several people around me looked over and stared at me like I'd lost my mind.

"Am I the only one who can see you?"

"Right now, yes."

"You can control who sees you?" I said a little too loudly; causing more people to look over.

"Yes."

"Think you can teach me how to do that?" I said under my breath with a grin.

"I think you'd have to be a ghost." She looked at the ground and added, "And you don't want to be a ghost."

"It might be a better alternative right now." I wiped at a tear that escaped down my cheek.

"Do you have a dagger?" she asked randomly; glancing around with paranoia.

"I have one that my mother gave me," I told her, confused by the sudden change in subject. She scooted closer to me and spoke softly.

"A divine dagger is the only thing that can kill an immortal. You must promise to take it on your journey."

She glanced around again. "You will be at a disadvantage in her river."

"Her...river?"

"Nadia's river," she explained. It took a moment before I realized what she was talking about. Nadia was a nymph. She was attached to a certain body of water. Was that body of water in the Underworld? I guessed that would make sense. A shadow of dread washed over me.

"Which river is hers?"

"The River Styx," she answered ominously. Of course. Why would it be any other river? I put my head in my hands. Things were going from bad to worse.

"She already has what she wants. Why doesn't she just leave me alone?" I asked; desperation evident in my tone as well as in the frustrated tears that once again rolled down my cheeks.

"She doesn't want you to figure it out."

"Figure what out?" She jerked her head to the left and her features turned to stone.

"I have to go." She began to fade.

"Bianca, wait! Figure what out?" But she was already gone.

"Stasia?" I looked up into the eyes of Willow and Liam. I quickly wiped some rogue tears off my chin. Willow sat down beside me and put her arm around me.

"Do you want to leave?" she asked gently.

"It's okay." I looked down at my hands and ran a finger over my trace; noticing that it looked slightly dulled.

"You just say the word and we'll bounce." Carmen came up to stand in front of me with Ricker on her heels.

"Plus, Dr. Drake is calling...." Phoebe bounced up on my left and kissed me on the cheek. "We wouldn't want to leave him waiting."

"Yeah, the last thing I need is to have some insane dead guy stealing my heart," Carmen said.

"I thought I already did?" Ricker sneered; putting an arm around her.

"Maybe I'll let Dr. Drake steal my heart after all." She imperiously lifted an eyebrow at him.

"It's too late for that." He pretended to tear her heart out as she wiggled away from him. A light change of color in my peripheral vision had me turning my head to the right - just in time to see a small gray tendril twist and writhe; vanishing behind several dancers about twenty yards away.

On my feet in seconds, I pushed away from my roommates and launched into the dancing throngs of monsters, witches and fairies. With my head on a swivel, I spotted a second gray tendril as it precariously hovered above the head of a younger girl dressed up as Pocahontas. I watched in horror as it spiraled down onto her shoulder and slid around her neck. As I was about to reach out and swat it away from her it disappeared into thin air. Pocahontas shot me an odd look, but I continued past her in pursuit of the allusive evil smoke.

It reappeared several yards away, floating innocently and flippantly through the cool night air. I concentrated on keeping it in my sight and followed it across The Hole. Suddenly obsessed with the tiny tendril and fearful for the hundreds of people gathered in celebration, I scanned every shadow and stone ledge in search of the only evil being I knew to produce such smoke. The loud music faded behind me as I followed a sidewalk around the History building. The festive ambiance created by the Halloween party in The Hole faded with it; eclipsed by a more sinister darkness that I felt weighing on my heart. Even the shadows scaling the sides of the stone buildings were darker. I could feel them watching me; imposing and leering above amongst the scraggly shadows of the tree branches.

A stinging sensation on my hand had me glancing down. I jerked away when I spotted several gray tendrils attempting to wrap around my left wrist, around my trace, which had begun to dull in brightness. Looking in every direction, I still only found my ever-watchful night companions: the towering trees and ever-taunting shadows. A movement to my right quickened my pulse immediately and my breathing spiked. Feeling vulnerable and exposed out in the open, I willed my feet to walk.

With horrifying slowness, the number of pinpricks nipping at the bare skin of my back increased in number and I began to feel the same sensation along my arms and the sides of my face. I stopped midstride, squeezed my eyes shut, and then spun around as if evading a swarm of killer bees. Considering a swarm of killer bees would be an upgrade from my current situation, I had little faith that my futile attempt to work, but that wasn't going to stop me from trying. Suddenly, I felt a strong presence right behind me. Spinning around on my heel, I braced myself for what I would find.

"Stasia?"

"Phoebe!" My crudely constructed resolve shattered and I began to shake uncontrollably.

"What are you doing out here?" She grasped both my arms in concern.

"I just thought I saw something." I shrugged my shoulders and tried to play it off as no big deal. With Phoebe's presence came immediate relief from the prickling sensation. I searched our immediate area out the corner of my eyes for any movement.

"Haven't you watched scary movies?" She put her hands on her hips.

"Huh?" How did we go from me seeing things to scary movies?

"Something bad always happens when a person walks off by themselves because they saw something or heard something. The only thing worse is when the dumb girl runs up the stairs when the killer's after her." I linked arms with her and let her chatter on as we walked back to The Hole. "I mean, where does she think she's going to go?

Her bedroom? The roof? It's tragic, really. So I'm going to have to make you promise to never be the dumb girl in the scary movies."

I smiled at her; insanely grateful for her innocent approach to the situation. "I can assure you I will never be the dumb girl in a movie. I'm a horrible actress."

"Well that's a relief. You had me worried!" she exclaimed with a smile.

Upon returning to The Hole I saw the party was still in full swing, so I tried to lose myself in the mass of people dancing and laughing. I blocked out anything related to Finn, Nadia, or my journey, and just pretended I was a normal girl dancing with my friends at a normal Halloween party. I pretended there were no evil princesses trying to steal my soul. I pretended my boyfriend wasn't betrothed to the aforementioned evil princess. I pretended I didn't have to travel to the Underworld in order to fulfill my destiny and become an immortal. And it worked. Until we left.

"That wasn't break dancing...that was broke dancing." Carmen jumped down off the stone wall she was using as a balance beam and sneered at Ian.

"It's called B-boying or street dancing," Ian replied in all seriousness. "And it's not as easy as it looks."

"All I know is that it looked like you were having a seizure." Carmen did a bad impression of Ian's popping and locking moves; leaving us all gasping for breath from laughing so hard. We left the party and were walking down a shadowed road on the marsh side of the island towards the infamous haunted Drake House. Large live oak trees covered with Spanish moss flanked both sides of the road. The elegant moss hung from their deformed branches as it swayed in the ocean breeze, which enhanced the spooky factor tremendously.

"You're a regular JabbaWockee, Carmen," Phoebe told her sarcastically.

"What'd you call me, Vampy?" Carmen stopped mid-step and turned to face her, then gave her a sympathetic smile. "I need to pray for you." She bowed her head, mumbled something inaudible and looked up; shrugging her shoulders. "Nope, too late. Your soul's not salvageable."

"It's alright. I'd rather be a vampire for the rest of eternity anyway. I'm starting to get used to my fangs." Phoebe touched her teeth extensions delicately. "Just think how fast I'll be able to eat corn on the cob!"

"What in the world is a jabachoochie?" Willow furrowed her eyebrows.

"JabbaWockee," Phoebe corrected her. "It's that group that was on America's Best Dance Crew a while back. You know, the hip-hop group competition?"

"I have no idea what you're talking about. Ouch!" Willow screeched as Phoebe stepped on her long fake hair; ripping her head backwards.

"Oh! I'm sorry!" Phoebe jumped back.

"Let's see if we can get this under control," I muttered as I stepped over to Willow and began gathering and twirling her hair into one massive bun on top of her head. The whole group stopped with us, watching and snickering.

"I think you should keep the extensions in. Gives you that 'damsel in distress' look," Ricker joked. "Or is it the big jelly doughnut look? I can't tell the difference."

"Your real hair is much more beautiful." Liam put an arm around Willow, who was staring daggers at Ricker.

"Hey….guys?" Carmen murmured; her tone deadpan. A horrified expression was frozen onto her dark features, and we turned to see the reason all the color had drained from her cheeks. "Is....is that it?"

Directly in front of us was the quintessential haunted house of childhood nightmares and horror movies, positioned on a decrepit acre of dried, decaying leaves. The ragged branches of a lone live oak tree had been stripped of its foliage, which now lay scattered below. No other trees on the island had begun to shed their leaves yet, and the stark contrast chilled me to the bone. Once you were able to move past the layer of brown leaves and the overgrown stone path that used to be a driveway, the main attraction took your breath away.

The Victorian style manor was extremely out of place on an island of beach homes. Its majestic wraparound porch was warped by the destructive forces of nature, but it still looked to be intact. Ruthless vines of ivy were devouring the entire structure inch by inch, and the majority of the light gray paint had been peeled back from the exterior due to years of relentless salt, wind and sand.

Several dormer windows were perched on the third floor overlooking the dreary landscape. The suffocating darkness and mass of vines drenched the house in mystery; hiding its secrets from the world. It looked...patient. As if waiting for something. Or someone. I felt a gentle push from behind.

"Go ahead Stasia, you go first," Carmen urged.

"The only way I'm going in that house is if every person out here goes in with me." I stared at the drab, wooden front door that probably hadn't been opened in eighty years. "And even then, you might have to drag me inside."

"What's the big deal? It's just a house. Just because an entire family was gutted inside doesn't mean it's haunted." Ricker rolled his eyes.

"What are you waiting for, then?" Carmen mocked him with a raised eyebrow. "I mean, since it's not a big deal and all."

Sensing a shift of movement on the road, I glanced down and followed a sheet of sand sliding across the road before gathering at Phoebe's feet. I met her gaze and smiled sympathetically. I knew from my own sand experience how comforting it could be.

"Yeah, man." Ian stared at the house as if it would come alive at any moment. "That's all you."

"Ya'll are pathetic." Ricker shook his head and strutted toward the house with a purpose. Shaking out his arms and tilting his head back and forth like a boxer readying for a fight, he jogged up the front steps with confidence, turned the knob and disappeared into the house. We held our breath as we waited for him to reappear.

"See?!" He popped back into the shadowed doorway with a triumphant smile shining on his face. "Ya'll were getting all bent out of shape for no-" Without warning, he was yanked from behind by an unknown force; leaving us with only terrifying silence and the gaping hole of an empty doorway. Carmen started running first, but we all followed and made it to the door at the same time. Without hesitation, we crossed the threshold and were instantly swallowed up by the blanket of darkness within.

"Ricker!" Carmen screamed at the top of her lungs with obvious desperation and fear. Any apprehension I had about the house was wiped clean the second Ricker was attacked. Now adrenaline and determination were my only driving forces. The interior of the house melted together in a cacophony of dark shapes and shadowed doorways. The dust that settled across its depths was at least three inches thick and quickly collecting in our lungs. I grounded my feet, centered my thoughts and concentrated on the open front door. All I had to do was think about a large gust of air circulating through the house and it came to fruition. I closed my eyes, focused on the air and pictured it swirling through each room, over the walls, and around the corners; hoping to clear the dust.

"Remind me never to piss Stasia off," Ian whispered and I heard Phoebe snicker.

When I opened my eyes, the wind receded. What it left was a dreary (although dirt-free) vacant shell of a house void of any color. The darkness of night erased all ability to distinguish one room from the next as we feverishly searched for Ricker. We all had the same idea of turning on our cell phones to use as flashlights; careful not to step on any old, rickety boards that could end up hurdling us into oblivion.

"Ricker!" Carmen shouted into the empty house again; panic-stricken. A light scraping sound from the corner brought our attention back to a room I assumed was the library. Floor to ceiling shelves that had once held masses of books, now held spider webs and dead cockroaches. Thick, velvet tapestries muted the windows and a once elegant brass chandelier hung haphazardly from its base. As a figure stepped out from behind one of the long window dressings, we all gasped.

"Were you worried about me?" A crooked smile washed over the figures handsome features.

"Ricker!" The raw emotion in that one word almost tore me apart as Carmen flew across the room towards him. Relief, anger, happiness, and frustration were heavy in the two syllables making up his name. "What the hell are you doing!?"

"I figured it was the best way to get ya'll in the house," he retorted sheepishly. Tears had started to roll down Carmen's cheeks as she stepped up to Ricker and slapped him across the face.

"Scare me like that again and I'll rip you apart piece by piece."

"That's my girl," he murmured adoringly with a grin before his eyes dropped to the floor. "I'm sorry Carm, I didn't mean to scare you." She stepped even closer and the second slap I expected was replaced by a hug.

"It's a good thing you showed yourself, dude. Stasia was conjuring up the elements to hunt you down," Liam informed him with a chuckle.

"Finn would be proud," Ricker quipped with endearment before realizing what he'd said. My chest threatened to cave in on itself, shattering my heart along with it, but I pushed the feeling away and frantically tried to think of something else to talk about.

"Did you see any ghosts while you were hiding?" I forced a grin. Relief washed across his eyes and he smiled back.

"Spiders the size of Volkswagens and one massive cobweb," he chuckled. "Scariest moment of my life." He glanced at Carmen before correcting himself. "Make that the second scariest."

"Hey guys! Come look at what me and Ian found!"

Twenty-Nine

We gathered behind Phoebe in the dim hallway as she brushed her fingers over what looked to be a large, imposing oil painting in a gilded metal frame. As she worked, faces slowly began to emerge. A young girl with dark hair and small eyes. A lanky boy resting on a stool. A beautiful woman dressed in a ruffled smock. She uncovered two more girls, another boy, and a handsome older gentlemen standing behind his family.

"The Drake Family…" Phoebe breathed in fascination.

"They look…stuffy," Ricker commented; squinting his eyes and leaning in closer.

"Way back then people didn't smile for portraits or pictures. Think you could smile for an hour while somebody painted you?" Liam contested Ricker.

"Depends. Am I naked? I'd be smiling if I was naked." Ricker continued inspected the painting despite Carmen's light punch square to his stomach. He looked at her with his best sad, puppy dog eyes. "What?"

"Look at that little girl. She doesn't look too good," Ian interrupted thoughtfully.

"Maybe she was one of the girls who died," Phoebe surmised. The small-eyed girl was clearly emaciated; her clothes hanging limply on her slight frame.

"I can't believe he killed his family," I thought out loud while I examined Dr. Drake carefully. He could have been any normal middle-aged father from his time, with salt and pepper hair, a muscular build, and pencil thin mustache.

There was a hint of pride evident in his features as he gallantly held his wife's much more petite hand; furthering my suspicion of the events that resulted in his family massacre. A resounding thump came from upstairs and we all stared wide eyed at each other, trying to decide if we should run for our lives or go investigate. My feet were leaning heavily towards running away from the house as fast as possible.

"Probably just a mouse." Ian shrugged his shoulders, but his eyes widened when we heard an even louder thump directly above our heads. "A very, very big mouse…?"

"I'm outta here," Carmen muttered and took off towards the front door. We started to follow when a scream filled the house with terror. Carmen's scream. She was standing in front of the door; unmoving except for the shaking of her hands.

"What happened?" Liam called out to her.

"It just shut…" she started, paralyzing fear causing her to stumble over her words, "…by itself!"

"It was probably just the wind," Ricker tried to console her. She turned around to face us with a spark of madness in her eyes.

"There was no wind and I was nowhere near it. It just shut all by itself." She swung back towards the door with her mouth still hanging open.

"Well then we'll just open it back up. That's what they make doorknobs for." Ricker walked up to the door and grabbed the handle. There was a loud pop and his body was thrown backwards; crumpling onto the hard wooden floor. He stood immediately, dusted himself off and made a beeline for the same door.

"Ricker I don't think that's a good idea-" Liam started to warn him, but it was too late. He grabbed the doorknob and was sent flying once again; landing hard on the floor. Carmen back away slowly, cautiously kneeling next to him – her eyes fixed on the closed door.

"I am not in the mood to die tonight," she muttered under her breath as she helped him back up. I looked around for a window, but the closest one was back in what would have been the kitchen.

"Maybe we could open a window and get out that way?" My suggestion was met with stares of uncertainty, so I forced my legs to walk into the would-be kitchen to find out. The floor beneath my feet let out a low groan as I reached the center of the room. As if speaking to each other, the substantial wooden door to the kitchen slammed shut behind me and I heard a distinct click at the window. I ran over to the crumbling, pane window and attempted to wrench it open to no avail. The lock wouldn't budge and the stronger my fear became, the sweatier my hands turned. That definitely didn't help my already compromised dexterity skills. I ran back to the door and tried the knob. It wouldn't even turn.

"Hey! Let me out of here!" I pushed against the door and started jostling the knob as I hard as I could.

"Stasia?" Phoebe's surprised voice came from the other side of the door. And then with renewed panic as she also tried the knob with no luck. "Stasia!"

"The door won't open!"

"Hold on!" I heard her walk away, followed by mumbling as the group decided what to do. I scanned the bare cabinets and empty holes where an oven or ice chest would have been. When I glanced back towards the door, I cried out in unadulterated fear. Blood. Everywhere. It covered the door, the ceiling and the walls. I watched in quiet horror as a word was methodically etched across the wall in deep red.

Penance.

My lungs squeezed as panic wrapped around my throat and shattered my courage. "Get me out of here!" I screamed, and started banging on the door. "Phoebe!"

I listened intently but was only met by deafening silence on the other side of the door. Where did they go? Did they get out through the front door? Did they leave me? I quickly noticed that the word had disappeared, but the blood that stained the walls was now flowing down in earnest now; puddling on the floor at my feet. This wasn't real. This wasn't real. I closed my eyes and repeated it over and over. This wasn't real.

I steeled myself and opened my eyes, and with a momentary wave of relief I let out a sigh. The blood was gone. I twisted my head back and forth, hoping I wasn't just seeing what I wanted to see. I reached my hand out and lightly touched the door with my fingertips. Completely dry.

"Phoebe!" I yelled for her again, but was only met by more hair-raising silence.

"Murderer!" A deep voice boomed behind me. I twisted around and met the angry eyes of a handsome middle aged man. "You made me do it! You did this!" he boomed. I took a step back and fell against a cabinet. He was covered in blood. His hands, his white shirt, even his trousers were drenched in crimson. My heart was jumping out of my chest but I did my best to calm down and speak clearly.

"I don't know what you're talking about! I didn't make you-" I pleaded with him.

"You're lying!" he boomed again, moving closer. "You made me kill them!"

"It wasn't me! I promise – Dr. Drake - please!" I covered my head but no retaliation came. I peeked out to see his face contorted in confusion.

"Drake?" He stood straighter, seemingly deep in thought.

"That's... that's your name. I saw you. In the painting."

"I killed them." He stared at me, fascinated. "She wanted their hearts."

"Who did?" I asked, suddenly terrified.

"Get out." His features hardened and he backed away.

"But Dr. Drake-" I reached for him.

"Get OUT!" he yelled at me, and suddenly faded away.

"Phoebe!" I pressed my ear up against the door and tried to hear something, anything.

"Carmen, don't!" I heard Willow gasp, and the sound of bodies hitting the floor turned my stomach. Furniture scraped across the floor and I heard more scuffling.

"What's happening to him!?" I heard Carmen scream.

"Carmen!" I yelled out. "Phoebe!"

My response was more muffled yelling and thumps, followed by a shrill scream. Then I realized the blood was back; once again dripping down the door and walls. I moved away as it ran down the cabinets. Now trapped in the middle of the room, I couldn't escape the thick mass of red liquid.

"Scared of a little blood?" a voice mocked me. "Oh, boo freakin hoo."

"Nadia." I spun around and immediately ran at her; anger erupting through every cell of my body. "You're the 'she' he was talking about, aren't you?!"

"I needed some hearts," she shrugged with a smug grin. "Don't let him fool you – he was all too happy to mutilate his family. I just gave him a little push."

I glared at her in disbelief. She truly was evil. In a fit of rage I tried to tackle her, but she simply disappeared; causing me to land hard against the blood soaked wall.

"You're gonna have to do better than that," she snickered from across the room; crossing her arms over her black leather mini dress. "So, how's our handsome dark prince? Oh that's right. He lied to you. Broke your fragile little heart." She stepped closer and smiled. "You're welcome."

"When I become immortal, I will hunt you down...." I hissed at her.

She started laughing and shook her head at me in pity. "You really are a riot, Stasia." She moved closer to me and the evil tendrils began to seep from her skin and into the air. Her golden skin shimmered as her anger grew. "You won't make it ten minutes in the Underworld. And if you dare step foot in my river-"

"What, Nadia?" A streak of boldness shot through me as I stepped towards her. The fear that had encased me earlier seemed to melt away, giving way to a seething rage. "What are you going to do?"

Her honey eyes darkened at my challenge. "I wouldn't want to ruin your pathetic story by giving away the ending. Patience, dear girl. Patience,"

I stepped towards her again. "Let me go, Nadia."

"Funny how you keep saying that," she chuckled. "If you think you're such a badass, get yourself out." She smiled wickedly and promptly disappeared. I ran to the door and tried the knob before resorting to banging on it once more.

"Phoebe!" The silence I was met with sent a wave of panic through me. I had to think. I looked around for something solid to break the glass window with.

"Why did you do this to us?" I froze as two small girls stared at me with nothing less than pure hatred. Their beautiful green and blue dresses were smeared with blood, culminating on their chests.

"I didn't do anything!" I shouted. "She's controlling you-"

"Don't yell at my sisters." The deadpan voice of another child sent my mind reeling as I took in the emergence of two boys; one ghostly white and the other covered in blood like his sisters. They surrounded me and began backing me into a corner as they stared at me with menacing eyes and hateful sneers. Their bodies shifted and blurred as their anger grew.

"You have to pay," one of the girls hissed at me. In the back of my mind I knew Nadia was controlling their ghosts, but their horror of coming face to face with four dead children was too much for me to process.

"It wasn't me!" I yelled at them, but they continued their slow, methodical approach.

"Stasia!" I looked behind the dead children to see that Bianca had appeared.

"Bianca! Do something!"

"You're stronger than them! Use your abilities!"

My heart was beating out of my chest and I'd lost control over my arms and legs. I couldn't think straight enough to figure out what to do with my abilities. Frozen to the spot, I could only watch them advance.

"Bianca!"

"Say you're sorry," one of the girls demanded quietly. I thought I heard Nadia cackle from somewhere far away.

"Bianca!" I met her gaze across the room and saw she was crying.

"I can't! She's pulling me back! I'm trying to fight her...." I watched in horror as Bianca faded. Nadia's laughter began to fill my ears and I squeezed my eyes shut.

"Say you're sorry," the other dead girl repeated, louder and more forcefully; bringing my attention back to them.

"No!" I yelled at them, hysterical with fear. "Get away from me!"

"Then you must die," the sickly boy said plainly; producing a knife and plunging it into my heart.

Thirty

I was floating. It felt so effortless and peaceful, I could have sworn that I'd been airborne my whole life. The freedom was undeniably liberating and soothing. Well, except for that awful rushing sound. Why was it so loud? Not to mention, it sounded like it was coming from inside my head. But that couldn't be right. Maybe if I tried hard enough I could make it stop. Not only did my attempt not work, the rushing noise actually kicked up a notch. I decided to give up and resume my peaceful floating instead, as the numbness in my mind scrambled my thoughts and confused my memory. I couldn't figure out why I was floating or how I got here, wherever 'here' happened to

be. I decided to open my eyes. A blinding light pierced my sensitive retinas and I snapped them back closed immediately. The darkness was less painful. Darkness. A pair of bright blue eyes flashed in front of me and I smiled. They were a startling mixture of light blues and grays; captivating my every thought. They blinked and disappeared, and an intense sadness washed over me and knocked against my recently frozen heart.

I was so lonely. Empty. I wanted the eyes to come back. They brought warmth. Comfort. Happiness. He was the only one who could save me; bring me back to the whole person I once was. Now I was shattered; pieces scattered about, never to truly be complete ever again. The lines had been drawn. The damage was done. It was a cruel world, indeed, that would manifest the only cure from the very source of the pain and agony. I needed his touch, the warmth of his skin and the strength of his arms. I needed to hear his voice and see his heartbreaking smile. I desperately needed to feel the security his dark embrace always brought with it. He was my salvation as well as my inevitable undoing. In his capable hands my heart craved acceptance and love, only to be crushed beneath the pressure of his betrayal.

The dizziness took over and I squeezed my eyes shut. Next, I was sinking and finally…a lightness. I opened my eyes only an inch; anticipating the now familiar blinding pain that sunlight produced. But thankfully it was dark and the moon provided enough light to make out my surroundings. Four earth toned stone walls caged me inside, creating a perfect square. The walls reached impossibly high and allowed only a small view of the night sky above. No sounds penetrated its solid walls, but I could sense the ocean was near. I felt its promise of security calling to me. Where was I?

As my eyes adjusted to the shadowy features of my prison, I began to make out distinct shapes. A chest of drawers. A chair. A desk. A bed. A very comfortable looking bed. My tired mind and body ached to lie down and escape into the world of pillows and blankets that beckoned. Then I realized that the mound on the bed was moving. Immediately on the defensive, I held my breath and pressed against the wall nearest to me. When the mound of covers didn't sit up or make a noise, I relaxed slightly but still kept my eyes fixed on the bed. I heard someone breathing. Were they sleeping? I tiptoed carefully to the side of the bed and peered over at its contents. At least eight pillows protected the sleeper from the stone wall next to the bed, and a fluffy white down comforter blanketed the bed's owner.

As curiosity won over logic, I carefully moved the covers back to where I assumed a head should be. I found a foot instead, and the roughness and size told me it belonged to a guy. The leather anklet holding four black beads told me exactly which guy the foot was attached to. Finn. I jumped back and clamped a hand over my mouth to prevent any hysterical sobs from breaking loose. Monstrous tears immediately blinded me and continued to roll down my cheeks as I allowed my eyes to release the feelings I couldn't vocalize.

Not realizing the toll my restraint was taking on my body, my legs failed beneath me and I slid to the floor. I leaned against the cool stone wall, taking deep breaths and crying for what seemed like hours. Finally the tears subsided to a slow trickle and I was able to get to my knees. Unbeknownst to me he had wrenched back the covers during my breakdown; revealing his bare torso and painfully handsome face. The need to look into his eyes was comparable to a punch in the gut, taking my breath and causing me to collapse back onto the hard floor. The desire to crawl in the bed with him and wrap myself up in his body shattered my heart again and again.

I held my breath as he mumbled something in his sleep. The tenor of his voice reverberated through my soul and I lifted myself back to my knees; allowing my eyes one last guilty pleasure. I knew it would hurt me later tenfold to even entertain this moment of weakness, but the void in my heart yearned to be filled; even if only temporarily.

"Stasia…," I heard him mumble, bringing back the tears in earnest. Holding back the sobs, my entire being became numb with pain. Too weak to resist, I reached out and touched his hand ever so tenderly. Still asleep, he moved his hand to lie on top of mine, filling me with an instant and overwhelming joy. I let it consume me and warm my heart. Eventually my eyes grew heavy and tired, so I rested my head on the mattress beside his arm and closed my eyes.

"I think she's waking up," a voice said; sounding very far away.

"Give her a little room. She'll be confused when she regains consciousness."

"Why is she so pale?"

"Her energy will soon be restored. As soon as she wakes up, her body will begin the regeneration process immediately." I didn't know who they were talking about, but it didn't sound too promising.

"I hope so…."

"Stasia, honey?" My stream of random thoughts perked up at my name. "It's time to wake up now." Wake up? Why in the world would I want to do that?

"Stasia?" Willow! I tried to open my eyes, but the brightness scorched them and I squeezed them shut again. I struggled to move, which immediately brought on extreme pain and pressure. This was quite unfortunate. I couldn't imagine that never moving again was a viable option. I realized I was lying on something grainy and warm. Sand? Was I on the beach? Why was I on the beach? I attempted to open my eyes again, and amongst the piercing flashes of light, I saw several faces peering down at me with concern.

"Somebody turn off the lights. They hurt," I heard myself say; still feeling somewhat detached from my body. Somebody snickered, and I remembered getting perturbed at whoever it was that found fifth degree burns on my corneas to be humorous.

"You can keep your eyes closed, but I need you to tell me how you feel," said a voice I couldn't quite place.

"Am I in my body?" my voice asked mechanically. I heard hushed, panicked whispering. Then the voice spoke again.

"Yes dear. Did you leave your body?" she inquired gently.

"I went to see Finn," my voice said and I felt my mouth turn up into a smile. I heard several gasps and more hushed whispering.

"You're back now. You're okay now," she consoled me. I just wanted to remember whose voice was speaking to me. She sounded so familiar! The next time I squinted my eyes open, the light didn't hurt as much, and I was able to see flashes of white sand and deep blue water dancing in front of me, along with a collage of faces. Phoebe. Willow. Carmen. Liam. Natasha. Natasha?

"Natasha?" I croaked my thoughts out loud and tried to lift my head. A sharp pain shot through my body without warning.

"Yes dear. I'm here."

"Oh, good." The sharp pain receded into my chest and I laid my head back down with a thump. I immediately thanked the sand for being so soft. A light pulling sensation was my answer, and the pain in my chest disappeared altogether.

"Where am I?"

"We brought you to the Fortunate Isle. You needed the Isle's essence to heal your body." Natasha explained.

"Heal? Am I hurt?" I asked, completely perplexed. No wonder I was in pain.

"You were stabbed, but we got to you in time. The Isle's water has healed you to a point where your own cells will be able to regenerate."

"Stabbed?!" I tried to sit up but quickly reminded by another jolt of pain the reason I was lying down in the first place.

"Easy, trigger," Carmen chuckled. Somebody stabbed me? The little boy. The two little girls. As the memory came slamming back, so did the excruciating panic.

"Those kids-all that blood-Is everybody okay?" Panic clenched my stomach.

"Shhh...you need to rest. We'll talk about it later." Later. For some reason 'later' seemed like a luxury I didn't have, but I couldn't remember why. Not feeling up to searching my memory banks, I closed my tired eyes and fell into a dreamless sleep.

The next thing I knew, I was being carried. A soft wind flowed along the bare skin of my legs and my senses reveled in the decadent smells of sage and lavender. Without fully opening my eyes, I could tell it was twilight. The absence of bird calls, the cool breeze, and an odd sense of just…knowing were my only clues.

I also sensed something else. A recognition. A welcoming. I could feel the energy of each tree. Each shrub. Each small animal foraging. They stilled as we travelled by; acknowledging our presence. Or was it just my presence? Something else whispered to my heart and soul. The jewelry lying against my skin warmed slightly, and a frenzied energy began to race through my veins. Both of my traces warmed and I knew. I was home.

"I don't see a house," I heard Carmen announce.

"You're correct. But that doesn't make it any less real, child," Natasha answered wisely.

"So, do we do a dance? Say a chant?" The corner of my mouth lifted in response to Phoebe's questions.

"Maybe we should ask the future Goddess who's pretending she's still asleep," Willow snickered. Damn.

"I'd really like to see you guys do that dance," I retorted softly; immediately surprised at how much better I felt. My chest reflected a dull ache, but it was only slightly uncomfortable. I knew the island was healing me, and one dip in Thetis's estuary would fix me right up. I knew about the magical qualities of the water on the Isle because it healed me the last time I was on the brink of death. Apparently I was making a habit out of that these days.

"As would I," the voice of the person carrying me said. Liam? He was just as strong as Finn; supporting my weight effortlessly as we stopped in front of the intricate wrought iron gate.

"Stasia! It's your trace!" Willow exclaimed as she ran up to the gate.

"Careful, Willow," Natasha warned and then turned to Liam. "Move Stasia closer. The house will feel her essence." Liam carefully stepped forward inch by inch with a slowness that made me giggle.

"It's a house, not a volcano. It's not going to hurt you." I smiled up at him. I looked to the right and took in the same meadow I'd seen the first time I came to the Isle, spreading out before us just past the gate. Then I remembered the lightning. I guess that could technically hurt us. Maybe I spoke too soon. I felt my trace burn and the gasps told me the house had appeared. No dramatic entrance, no natural disasters or lightning. One second it was invisible and the next, a sprawling, majestic home stood before us. Unlike the last time I arrived, the home and surrounding gardens were immaculate. The mangrove trees still dwarfed the manor with their size and stature, but nothing could compare with the home's beauty. Not even the gardens overflowing with the colors of autumn displayed by the mums, goldenrod and Russian sage.

"That's unbelievable," Liam muttered in amazement.

"So it recognizes her?" Carmen asked with shock swiftly spreading over her dark features.

"That's right," Natasha confirmed. "She awakened the island, as well as the house, the first time she arrived."

"Wow," I heard Willow breathe.

"I think I can walk now," I informed Liam. He gently tilted me forward; allowing my feet to land softly on the grass below. As soon as my feet hit the ground, the frenzied energy rushed through me like an electric current. I closed my eyes and sighed with happiness, then pushed open the ornate gate crawling with ivy and led everyone down the stone path. The sandstone exterior of the house shaded with the warm colors of sunset set my heart on fire. Its gothic majesty wasn't lost on my roommates, who were still gawking like it was their job. As I stepped onto the first step leading towards the door, it clicked automatically and swung open slowly.

"You better say it's supposed to do that." Carmen narrowed her eyes at me suspiciously.

"It's supposed to do that," I snickered back at her. As we entered the grand parlor, my focus fell on one thing only. The fountain. Namely the estuary that lay hidden below the fountain. And it was calling to me. As everyone else scattered around the room to appreciate the many wonders it held, I walked straight to the fountain. I stood on the edge and peered down into the shaded water below. It was also fairly dark in the house as well. Before I could complete the thought, several lights including the crystal chandelier hanging over the staircase flared to life. I could definitely get used to that.

"You better say it's supposed to do that," Carmen hissed at me from behind Phoebe, whom she'd jumped behind in a brief moment of fear.

"I honestly didn't know I could do that." I smiled widely at her, enjoying the connection I had with the house. It was almost as if it were an extension of myself.

"What are you doing?" Phoebe asked curiously just before I stepped off the ledge of the fountain; submerging my body in the soft, healing waters of the estuary. I automatically took a deep breath of water and marveled at the warmth it sent through my body. It was dark, but I could still see relatively well...so I wasn't expecting what happened next. The algae on the walls of the underwater cavern began to emit a blueish glow, illuminating the underwater room with an ambiance of magic. My trace shimmered blue right along with them and I continued to swim in circles, enjoying the feel of the water gliding over my skin.

"Hello, dear. I see you've found your mother's favorite hiding place."

I whirled around at Natasha's soft voice to see her descending from the fountain with a nostalgic glow lighting up her face. Her flowing black pants and lacy top danced in the water as she swam to me.

"You can breathe underwater, too?" I asked, completely shocked. She smiled at my surprise.

"I have an affinity for killer whales," she explained. "Therefore I have the ability to breathe underwater." I thought about what she said and tried to wipe the utter disbelief off of my face. I didn't know why it was so surprising - Finn could breathe underwater, and it would only make sense that his mother could as well. I was still trying to figure out how one would come to the conclusion they had an affinity for killer whales when I registered her first comment.

"Did you know my parents well?" I questioned her.

"Yes. Your mother was a brilliant leader and your father was a loyal, loving husband; he was the foundation of her strength and happiness. They loved you very much. They would be proud of you, Anastasia." She touched my arm. "I know I am."

As I allowed her endearing words to touch my heart, I remembered Finn's betrothal. The walls of my heart slammed shut and I twisted away from her.

"Why are you here?" I said harshly.

"Your friends brought you to my house last night when they found you in the kitchen. They knew I could help," she explained with concern.

"Last night?" Anxiety clutched my chest. "What's today?"

"Today is November first."

"That means…"

"You will need to leave for the Underworld at midnight." As if that realization wasn't enough, it would also be Finn's eighteenth birthday. The day of his fight. The day he would be betrothed to Nadia. I spun around to face her again, anger spreading through my veins.

"Why didn't you tell me Finn was betrothed?" I spit at her with venom in my voice; instantly feeling guilty. But I deserved an answer. I had trusted her! I thought she cared about me. I waited as she took a deep breath and her features settled into sadness. It seemed like she had aged considerably since the last time I saw her. Being the mother of the future Prime must take its toll on a woman.

"It wasn't my secret to tell, Stasia," she answered calmly; instantly infuriating me.

"Apparently it wasn't anyone's secret to tell, since I had to hear it from Nadia!" I yelled, exasperated.

"I am so sorry, dear." She reached for me but I swam farther down into the cavern; running my fingers over the fronds of kelp to calm me down. Several of the massive seaweed stalks swayed in my direction and I allowed them to wrap around me, comforting me and showering tiny electrical currents across my skin. Natasha kept her distance, but I wasn't done talking.

"And now it's too late. Tomorrow is his birthday." Tears burned in my eyes and I let them melt into the surrounding water. "It's too late."

"Finn is very wise. He does nothing without forethought and careful consideration. I trust he has a plan." She swam closer. "He loves you." Her words only succeeded in eliciting an onslaught of sobs as my sadness pulsed through me. I wiggled out of the seaweed as she gently hugged me and I pulled her close; craving a supporting touch. She let me cry for several minutes before she pulled away and met my eyes. The dark red stone around her neck glistened and seemed to catch fire in the blue light of the algae. It was magnificent.

"It was a gift from Finn's father, Charon." She smiled lovingly and grasped it in her hand.

"It's gorgeous. What kind of stone is it?"

"Fire agate. It represents the Underworld." Fire agate. That was the stone hidden within the black onyx Finn had given me, and the same stone hanging from Nadia's necklace. Now it made sense why it would act as a beacon for anyone who knew its meaning. Bianca said it would call to Nadia. Finn said it would act as a beacon for my mother in my reveries. What else could it do? Would Charon also recognize the black onyx and fire agate stone Finn had given me? The possibility of bumping into Charon while I was in the Underworld did little to make me feel better.

"If Charon is in the Underworld, how do you ever get to see him?" I asked her curiously. Talk about a long distance relationship. Then something else occurred to me. "And how is that possible? Doesn't your soul have to be connected to the Underworld in order for you to be married?" She patted my hand and smiled.

"You are correct, but Charon comes and goes from the Underworld at will. He visits often. Secondly, there is much you do not know about me. I am a descendant of Hecate, as was my mother. Hecate is a Goddess of the Underworld, so I am connected to the darkness. I am also connected to the sea, as my father was a Tyde."

"But…Hecate? Wasn't she technically a witch?" What we read in History class painted a picture of dramatic displays of sorcery and witchcraft.

She chuckled at me. "She is the Goddess of magic and witchcraft, so I suppose she could be classified as such." This was one of the most fascinating things I had ever heard. Descendant of Hecate and a Tyde? She was the ultimate double threat.

"So what kind of abilities do you have?"

"I have a connection with all herbs and plants, as well as the moon. I have the ability to work enchantments."

"Like a real witch!?" I blurted out.

"Technically, yes - although the term 'witch' is fairly recent in the history of the world. In its rawest form it isn't the hocus pocus you see in movies. I simply call upon the elements to assist me. Very much like yourself."

"Wow." I was utterly impressed.

"My connection with the moon, along with my Tyde heritage, allows me to manipulate the ocean tides as well."

"Wow." For some reason that was the only word I could say. Suddenly it made perfect sense as to why she would be able to help me reach the Underworld. The anxiety I carried with me for a month lessened slightly and I felt safe in her capable hands.

Suddenly, I remembered the other items I'd planned to bring with me on my journey.

"My valise! I need it-"

"Willow made sure we had it before leaving Lorelei. It awaits you, along with several changes of clothes that she also packed for you," she explained. Relief flooded my system, followed by fear.

"So…how long do I have?" I asked apprehensively.

"Five hours," she said plainly. "I have everything we will need."

"To kill me?" I squeaked.

"Technically, yes," she confirmed. I could hardly contain the bile that fought its way up from my stomach, threatening to force its way out. Noticing my discomfort, Natasha linked arms with me. "You should be feeling almost back to one hundred percent, yes?"

"Except for the permanent panic that's taken up residence in my chest, I'm great," I told her sarcastically

241

with a smile. My entire body did feel incredibly strong, and my mind was revitalized as well.

She laughed and her cool blue eyes turned comforting; reminding me of another set of eyes. "Everything is going to be fine, dear. Let's head back up and make sure your friends haven't gotten lost in this mansion of yours."

After pulling our wet bodies and clothes out of the fountain, we met four sets of wide eyes staring at us in confusion. I shook my hair out and took the towel Natasha offered me.

"Hidden underwater cavern," I disclosed simply.

"That's it. I'm moving in." Carmen put her hands on her hips. "I am in love with this place."

After changing into the dry leggings and t-shirt Willow packed for me, we gathered in an upstairs loft overlooking the gardens that cascaded down the wide expanse of the back yard. Two large couches and one loveseat faced the ceiling-to-floor windows that covered one side of the room. We feasted on the three bags of chips Willow brought from our suite as we discussed the events of the night before.

"So you didn't actually see any ghosts?" I asked them in disbelief.

"We could tell something had taken hold of Ricker, but we never actually saw anything. Well, besides the furniture flying around the room. We definitely saw that." Carmen shook her head in disbelief.

"I can't believe he broke his arm." I shook my head. At some point during the scuffle, a table lifted on its own and was launched at Ricker. When he shielded himself from it, his hand took the full force of the blow; snapping the bones of his forearm. Ian was currently nursing Ricker's bruised and battered body back at Lorelei.

"Did you see any blood running down the walls or anything?"

"I don't think so," Phoebe answered as she stuck her arm in a bag fishing for chips. Her eyes widened and flickered up to mine. "Why? Did you?"

"It was everywhere," I whispered, remembering the horrifying scene.

"I still can't believe you got stabbed....by a ghost." Willow looked close to tears. "We should have been there for you."

"You wouldn't have been able to get in. Nadia made sure of that," I huffed.

"When we got the door open, we just saw you slumped over on the floor with blood all over you. We still don't know what that little bastard stabbed you with," Carmen complained. I thought back to the knife I saw in the small boy's hand right before he tried to kill me.

"It was a knife," I told them, my tone weary. "They thought I was the one that killed them."

"They?" Phoebe squinted at me.

"I saw all of them - Dr. Drake...his children..." I rubbed my temples. "Nadia made him do it. She needed their hearts."

"For what?" Phoebe gawked at me.

"I have no idea. All I know is that she is pure evil."

"You'd have to be to force a father to kill his entire family and rip their hearts out." Carmen agreed with disgust.

A buzzing sound had Liam pulling his phone out. "Oh wow," he muttered as he read it several more times before looking up at us with wide eyes.

"That was Ricker," he announced solemnly. "Apparently, Priscilla's body was found this morning near campus." We all looked at each other as he confirmed what we were all thinking. "She's dead."

"Dead?" I gasped.

"Are they sure?" Phoebe sat up. His phone buzzed again and he took a moment to read the text.

"There doesn't look like there's any foul play. It must have been a heart attack or something."

I was leaning toward the 'or something' possibility. Although the prospect of Priscilla never harassing me again was tantalizing positive, I had a very bad feeling Nadia had something to do with her demise. If she decided to steal Priscilla's soul, the crime scene would show no foul play. Her soul would have been snatched cleanly from her body.

"Wow," Carmen breathed. "I mean obviously, I'm not her number one fan, but nobody deserves to just keel over dead like that."

"The police are investigating what happened, but Ricker said everyone on campus is coming up with their own theories," he informed us with a shake of the head.

"You don't think..." Willow met my gaze and I knew her thoughts were running parallel to my own.

"I don't know. It sure is a huge coincidence..." I started.

"She might be waiting for you in the Underworld. Maybe this is all part of her 'Ruin Stasia's life' plan." Carmen shrugged her shoulders.

Liam, who had been thoughtful since Ricker's text, stood and began to pace. He looked very beach prep, wearing khaki linen pants with an untucked white button down shirt. He was chewing on his bottom lip, and his tense body language told me something was on his mind. Something important. He glanced at me several times before stopping in front of me.

"I need to tell you guys something." He sighed and gestured for Natasha to come back in the room and sit down. "It's about Finn."

Thirty-Two

"What is it, dear?" Natasha spoke softly, but her blue eyes were now swirling with intensity. A paralyzing panic took my body captive while we waited for Liam to continue. He stared at Natasha for several seconds and then glanced at me again.

"Finn confided in me several weeks ago," he began with downcast eyes. "He was adamant that our conversation stay between just the two of us. But as things have become increasingly complicated and I'm beginning to understand the magnitude of his decision, I need to tell you."

"Is he okay?" Natasha prompted. Liam nodded and I felt her breathe a sigh of relief beside me.

"He has decided," Liam paused and took a deep breath, "to deny his destiny as the future Prime; exiling him from both the Sons Order and the Underworld."

A moment of shocked silence passed as Natasha's hand flew up to her mouth and she just shook her head back and forth. Willow, Carmen and Phoebe were speechless, and I was so confused by what I just heard, I couldn't reconcile his words. Deny his destiny? Deny the one thing he'd been preparing for his entire life? Why would he do that? Why would he give that all up? Nadia. As my blood began to boil, I quickly found my voice.

"Is this Nadia's doing? Is she making him do this?" I yelled at Liam frantically. I clasped my shaking hands together tightly and forced myself to think straight.

"No," Liam whispered.

"No, what?" I urged. How could she do this to him!? She would have to answer to me. She would not get away with this.

"He's not doing it for Nadia." He held my now irate gaze with intensity. "He's doing it for you."

Natasha let out a gasp as understanding washed over her features. Unfortunately that understanding wasn't reaching me. Why would he give up his destiny for me? I would never ask that of him!

"But…why?" As my legs began to shake as hard as my hands, I stumbled back to the couch and sat down in a heap of nerves.

"It's the only way he can be with you," Natasha responded for him; tears collecting in her eyes.

"But I would never ask him to do that! He can't deny the one thing he's worked his entire life for! It's who he is!" I screamed at them as they all stared back at me; still in shock. A war began to rage between my heart and head. My heart rejoiced at the sacrifice he was willing to make to be with me, but my head was screaming at me to stop him from ruining his life. It just wasn't right. He couldn't give up everything. Not for me. Didn't he lecture me about the weighty responsibility we both had to lead and protect our Orders? Didn't he explain how many people were counting on us? And he was willing to throw it all away. For me.

"When was he planning on doing it?" Phoebe asked Liam slowly.

"He's planning on announcing his denial during his fight tomorrow night," Liam told us and Natasha gasped again.

"But he can't!" I cried as my opposing emotions clashed; each fighting for attention. I wanted to be with him more than anything, but I wasn't willing to sacrifice his destiny. Not for me. We'd figure out another way. There had to be another way.

"He can. And he fully intends on going through with it," Liam declared.

"Natasha, please don't think I want this-" I started to plead with her.

"My dear, true love is a strong force. It is the one thing in this world that's stronger than fate." She faced me as tears rolled down her cheeks. "Once set in motion, it is unstoppable."

I put my head in my hands. I had to find a way to stop him. Unable to sit down any longer, I stood and walked out of the room; drowning in my own thoughts. My feet took me to the fountain. Not wanting to ruin another set of clothes, I sat down on the ledge and dangled my feet in the water.

Could it be true? Was Finn willing to give up everything just to be with me? Guilt crashed into me, knocking the breath out of me and sitting wholly on my shoulders; causing them to slouch forward with grief. Maybe if I'd given him more time to explain…maybe if I didn't make him feel so bad…maybe then he wouldn't have felt that he had no other choice. That was when it hit me - this was his only choice. He knew there was no other way. But the difference was that it wasn't my only choice. I would find a way around this. I wouldn't let him throw away his destiny. The Sons needed him, and I knew he would never be whole again without his Order. Without the connection to the Underworld. Without his father. My heart shriveled and threatened to shatter at my last thought. I knew what it felt like not to have a father, and I wouldn't let Finn live like that.

"You are worth it."

Natasha climbed onto the ledge of the fountain and sat down beside me.

"No I'm not. I could never take the place of his Order, his destiny, his family…" My voice broke on the last word and I choked back a sob. Natasha put a comforting arm around me and sighed.

"There is a way-"

"I'll do it," I proclaimed immediately.

"Hear me out, dear." She patted my hand. "It isn't that easy."

"I don't want easy. I want possible," I assured her.

"Persephone, the Queen of the Underworld, wasn't always connected to the Underworld. She became connected after she-"

"-ate a pomegranate from the grove," I finished for her. She nodded gravely.

"It connected her...but it also trapped her," she continued, as her eyes searched mine to ensure I understood the gravity of this new possibility. "Forever."

"So, eating a pomegranate would connect my soul to the Underworld, therefore allowing Finn to be with me," I connected the dots. A bubble of hope began to grow in my heart and I laughed out loud. "It's such an easy fix! I'll just have to find a way to take a pomegranate from the-"

"No, Stasia." She placed both hands on my cheeks, forcing me to focus on her next words. "Don't forget the most important part. You would be connected to the Underworld, because you would be trapped there."

My hope bubble sprung a leak and deflated into a limp, worthless fraction of its former self. I could eat the pomegranate that would forever connect me to the Underworld and allow me to be with Finn...only if I gave up my own destiny. Another slice of anger cut through my heart and I faced Natasha.

"This isn't fair, Natasha! I love him! Who cares if I don't have a connection to the Underworld!" I threw up my hands in frustration.

"The decisions of the Queen affect us all, Stasia. But she is the Queen. Once decided, her choices cannot be challenged. She will not hesitate to punish those who stray," she explained ominously.

"Just because she's pissed off about her own past, she wants to ruin everyone else's?" My voice rose as the helpless feeling burned inside of me. "Where's the decency in that?"

"She is very bitter, and she is very powerful. That is a lethal combination. And one that must be respected."

"I want to go now," I declared through gritted teeth.

"There are two more hours until midnight," she said gently. "It is best to-"

"I don't care what's best!" I lashed out at her, immediately regretting it and lowering my voice. "I have to do something. I can't sit around and stew on this for two more hours. There's too much at stake. Please Natasha," I pleaded with her. She searched my eyes and let out a breath.

"As you wish. But you must promise to follow my instructions without fail. It is vital to the awakening once your soul is ready to return." I nodded. Suddenly my own death seemed insignificant and petty compared to the all-consuming anger that now coursed through my body.

"Once your soul separates, you will realize right away it is much different than a reverie," Natasha disclosed. "The link between your body and soul will be almost non-existent. When the link between the soul and the physical body is severed, the universe strives to scatter the energy and re-allocate it elsewhere."

"Does it do that to body-less souls? The ones who have really died?" Phoebe asked curiously.

"No. Once the body dies, the soul goes through a slight transformation. Its energy is no longer of use to this realm," she explained to Phoebe quickly, and then turned her attention back to me. "It will feel as if you are literally being pulled from every direction. It can be very strong at times, but don't panic. You are strong enough to resist it. The essence of who you are at your core is the one thing that will prevent the re-allocation of your energy. If you center yourself and continue to look inward, you'll be fine."

"How will I find the entrance to the Underworld?" I seriously doubted that a neon OPEN sign would be blinking in Persephone's window. Although that would be extremely helpful.

"The Underworld will find you."

"Let's say the Underworld is taking the day off-" I began, but quickly shut my mouth when Natasha sent me a look that told me this was not the time for jokes. It was an automatic self-preservation mechanism that I couldn't seem to shut off. Thankfully Carmen spoke up.

"And this serum. You know for a fact it works?" she asked Natasha cynically from her seat beside me on the couch.

"I would not allow anything to enter Stasia's body that was not fail-proof." The dark tone blanketing Natasha's voice prevented anyone from arguing with her.

"Then I'm going with her."

"What?!" My head jerked over to Carmen in the hopes that she had momentarily lost her mind. Unfortunately, her unwavering gaze met mine and I knew that trying to talk her out of it would be pointless.

"I'm going. I don't care what you say." She raised an eyebrow at me; daring me to challenge her.

"Me too," Phoebe declared.

"No!" I pleaded. "This is too dangerous!"

"I'll stay here with Natasha and Liam to help protect your bodies," Willow offered; confessing to me that this plan had already been decided upon behind my back.

"Liam, please talk them out of it." I sent him an imploring look.

"I know from personal experience, it's always beneficial to surround yourself with the people who love you the most." Well he was obviously no help.

"He has a point," Natasha conceded.

"You're willing to risk an eternity in the Underworld...for me." I stared at them and waited for them to start laughing and tell me they were just kidding. They had to realize how ridiculous this sounded. What if their souls didn't make it back? They would be trapped forever!

"Yes, I would not hesitate to risk my life for you," Carmen proclaimed seriously.

"Ditto," Phoebe said as she put her hands on her hips. A wave of relief washed over me and I threw my arms around Carmen. Phoebe hopped up from the loveseat and joined the embrace. Tears were streaming down my face as I sat back and struggled to understand why everyone in my life was willing to risk everything for me. It was just ludicrous! But the relief was so great, I had no more argument left in me. To have two of my best friends with me on my journey was more than I could ever ask for. The hard truth of the matter remained at the forefront of my mind, however. The stakes had just gotten much, much higher.

Thirty-Three

"I feel like we're starring in some Syfy movie about a handsome devil of a man who genetically alters peoples' bodies for kicks."

"You watch way too much late night television, Phoebs." Willow laughed at her dark imagination.

"I can promise you there will be no body altering on my watch," Liam humored her, as Natasha continued to make sure we were comfortable. All three of us were lying on three tables that we gathered from around the house. We had pillows and blankets, but I wouldn't say 'comfortable' is how I would ever describe laying on a table. Natasha and Liam needed to be able to get to each of us in order to check our bodies' serum levels while our souls were in the Underworld. Willow was sitting patiently in an arm chair watching Liam's every move. The crease between her forehead and the worry in her eyes made me uneasy. Although I was still more than ready to do this, I was having doubts about my ability to pull it off.

Natasha produced three surgical needles and a large vial of cloudy, cream-colored liquid and handed them to Liam, who began to measure out the initial doses. Phoebe, who had been entertained by her own imagination moments before, was watching him with a look of pure terror. I could tell her hands were shaking as she proceeded to bite off every nail she had. Liam inserted the needle of each syringe into the vial of liquid and pulled out a specific amount; lying it down on a tray before moving to the next one.

"I think I'm gonna be sick," Phoebe forced out; promptly hopping off the table and running to the bathroom. Willow followed after her and I shared a nervous glance with Carmen. I was on the verge of having an anxiety attack myself. It wasn't long before Phoebe was back, looking only slightly pale. She forced a smile and climbed back up onto the table.

"So tell us more about how the serum works," I urged Liam; hoping to calm our nerves if we had more information about what would be happening in our bodies. As Natasha gathered gauze and alcohol, Liam sauntered over to us.

"Your parasympathetic nervous system, housed in the medulla of your brain, slows your heart rate naturally by releasing a chemical called acetylcholine," he started to explain.

"Let's try that again, but in English this time," Carmen insisted, and Willow giggled from her chair. Liam chuckled and glanced shyly back at Willow.

"The serum will begin by slowing your heart rate down to five beats per minute. A normal heart rate is between sixty and one hundred beats per minute."

"Wow," Phoebe breathed.

"Consequently, your breathing will slow to a rate almost unrecognizable by even an RPM machine." We stared at him blankly and he grinned. "Respiratory Profile Monitor. The serum basically tricks your brain into believing your body is dead. However, it doesn't allow it to send the signal to your organs for them to shut down. So your body will be doing a balancing act while you are gone; teetering on the brink of actual death. We will monitor the serum levels to maintain the correct percentage." Phoebe's face immediately drained of all color.

Liam handed the syringes to Natasha as she added, "Once your body reaches the minimum level of heart and breath rate, your soul will easily detach; also believing the body is dead. When you return, the force of your soul reconnecting will literally awaken your body."

"If we return," Phoebe corrected her shakily.

"When you return." Natasha raised a dark eyebrow at her and proceeded to give us our instructions. "Now I need you all to lie back and try to relax while we inject the serum."

"Oh yeah, 'cause that sounds about as relaxing as a bathtub full of acid," Carmen muttered. I heard Natasha snicker as she wrapped an elastic band around my bicep; restricting the blood supply so she could find a good vein. I'd seen nurses use the same technique while taking blood. She inserted the long slender needle into the crook of my arm with expert precision and a tiny prick, and then slowly emptied the creamy liquid into my bloodstream. It was colder than my body temperature and I felt it as it spread through my arm, up my shoulder, and into my heart. While Natasha tended to me, Liam administered the serum to both Phoebe and Carmen.

"So how long does it take for this stuff to kill us?" Carmen asked impatiently.

"Anywhere from ten to twenty minutes," Liam answered. Carmen narrowed her eyes at me and Phoebe.

"If you get there before me, you better wait. I'm not going gallivanting around the Underworld all by myself."

"I'll be the one hiding under a rock," Phoebe whispered and let out a nervous giggle.

"Let's go over a couple of things before you begin to lose consciousness," Natasha instructed while cleaning up the supplies. "You have the map?"

"Safe and sound," Phoebe answered, patting her pants pocket. Willow had made an index card-sized replica of Finn's Underworld map for me to take on my journey. Phoebe was now tasked with keeping it out of harm's way.

"And Stasia, you have the dagger, the black onyx balefire, and the piece of rope," Natasha confirmed. Something told me I was still missing something important.

"Hey Willow, will you grab the white stone out of my valise? I think I want to take that with me too," I requested.

"White stone?" Natasha's interest piqued.

"It's just a stone I found at a shipwreck site on the Outer Banks." I shrugged.

"Have you figured out what the piece of rope is used for?" she inquired.

"Not yet, but it can't hurt to bring it along."

"Very true," Natasha agreed. Willow came back in the room and handed me the white stone. Natasha materialized beside my table.

"May I see?" She brought the stone up to her face to get a good look at it. "Moonstone."

"Moonstone?" I'd never heard of a moonstone before.

"It may indeed come in handy." Natasha grinned knowingly and handed it back to me. "It helps in the foretelling of the future, as well as enhancing intuition."

"That's either a crazy coincidence or you were meant to find that," Phoebe commented. I rolled the stone back and forth in my palm. It was definitely curious that I would find a random moonstone in the middle of the ocean.

"Now girls, I need you to listen to me very carefully." Natasha sat on the edge of Phoebe's table and made eye contact with each of us separately. "You must avoid any fruit you find in the Underworld." Her intense gaze paused when it reached me. "And you must not drink from the River of Forgetfulness, no matter how thirsty you may be."

"I think we can handle that." Phoebe nodded dutifully. Natasha's features turned solemn as she continued.

"When it is time to return and you find yourself at the Gates of Horn and Ivory, there are two things you must remember above all else. Do not give in to your fears and do not lie to yourself."

"That sounds simple enough," Carmen retorted, but I could see the unease in her dark eyes.

"I agree that it should be simple, however the soul is a self-serving entity at its core. Pride and insecurity can always lead us off our true path. The key is accepting the bad that haunts our souls, as well as the good. We all have both within us."

As she spoke the last sentence, I realized that the serum was beginning to take effect. I was feeling a little woozy and I could feel my reflexes and movements slowing considerably. I looked over at Phoebe and Carmen, who looked to be having trouble focusing on Natasha as well. All I wanted to do was close my eyes and go to sleep.

"I think it's working," I warned Natasha.

"My mind seems to be slowing down," Phoebe added.

"That's nothing new," Carmen quipped, but her words came out slurred. I gave in to the heaviness and allowed my eyes to close on the only realm I'd ever known.

People say that when you have a near death experience, your life flashes before your eyes. I can say something flashed before my eyes during my more-than-near death experience as well, but it was only one image. Deep blue eyes. They stared into the recesses of my soul, shining with acceptance and love. They swirled before me like a kaleidoscope; making me dizzy. As they returned to a stationary position I noticed they had gotten tremendously closer. I couldn't see any other features. All around them was only darkness. As I focused on the light blue and gray flecks within them, I became completely absorbed in their magic. Suddenly I found myself being sucked into them; speeding faster and faster towards the stormy sea of dark blue. As I plunged into their depths I felt myself being stretched and pulled in several directions. I instantly fought to center myself, which was easier than I thought it would be. The blue disappeared and was replaced with a warm, soothing darkness, and then...there was nothing.

My feet were wet. And cold. I looked down to see myself standing in the middle of a river. Metallic-looking rocks and imposing boulders lined the banks as the silvery water rushed by in a steady cadence. There was no grass, no trees and no shrubs accenting the sides of the river. Only the massive boulders surrounded by smaller river rocks; a wide array of bronze and copper tones glittering beneath the water. The banks of the river were covered in a shimmering white substance that appeared to shift and blur as my eyes moved across it. The sky above was a golden yellow hue, but there was no warm sun shining down on me. I craned my neck in each direction, but it didn't appear the light was coming from one particular source. It seemed to reflect and bounce off of everything it touched; enhancing the metallic qualities of the landscape around me.

A dense fog flanked both sides of the river, not allowing as much as a glimpse into what lay ahead in either direction. I wasn't sure if I should move or stay where I was. In the middle of contemplating my next move, a slender ribbon of silver twisted and hovered beside me. I held my breath and immediately froze in hopes of not antagonizing it. A flash of memory took me back to a previous reverie I had before I came to Lorelei and stumbled upon my destiny. Finn had been surrounded by hundreds of silver ribbons (right before they attacked me) and he told me I shouldn't be there; that my heart wouldn't survive. Had my soul somehow jumped realms without my knowledge? Was that even possible?

Before I knew what was happening, the single silver ribbon began to writhe and lengthen; becoming more opaque. Still holding my breath, I watched wide-eyed as it began to take human form. It almost looked like…Carmen? No way. Right before my eyes, her features became more distinct and she opened her eyes. She glanced around skeptically and finally looked down at her feet.

"Why are we standing in the middle of a river?" she complained, although I continued to be in shock at what I had just witnessed. She met my startled gaze. "What?"

"Whoa," was all I could say.

"What is it? Is something wrong with me? Am I missing a body part?" She began to frantically look herself over, running her hands over her face. I let out a hysterical giggle.

"Not at all, I seriously just saw-" I began.

"What the hell is that?" she interrupted in a low voice, staring at something to our left. When I followed her gaze I saw another silver ribbon appearing. We watched in silent awe as it writhed, became opaque, and took on human form; eventually turning into the Phoebe we knew and loved.

"Oh. My. God," Carmen croaked.

"Why are we standing in a river?" Phoebe looked at us in confusion. "And why is Carmen staring at me like that?"

"We just watched your soul appear and turn into human form," I explained.

"That's what that was?" Carmen looked at me wide eyed.

"I believe so." I grinned at her.

"Did you guys go through the tunnel?" Phoebe exclaimed with elation.

"Tunnel? No, I saw some kind of-" Carmen began, when she lost the ability to talk. What could only be described as a shockwave travelled across the river and right through us, knocking us slightly off balance and taking our breath away. When I looked back at the bank, I noticed the fog had disappeared. Something else had taken its place.

It was surreal in its majestic appearance. There were no words to accurately describe the beauty of what stood before us. Its massive trunk was the thickness of four Cape Lookout Lighthouses pushed together, and stood at least twenty stories high. Only the bottom portion of the canopy was visible to us standing so far below, but the mass of branches and lush green spread out for at least a hundred yards on all sides. It emitted a brilliant inner light, spreading throughout its entire length, down to each leaf. That was when it hit me. I had seen this tree before. In Nadia's mind.

It was the last image I saw when I accidentally accessed her memory. It was mesmerizing in her mind's eye, but it was beyond belief in real life. As with everything else, it had a metallic quality to it. The trunk was dark copper and the leaves, although green, shimmered with an effervescent frosting.

"The Forbidden Tree," Phoebe whispered as she studied the pocket-sized map of the Underworld.

"Is that where the entrance is?" I inquired.

"It looks like it." She squinted at the paper. "But I can't tell exactly where."

"Well there's only one way to find out." I smiled and took the first step towards the Underworld. We carefully made our way across the river and over several boulders before reaching the bank. The white I saw was a soft layer of silt that shimmered and blew around our feet as we walked toward the Forbidden Tree. It was extremely soft and reminded me of the sand on the Fortunate Isle.

It didn't take long before we were almost beneath the massive branches looming high above. The only sound was the river at our back and a slight humming that seemed to be coming from the tree. Along with the humming, the tree smelled sweet and intoxicating. I took a deep breath. It was a cross between sweet mint and basil leaves that filled your senses and lifted your spirits. I tilted my head back and scanned the lower branches for any fruit, namely pomegranate, but I only saw foliage. I hoped this wasn't the only tree it might grow in, considering how high up they would be. Despite Natasha's warning, I had every intention of taking a pomegranate back with me. I couldn't let Finn throw his life away. If I had to eat it to convince him of that, then so be it. We would worry about the nuances of my being trapped in the Underworld forever at a later date. There had to be a way around it.

We painstakingly tiptoed around the trunk; anticipating that the ground would split and swallow us whole at any moment. The white silt beneath our feet turned to a dark rust color as a large forest of trees came into view up ahead. Far from the massive size of the Forbidden Tree, they were much smaller in stature and more like the trees back home. The only difference was the same metallic tones that were becoming a common theme.

"Does everything look metallic to you guys, too?" I asked.

"I was just thinking the same thing," Carmen agreed, nodding her head.

"It looks like somebody spray painted everything with Rustoleum," Phoebe added.

"Maybe we should do that to our suite when we get back." I smiled at them and we continued toward the forest of trees.

"We'll start with your bedroom." Carmen smirked at me.

"What's that?" Phoebe pointed up ahead. "It's not on the map…"

"It looks like…a bridge?" I strained my eyes to focus on the odd shape up ahead.

"I think it's another river," Carmen guessed, "and the bridge is how we cross." Unfortunately as we continued, it became painfully obvious we wouldn't be crossing something as mundane as a river. We stopped several yards away and gawked at each other in disbelief. A wide chasm divided the terrain we currently stood on from the land on the other side of the bridge. The gigantic fracture was about one hundred yards wide, and straddled by a rickety bridge no wider than three feet.

"Stay here," I instructed as I gathered my courage. "I'm going to go take a look."

"Not a problem," Carmen retorted without taking her eyes off the giant crevice. I walked closer; sweeping my eyes along the landscape just in case. As I approached the edge of the divide, a bout of vertigo swept over me and I found back nausea as I peered down below. There was no end to its depths. The bottom was not visible, so it eventually faded to nothingness. I looked to my left and right, searching for a different route, but it stretched as far as I could see in both directions. The bridge was our only option. Feeling defeated, I jogged back to Phoebe and Carmen; a full blown panic attack building in my stomach.

"What did you see?" Phoebe squeaked as she bit off what was left of her nails.

"It's so deep I couldn't see the bottom," I sighed. "And our only option of getting across is the bridge."

"That bridge?" Phoebe squeaked again and glanced over her shoulder at it.

"That bridge," I confirmed solemnly. Her fear was definitely warranted. The bridge looked miniature in comparison to the massive black hole it crossed. It also had no support beams or suspension cables, even though it reached so far into the distance. I was hoping they were invisible. That's what I told myself, anyway.

"Do you think Persephone will be on the other side of it?" Phoebe struggled to read the map. "Those trees should be part of her grove."

"Let's just concentrate on not falling to our second deaths for right now." Carmen wiped her forehead and looked at her wearily. "We'll worry about Persephone later." Phoebe tucked the map away and nodded her head in determination.

"Here goes nothing," I muttered. The shakiness in my legs increased with every step I took. And that was not conducive to crossing a giant crack in the earth on a tiny bridge. We slowed when we reached the entrance of the bridge, and Phoebe and Carmen shot each other a terrified look. I stepped up first, but as I noticed the large gap in between the wooden slats that made up the bridge, my feet were having second, third, and even fourth thoughts. A strong wind blew continuously from below and I pulled my hair back into a ponytail.

"Just hold on really tight," Phoebe suggested gently.

I looked back at them one last time and gradually placed my hands on the rope-like railing. The first step was the most difficult. The second and third were slightly easier, but 'easy' was definitely subjective in this type of situation. I did my best not to focus on the black emptiness beneath my feet, hoping to prevent a misstep or catastrophic loss of balance. I made it about five yards before calling back to Phoebe over my right shoulder.

"It actually feels pretty sturdy!" I steadied myself once again and continued.

"Okay! I'm coming out!" Phoebe yelled back. I made sure not to turn around and look, for fear of losing my balance. The other side seemed a lifetime away and my still-shaking legs reminded me of the anxiety that pulsed through me.

"Come on Carmen!" Phoebe hollered at her from behind me.

Not hearing a response, I automatically looked back to make sure Carmen was alright. A wave of vertigo hit me again and the entire world tilted sideways, making me dizzy. I instantly dropped to my shaky knees and placed a death grip on the railing.

"Stasia! Are you okay?" Phoebe called out to me.

"I think so," I tried to yell back. Thankfully, I was able to see Carmen stepping onto the bridge before the vertigo hit, so I forced myself to concentrate on simply placing one foot in front of the other. Not able to see behind me, I couldn't tell how far I had gone. I fought the urge to find out as each step seemed to take a lifetime.

After about twenty more excruciating minutes, I neared the end of the bridge. With adrenaline moving me forward and fear fixing my eyes on what appeared to be a stone square platform up ahead, a shower of relief hit me when I stepped over the last wooden slat of the bridge. When both of my feet made it onto the stone platform attached to solid ground, I collapsed to my knees. The stone sparkled with flecks of silver and bronze; captivating me. I had to shake myself mentally to divert my attention back to Phoebe and Carmen.

Phoebe was farther along than I had expected, so she made it to the platform not long after I did. We both watched anxiously as Carmen stalled several yards from us. Her dark features were pale, and when she looked up briefly I recognized the terror flashing in her eyes. I got to my feet and carefully walked to the end of the bridge.

"You're almost there, Carmen. Just a little bit farther. You can make it," I urged her gently.

"I'm kicking your ass as soon as I make it off this thing," she threatened.

"As soon as you're off this bridge, you can do anything you want," I snickered; appreciating the extent to which she and Phoebe were willing to go for me. "Just keep walking."

"Careful what you ask for," I heard her say under her breath, but she began to move forward again. Several minutes later, she extended her hand and I pulled her towards me and the stable platform. Instead of attacking me as she had threatened, she wrapped her arms around me and squeezed tightly. I tried to calm her when I noticed she was shaking uncontrollably.

"Thanks Stasia." She grinned at me and winked. "I wasn't sure I was going to make it. Turns out I just needed something to look forward to."

"Look forward to, indeed."

We all gasped and twisted around in the direction of the velvety sound of her voice. She stood tall and regal mere feet away from us on the same platform. Although there was no sun in the Underworld sky, the angelic woman standing before us was pretty close to it. As with the sun, it almost hurt your eyes to look directly at her. She had a golden, ethereal glow that dulled everything around her in comparison. Thick golden hair was braided down her back and what looked like actual strings of gold were woven through it. Flowing white fabric was wrapped haphazardly around her body and secured around the waist with a thick gold band. Her bare arms were adorned with countless gold bangles and a massive yellow gold pendant hung from her neck. A heart shaped face held full lips and perfectly straight nose. When I met her gaze, my entire body froze. She had Nadia's piercing golden eyes.

"Persephone," I breathed unwittingly.

"It would appear the Day of the Dead is upon us." She inspected each of us individually; her golden eyes seeing much more than our physical appearances. "You have come to fulfill your essence," she stated simply, and my heart skipped a beat. I hadn't been expecting her to know who I was. I raised my chin slightly and stood up straight.

"Yes," I proclaimed with dignity.

"Antiquity trace," she commented; clearly intrigued by my newest addition. "Very interesting."

Her curious gaze did not deter the excitement I felt at finding out what my trace stood for.

"It's a pity your parents wanted nothing to do with you," Persephone provoked with a conspiring gleam in her eye.

"You and I both know that was not the case," I shot back; assuming if she knew who I was, she had encountered my parents when they were killed and came to rest here. The corner of her mouth lifted ever so slightly as if I had passed some kind of test. I noted that there were no smoky tendrils swirling around her body. Maybe it was only her daughter who was filled with pure evil.

"It still remains to be seen if their many sacrifices were in vain," she challenged me with a smirk.

"I don't have to prove my worth to anyone." I held her gaze. "The fact that I'm here should suffice as your answer."

"Stasia..." I heard Phoebe hiss behind me in warning, but I held my stance easily. I refused to let anyone doubt my integrity, especially not a jaded, bitter queen. Unfortunately for Phoebe, her warning only diverted Persephone's intense deliberation onto her. Phoebe visibly squirmed under her powerful stare, but Persephone only smiled.

"A muse; so innocent and naïve," she declared softly. Her expression quickly changed from a smile to a sneer as she shook her head in disgust. "Love is such a fickle thing. Don't expect it to last. He will inevitably become bored and move on to someone else. They always do." As Phoebe shrank back in horror at her words, Persephone moved her piercing stare to Carmen.

"A protector," she labeled her and then narrowed her eyes. "And very hard to read; a strong spirit. Too strong. You often become blinded by it."

"Strong is a good quality," Carmen carelessly defended herself.

"Strong is a prideful quality," Persephone snapped at her, and then lowered her voice quickly. "But one I can appreciate."

She returned her overwhelming gaze to me as I began to grow impatient. Not knowing how much time had already passed, I was anxious to continue. She stepped towards me and her golden eyes became stormy and defiant.

"I deny you admittance," she announced with venom. The finality of her denial caught me off guard, but I soon recovered and took a step towards her with renewed confidence. Ending my journey at the entrance was not a viable option.

"That's not good enough," I countered with conviction. She moved closer still and grinned wickedly at me.

"And why do you propose I step aside and allow you entrance, young Goddess?"

"It's the right thing to do," I affirmed.

"According to whom?"

"Every day I wake up is a day I've fought for. Every mistake, every laugh, every tear and every sunrise - I've earned through years of abuse and pain. I carry those memories with me as a reminder of who I am and what's truly worth fighting for. And if you aren't able to see that, I'm afraid your soul searching talents are highly suspect."

Her now shining eyes met my gaze and her beautiful features softened. In that brief moment, I felt her darkness. Slightly chilled around the edges with a glowing warmth within, it reached out and enveloped me. The next second it disappeared and she straightened.

"You are bestowed admittance."

"I think I need a change of pants," Carmen testified.

"Eww. Spare us the details," Phoebe attested, making a face. After Persephone allowed us entrance, she immediately vanished. No goodbye, no good luck, no nothing. It was more than a little unsettling, and the anxiety-related nausea churning in my stomach reminded me that I had just held my own against the Queen of the Underworld. I didn't know I had that in me! I shook out my hands as we continued along a winding path that, according to the map, would lead us through the groves. I hadn't realized I'd balled them up throughout the exchange with Persephone until a stinging on my palm alerted me that my fingernails had broken skin.

"Between the 'bridge-o-death' and our little chat with the Queen of the Damned, I've decided I should carry a gun at all times; whether it's to defend myself or to put myself out of my misery," Carmen rambled on nervously. "It's a win-win situation, really."

"I don't think a gun would do much against Persephone," Phoebe reminded her.

"That's not going to stop me from trying. At least I'd go down fighting," Carmen declared. I slowed when I recognized the trees on my left.

"Pomegranate trees," I said under my breath.

"What'd you say?" Phoebe asked as she followed my gaze.

"I just...those are the same kind of trees that were at the Sons' Cimmerian Ball," I alleged. "Remember? They were around the dance floor."

"Oh yeah, I do remember that now." She grinned dreamily at a memory only she could see. As we moved forward, I noticed just how peaceful and serene the Groves really were. The fragrant aromas of the flowering trees made a convincing case that we were simply strolling through a lush garden; enjoying a nice Saturday afternoon. Unfortunately, the otherworldly metallic shimmer of every tree reminded me just how far we were from nice Saturday afternoons and lush gardens.

"How much further do we have to go before we make it to Charon's Marsh?" I consulted Phoebe. She inspected the map, glanced around briefly and then folded it up carefully; tucking it away in her pocket. Carmen and I stared at her as we waited on her answer.

"I have no idea," she shrugged.

"What do you mean you have no idea?" Carmen argued, and held out her hand with impatience. "Give me the map." As we all hovered over the not-to-scale mini map, we could only speculate as to how far into the Groves we had travelled. We knew we were headed in the correct direction, but it could be another ten minutes or an hour for all we knew.

"Let's pick up the pace," I instructed. After we jogged what felt like another two miles, the rust-colored dirt of the path began to harden and shift to a charcoal-like black dirt and we finally came to the edge of the Groves.

"Charon's Marsh should be straight in front of us," Phoebe surmised. We wearily stepped off the Groves' convenient path and noticed the Underworld had begun to transform into a darker, more menacing landscape as the Groves shrank behind us.

"I think this is it," Phoebe said as she inspected the map once more. We came to a stop at a place where the dirt under our feet met a line of tall grass. A dense fog hovered above the marsh, masking its true size; the lack of color creating a lackluster feeling in my soul. Although there were patches of grass as well as shrubs and tall weeds that surrounded the marsh, they were all variations of bronze, silver, and black. Even the water of the marsh appeared to be dark as midnight as it lay completely still; hiding immeasurable secrets of its own. The rush of what I guessed to be a waterfall was the only sound besides our own labored breathing from running. The most disconcerting aspect, however, was the smell.

"Why does it smell like a Bath and Body Works store when we are clearly in hell?" Carmen articulated my own thoughts with a terrified sheen in her dark eyes. The soothing fragrance of wild honeysuckle and cherry blossoms filled our senses, which was a direct contrast to our dismal surroundings.

"Maybe it's coming from one of the other parts of the Underworld, like the Elysian Fields or the Asphodel Meadows? Finn said they were considered to be like heaven..." Phoebe brainstormed.

"I think you might be right, Phoebs." I smiled at her, thankful she had been paying attention when Finn explained the map. I had been too busy trying not to pass out the whole time.

As directed by Finn several weeks ago, we took a right and followed the banks of the marsh. I couldn't fight the feeling of extreme isolation that hugged tightly at my fickle nerves. Persephone was the only being we'd met thus far. Not that I was necessarily chomping at the bit to meet any tortured souls (or even sprightly souls) - but still.

The constant roar of the waterfall continued getting louder the farther we walked, but we were straining to see anything through the fog. Knowing we were getting close to the River Styx, a ball of jitters manifested in the pit of my stomach. I was almost one hundred percent sure Nadia would be lurking near the river she was connected to, eagerly awaiting the opportunity to ruin my chance of completing my essence. It was only a matter of time. I looked at Phoebe and Carmen with regret as I remembered what I hadn't told them yet.

"There's something I haven't told you guys yet. Nadia is, in fact, a river nymph." I continued hesitantly, "The River Styx is the river she's connected to, so there's a pretty good chance she'll be here somewhere."

Watching for their reactions, I was taken by surprise when Carmen burst into a fit of giggles. Phoebe's green eyes darted towards me with worry written all over her face.

"Carmen?" I addressed her apprehensively. Maybe this place was getting to her. She stopped laughing long enough to focus her wild eyes on me.

"Of course!" she exclaimed; throwing her hands up and flashing a deranged smile at me, which was emphasized by the maniacal look in her eye. "Of course it's her river! This is wonderful!"

"Carmen..." Phoebe tried, but Carmen didn't hear her.

"I was just saying to myself: What would make this diabolical journey even more exciting? The wicked Princess of the Underworld, that's what!" She clasped her hands together with joy as Phoebe and I shared another concerned look.

"Come on, Carmen, let's keep moving," I urged her. "We'll deal with Nadia if we have to. Until then, we'll stay on course."

"But I want to see her!" she pouted. To mine and Phoebe's dismay, she began to call for her at the top of her lungs. "Nadia! Nadddddiiiiiiaaaaaa!"

Phoebe immediately clamped a hand over Carmen's mouth and delivered a stern message in a hushed whisper. Carmen nodded her head obediently and Phoebe carefully released her.

"Let's keep going," Phoebe advised gravely as she clutched Carmen's hand and pulled her along.

Finally we came upon an imposing hill dotted with bronze boulders, pockets of silvery clover, and an array of loose, golden pebbles. We climbed the hill with laborious slowness; weaving in and out of the multiple rocks and avoiding smaller boulders that just our weight could dislodge and send rolling down the hill. Carmen had grown especially quiet and reluctantly followed Phoebe's lead, and I was getting more and more worried about her deteriorating mental state. I couldn't tell if she was in shock, or just couldn't digest everything that was happening. Either way, I hoped we could snap her out of it before it was time to go back. I would never forgive myself if Carmen became trapped here.

As Phoebe and I worked together to heave Carmen over the crest of the hill, we noticed that we were unexpectedly facing a wide river of angry, black water. Unable to discern the riverbed, I had no idea how deep it was or what challenges waited beneath. The torrent was so powerful, it dislodged several large rocks while we looked on and quickly carried them downstream. Suppressing my fear and keeping a keen eye out for Nadia, we continued following the riverbank until the roar of the waterfall could no longer be heard.

"Oh my God, Stasia, look!" Phoebe clamored, and pointed excitedly across the river. My mouth dropped and tears instantly sprang to my eyes. What lay across from us brought only one word to mind: 'Paradise'. Its effect on me was immediate and overpowering. I had the strange impulse to negotiate the river's violent waters in order to immerse my soul in the euphoria that waited just on the other side.

From our position on the bank, the vibrant colors were shockingly intense. I took in the bright flowering trees, fields of golden wheat, lush orchards, and what looked to be a cluster of shimmering buildings that all appeared to blur and shift when I looked directly at them. Shadowy forms in the distance drifted lazily back and forth, as if enjoying a walk in the park. The intoxicating aromas we smelled earlier were slightly stronger, and it was clear now where they had been coming from. I was utterly mesmerized by its beauty and I knew without a doubt that we were looking at the Elysian Fields; the place where the divine souls reside.

I could sense it far better than I could actually see it. Just as I'd felt the warmth of darkness, I could feel the cool breeze of divinity. It washed over me like a summer rain shower; cleansing and revitalizing my soul.

"The Elysian Fields..." Phoebe exhaled.

"It looks like Candyland!" Carmen's hysterical giggle brought me back to reality. I wrenched my attention away from the wonderment in the distance and focused on the reason I came - the river. I scanned the landscape, still surprised we hadn't encountered Nadia, but found something almost as disturbing. Lining the banks of the river was a thick mass of intertwining vines. The gleaming white hue of the vines created a daunting barrier between me and the raging waters. They were the very same vines that spiraled around the lightning bolt of Nadia's menacing trace.

Assuming that nothing was what it seemed in the Underworld, I had a disturbing feeling that the vines were not to be underestimated, especially since I would have to wade through them in order to reach the water. According to Finn's instructions, I had to submerge my body in the river and allow it to take me downstream, over the waterfall, and into the marsh. Although the river's current was much faster than I expected, the part that involved my body falling over a large waterfall was what was creating a precise pain in my temple.

I returned my attention to Phoebe. "After I'm in the river, take Carmen back down to the marsh and wait for me there."

"What if you get into trouble?"

"If I'm not out in thirty minutes, you and Carmen should continue to the Gates without me and get out as soon as you can."

"No. I'm not leaving you." She frowned at me in disagreement.

"You have to take care of yourself and Carmen. I'll be fine." I placed a comforting hand on her shoulder.

"You should listen to her, Phoebe," a cynical voice responded. Her slight frame stood amongst the white vines; a smug look on her young, angelic face.

Bianca.

"Bianca?" I whispered in bewilderment. "But…"

"But what?" she raised her eyebrows at me.

"You aren't allowed to be here."

"It would appear the rules don't apply to me." She shrugged and flashed a devilish grin. Although she wore the same blue dress, all traces of blood and gore had been erased. Her shy, timid persona had been replaced with a confident, aggressive imposter, but the clearness of her voice was evidence that Nadia was not influencing her.

"You always were the favorite," crowed another voice. We spun around to see none other than Priscilla standing to the other side of us.

"Priscilla!" Carmen cheered joyfully. "Look guys, she's not really dead!"

"Carmen, be quiet!" Phoebe hissed. I shifted my baffled gaze back to Bianca and struggled to comprehend what was happening.

"You know each other?" I asked Bianca incredulously.

"Don't you see the resemblance?" she cross-examined; matching my incredulous tone. I looked over my shoulder at Priscilla and then back at Bianca. How could I have been so blind?

"Cissy," I muttered in disbelief. Bianca was a Siren…just like Priscilla. Bianca died twenty years ago, but if she were still alive, she would be about Priscilla's age. A thick cloud of dread hovered above me as understanding hit hard. Priscilla was the twin sister Bianca had spoken so fondly of.

"You didn't really think I hadn't stayed in contact with my own twin sister, did you?" she mocked me as she pouted with feigned compassion. "Oh...you did."

"You lied to me," I accused her, still in shock. Her betrayal cut deep.

"You made it so easy! You wanted to believe I was scared of Nadia. You wanted to believe I was lost. You wanted to believe I was your friend."

"Quite presumptuous, if you ask me," Priscilla cackled.

To my surprise, Phoebe spun on her heel and snarled at her, "Nobody asked you."

"I am only loyal to Nadia." Bianca looked past me and winked at Priscilla. "And my sister."

"The monster who stole your soul?" I questioned her faulty logic.

"There's a monster?" Carmen whimpered in a child-like voice, before Phoebe silenced her with a harsh look.

"She didn't steal it." Bianca glowered at me. "She saved it. She takes care of me."

I turned my questioning gaze onto Priscilla; still wondering how they couldn't see Nadia for what she truly was. "And what about you? Did Nadia 'save' your soul as well?"

"Not all of us can be as amazing as my sister. I strove to be what Nadia expected of me while I was alive, but she believed I would be more useful in my soul form. And she was right." She beamed; proud of herself. 'Delusional' apparently ran in the family.

Keeping her green, calculating eyes on me, Bianca meandered out of the vines and drifted closer to Phoebe and Carmen. I noticed Priscilla advancing on me; strategically trapping us in the middle. I kept the conversation going and tried to figure out what to do. I had no idea what type of weapon would work against body-less souls. If they were already dead, how could I kill them? But if Nadia simply stole their souls, did that mean they were actually dead? Too bad there wasn't an instruction manual to go along with the Underworld. Then another thought came to me and I narrowed my eyes at Priscilla.

"What about the Sirens? Are you not loyal to Keto anymore?"

"Who do you think brought Nadia to Lorelei in the first place?" Priscilla hissed at me. "Keto chose me to help Nadia!"

"Of course she did," I muttered; my tone heavy with sarcasm. Inside, my blood reached its boiling point. Keto wasn't as noble as she led me to believe. She wasn't going to wait until I was immortal to challenge me. Instead, she brought in reinforcements…Nadia being the supreme choice.

Priscilla moved even closer. "They will both be quite pleased when I tell them we've gotten rid of not only you, but two other annoying Tydes as well!" At this, I stepped towards her.

"Leave them alone!" I demanded through gritted teeth. Priscilla nodded at Bianca, who immediately closed her eyes, opened her mouth and began to sing. Although I had heard a Siren's song before, Bianca's was unlike anything I'd ever experienced. The seductive notes were impossible to ignore as they wrapped around me like a vice grip and filled my mind to capacity. I instinctively centered my energy and pushed the song out of my mind and as far away from my body possible. Unfortunately, I knew Phoebe and Carmen were still completely vulnerable. When her notes reached several octaves higher, Carmen collapsed in pain. Phoebe quickly followed; clutching her ears and writhing in agony.

"Stop it!" I shouted at Bianca, at the same time Priscilla wrapped her arms around me. I twisted at the last moment; ensuring she didn't get a solid hold on me. I was able to free my left arm, and I punched her as hard as I could in the stomach; causing her to loosen her grip. I pushed her off of me and ran at Bianca. Her deep green eyes opened with the speed of light; shining with vengeance and welcoming my attack. Her image blurred as she continued to sing and I was knocked down by a pulsing shockwave that exploded though my mind and scorched my eyes. Thrashing on the ground, I squeezed my head in an attempt to rid myself of the painful spasms. Smaller shockwaves now pinpointed the front of my brain; severing all activity and paralyzing me. Still fighting past the insufferable sharp pangs, somehow I managed to open my eyes and shuffle onto my hands and knees. I began to crawl towards Bianca at an agonizingly slow pace as the screams of Carmen and Phoebe became more desperate.

The air was suddenly knocked out of me when Priscilla's foot connected with my stomach; sending me crashing over on my side and gasping for breath. As Priscilla pushed my shoulder down and prepared to hit me, I bent down and wrapped my shaking fingers around the handle of my dagger. My trace quickly warmed at its proximity, but the aquamarines and diamonds felt cool in my palm as I unsheathed it from my boot. Waves of energy and calm determination shot up my arm and into my heart; helping me push out Bianca's unrelenting shockwaves and throw Priscilla off of me. I scrambled to my feet and she tried again to grab me from behind. I spun around on her and sunk the dagger into Priscilla's shoulder with a quickness that surprised even me. She screamed and released me before crumbling to the ground.

Bianca suddenly stopped singing when she saw Priscilla on the ground, squeezing her shoulder in anguish. Her deep green eyes became inflamed and a fierce anger took over her features. I noticed a light layer of smoke tendrils lifting from her transparent skin. Evil personified, just like Nadia. As I watched Bianca advance on me, I spotted Carmen and Phoebe lying motionless on the ground in my peripheral vision. When Bianca reached me, the anger in her eyes changed to a burning hatred and the smoky tendrils immediately grew in height. Before I could move, she tackled me to the ground and slammed my skull against it; muting my senses and sending a black cloud of numbness around the edges of my vision. Pulling power from the stones of the dagger's handle, another surge of white hot energy coursed through me and I successfully pushed the darkness back. She slammed my head into the ground a second time, and then produced a smaller knife from her dress pocket.

I caught her wrist as she swung it down towards my chest with fury. I struggled to shove the knife away from me and inadvertently met her frenzied gaze. Her lips lifted into a vengeful smile and out of nowhere, an idea hit me. As I held her gaze, I concentrated on centering my energy and reached out to her mind. Just as I'd hoped, her smug expression morphed to shock as a litany of images flashed before my eyes. A tall woman with flowing blonde hair. A young boy smiling and laughing happily. Her own body covered in blood. Nadia's face. A younger Priscilla running alongside her. Nadia lashing her with some kind of glowing whip. My own face, confused and terrified.

"Get out!" she yelled, as she snapped her eyes shut and recoiled in an attempt to rid her mind of my spying eye. I took the opportunity to rip her off of me and roll on top of her. The dagger in my hand warmed as I held it above her, prepared to plunge it into her chest. I was met with the frightened eyes of a young girl; vulnerable and defenseless.

"Please Stasia, don't send me there! Please!" she screamed in terror.

I faltered as her fear washed over me, and a momentary pang of sympathy stalled my anger. With her features returning to the young, innocent face of a girl, I hesitated a second too long. When I started to pull my dagger away from her, she laughed demonically and stuck her knife into my stomach. Pain exploded from the newly formed wound and my rage returned with a vengeance; strengthened by the added layers of betrayal. I lifted the dagger easily and brought it down into her chest.

"No!!!" I heard Priscilla scream behind me. Bianca's eyes closed and she quickly began to fade below me. Her form shrank from a human one to the familiar thin ribbon of silver, which appeared to then be sucked up and away towards an unknown source. I held a hand over the bloody cut in my abdomen and struggled to stand. Priscilla was doing the same, but with the intention of attacking me again. As blood began pooling in my palm and running down my arm, I stumbled over to Phoebe and Carmen, who were still unconscious.

"Phoebe! Carmen!" I shook them frantically. Phoebe finally groaned and made an effort to open her eyes when I felt it. A prickling cloud of cold, aching evil wrapped its tendrils around me and tightened; slicing my skin and yanking me down to the ground. I struggled against it, but only succeeded in cutting my skin further.

"I'm really getting tired of you." Nadia materialized beside me and glared down at me as I lay helpless on the ground. Her eyes flitted up toward Priscilla with icy hate. "And you."

With a flick of her hand Priscilla screamed, sank to the ground and began to fade. As her soul morphed into a silver ribbon, she followed the same path as her sister and disappeared from sight. Nadia muttered something with irritation and then faced me once again. Her honey eyes flashed and her skin and hair sparkled of the purest of gold. It was more apparent than ever that she was connected to the Underworld. The evil tendrils floated off her skin, which alluded to the firing inferno burning just below the surface. She wore a tight bronze skirt with a flowing white blouse that highlighted her golden skin. She shook her head disparagingly at me.

"I suppose if you want something done right, you have to do it yourself." She glanced at Phoebe and Carmen, rolled her eyes and growled, "Get up."

With another flick of her hand, they were swiftly hoisted to their feet; instantly regaining consciousness. I watched as Phoebe's anger began as a slow simmer within her narrowed eyes, and then roared to life when she attempted to move and couldn't. I froze in fear as the white vines at the bank untwisted and slithered towards my roommates. Shaking myself mentally, I struggled against the tendrils that held me down while the taunting vines curled around their legs, torso and arms with painstaking slowness. Carmen receded further into herself and looked on in eerie silence. Phoebe struggled against the death grip of the vines, but Nadia only succeeded in looking bored.

"Leave them alone!" I yelled at her. "They don't have anything to do with this."

"You did this." Her eyes sparkled with madness and her words caused a memory to resurface. "This is your fault. You killed them."

"No!!" I screamed. Nadia just smiled and flicked a finger at Carmen and Phoebe. Instantly, the vines tightened and cut off their ability to breathe. Carmen's eyes bulged while Phoebe continued to struggle.

"Carmen! Phoebe!" I called out to them, feeling utterly helpless and inadequate as my roommates were strangled to death in front of my eyes. Nadia glanced down at a non-existent watch on her wrist.

"Time to go," she claimed, as if we were simply late for an appointment. She flicked a finger at the vines again, which promptly lifted Phoebe and Carmen off the ground. I felt myself also being lifted as the evil tendrils continued to slice through my skin. "I'm taking you where you belong."

She brushed her hair off her shoulders, smirked at me in victory and snapped her fingers. "Hell."

Thirty-seven

Silence. It precedes many things. The punch line of a joke. The deafening boom of fireworks. A much deserved standing ovation. But for us it preceded a terrifying experience that we would never, and could never, forget. The moment Nadia snapped her fingers, we were transported somewhere that no nightmare, no fear, no dark corner could ever compare with. It truly was Hell: Tartarus.

"Stasia?" Phoebe whimpered quietly next to me.

We found ourselves standing on parched soil that was blacker than black; staining everything it touched. Our clothes were quickly covered in the suffocating soot and I felt it collecting in my lungs. Nadia and her evil vines had disappeared, but the relief I should have felt was easily trumped by my sinister surroundings. The wasteland of Tartarus seemed without end or reprieve. But it wasn't the scenery that had my heart squeezing with horror. It was the inhabitants of the wasteland around us.

Suspended at least twenty feet off the ground in every direction were thousands of tormented souls littered the landscape; held captive not only physically, but emotionally and spiritually as well. I focused on one in particular closest to us. From the churning red haze of the sky, a thin rope of fire was attached to a gold shackle encircling his neck. From the ground, a similar rope of fire stretched upwards and secured his ankles. Both ropes were pulled taut, leaving him suspended indefinitely.

As I took in the countless other souls imprisoned in the same way, I could feel something resembling evil, but unlike Nadia's smoke, it was much less organized. It felt more like a boiling madness that pressed against me; poking and prodding to wiggle its way in. I pushed it away and envisioned my mental barriers so I could think straight. I also felt an overwhelming hopelessness that threatened to suck the energy out of me.

"Phoebe, don't move," I warned her in a low voice; unsure as to what would happen if someone or something figured out there were three new residents.

"Make them stop screaming!" Carmen yelled at the top of her lungs; thick with agony. She gripped her head and squeezed her eyes shut; crouching down to her knees. "Make them stop!"

I glanced at Phoebe, who was attempting to comfort her with a pained expression. The screams of the souls were apparently lost to us. I could see their grotesque mouths stretched open as they struggled against their binds, but all I heard was silence.

"Why don't we hear them?" Phoebe glanced up at me with trepidation.

"I don't know," I whispered, feeling completely defeated.

"Make them stop!" Carmen screeched again, even louder.

"We need to get her away from them," I advised Phoebe. I closed my eyes and sent out some intuitive feelers in the hopes I could sense which direction we needed to travel. To the north, west, and south I felt only more madness and hopelessness. To the east, I felt a slight trickle of light that washed over my skin like a breath of fresh air.

"This way."

Phoebe pulled Carmen upright and we both supported her weight as she continued to fight against the screams. We half-carried, half-dragged her for what felt like miles over the scorched, blackened earth. The endless amounts of soul we passed continued screaming silently as they were tortured relentlessly by an unknown source. At last I could see a clearing up ahead, but I had a foreboding feeling that it wasn't necessarily a good thing. Once past the forest of screaming souls Carmen was able to walk on her own, but completely drained and still in shock, she remained unresponsive. We held her hands and continued to walk. The trace on my arm had grown murky and dull under the weight of delirium pressing in on us. The wound from Priscilla's dagger and the slashes from Nadia's evil had stopped bleeding, but the damage was done. Every move stretched and reopened each one, which burned incessantly and reminded me I was still very mortal.

We arrived at a wall of misshapen branches that arched towards the sky and then fell back down to the parched dirt; creating hundreds of scraggly tunnels. A layer of a black, moss-like substance hung over most of the branches; preventing us from seeing more than a couple of yards within. They stretched out all the way to the horizon in both directions, and appeared to be our only option. I closed my eyes again and felt that same sliver of light, and instinctively knew we were heading in the right direction.

"Carmen, do you think you can make it through here?" I asked her; enunciating my words to make sure she understood. Her blank stare reinforced the feeling of speaking to a toddler not yet able to understand me. Her warm dark eyes had turned distant and lifeless, void of any comprehension or emotion. I sighed, took her hand, and gestured for Phoebe to follow me. We knelt down and made our way through the dizzying maze of scraggly branches and misshapen trees. Beneath the canopy of black moss, the world became even more shaded and bleak. A mildewy stench filled my nose and a slight burning irritated my eyes. I sensed something around us and caught glimpses of things that darted in and out of the shadows, stalking us. We pushed on, climbing over and through branches, often tripping on camouflaged roots. The presence I felt began to multiply, and I knew we were being followed by not one, but a group of....something. I could feel their elation, as if anticipating something.

"Did you see that?" Phoebe whispered in terror as a shadowed figure dashed in front of us.

"I think we're being followed," I informed her in a low voice. All of my senses switched to high alert when a hair-raising scratching sound filled the air. Carmen stopped dead in her tracks and became rigid as she stared at a spot in the distance with an expression that gave me chills. She looked...possessed.

"Stasia watch out!" Phoebe turned abruptly; shielding Carmen from whatever had abducted her mind. I looked forward just as a being stepped out from behind a blackened, dead tree. It looked human enough, but was hunched in such a dramatic fashion that it was impossible to know for sure. Skin and muscle hung from its exposed bones and it stood at least eight feet tall. I grabbed Phoebe's hand and quickly dragged her and Carmen sideways and around a thicket of branches that scraped my arm as we ran by. With Carmen's rigid movements and the amount of obstacles blocking our way, we didn't get very far. Another being leapt into our path and a chill went through my body when my eyes landed on her. Limp black hair hung over her cheekbones and her shining black eyes bored into mine. Her skin and muscle were all intact, but a torn, dirty maiden dress hung off of her. Her demon eyes fell onto Carmen, who began to walk stiffly towards her.

"Carmen! Don't!" I pleaded. Phoebe lunged forward and grabbed her arm, but Carmen pushed her so hard that Phoebe went flying backwards and landed hard on her back. In a moment of clarity, I jumped in between a possessed Carmen and the decrepit woman. Carmen looked right through me, her face contorted unnaturally.

"Carmen! Listen to me!" I put my arms out to stop her from walking. "Stop!"

Realizing that my tactic wasn't working, I wrapped my arms around her and easily pushed her to the side where she landed in a limp heap, unmoving. I turned just in time to see the skin melt off of the woman's face, as more and more of the beasts showed themselves. The woman lifted her arms slowly and glanced around at the others; signaling them to drift back into the shadows.

"Stasia! Help me!" Phoebe shouted from several yards away. Thick black vines had pushed up through the ground and were wrapping around her legs. I ran to her side and attempted to cut them away with my dagger, but they could have been made of steel for all the good it did. As the woman continued to slowly raise her misshapen arms that continued to drip skin, more vines pushed through the earth below me and crawled up my ankles. They secured themselves around my thighs and I fell to the ground as they methodically inched their way up to my waist. The harder I fought, the tighter they became. I heard Phoebe's screams as she was dragged across the ground past me. Carmen had also succumbed to the vines and they began to drag her away as well.

"Let me go!" I screamed hysterically as I was hauled across the parched landscape. The layers of soot stirred up by my body pressed into my eyes, ears and mouth. I felt every root, every rock and every bump as I was raked across the ground. Self-directed anger shot through me when I realized that all of the abilities and affinities in the world didn't help me when I wasn't near the ocean. I felt my energy being sucked from me, seeping into the dry dirt.

I closed my eyes and gave in to the pain, the hopelessness and the numb fear that attached to my mind. My world became filled with a never-ending blackness; pain and misery wrapping around my heart and keeping me company while my wounds were reopened and my blood smeared behind me. When I finally felt the movement stop, I was unable to move or even open my eyes. Limp and fading into unconsciousness, I barely heard Phoebe's shouts. She was laughing. Or was she crying? I couldn't quite make it out. I just wanted to rest. I'd feel better after I went to sleep...

"Wake up!" I felt my body being shaken violently and my eyes flew open. Phoebe's tear-streaked face hovered above mine. The black soot covering her skin and hair made her wild, panic filled eyes that much more startling. "Get up, Stasia! Get up!"

I attempted to talk but it just came out as a groan. I lifted myself up on my elbows and twisted into a sitting position. A burning heat was scorching the right side of my body, and I cringed away from the red glow that suddenly filled my vision.

"What is that?" I asked hoarsely, squinting and shielding my already burned and torn skin. She pointed to the source of the glow, and an intense fear crept up my spine. An angry river of lava flowed slowly and silently towards the dark horizon; bubbling and devouring everything in its path. Carmen's dead eyes flashed in my mind.

"Where's Carmen?" I insisted and swiveled my body; searching for her.

"Over there," Phoebe squeaked. I followed her stare to a figure that was standing dangerously close to the river. I was about to call out to her when she turned abruptly and began walking towards us. She strode right past us, twisted on her heel and stared down at us.

"Carmen! What are you doing?" I yelled at her with desperation; determined to get through to her. But instead of answering, she began to chant in a foreign language as she focused intently on the lava. While she chanted, small streams of lava travelled up the black earth and wound towards us. Still unable to stand, I crawled frantically away from the heat I could feel nipping at my feet. Phoebe was able to move faster, so she was several yards ahead of me when the earth opened up. The lava burned its way through the crumbling soot easily, creating a wide gash I couldn't crawl away from. The dirt gave way beneath my fingers and as it slid down, I was helpless to stop my body from following. I twisted onto my stomach and clawed at the deteriorating ground in vain.

"Phoebe!" A wave of soot muffled my scream as it filled my mouth. I lost sight of her as my body went over the edge. Expecting the powerless feeling of falling, I inhaled sharply when I abruptly stopped; my body precariously dangling over the void below. In another split second, I was sprawled on the ground mere yards away from the river and the conjured lava streams. I convulsed onto my side as my lungs struggled to expel the dirt I'd breathed in. The tears in my eyes succeeded in washing my eyes out enough so I could open them briefly, and the world sloshed and blurred as the tears continued to flow. I felt a hand squeeze mine and I turned my head to the right. The tears poured down my face; clearing my vision further and revealing my rescuer.

A wave of cool, refreshing sea water crashed over me and washed away my pain. It soothed every cut, every burn, and even the knife wound I could still feel throbbing in my abdomen. The smell of sea grass wafted around me and sent a comforting numbing sensation through my mind.

"Try to breathe slowly, baby girl." Her voice was like a ray of sunlight in a world of infinite darkness, and I immediately recognized it from her own memories. I lifted myself up on my elbows and gazed up at her, consumed with wonder and astonishment.

"Are you...?" The cadence of my voice scratched my throat. "Are you...Thetis? My...mother?"

"Yes, Pasha," she whispered, and I didn't miss the overwhelming emotion in her voice at the nickname she, herself, had coined. I lifted myself all the way up into a sitting position and met her wise, aquamarine eyes. They shone with fresh tears and her joyful smile lifted my heart. Suddenly overcome with emotion, I collapsed into her waiting arms. It was a place I never thought I would find myself, and I never wanted to let go.

"Pasha, we must move. We must go." Knowing she was right, I released her but couldn't take my eyes off of her. She was breathtaking. Her flowing white dress was untouched by the dark, sooty soil below, and her hair washed over her shoulders in a symphony of blonde and silver. She took my hand and assisted me to my feet. As a shuffling sound drew my attention to the landscape behind us, a throng of decrepit beasts closed in on us. I turned to run, but Thetis wrapped her arms around me and muttered something under her breath. In a split second we were on the other side of the River of Fire watching as they retreated back into the forest of branches. My stomach dropped when my thoughts shot to Carmen and Phoebe. My despair didn't last long.

"Stasia!" I was attacked from the side as Phoebe embraced me in hug; knocking me to the ground.

"Hey Phoebs." I smiled weakly and she hugged me tighter.

"She saved us! Thetis saved us!"

"How's Carmen?" I managed beneath her weight.

"Well, she's…alive."

I looked over Phoebe's shoulder at Carmen, who stared sightlessly and sat rigid and motionless on the ground.

"Come, girls. It is not time to rest just yet." Thetis smiled down on us.

Together we helped Carmen to her feet, but she resolved to trail behind in a trance-like state as we put distance between ourselves and the River of Fire.

Thetis slowed and took my cheek in her hand. "Who did this to you?"

"Nadia," I told her apprehensively. She could be great friends with Nadia for all I knew. Extremely unlikely, but still possible.

"That doesn't surprise me." An irate determination spread across her features. "We must hurry and get you back to the River Styx. She could be waiting, but either way she'll know when you are in the river." I averted my gaze to Phoebe.

"Phoebs, take Carmen and get out of here," I instructed.

"But St-" she began to object.

"You have to get Carmen out of here. She needs you, Phoebs. I'll be fine, I promise."

"I assure you that I will escort her to the River Styx and she will easily find the Gates, once she completes her essence," Thetis consoled her with a warm smile. Phoebe considered our words for a moment and eyed Carmen warily.

"Okay. I'll let Natasha know what's going on." She nodded at me.

"Natasha..." A faraway look fell over Thetis's eyes. "Please tell her I think of her often."

"I will!" Phoebe walked over to Thetis and took her hand. "It is such an honor to meet you. You're amazing!"

"As are you, Phoebe." Thetis kissed her on the forehead and patted her hand. Phoebe gave me another hug and began the task of dragging Carmen back to the Gates and getting back to their bodies. I turned to Thetis.

"How did you know...?" I trailed off.

"Why - the moonstone, of course." She smiled at me knowingly.

"The...moonstone?" I furrowed my brow and reached into my pocket. I pulled out the white stone and it warmed at my touch.

"Come," she contended with a grin and held out her hand. I stepped towards her and she wrapped her arms around me; muttering once again. In a flash, we were transported out of the dreary landscape and back to the River Styx. Thankfully, this time we were on the opposite side.

"I cannot take you farther into Elysian, but I can promise your safety here. Nadia cannot walk this land."

"Why not?"

"I think you know the answer to that, Pasha." her eyes smiled at me; amused.

"Evil?" I guessed.

She nodded proudly and continued our previous conversation. "As you are aware, aquamarine is my stone...and now yours. However, the moonstone originates back many, many centuries, back to your grandmother."

"My...grandmother?"

"Your grandfather's name was Nereus and your grandmother was Doris. Her stone was the moonstone." I peered down at the white stone in my hand that I knew stood for foresight.

"I found it at a shipwreck," I said in a low voice, sadness washing over me at the memory of Finn.

"I know," she admitted slyly and winked at me. "I instructed Finn to place it there for that very reason."

"You...he put it there?"

"I knew that once you returned, you would have to take your journey. I wanted to know when you arrived. We are not the only ones who wear aquamarine, but only a select few have a connection to moonstone. If I were to sense it, I would know that you had finally arrived to complete your essence. When Finn communicated your return, I instructed him to make sure that you obtained it. But you needed to be drawn to it in order to feel your own connection to its essence."

"I had an odd feeling that I should bring it with me on my journey," I thought out loud; also marveling at Finn and my mother conversing about me. For some reason that brought heat to my cheeks.

"Your grandparents would be so proud of you," Thetis whispered as sadness trickled into her beautiful eyes. "Unfortunately they did not know of your birth. No one did, except for a select few." As a tear ran down her cheek, I took her hand.

"I know. I saw it happen...in your memory." Her face instantly lit up at my words.

"You have antiquity! Oh, Anastasia - that's wonderful!" she rejoiced, and eyed my newest trace. "The infinity symbol, of course! I should have known..." She beamed at me as she reached out and gently touched my cheek. Unable to stop myself, I told her all about the last four months of my life; my abilities, my affinities, my friends...and my complex issues revolving around Finn.

"I can't let him give up everything...for me." I searched her eyes for an answer. "I love him, but that's why I can't allow him to do that."

"Love is a powerful force. It's also much more potent than evil." She emphasized the word 'evil' and gently patted my hand. "Always remember that. You will know what to do. Listen to your heart and decide what you are willing to sacrifice, my dear Pasha." I held her gaze and tears began to collect in my eyes. I couldn't believe she was actually sitting beside me, giving me advice. I felt the gaping hole that had been created so long ago in my heart finally begin to close and mend.

"Thanks, Mom," I whispered, testing out the word Mom. It felt surprisingly at home on my lips. She embraced me in a hug.

"It is time," she proclaimed. I nodded and we stood; both of us eyeing the raging river several yards away. She stepped in front of me, ensuring that she held my entire focus.

"I love you Anastasia, and I am very proud of you. You are more amazing than you know. If I could do it all over again, I would gladly sacrifice my life for yours once again. You are worth it." The echo of Natasha's words resounded in my heart. Her expression became intense as she continued. "I need you to listen very carefully to what I'm about to tell you."

"Okay." I held my breath in anticipation.

"Your father is alive," she divulged, and my heart skipped a beat while my legs turned to bricks. I felt the look of shock on my face and I tried, to no avail, to speak. Thankfully, I didn't have to. "You must find him. He is waiting for you."

"Where…where is he?" I forced air out of my lungs and made myself speak.

"An island. He is being held captive." My reveries about the older man came crashing back to me and I felt my mind shift with clarity at this new revelation.

"I think I've seen him - in a reverie," I breathed; the piece of the puzzle clicking in my mind and filling my heart.

"That does not surprise me. Your soul knows where to find him. You will also find the conch shell I left you to be useful in your search," she hinted, with an enchanting light in her eyes. As I became speechless again, she put her comforting hands on my shoulders. "But right now, Pasha…it is time to fulfill your destiny."

I swallowed and focused on the task at hand. As if Finn, my friends and the entire Tyde Order weren't enough motivation, now I knew that my father was alive. And waiting for me. A surge of renewed energy shot through me and I stood up straight; smiling confidently at my mother.

"I'm ready."

Thirty-Nine

Glancing over my shoulder one more time at my mother, I drew a deep breath and leapt into the raging rapids below. The dark water didn't hesitate to draw me under, and I automatically took a deep breath. As the water filled my lungs and circulated through my body, I realized with horror that I'd made a mistake. As if I had swallowed a mouthful of fire, dancing flames licked at the insides of my body; scorching my throat and burning my muscles. I clamped my mouth shut and desperately held my breath. As the water continued sizzling through every cell, I flowed downstream within the rapids and did my best to avoid any large rocks. I had no idea how much further I had to go, but I knew I couldn't hold my breath for much longer.

Helpless to control the monstrous, angry river that I was currently in the grips of, I held on for dear life. As the need for oxygen starved my brain and muscles of clarity and energy, I fought to get my head above the water. Unfortunately, the strength of the current rolled me over and tossed me in every direction except for up. Feeling the fuzzy blackness knocking at my consciousness, I opened my mouth and again breathed in the scorching water I was submerged in. Once again it surged into my lungs with ferocity. Despite the scorching heat, I felt it revitalize my muscles and lessen in its intensity, so I continued to take in deep breaths, ignoring the pain. Clarity returned and I was able to think about what was happening. Miraculously the more breaths I took, the less it burned.

Like salt on a wound it was a pain I'd never experienced, but as it burned, it healed. As it faded, it made me stronger. As it disappeared completely, I was reborn. Allowing the river to take me ever closer to the waterfall, I was no longer scared. This is what I was meant to do. I closed my eyes and smiled; welcoming the ferocity of the water I was immersed in.

Just as I was marveling at the increasing intensity of the water, I felt my legs drop over the top of the waterfall. Suddenly my head was yanked backwards as something latched onto my hair. My neck twisted painfully as I fought to be released and I met the searing gaze of Nadia. While the rapids rushed over my body, bound for Charon's marsh below, Nadia was pulling me back up. A calm determination fell over me and in that moment, there was nothing that would stop me from going over that waterfall. I reached up, grabbed her wrist and wrenched it sideways as hard as I could. I felt the breaking of her bones and heard her shout, but she continued ripping me away from my destiny. I reached down for my dagger, but with the opposing forces working on my body, I couldn't reach it. My hand brushed my pants pocket and I remembered the piece of rope within. I was able to pull it free with two fingers and wrapped my had around it. Not knowing what to expect, I blindly swung it up towards Nadia and felt it warm and soften.

Nadia's scream told me something was happening but I didn't know what until I saw the tail end of something silver whipping around in the water. I swung again and was able to see the now silver and much longer rope make contact with Nadia's leg. It wrapped around her calf and she screamed again as it appeared to burn her skin. In her attempt to rid her skin of the rope, her grip loosened and I was able to slip out of her hands. The current swept me back down the river. Then I was falling.

I knew I was in the waterfall, but every ounce of my essence was telling me I was no longer just in the waterfall,

I was a part of it. Its foaming energy merged with mine and rushed within. A flash of light lit up the world around me, and I was suddenly lying on something soft. I instantly knew what had caught me. The ocean. I smiled as I heard it calling to me; singing. I felt its welcome embrace and acceptance as I silently sank beneath the surface. Unable to move, I drifted down to the fine sand on the bottom and watched the light from the sun scatter and create magnificent prisms above. Wobbly bubbles began to form and rise all around me. As they ran over my skin and sent tingles through me, I watched as they floated soundlessly to the surface.

My attention was caught by a small shadow that drifted downward; gently swaying like a feather in the wind. The closer it got, the brighter it became. It shone a brilliantly bright aqua; pulsing and flashing silver beams from its depths. No longer a shadow, the bright ball of light halted right above my chest. I looked on, mesmerized, as it began to spin at an incredible speed. Completely entranced, I almost missed the moment when it plunged into my body with an immense explosion, sending me spiraling down, down, down....

I hit the marsh with incredible speed and allowed my body to float back up to the surface on its own. Once my face broke the surface, I sucked in a breath of oxygen and let out an exalted cry of joy. Everything was brighter, sharper. I could distinguish each individual aroma drifting along the breeze and discern the smallest of sounds; easily pinpointing where they had originated. I kicked to the side of the marsh and lifted myself up onto the bank. The waterfall had once again succumbed to the veil of dense fog; keeping it, as well as the marsh, hidden once more. I turned my attention to the next obstacle. Getting home.

I knew Nadia would be looking for me, which meant I needed to get out of there as fast as possible. I took off in a sprint along the banks of the marsh and picked up the pace as the River of Forgetfulness flowed gently to my right. If the map I memorized in my head was correct, once the River of Fire was visible on my right, I would be nearing the outskirts of Groves, as well as the Gates of Horn and Ivory. I could have run for miles without becoming winded as my newfound strength coursed through me and recharged my muscles every several minutes. When the heat of the River of Fire swelled up beside me, I spotted the Groves of lush trees on my left. I only slowed when I reached the mouth of a towering white arch. It reminded me of the arch in St. Louis that I'd seen pictures of. It was a pearly white, smooth stone and stood impossibly high. I glanced over my shoulder to make sure I hadn't been followed, when I saw a small tree on the outskirts of the Groves. Deep red fruit hung from its branches. Pomegranate.

Without hesitation, I jogged over to the tree and quickly plucked one of the lower hanging pomegranates from a branch. The round fruit fit perfectly in my palm as I clutched it carefully and ran back to the Gate. Standing before its grandeur, I wished for some kind of instruction or a hint as to what to do next. Did I just walk through it? Did I need to say something? Had Carmen and Phoebe made it through without an issue?

"You have succeeded," a velvety voice stated simply. Persephone, in all her glory, appeared directly in front of me; creating a barrier between me and the Gate. "What do you plan to do with your newfound essence?"

"I'll become the rightful leader of the Tydes," I proclaimed with an inner pride.

She nodded. "Your destiny."

"That's right." I held her gaze.

"If that is so, young Goddess, then why do you feel the need to take back a souvenir?" She sneered at the hand that held the pomegranate.

"It's just...insurance," I stumbled, and she chuckled softly.

"You would give up everything…" She shook her head at me in disappointment. "Then you are a fool. No man is worth any level of sacrifice. Not even Finn." My heart jumped at his name. She sensed my surprise and smiled wickedly. "Love is a figment of your imagination. It isn't real, sweet Anastasia. We create love. Love destroys us. The end."

"Real love is worth any sacrifice," I countered. "My heart goes out to you and to the sacrifice you were forced to make."

"And yet you consider making the very same sacrifice. Voluntarily."

"If it comes to that."

"I find your idealistic view endearing; however you will find that there is no love greater than self. We are selfish beings who will always put ourselves first when presented with the choice. You are no exception, Anastasia."

"Have you ever been in love?" I inquired with genuine curiosity.

"Yes," she retorted, and her golden eyes hardened. "And it destroyed me. Now leave." She narrowed her eyes at me and I knew I had outstayed my welcome. I was also eager to get back to my body and to find Finn. I could only hope that I still had enough time.

"Thank you, Persephone," I obliged gratefully. Her face softened and she disappeared without another word.

I turned my attention to the Gate towering above me. I decided that the best plan of action was to simply walk through it and let it take me where it may. Fearlessly, I strode beneath the looming arch. But when I stepped onto the cusp, the smooth white stone above disappeared and I found myself in the middle of a field of wildflowers. A light breeze lifted my hair and flowed over my skin. The soft smell of lavender soothed me and I turned around slowly; taking in my new surroundings.

A small girl appeared in front of me. Her thick blonde hair hung over her face and her blue eyes widened in fear. As she struggled to lift her arms, the sun glinted off of the gun she was gripping tightly in her small hands. She met my surprised gaze and pointed it directly at me. I recognized her wrinkled pink shorts and stained white shirt, but the image on the underside of her left wrist cemented my assumptions.

"Hannah," I attempted calmly. "Put down the gun."

"No," she insisted, lifting the gun higher. A paralyzing fear crept up my spine when I realized she could pull the trigger at any moment. Was she real? Was the gun real?

"It's going to be okay. Everything's going to be alright," I promised her in a soothing tone.

"Liar!" she screamed at me; jostling a memory of Natasha's wise words. 'Do not lie to yourself'. I sighed and tried a different approach: brutal honesty.

"You're right. That is a lie. It's not alright. It's not okay. Things are going to get worse - much worse. You're going to be scared. You're going to want to die. You're going to want to give up." She listened to my words intently and began to lower the gun, so I continued. "But you're stronger than you give yourself credit for. You're going to make it. And trust me when I tell you that you're worth the fight."

She stared at me in disbelief for a moment more, and then dropped the gun and ran into my arms. As I wrapped my arms around her, she disappeared and I was below the Gate once more. The smooth, white stone had morphed into an arch of interlocking horns. I smiled to myself and took the next step.

I gasped for air and began to cough uncontrollably as a wave of nausea crashed over me.

"Get her some water!" I heard Natasha shout at someone. Her voice softened and I sensed her lean over me.

She placed a cold washcloth on my forehead and stuck something under my nose that smelled of garlic. It instantly calmed me and erased the nausea twisting within my stomach. I slowly opened my eyes.

"Natasha?"

"I'm here, dear," she answered tenderly. I didn't miss the smile in her voice.

"I did it," I breathed in relief. She chuckled and helped me sit upright to drink from the glass of water Liam handed her. It felt amazing to my throat, which had swallowed at least two gallons of black soot. I pulled up my shirt to inspect the stab wound in my stomach, only to realize it had closed and was only a tender pink scar. The scratches down my arms and legs were also in the process of healing.

"How'd that happen?" I said under my breath. The answer came to a screeching halt just inside the doorway as Willow let out a squeal and catapulted herself towards me.

"Oh Stasia! You made it!" She held onto me tightly. "I was so worried! Did you go over the waterfall? Did you complete your essence?"

"I did it." I grinned weakly. "I also met my mother."

"That's what Phoebe said!" She jumped up and down and hugged me again, and my thoughts went to my other roommates.

"So they're okay?" I asked, hopeful that Carmen had returned to normal once she had awakened in her body.

She nodded solemnly, but Liam frowned in frustration and gave me the somber news. "Phoebe's fine - she's resting in another room. But Carmen is...troubled." My heart squeezed as I remembered her blank, lifeless eyes staring into the distance.

"I don't know what happened. Something took hold of her and wouldn't let go," I voiced my thoughts.

"She's in there somewhere. We'll find her." Natasha smiled encouragingly. "Ricker flew in to be with her, but she's still not talking." If both Liam and Natasha were here, did that mean…?

"What day is it? What time is it?" I shrieked as I jumped off the table. "I need to get to Finn!"

"Take it easy, Stasia." Natasha grabbed my arm and steadied me before I fell against a cabinet. "You've made it back just in time. It's only eleven o'clock…at night."

"Eleven o'clock?!" I shrieked again. "That's not just in time! I'll never make it!" Tears began to build behind my eyes and my legs started to shake.

"You underestimate me, Anastasia." Natasha grinned at me with a twinkle in her eye. "And you should never underestimate a witch."

"Never," I promised her quietly, and secured the pomegranate in my left hand.

Before changing into a pair of clean jeans and a black hoodie, I did what I could to scrub off the black soot from the Underworld while Natasha brought me up to speed on Phoebe's condition. She was perfectly healthy except for a touch of exhaustion and anxiety. Natasha worked up an herbal remedy that would keep her in a deep sleep until her body and mind were able to recover. She wanted to be careful with Phoebe's state of mind, considering the condition of Carmen's. Willow and Ricker were tending to Carmen, but she was still unresponsive. Willow was working her healing magic and Liam was working on a couple remedies to try, so Natasha remained optimistic; but I had the feeling she was only trying to prevent me from worrying.

She led me out to the grand parlor and turned to face me abruptly. "Do you trust me?"

"Yes," I declared.

"Then close your eyes." I did as she instructed. Without a word, she placed her hands in mine. I began to feel a modest spinning sensation as a cool wind blew up around us. I peeked out of one curious eye and instantly wished I hadn't. The air wasn't blowing or spinning, we were. A continuous blur of colors wrapped around us and the ground beneath our feet was no more. I closed my eyes and held onto Natasha for dear life. For the sake of my nerves, I was glad when I felt solid ground beneath my feet and Natasha released my hands.

"We have arrived," she announced joyfully. I cautiously peeked out of one eye and glanced around timidly before opening the other. We stood on a rocky beach full of boulders; the largest of which was taking the full force of the ocean's fury. The sea spray showered over us and I tilted my face up to welcome its cooling mist. The proximity to the ocean felt like coming home. It filled me with the reassurance and happiness that I greatly missed while in the Underworld.

As a smile spread across my face, I felt a trace of warm darkness wrap around me and my heart stopped. Finn.

"As long as you're with me we shouldn't have a problem getting into the coliseum, but we may have to improvise in order to get you close enough to Finn." I patted my jacket pocket where I'd hidden the pomegranate and nodded in agreement.

I followed her up the rocky beach towards a large cliff that towered high into the night sky. Unsure as to how we were going to scale the massive rock face, I was extremely relieved when I spotted what looked to be a tunnel. It was an unassuming arched entrance about ten feet wide and eight feet tall.

"This is the back entrance," Natasha whispered to me; her eyes fixed on something ahead of us. The back entrance? What I thought was a rock face was actually the back side of the coliseum I'd seen in my vision. As we made our way through the dim tunnel, we began to hear voices up ahead and Natasha whispered to me over her shoulder.

"I think your best bet is to stay on this main level. I'm allowed one visit before the fight starts. You will follow me to his room, but the security will be extremely heavy so you need to make sure you are not seen. They will keep him there until the beginning of the fight," she glanced down at her watch, "which is in fifteen minutes. He will be escorted to a platform where he will wait for the signal to enter the arena."

"Okay." Knowing what was at stake, I had to deliberately calm down my frantic thoughts and shaking legs.

"Once on the platform, he will be alone for only a couple of minutes. That might be your only chance." She took my hands in hers. "Good luck, dear. And remember, if you are unable to convince him, do not feel guilty about his sacrifice. My son's happiness is all that matters to me - not the Prime position, not the Underworld, not even the Sons. He loves you. You make him happy." Tears collected in her bright blue eyes.

"Thank you so much, Natasha." I hugged her fiercely "For everything."

"Time to go." She smiled, smoothed out her clothes and took a deep breath. I nodded and began to follow her down the tunnel. We veered to the left and I could just make out a larger room up ahead. Natasha put her hand up to signal for me to stop, so I pressed my body against the rock wall and looked on in silence as she continued. Two men dressed in black suits stepped forward, seemingly out of nowhere. They nodded respectfully to her.

"Welcome, Natasha," one of the men greeted her. "Finn is awaiting your arrival."

"Thank you," she obliged. The two men stepped aside and I leaned forward slightly in order to see Natasha open a thick wooden door, slip inside and close it behind her. I leaned back against the wall and scanned the tunnel for any nook or cranny that would fit a person. I couldn't very well lean up against the wall while they escorted him out to the arena.

Several yards away, there was a crack in the wall where I thought I might be able to squeeze myself into. Wryly, I thought the fact that I hadn't eaten in at least twelve hours should help. As if on cue, my stomach rumbled loudly. The acoustics within the stone tunnel were not conducive to someone who did not want to be seen or heard. I inspected the crack in the wall and decided I could fit. I turned sideways and shimmied my body inside. It was extremely uncomfortable, considering that several stones were sticking into my back and legs, but it worked.

After about five minutes crammed into the crack of the wall, I began to develop a fear of small spaces. I held my breath as I heard a click and then soft footsteps coming down the hall. Natasha padded by, tears streaming down her face. As silence fell over the tunnel once again, my stomach became one big ball of nerves and my forehead broke out in a cold sweat. I closed my eyes and tried to take several deep breaths, but it did little to calm me. I had no idea how I intended to pull this off. Even if I somehow made it to the platform, I had only minutes to convince him not to deny everything he'd worked for up to this point.

"Let's do this." The sound of Finn's voice created an explosion of emotions that rocked me to the core. Tears sprung to my eyes, and it took everything I had not to run to him and throw my arms around him. As their footsteps echoed off the tunnel walls, adrenaline began to pump through my veins and all of my already heightened senses went on high alert. The world stopped once I caught a glimpse of his handsome face as he walked by with the two men in black suits. They were explaining to him what would happen next.

"...your axes are already in the arena, and you will wait until given the signal to enter..."

I shimmied back out of my crack in the wall and instantly took a deep breath. I made a mental note not to make a habit out of hiding in cracked walls. I looked back towards the direction they had come to make sure the coast was clear, and then I crouched down and followed the sound of their voices. As we rounded a corner I began to hear the crowd above. The rhythmic pulse of their stomping feet matched my own beating heart and I felt each stomp deep within as it sent pulses through my body. Their chanting voices reminded me of my vision as a blast of light filled the corridor. I peeked around the wall to see Finn's dark figure standing alone on a black raised platform; the sounds of the arena beckoning to him from only feet away. Wearing black shorts and no shirt, he matched the image I remembered. His hands were at his sides, wrapped in his signature leather gloves. The immense sound became deafening as the crowd became more impatient. Knowing I didn't have much time, I decided to move.

I looked around quickly to make sure that no one else was around, and then stepped around the corner towards the platform. Right before I got to the three small steps leading up to him, a loud horn sounded from the arena and Finn began to walk into the arena. With my heart in my chest I leapt up the steps; missing one and crashing down onto my knees.

"Finn!" I shouted out to him, but the sound of the crowd drowned out my cries. I watched in quiet horror as another figure began to walk towards Finn from the other side of the arena. Maddox. Also wearing black shorts, his strong chest tensed with each step he took. I scrambled to my feet and pressed my back to the wall, peering out of the doorway. The height of the arena was dizzying, and it was packed to capacity with cheering spectators. The bright lights I had seen in my vision were shining down onto the black circle Maddox and Finn now stood in. They halted their steps and silently nodded their heads at each other respectfully.

Maddox's dark face was serious and menacing as he fixed his eyes on Finn's. They looked very similar, although Maddox's features were slightly harsher. His blue eyes flashed as another horn sounded and the crowd erupted. Confusion swept over me and I tried to figure out why Finn hadn't stopped the fight yet. Was he waiting until he killed Maddox? My thoughts were interrupted by a shrill bell that signaled the beginning of the fight. They immediately knelt in a defensive stance and began to circle one another. Finn was the first to lunge at Maddox; immediately connecting his punch to Maddox's jaw. Unphased, Maddox punched Finn in the stomach; pulling his head down and kneeing him in the chest. With a pained expression, Finn straightened and lunged again. Punch after punch was thrown until they were both bloodied and bruised. Maddox's left eye had swollen almost completely shut and Finn's lip was gushing blood. I realized they both healed extremely fast, which must be part of the difficulty of the fight. Finn connected one last punch and a wave of crimson cascaded from Maddox's nose. I cringed when he fell to the ground and immediately hopped back up to his feet.

The horn sounded once again and they both stopped and stepped away from each other. I jumped when the shrill bell sounded two more times, and then watched as they lunged for their weapons with quiet speed; Finn holding his double blade axe, the diamonds and black onyx on the handle glinting in the lights. Maddox gripped a sword with a thick, curved blade and my heart began to beat wildly. Finn expertly swung the double blade axe around his head and body, causing Maddox to follow its every movement in preparation for when he swung it at him. Both experts at their weapons, it was more like watching a dance than a fight. Their movements were fluid and precise, each darting out of the way at the last moment. Every swing of Maddox's blade, every lunge he made stirred a terror in me that wouldn't let go.

It took all of my effort to keep my legs from running out there to protect him, although I was fully aware I was ill equipped to do so - and that was an understatement. Finally, after ten minutes of agonizing tension, the horn sounded again and they stepped away from each other. Finn's face and body were already beginning to heal from the first round, but I could tell the fight was taking a toll on him.

Maddox was favoring his left leg, but his focused eyes stayed on Finn the entire time.

Suddenly, something began to push up through the earth around the black circle where they stood. Three more circles broke through the earth, each containing hundreds of spikes at least a foot tall; the tips menacingly sharp. It would only take one missed step to result in one of them becoming impaled. A terrified sob rose from my chest and I clutched my stomach, suddenly feeling nauseous. The bell sounded three more times and when I tried to look away, I couldn't. They began to circle each other again and I remember thinking how much I just wanted it to end. No matter the outcome, it was torture to watch the person you loved get beaten to death.

As they swung their weapons, Finn's axe connected with Maddox's blade; sending the sword flying out of the circle. Finn swiftly swept Maddox's legs out from under him, causing him to crash down; his head missing the spikes of the first circle by an inch. Finn jumped on top of him, but surprisingly he set down his axe. He began to untie his gloves, using them to tie up Maddox's arms and legs. The crowd mumbled as they attempted to figure out what Finn was doing, and why he hadn't ended Maddox's life already. From my position I could also see Maddox yelling something at Finn, and Finn simply shaking his head at him solemnly.

The crowd quieted automatically when Finn stood and acknowledged them. My heart plummeted and I knew what he intended to do next. He put his hands up and addressed the audience.

"Sons, ancestors, and friends; you've come here tonight to witness the crowning of a new Prime. However, I have made a decision to-"

"Finn! No!" Before I could stop myself, I was running. I heard a collective gasp from the crowd as they saw me, and Finn turned. When his gaze met mine I felt his darkness reach out to me and embrace me. His face turned from determined to shocked in under a second as he gawked at me in silence. I stopped just before the first row of spikes and caught Maddox's good eye staring wide-eyed at me.

"Please don't! You can't do this! You can't give everything up!"

Without a word he walked out of the circle, through the spikes and came to a stop in front of me. In his eyes I saw the desperation that motivated him, the love that drove him, and the honor that bound him to his destiny.

"Pasha," he whispered in astonishment.

"I know what you're planning to do and…" the tears began to fall, "I can't let you do it. We'll find another way!" I pleaded with him, but he simply smiled.

"This is the only way. Once I am bound to Nadia, you will be lost to me forever."

"If you do this, you'll lose everything!"

"But I will gain the one thing I can't live without." He took my hand and gently kissed it, then he quickly turned and walked back to the circle where Maddox was thrashing around, cursing at him. Finn addressed the audience again. "My destiny is my own to accept or deny. And on this fateful night I choose-"

"Finn, no!" I produced the pomegranate from my pocket, realizing there was no other way. When I held it up in my palm the crowd gasped and Finn's face paled with horror. I spoke steadily and only to him, "Fulfill your destiny. We will be together in the Underworld."

"Stasia don't!" No sooner than his words were out, I brought the fruit to my mouth and sunk my teeth into it while my mother's words echoed in my mind: 'Listen to your heart and decide what you are willing to sacrifice, my dear Pasha'. I watched in slow motion as he ran out of the circle towards me. A forceful wind blew me backwards and then the world around me disappeared.

A light breeze flowed over my skin and ruffled my hair. The soft ground beneath me smelled of spices and herbs. I slowly opened my eyes and lifted myself up onto my elbows. I was lying in a sort of garden. Sweet mint, basil and paprika plants had been flattened beneath my weight.

"You surprise me, young Goddess."

I twisted around to find Persephone perched on the grass with her legs tucked underneath her body mere feet away from me. I took several deep breaths and mimicked her position. We were in the middle of an expansive garden flanked by a magnificent golden mansion. Despite the beauty surrounding me, I could only put my head in my hands and I began to cry. The fear and stress of the last twenty-four hours exploded within me and slowly drained into the soil that supported me.

"I couldn't let him do it. I love him." I continued to sob.

A demonic laugh wafted up from our right, and I looked over to see Nadia making her way up the path towards us. I began to stand, feeling way too vulnerable in a sitting position, but Persephone grabbed my arm and held me where I was.

"Stupid, stupid Stasia." She chuckled again and put her hands on her hips. "You think you've done something noble, but all you've accomplished is trapping yourself in the Underworld, allowing Finn and I to live out the life we are meant to have." She winked at me. "I'll tell him hi for you."

This time I stood, fully intending to tackle her when Persephone also stood. "Silence, Nadia."

Nadia furrowed her brow. "I'm just telling her what she should already know."

"What matters to me is that Finn fulfills his destiny - because for every evil being like you, we will need a noble, good leader like him!" I spat at her.

"Ugh, really?" She raised an eyebrow. "Give me a break. Who do you think you are? You're no martyr. Why don't you just stay down here with my mother and leave the real leadership to the ones who can handle it?"

Holding her gaze, I stepped up to her. "A leader does not demand from weaker beings. A leader does not take advantage of her abilities. She leads from within, with dignity and grace. She always puts herself last and she is willing to sacrifice for what is right." I stepped even closer as she gawked at me with wide eyes. "You will never be a leader," I hissed at her.

"Anastasia." I turned to Persephone and she motioned for me to stand beside her. "Come." With one last glance at Nadia, I turned and walked to Persephone. She put her hand on my shoulder.

"Never have I met a woman more willing to sacrifice for the man she loves, and willing to fight so hard for what is right. You have proven me wrong, young Goddess. And for that, I have decided to give you amnesty."

"What!?" Nadia lashed out, but Persephone held up her hand.

"I also dismiss your betrothal to Finn." She sighed and eyed her daughter in disappointment. "It pains me to say this, but you truly do not deserve him."

"Mother!" Nadia gasped, and Persephone smiled kindly at me.

"I grant you amnesty, Anastasia. Use my pardon wisely."

"No!" Nadia screamed, and my world once again went black.

The roar of the crowd above hit me with a force that caused me to snap open my eyes. My head fell to the right when a sudden movement caught my attention. I looked over just in time to see Finn drive his axe into Maddox's chest. He quickly yanked it out and angrily threw it across the arena. He knelt and quietly spoke to Maddox as he leaned over him; hugging him with urgency. My eyes filled with hot tears and an overwhelming pride filled my every cell.

I was lying near the wall of the arena covered by a blanket and flanked by two guards. It would appear that no one had noticed my reappearance just yet. Two more men ran onto the arena floor and struggled to wrench Finn off of Maddox's body. He collapsed into a heap of tears and defeat as they dragged Maddox's body away; the crowd cheering and chanting Finn's name.

Too exhausted to move, I simply called out his name. "Finn..." He either heard me somehow or felt my essence, because his eyes lifted and met mine automatically. In that moment the world disappeared and all that was left was us. His darkness reached out to me as he stood slowly. The crowd, seeing his attention diverted, began to murmur and gasp as they laid eyes on me.

Finn continued to make his way over to me and they quieted and seemed to hold their breaths. I forced my body to turn on its side and I painstakingly lifted myself up to my knees. He stopped in front of me and fell to his knees as well, grabbing my arms and supporting my weight.

"Oh Stasia, I'm so sorry." I silenced him with my finger and smiled through my tears. His own tears continued to fall as I wrapped my arms around him and brought my lips to his. My heart exploded into a million pieces; raining down on us and blanketing me with euphoria. The crowd in

313

the arena erupted into cheers that I felt all the way down to my soul. He glanced up at me in surprise.

"You have darkness in you... I can feel it..." he said only to me, amazed. "But how...?"

"Persephone pardoned me," I laughed from the joy I felt, "and she dismissed your betrothal." Finn simply shook his head at me in astonishment.

"And here I thought I was going to be the one to find a way around it and save the day." He chuckled. "I should have known you'd show me up."

"It's what I do," I teased him.

"And loving you is what I do," he whispered, and embraced me again for another passionate kiss. The incessant chanting of the crowd drew our attention back to our audience, who was demanding the induction of their new Prime.

"Your Order awaits." I grinned up at him with pride. The arena floor was quickly cleared and a rolling platform was brought out for the ceremony. As Finn was ushered up the steps, he refused to let go of my hand.

"I don't belong up there," I hissed at him.

"Of course you do." He smiled at me and dragged me up the stairs as my cheeks flushed and my heart beat wildly.

"This is amazing," I marveled at the pomp and circumstance surrounding us. Finn simply grinned at me.

"Just wait until your eighteenth birthday. You haven't seen anything yet."

We were soon joined by Natasha, who hugged me before hugging Finn - drawing a laugh from the crowd - and finally by Charon. I recognized him as the same older man I saw Finn talking to the night of the Ball. He looked to be in his late fifties with salt and pepper hair and warm blue eyes.

"I have heard a great deal about you, young lady." He bowed to me. "My son is a better man with you by his side."

"Thank you," was all I could manage. Charon produced a staff that was covered in black onyx, with an immense diamond adorning the top. He beat it three times on the platform in quick succession and the crowd quickly quieted.

"Tonight I induct my son as your new Prime! This is a new era for the Sons' Order. One which will flourish and shine beneath his strong hand." He turned and held out the staff to Finn, who stepped towards him and grasped the staff as well. They both closed their eyes and muttered something inaudible, then they met each other's gaze and slammed the staff down onto the platform with a loud boom. An intense light shot up from the top of the staff and a thumping shockwave flew outwards. When I looked back up at Finn, my breath caught. An inner glow I'd never seen before was shining from him. His eyes were brighter and he stood taller with an inner dignity. Charon released the staff and turned around. When he held his arms up, the entire stadium bowed to Finn. It was a surreal and majestic experience, and the pride I felt was magnified each time I looked up at him. He diverted his shining eyes to mine and placed his hand on my neck, lifting my chin with his thumb.

"No matter what, you will always be my true destiny." He brought his soft lips to mine and I felt my legs melt as my heart soared. I knew in that moment that I was exactly where I was meant to be.

When the crowd sat back down, a loud clapping brought everyone's attention to a newcomer, who had just entered the arena. She sauntered towards us with an air of arrogance I was beginning to despise. Her bronze skirt had somehow inched higher up her thighs, and the white blouse had been replaced with a tight black one. Her peep toe leopard skin stilettos tapped impatiently as she stopped just short of the black circle and platform we currently stood on.

"Bravo! Bravo!" she cheered cynically. Her eyes fell on me with a hatred I could feel before her gaze slid to Finn with a smile dripping with evil. "Hi love, remember me?"

"What are you doing here?" he asked calmly; his anger sizzling just below the surface. She smirked at him and then her golden gaze pierced mine. Her features darkened considerably and the evil tendrils began lifting off of her sparkling, golden skin.

"Taking back what's mine," she growled. Before I knew what was happening, she lifted her arms and ripped Finn's soul from his body. His soul-less body flew backwards and landed hard on the circle below with a heart-stopping thump.

"Finn!" I screamed as the arena erupted into chaos around us. She gave me one last, devilish smile and I saw Finn reach for me before they both disappeared. As I met the horrified eyes of Natasha, I knew the real fight had just begun.

To be CONTINUED...

Want more? Read on to catch a sneak peek at the prologue for the third book in the Daughters of the Sea Series!

Chosen (Daughters of the Sea #3)

Prologue

A crisp, biting wind swirled through the open window; lifting the thin sheet draped over his aching body. The night surrounding his isolated room was dark and still when the roar of the ocean's waves was interrupted by an entrancing melody. The full moon shone into his tired eyes as they cracked open at the faint singing; its silver glow pulling at his conscious. He wrapped the tattered sheet around his body and slowly made his way to the window. The night sky above glittered with the dancing of stars, while the radiance of the moon highlighted the rolling waves below.

The bubbling surf raced up the beach until its energy was spent; tugging on the sand and rocks below as it retreated once again. The cool breeze swept through his gray beard and he squinted his eyes at the beach below. With each fallen wave, the glow grew brighter. Hundreds of magnificent blue lights sparkled within the water, creating a magical blanket of effervescence along the water's edge. He had only seen this phenomenon once before…many, many years ago. It was a type of plankton that glistened a beaming blue when it was stirred up; however, he knew it was typically only found farther out in the ocean. Its unexpected arrival on land had his suddenly guarded eyes scanning the beach. That was when he saw her.

The sheer white fabric of her flowing dress drifted in the breeze as she glided in a wide circle; dancing and spinning with a power he felt down in the core of his tired soul. She was spellbinding and beautiful - and deadly. The captivating symphony of her voice cascaded down the stone walls of his prison and whirled around the crescent-shaped beach below. Her wild, curly dark hair was accentuated by streaks of silver as it blew around her pale face. Eyes closed, her skin shimmered silver in the light of the moon above while she continued her trancelike dance. Loose silver ribbons lifted from her wrists, ankles, and hair where they were loosely secured. They created an illusion of fire; its sparkling flames shooting up into the air and around its writhing center. He shook his head and closed his eyes to snap himself out of her allure.

As the singing faded slightly, he looked on as she stopped twirling and raised her thin arms into the air with closed fists. She tilted her head back; her dark hair falling down her back, her body now fully embraced by the moonlight. She herself emanated an eerie glow. She wasn't just dancing amongst the night, she was a part of the night. The moonlight that caressed her angelic face also shone from within. She stood perfectly still for what seemed like hours while the ever-moving world around her continued its pace. Finally, she slowly dropped her arms and flashed open her palms. What appeared to be small crystals scattered around her onto the sand. They shimmered and flickered as they brightened further.

She raised her arms again very slowly, making the circle of crystals hover in the air around her. As they started to spin, they took on the appearance of a solid ring of light. Her arms continued to lift, taking the ring of light higher and higher. A bright flash caught him by surprise and he stumbled backwards; shielding his face. After regaining his balance he approached the window once more, only to see the ring of light had disappeared, as well as the glowing plankton. All that remained was her.

She stood rigid and silent as the surf swept over her feet and rushed back toward the waves. She swayed gently from side to side and he realized how innocent she looked.

Her small stature was a reminder of who she used to be, but he knew better. He knew what she was capable of. In a flash, she twisted her head and locked him in her chilling glare. The startling silver of her eyes chilled him to the bone and had him slowly backing away from the window. Amongst the dark shadows of his room, he stared at the long ray of light cast across the floor by the moon. He knew what her witching hour display meant. He knew it with certainty. A creeping cold slithered up his spine and squeezed his heart. They were running out of time.

Acknowledgements

I want to thank Stacy Sanford for being my best friend and supporter. I would not have been able to stumble down this incredible journey without you!

The Daughters of the Sea Series

About the Author

Kristen Day is a native North Carolinian who, in true southern fashion, is addicted to sweet tea, baked goods and football. She graduated from Appalachian State University and bleeds black and gold. When she's not kayaking or making jewelry, she writes paranormal romance and urban fantasy novels. Forsaken is the first novel in the captivating and addictive Daughters of the Sea series.